Praise for The Blood:

"This is a real page turner, a wonderful story with great action, plus a travelogue of Europe. Impressive!"

"Welcome, Mr. L.G. Rivera, to my list of 'must-read' authors."

"The book is fast-paced and takes you from horror to romance to adrenaline-pumping action with mastery. I was also surprised by the thorough research as well as the very relatable characters found on every page."

"I really enjoyed reading 'The Blood' and I would recommend it to anyone who likes a historically based great adventure story."

Also by L.G. Rivera

Dammed

Sunk

Short Stories:

Maggie Moo

The Life Coach

Coming Soon

Agobio

Z+

and

The exciting sequel to The Blood:

The Bones

THE
BLOOD

L.G. RIVERA

Published by Studio 223 Productions

Cover Design by H.D. Bradford

Library of Congress Cataloging-in-Publication Data
Rivera, L.G.
The Blood / L.G. Rivera.

ISBN 978-0615492254

Printed in the United States of America
Published in the United States by Studio 223 Productions

Studio 223
PRODUCTIONS

THE
BLOOD

For Mom and Dad

PART 1

The women wept, watering the dry earth. John looked up through his own tears at the man he had loved, disfigured and dead on the cross. One of the women handed him a cloth. "He bleeds," she said. John rose up, legs weak, and approached the centurion. "Please, the blood," John pleaded. The centurion simply nodded. John approached the foot of the cross, hearing the cries and whimpers from the two still alive to either side. The centurion motioned to another guard, who brought the short rough-hewn ladder and placed it against the cross. John climbed, the smell of death, blood and dust strong in his nostrils. He pressed the cloth to his Master's disfigured face, collecting the blood flowing freely from the nose and mouth. Awkwardly, John wrapped the cloth around his Master's head, covering Him and collecting the blood. He climbed back down, nodding at the centurion, and walked back to the women. John looked at the blood on his hands, then fell to his knees and sobbed.

CHAPTER 1

Italy, 35,000 feet over the Alps
May 21, 2025   10:22 a.m.

Saleem Al Barat carefully adjusted the airspeed. He had done this many times before, though only on the simulator. This time it was real. This time there would be no return.

He looked down at the dead pilot on the floor of the cockpit. The .22 had done its job. Just one soft pop and the bullet had unleashed death through a tiny hole in the pilot's skull.

It was a shame, really, Saleem thought. He liked the pilot; the man had taught him much and had been patient with him as he learned. It was a shame about the plane, too. The 787-200 was like a flying mansion, outfitted for royalty. Saleem did not know if the Sheik had willingly donated the plane for the mission. If he had, it was a great sacrifice. Three-hundred million euros at least worth of sacrifice, not an insubstantial amount even for a Sheik.

The mission had been well funded from the start. He thought back to when he'd first been approached in Paris. The mission leader, the big Moor, had assured a lifetime of prosperity and comfort for Saleem's family. It was this thought that comforted him now.

Saleem's palms sweated. He banked the plane away from its intended flight path to Bahrain and pointed it at Turin. Beneath him, the Italian Alps unscrolled slowly and majestically, the great peaks of ice and rock reaching silently for heaven. His heart beat faster in spite of the serene scene and the months of training. Saleem closed his eyes and prayed. *Allah, grant me strength.*

In the simulator, every time he'd hit the Cathedral the computer had reset immediately, placing him instantly back in clear blue skies. This time there would be no reset. This time there would be only paradise. He smiled. The irony of entering paradise through the door of the infidel's Cathedral was not lost on him.

"*Allahu Akbar,*" Saleem whispered under his breath.

He throttled the plane and the airspeed climbed steadily. The blue skies and snow capped mountains reflected in his obsidian eyes. Turin rushed towards him. It would not be long now.

Turin Cathedral, Capella dela Sindone
Turin, Italy
May 21, 2025   10:23 a.m.

"Ah hell, where is he?" the short bespectacled man asked, calling out. His words rang loud in the stone walls of the large chamber.

"I don't know, but we can't take the sample without him, Bart," another man, tall and thin, said. "Protocol. It'll be undocumented. Not official," he added.

"Dammit, I know that Victor," Bart Bickle, the short man, spat out. Others in the chamber that had been busy at their instruments looked up now.

"*Signore*, language." Father Vittorio Sella's words were crisp, authoritative. "Do not forget where we are — in the presence of the Most Holy. The very burial Shroud of Christ."

Father Sella took his gaze away from Bickle and cast it on the Shroud. The Shroud hung resplendent, bathed in light from the LED spotlights. The golden honey-colored ancient cloth contrasted brightly against the dark wood frame. Outside of its protective case, it seemed to glow. The faint outline of a man, of Jesus Christ millions believed, waited patiently and serenely for the scientists gathered in the room. Some of them stood to the side and stared, like millions of pilgrims had over the centuries. Others busied themselves with their instruments.

"Sorry," Bickle said quickly and insincerely. "Just frustration, you understand."

Father Sella nodded his head patiently.

"I mean, it's been what," Bickle went on, "over twenty years since we've had a Pope that would allow new research? Forty years since the last meaningful examination? With forty years of advances in the sciences ready to shed new light on this. And we're waiting on one man? One," Bickle paused and bit his tongue, "darn man. And an historian at that," he spat out with disdain. "I mean, why do we need him?"

"You know the rules, Bart," Victor Salayar said. He held up his long index finger. "We must have one project head here at all times for the taking of samples. And yours is the most important sample," Victor said, intentionally stroking Bickle's ego. He didn't like the man, but he was easier to work with when buoyed with self-importance.

"Bah," Bickle harrumphed, and waved his hand, "now you're just blowing smoke up my — chimney."

"It *would* be nice to get an accurate carbon dating this time," Victor said with sincerity.

"Bah." Bickle waved his hands again. "We all know that DNA is the thing this time around. That's what everyone is waiting for. The DNA samples. Isn't that right Ms. Lancaster?" Bickle asked, turning to the center of the room.

Dr. Leigh Lancaster stood in front of the Shroud, transfixed. Her short jet-black hair was silhouetted in front of the brightly lit Shroud. She stared in wonder at the ancient cloth and the faint imprint of the face. Lost in her thoughts, she did not hear Bickle.

"I said, isn't that right, Ms. Lancaster?" Bickle raised his voice though it was hardly necessary.

"Doctor," she corrected him without turning. "It's Doctor Lancaster. Isn't what right, Mr. Bickle?" Leigh asked, still facing the Shroud.

"That DNA's the thing this time. It's what everyone is waiting for. Waiting for you and your wondrous machine to peer into the DNA," he said.

"If you say so, Mr. Bickle," Leigh said, not allowing him to take her attention from the Shroud. She didn't like him. No one on the team did, she thought.

"I do say so," Bickle said. "An actual DNA sample from 2000 years ago? Or 700 years ago, depending on what you believe. That's what everyone wants, isn't it?"

"I suppose. But everyone wants to see what you come up with, Mr. Bickle. With the carbon dating," Leigh said, having learned the ego stroke trick days ago when they first landed in Turin.

"Another smoke blower," Bickle harrumphed. Still, his chest puffed out a little.

Leigh stepped towards the Shroud. She got closer, almost touching it. It was magnetic.

"I'm sampling this area next," she called out to a short blonde woman working at a computer at the side of the room. She rose and walked over to Leigh.

"Right here, Sally," Leigh said. She pointed at the bloodstain at the small of the back, where blood had trickled and pooled as the man had lain dead on top of the burial shroud so very long ago.

Sally Thomas looked at the area and noted it on her tablet. "I'll prep the sampler," she said. "It'll be ready to go when he gets back."

"How's the data from the other samples coming?" Leigh asked.

She checked her tablet. "Good. The computer is analyzing and stitching it all together," Sally said. "I have all the raw data streaming to your tablet," she added.

"Brilliant. Thanks Sally," Leigh said, touching her on the arm. "Now after that I'd like to sample this area at the neck here, but we have to be careful with—"

"So does no one know where he is?" Bickle's grating voice filled the chamber again, interrupting her.

Leigh narrowed her eyes and stared at the man.

"Aren't any of the other team captains available?" Bickle went on, loudly. "I'd like to take this sample and get out of here already."

Three captains had been appointed out of the team of fifteen scientists and experts; at least one captain had to be present at all samplings. Father Sella and two of his assistants had to be present at all times as well. The Vatican had decided that to minimize contamination and damage to the Shroud, only those that were actively working on the Shroud could be present. In practice, most of the scientists stayed in the Sacristy as much as they could to witness history in the making.

"Smith is in Milan for the weekend," Victor said, "and Giuseppe is in the hotel, sick."

"Well call him up, drag Giuseppe out of bed, get him over here," Bickle's voice filled the chamber again. He clapped his hands. "Let's go. Call him up. Or find that damn historian."

Leigh Lancaster closed her eyes and rubbed them. "I'll be right back," she said to Sally and gave a weak smile.

Leigh walked over to Victor, pulling him aside. "How am I supposed to get anything done with this?" she whispered, tilting her head at Bickle.

Victor nodded sympathetically. "I know, I know. But Bickle does have a point. We need the team captain here. We need him. Any idea of where he's off to?"

"I've got an idea," Leigh told him, squinting her eyes.

She walked over to a stainless steel table at the back of the chamber. Half the Sacristy, the side room at the back of the Chapel in the Cathedral, had been converted to a lab. Machines and electronics of every sort filled the back of the room, in jarring contrast to the gilded medieval decorations all around.

"I'm going to go find him," Leigh announced out loud, though mostly to Bickle.

"Finally," Bickle threw his hands up. "Glad someone's got the balls to do something."

This earned him another chastising look from Father Sella.

"Just let me check my sequencers and I'll go," Leigh said.

She picked up her iTablet computer, tapped out a few commands, and verified that the sequencers were working, churning away on the previous samples. She saw the letters streaming real time in a window on her tablet. *GTAACCATGATTACCAAXXCCAA....*

"Good," Leigh whispered to herself. She went to the sequencer, a refrigerator-sized machine, gleaming black with multiple readouts and flashing lights. The words "Tabor Applied Genetics Company," the genetics lab that Leigh headed, were etched into the side and lit from behind by cool blue LED's. Leigh gently, almost lovingly, stroked the side of the machine. She tapped out a couple of commands on the tablet and, satisfied, put the tablet computer in her leather bag and slung it over her shoulder.

"Boy, you take that thing everywhere," Bickle, who had been watching her, joked. "You take it to bed too?"

Leigh shot him an icy stare from her pale green eyes. "I do. That's not all I do with it either." She cocked an eyebrow and brushed past him. "Be back in fifteen, I hope," she called out to Victor and Sally, and walked out of the chamber.

Her heels clicked loudly and echoed off the stone walls. She parted the plastic curtain that had been put up temporarily, pressed through, then past a heavy ancient wooden door, and past another plastic curtain. She strode down a long rectangular hall, smiling at the security guard that sat at a desk at the end of the hall.

"*Arrivederci, doctore,*" the guard said and smiled at her.

"I'll be right back, Elisio," Leigh said and smiled to the young security guard. She passed the guard and came to a huge wooden door.

"I'll be here waiting for you," he said in his thick Italian accent, and winked at her.

Leigh smiled at the flirting young man and shook her head. She pushed the big door open.

Leigh emerged outside in the plaza, at the side of the Capella di Santa Sindone, the Cathedral's chapel that housed the Shroud. The chapel butted up to the Palazzo Reale, Turin's huge and ornate royal palace. Leigh walked across the Plaza Reale at a fast clip, sure of where to find him.

The Duomo Bar
Turin, Italy
May 21, 2025 10:33 a.m.

"Alfredo, *un otro sil vous plaise*," Jonathan Tremaine called out to the bartender.

"*Signore*, that is not even Italian, or much of French for that matter," Alfredo said in accented but perfect English.

"Alfredo, Alfi," Jonathan motioned him over, "*per favore, un altro*," he paused, "ah, dammit. How do you say it? Gin and tonic?"

"*Gin e tonico.*"

"Easy enough. Yeah, that. Another of that," Jonathan said, and flashed a big smile.

"Ah *signore*, you speak terrible Italian but tip very well. Are you sure you want another?" Alfredo asked, eyeing him. It was the man's third and it was still early.

"Yes I do. And I will tip well again. Healthy American tips."

"Then I will pour again."

"And a most generous pourer you are. I tip, you pour. See? History repeats itself."

The bartender cleared away the empty glass, looking at Jonathan.

"And don't worry. I'm a big boy. I can handle it," Jonathan said, reading the bartender's slightly skeptical look.

Jonathan had that large Midwestern build, square-jawed and handsome. He leaned against the bar, barely resting on the barstool, and looked around. The Duomo Bar was tiny and tucked into a nook on the Via XX Settembre, one of the main roads running north right past the Cathedral, where he should be right now. The bar had the distinct advantage of being open early, mostly for cafes and pastries, but they served liquor even at this hour. It was also conveniently less than three blocks from the Cathedral.

Jonathan closed his eyes and tried not to think about what was going on in there. He focused instead on the bar, drinking in its details. A young tourist couple sat drinking cappuccinos, examining a folded up map. An old well-dressed man sat at the other end of the bar, having an early snack of a panini and a small glass of red wine. Behind the bar hung a huge mirrored shelf with three-dozen bottles artfully arranged by size. He stared at them, then caught sight of himself in the mirror behind the bottles.

"You look like hell, buddy," he said to himself, staring in that mirror. He'd barely slept in three days and the Shutter was working overtime. Jonathan rubbed the stubble on his face and ran his hand through his sandy-brown hair.

The door to the bar swung open. Still looking in the mirror, Jonathan saw the petite form of Leigh Lancaster, dressed head to toe in black, walk in. He smiled to himself.

"There you are," she said.

"You found me," Jonathan said without turning around. "Have a seat. Have a drink."

"We need you. Come on."

"Only if you have a drink with me."

"It didn't work yesterday, what makes you think it'll work today?" Leigh asked with an amused look on her face.

"Well," Jonathan said and turned on the barstool to face her, "today, you need me." Jonathan smiled a broad smile.

Leigh looked up in exasperation. "Bloody hell. It's all children I'm dealing with."

"I agree. All the more reason to drink. Now sit." Jonathan motioned at the barstool next to his.

"Fine," Leigh said, exasperated, and took a seat.

Alfredo came over with a glass of ice with a twist of lemon, poured a healthy shot of gin and set a bottle of Schweppes tonic in front of Jonathan.

"*Un café,*" Leigh told the bartender, and then turned to Jonathan. "A bit early for that, isn't it?" she asked, pointing at the gin and tonic.

"Hey, it's after noon back home."

"No, it's three in the morning back home."

"Then it's last call, then," Jonathan said.

"We need you," Leigh said with all seriousness. "Bickle wants to take a sample. So do I for what it's worth."

"It's worth more than Bickle, that's for sure."

Jonathan poured the tonic. It fizzed. He stirred it with his pinkie and took a big slug of the drink, saying nothing. He looked in the mirror again and it happened. The Shutter went off. He stared glassy eyed for a moment, his mind reeling. His vision blurred, then all his synapses fired at once in perfect clarity. He caught himself and blinked.

"Jonathan?" Leigh shook his shoulder.

"Yeah?"

"You okay?"

"Yeah."

"You drunk?" she asked with a furrow of her brow.

"Not yet."

"You looked, I don't know, strange for a moment. Not all there."

"I wasn't."

"Is this that memory thing of yours?" Leigh asked.

Jonathan snapped out of it, returning fully. "Why? What? Who you been talking to?"

"No one. Everyone. Word gets around," Leigh said sheepishly.

Jonathan bit his lip.

"They say you have a photographic memory," Leigh said, and paused, sensing his discomfort.

"They?" Jonathan asked, staring into the mirror again.

"They. You know — them. The other scientists."

The café came and she poured half a pack of sugar in it. Jonathan took another drink. Neither spoke as they sipped their drinks.

"Listen, I don't know you that well," Leigh broke the silence. "Sorry, it was rude. I shouldn't talk about you behind your back."

"Don't be sorry," Jonathan shook his head. "It doesn't bother me."

Leigh took a quick sip of the hot café.

"Well, only a little," Jonathan went on, "but it's not you. It's this," he gestured at his head, circling it with his hand. "This wonderful gift I have," he said, sarcastically.

Leigh stared at her café now, a bit embarrassed.

"And it's not photographic. It doesn't work like that. There's no button. It just happens, like that," he snapped his fingers, "and then I can remember everything that moment. Even things I'd rather forget," Jonathan said softly and took a big pull on his drink.

Leigh stirred the café with a tiny spoon. "You okay?" she asked, genuinely concerned. She put her hand on his.

Jonathan brightened and flashed a big smile. "Never better. Now, please have a drink with me. A real drink. Then we'll go."

Leigh looked at him, then at a clock on the wall. "I'm never going to get you out of here until I have that drink, am I?"

"Nope."

Leigh sighed. "A Garibaldi, please," she told Alfredo.

"And a refill for me," Jonathan rattled the ice cubes in his glass. He faced Leigh. "Garibaldi? What the hell is that?" he asked.

"Campari and orange. Most people hate it."

"But you like it?"

"I'm not most people," Leigh said with a smile and brushed a stray lock of hair from her eyes, tucking it back behind her ear.

"No, you're not," Jonathan said and looked her up and down, though subtly. "You don't look like a scientist, or a famous one at that."

"Oh?" Leigh said in mock indignation. "And what exactly do I look like?"

"Like a singer in a punk band," Jonathan said without hesitation.

Leigh laughed. "Punk? No one's called me that in a long time. Vampire, yes, with all my black clothes, but punk — not in a long time."

Alfredo brought over the drinks.

"Cheers," Leigh said, and clinked glasses.

"Yes, definitely punk. You've got that British punk thing going," Jonathan said with a nod of his head.

"Why's that?"

"The accent, for one. And the tats."

Leigh rubbed her arm, pulling down on the long sleeve of her shirt that covered her tattoos.

"How did you know?" she asked, surprised.

"The first day," Jonathan said, "when you put your gloves on. You rolled up your shirtsleeves for a second. It's a nice tattoo, from what I saw. Nice work. Is it a full sleeve?"

"How did you—?" Leigh trailed off, still dumbfounded. She always wore long shirtsleeves, especially in professional settings, to hide her tattoos. "How could you see?"

"Photographic memory." Jonathan tapped his temple and grinned. "Remember?"

Leigh blushed, showing light pink on her ivory skin. "I thought it didn't work that way," she said.

"It doesn't. The Shutter just happened to go off right then, that moment," Jonathan said.

"The Shutter?"

"That's what I call it," he said. "It's like all my senses open for a millisecond and I can remember everything. What I see, smell, emotions, how my body felt, the whole lot."

"Oh really?" Leigh unsheathed the straw from its paper wrapper and took a sip of her drink. "So what is it? The tattoo, I mean. Let's see how much you can remember, mister," she asked, arching a skeptical brow.

Jonathan closed his eyes and breathed in deep. He was quiet for a second, then began to speak in a monotone.

"You're across the room. Your hands are ivory white and remind me of the marble of the '*Pieta.*' You're putting your gloves on and roll up your left sleeve for a second. I can see your tattoo and I look closer, surprised. I see the brown roots of a tree. There is grass at its base. There is something green, a vine or a snake, coiled around the tree. It is very detailed, even from a distance, very fine work, I thought, and I wanted to see more of it."

Leigh stopped in mid-sip. "Wow. That's very impressive. All that from a glance?"

"I was tired from the trip," Jonathan went on, trancelike. "I had been looking at the Shroud and heard you putting the gloves on, the rubbery stretchy sound loud and echoing in the Sacristy. Bickle was sitting in the corner reading the Economist. It was two thirty-seven p.m. and I had been awake for twenty-five hours. The instrument you had unpacked, a big black box, was lit up. The lights were red, green, green, green, yellow—" Jonathan trailed off and shook his head.

"Wow," Leigh said in amazement.

"Sorry," Jonathan said. "The recall gets me almost in a trance. It's kind of like a garden hose. When you close the valve, it takes some time for the flow to stop."

"That's amazing."

"Helped me pass history in school," he said, tapping the side of his head.

Jonathan raised his glass and took a big slug of the gin, almost no tonic now.

"I bet," Leigh said.

"So what's the rest of it?" he asked. "The tattoo I mean."

"You'll just have to wait on that one, cowboy," she took a sip of her Garibaldi. "But you were right about the snake. I'll give you that." She gave him a sly half-smile.

"The lady's all secrets," he said.

"Gotta have something to keep them interested," she said.

"I think you have a lot of interesting somethings, that's what I think." Jonathan said, smiling at her.

Leigh blushed again. "Hush, you."

"Alfi, *un altro, por favore*," Jonathan said and raised the empty glass.

Leigh gave him a disapproving look.

"I'm a big boy. I can handle it," he said. "I'm not a cheap date."

"Well I *am* a cheap date," Leigh said and took another small sip of the Garibaldi. "This one is all I need."

"What's that taste like anyway?"

"Here you go, cowboy." She slid the drink on the stainless steel bar top to him. It glided easily on a layer of condensation.

Jonathan raised an eyebrow, then took up the glass, holding the straw to one side with his index finger and taking a sip of the blood-red drink. He grimaced.

"If that's what I had to drink, I wouldn't drink," he said.

"Told you. Most people hate it. And that one is actually very well made."

Alfredo came by with a fresh glass and bottle of Schweppes tonic.

"Last one?" Leigh asked hopefully.

"Last one. Deal's a deal."

"Why are you here anyway, if you don't want to be here?" Leigh asked. "If you don't mind me asking."

"I do want to be here. Well, did want to be here," Jonathan said, pouring the tonic into his glass.

"What do you mean?"

"Well, the easy answer is the Old Man asked me. Personally. You don't turn that down. I'm sure he asked you too," he said.

She nodded.

"Gathering the best of the best to study the Shroud and all that," Jonathan said. He fished the lemon out of the glass and squeezed it. "That's why he asked you, right?"

"Well, I'm not, I — I don't consider myself the best," Leigh said and looked sheepishly at her drink.

"Ah, take the compliment," Jonathan said, waving a hand at her. "It's not everyone that invents a whole new way of sequencing DNA."

"I didn't invent it. I just — I just made it work. Standing on the shoulders of giants and such."

"What's it called again? Nano, nano-what?"

"Nanotube extraction," Leigh said.

"One day you'll just have to explain it to me."

"One day. Not now. We've got work to do now," she said. "Quit nursing that drink. You killed all the others," she added.

"This one I want to keep alive," Jonathan said and gave a short laugh. He stirred the drink with his pinkie, the lemon swirling lazily around.

"Well, I'm going to ask you again. Why are you here if you don't want to be here?"

Jonathan turned serious, the slight smile that was always on his face gone. "You've looked at the Shroud, Leigh. What do you think?"

"Well, I'm waiting to see what the data reveal. First I want to scientifically look at the—"

"Bullshit," Jonathan cut her off.

Leigh closed her mouth, a look of surprise appearing on her face. She was not used to being cut off. She was the head of her lab and everyone was always deferential to her, sometimes annoyingly so.

"You know," Jonathan said, nodding his head. "I've seen you look at it. You know. You've already made up your mind."

"Well as a scientist I have to acknowledge that I have a belief system and certain things have to be set aside and looked at rationally and from a scientific perspective—"

"Bullshit," Jonathan interrupted again. "You can stop all your science talk. I know it all. I've heard it all. At the end of the day it's no better and no more rational than Father Sella's belief. At least he's not lying to himself about his beliefs."

Leigh straightened up on the barstool, indignant. "I'm not lying to myself."

"What are you doing then?"

"I'm gathering evidence," she said.

"And why would you need evidence if you already believe?" Jonathan said, raising an eyebrow.

Leigh didn't answer him. "And what do you believe, mister? Is it the real deal or not?" she asked instead.

"It doesn't matter."

"Well that's a fine attitude for the head of our Shroud study team to take."

"Look," Jonathan said, gazing earnestly at Leigh, "I'm an historian. I study history, the past. The beautiful thing about history is that we keep repeating it. So if you know the past, you know the future."

"So what's the future? Why don't you believe our work here matters?"

"I'll tell you why it doesn't. Go back to the year 1353 for a second. To a tiny little town called Lirey in France. Out of nowhere, a knight of some renown, Geoffrey the First, let's call him Jeff, says he wants to build a chapel there. A chapel for the Most Holy Shroud it turns out. The very cloth that Jesus Christ was laid on in a tomb in Jerusalem. The very cloth that soaked up the blood that you're so intently studying now. The very cloth that was somehow, no one knows how, imprinted with his image when he was resurrected, if you believe that sort of thing."

Leigh shifted on the stool. "Yeah, yeah," Leigh said, impatient. "What's your point?"

"The point I haven't got to. We're still in 1353. Lirey, Jeff the Knight's village, becomes a place of pilgrimage, with people coming from near and far to see the Shroud. The Bishop at the time, a guy named Henri, denounces it as a forgery. This is the Bishop, mind you, the guy you would expect to push this sort of thing. Despite this, people still come to see. Some believe, some don't. Enough believe that they build a chapel for it. Eventually, the Shroud passes down, through marriages, to the Savoy family. They believe in it enough that they keep it for over 500 years. Enough people believe that they are able to build a very nice church at Chambery in France, and, later, the Cathedral here in Turin."

"Okay, thanks for the history lesson. What's the point?" Leigh asked again.

"Not done. Fast-forward a few centuries. May 25, 1898. The Shroud is exhibited here in Turin and a fellow by the name of Secondo Pia, an amateur photographer, uses this new technology called photography to take pictures of the Shroud. He's in the lab developing it when he goes cold. The negative of the Shroud shows up clearly like a picture of the face of a man. The Shroud itself is a negative image, you see, and the negative of that shows up as a positive. It can't be a fake then, right? I mean, how did medieval forgers know about photographic negatives and all that? Well, people descend on poor Secondo Pia like hounds, accusing him of fakery or worse. Some people believe, some don't."

"Okay," Leigh said and nodded, "I think I understand."

"Wait, one more," Jonathan said, raising a finger. "In 1978 a team of scientists much like ourselves is assembled and studies the Shroud for five days. They reveal that it is indeed blood on the Shroud and that it is human. They reveal that they have no idea how the imprint of the image got on there, but it was not paint or any known process. And, most infamously, they announce that the radio carbon dating revealed it to be only 700 years old. Not old enough for Christ."

"Which was later proven false," Leigh said. "Now that I knew. So what's the point?"

"So, some believed, some didn't. Even after the carbon dating, millions showed up to look at it, to pray to it, to venerate it. It didn't matter what the science showed. And we now know, here almost 50 years later, that the carbon dating was wrong. But they didn't at the time."

"So what's your point?" Leigh asked, getting fidgety.

"The point is this. History repeats itself. People will either believe or not believe that the Shroud actually wrapped Jesus, that it has his blood, his image. I saw it in your eyes when you looked at it. You believe. The science doesn't matter. And, also, that the science can be wrong. It's been wrong before. It'll be wrong again."

Leigh nodded. "I understand. But I still think it's important. We don't know what we'll find."

"There's one more thing."

"What's that?" she asked.

"They kill the messenger."

"What? What do you mean?"

"Poor Secondo Pia, the photographer. The carbon dating team in 1978. They pilloried them. The public, the press, all turned against them. People don't like having their belief system upturned. You're messing with dangerous stuff there, miss — reading God's DNA and all. Or not God's, and just a man's. Either way it turns out, you're bound to make more enemies than friends."

Leigh nodded solemnly. "I hadn't thought of that."

They were both silent a moment. Jonathan drained the rest of his drink.

"Finish your drink, if you can down that vile stuff," Jonathan said.

Leigh took a big swig, setting the straw aside. "There."

"You're not done, you still have half left. And I really need another," Jonathan said.

"Nope. That wasn't the deal."

Leigh sipped at the remainder of her drink. They were quiet for a moment. Jonathan stared at his empty glass, cradling it in his hands.

"I hate seeing it. That's why I don't want to go, why I don't want to be in there," Jonathan said quietly, looking up into the mirror behind the bar and avoiding his own gaze.

"What do you mean?"

"The Shroud. All that poking and prodding," Jonathan said. "I hate seeing it. That's why I don't want to go."

Leigh looked at him.

Jonathan sensed the question in her gaze. "Well," he began, "if it is the real deal, the Shroud of Christ, should we be poking and prodding at it? And if it isn't and we can prove it, why do it? Why crush the faith of millions? It's a no-win situation."

Leigh nodded gravely. "I hadn't thought of that either."

They were silent a moment.

"Enough of all this," Jonathan said, painting a big grin on his face, "you done with that awful drink yet?"

Leigh downed the rest. "All done."

"Grab your little bag, let's go get this done."

Leigh grabbed the bag from the top of the bar where she'd placed it.

"What's in there anyway?" Jonathan asked. "You always have that thing glued at your side."

"It's my tablet. Look," she brought out the Apple iTablet computer and swiped it on. "The sequencers are streaming the data from the sampling right to here."

Jonathan looked at the letters filling the window. *A T G G X C A T A T X X A T X G.*

"I know a little bit about DNA, the A's and the G's and T's and all, but what are the X's?" he asked.

"Holes. This sample is ancient. There are lots and lots of holes and gaps in the DNA. If we can get enough samples we can piece most of it together."

"Then what?" Jonathan asked.

"I don't know," Leigh admitted. "Then we have a full sample, is all. The decoded genome from 2000 years ago."

Jonathan nodded. "That's quite amazing. Let's get back to it, then." He laid down a fifty euro note on the bar. "*Arrivederci* Alfredo. *Danka Danka,*" he called out.

"Goodbye, sir," Alfredo said, "and learn *Italiano!*" he joked.

Jonathan laughed and got up. He was tall and towered over Leigh. He held the door open for her.

"Vampire, huh?" he asked her as they walked out.

CHAPTER 2

Outskirts of Turin, Italy
May 21, 2025   11:06 a.m.

Saleem al Barat was close.   The 787-200 was at V-Max, engines screaming. He was flying low, the altimeter counting down like a stopwatch. There was a five-story building in front of the Cathedral that he needed to clear. That had been the trickiest part of the simulation. More than once he had hit the building. There was no glory in the building, only death. But he had practiced many months and was sure he had the angle of approach right. He had watched videos of Hani Hanjour as he flew and struck the Pentagon back in 2001. Flying so low, so fast. A true hero, Saleem thought.

He closed his eyes and could see the simulator. Turin would unscroll below him and he would clear the buildings and plow into the front door of the Cathedral. *"Right into the heart of the infidels."* That is how the big Moor had explained it. "With so many targets available, why this one?" Saleem had asked. The big Moor told him this was a strike to the heart of the infidels. He had also told him not to ask so many questions. Saleem did not.

It was an easy mission. So much easier than a commercial hijack. You couldn't do those anymore. Too much security. Too many passengers ready to give their lives to fight you. But this one had been easy. He looked down at the dead pilot again, feeling a twinge of sadness. He'd been such a nice man.

Saleem put it out of his head. He was close. The attitude indicator, the artificial horizon showing the angle of approach, was almost flat. The 787-200, full of fuel, thundered across Turin. Such a shallow angle to clear the buildings. He was sure it was right. His heart beat hard in his chest and his palms sweated.

"Today, I will be in paradise," he said out loud. Only the dead pilot was there to hear.

Capella dela Sindone
Turin, Italy
May 21, 2025 11:07 a.m.

"Now we have two gone," Bickle complained.

"She'll be back," Victor said reassuringly. "They'll both be back."

"They'd better be. We've only got three more days and I'd like to process these first samples before we leave. Find out what year this thing is from. Bet you they were right all along. I peg it at 1350. I bet the thing is a fake."

Father Sella looked over at Bickle, then back at the Shroud. "Forgive him Father," he prayed under his breath.

Father Sella stood in front of the Shroud, in front of the imprint of the face. Such a serene expression, he thought. He looked down the length of it to the imprint of the back, to the dozens of dumbbell-shaped marks. Father Sella tried to imagine each mark, each a hit of the Roman flagellum, each a piece of flesh ripped out from His back. Each of Father Sella's sins there, paid for in His blood. His eyes started tearing up and he was alone with the Shroud, in His presence.

"*Grazie, Gesu,*" he whispered under his breath.

Via XX Settembre
Turin, Italy
May 21, 2025 11:09 a.m.

Jonathan and Leigh walked out of the Duomo Bar and onto the Via XX Settembre. It was warm out, and downright hot in the sun. They crossed the street to the shadowed side. Jonathan was content. He was nicely buzzed. The Shutter did not go off as much when he'd been drinking. The gin burned in his stomach and warmed his blood and made his head fuzzy and happy. Leigh made him happy, too. She was a smart girl, and light on the pretense, which he appreciated.

Leigh looked over at him. "What?" she asked.

"I didn't say anything."

"I thought you had."

"Maybe you can read my mind," Jonathan said.

"You know all us vampires can," Leigh said, opening her eyes wide.

"I still don't get vampire from you at all. Punk girl, yes."

"Neither one sees the sun much," Leigh said.

"That's true," Jonathan said.

They walked down the street in a comfortable silence for a bit.

"Did you know of all the attempts to destroy the Shroud throughout history?" Jonathan asked to break the silence.

"Do tell, Professor."

"Cute," Jonathan said and rolled his eyes. "Really, it's very interesting."

"How so?"

"Well, it's come so close to destruction so many times, but always escaped by some — miracle is one word, I suppose. Chance is another."

"Okay, I'm interested, Professor," Leigh said.

"In Chambery, the city in France where it was kept for almost 150 years, it was almost destroyed in a fire in 1532. A mysterious fire. It was saved at the last minute by a local blacksmith. It was so hot that the silver case it was kept in actually melted and dripped silver onto it, burning those little holes you see."

"I was wondering how those got there."

"And in 1997 it was almost destroyed again in another fire, arson most likely. A fireman named Mario Trematore axed the bulletproof glass open and took it out in the nick of time. And in 2017, there was that whole attempt with the car bomb. Surely you remember that. If it hadn't been for that guard, Pietro Costa," Jonathan said and paused, reflecting. "You know, it's almost like some force wants to see it burn and some greater force won't allow it," he said quietly.

"Do you believe?" Leigh asked, very serious. "In that greater force?" she added.

Jonathan sighed. "I don't know," he said and looked away. "Maybe. I used to. I don't. I don't know." Jonathan rubbed his face. "What does it matter, anyway?"

"It matters," Leigh said earnestly.

Jonathan stopped in the middle of the sidewalk, in the shadow of a tall apartment building. He turned to look at her and smiled a weak smile.

"Thanks," Jonathan said.

"For what?"

"For caring. For coming to get me," he said.

Leigh smiled and looked down at her shoes, embarrassed. "Anytime, cowboy," she said, looking up at him again. "Now let's get some work done."

They began to walk again when, suddenly, a great roar came from above them, filling the air with a horrific noise. A shadow of darkness filled the street and reached out for the Cathedral.

CHAPTER 3

Turin, Italy
May 21, 2025   11:11 a.m.

The buildings flew past Saleem. He held the plane steady at the correct angle, adjusting the trim ever so slightly. He saw the five-story apartment building rushing towards him, so close, and the Cathedral just beyond it. It was coming so fast, much faster than the simulation. He heard a crash and metal scraping. He'd hit something on the roof of the apartment. The plane gave a great shudder, but the momentum carried it through. Saleem kept his eyes open, seeing the Cathedral come upon him in a flash. This was it. In a moment, he would enter paradise. He heard a tremendous crash, which was the last thing he heard. Fire and searing heat consumed him. It was all he felt. And it seemed to last an eternity.

Capella dela Sindone
Turin, Italy
May 21, 2025   11:11 a.m.

Father Sella stood praying in front of the Shroud. In the background he heard Bickle still complaining, but it did not matter. He was somewhere else. The prayer was transporting him and God was being kind, filling Father Sella with light. It felt incredible. A part of Father Sella was vaguely aware that he was having a beatific vision, his first ever, but soon those thoughts were overwhelmed with a beautiful cool white light. Below him, he could see the Sacristy, the scientists looking up from their instruments at some great noise. Bickle, Victor, Sally, and the others, startled, looking towards the door, the room filling up with that beautiful cool white light. Father Sella saw himself standing in front of the Shroud. It too blazed in glory and light. And then it was no more.

Via XX Settembre
Turin, Italy
May 21, 2025 11:11 a.m.

It all happened in an instant. Jonathan and Leigh both heard the great roar fill the air and then a deafening crash. An immense concussive force hit them like a giant fist slamming them in the chest. Suddenly, almost as fast, a great cloud of darkness and dust rushed towards them, funneled by the narrowing street and gathering speed.

On instinct, Jonathan grabbed Leigh by the shoulders and they both fell into the portal of an apartment building, landing face down. The cloud of dust and rock flew past them with the vicious speed and force of a hurricane. In an instant they were encased in dust. Jonathan's first thought, oddly enough, was *Pompeii*. He wondered if this is how it had happened, how the hapless inhabitants of that city had been encased and killed in the hot volcanic ash. His second thought, which came naturally, was *protect her.* He sheltered Leigh, swinging open his coat and tucking her in, covering her.

Outside her protective cocoon, Leigh could feel dust and dirt and bits of rock flying past, like some great dustbowl storm. There was no time to think, no time to react, no time for fear. That would come later.

Jonathan held Leigh tight, their heads touching. They were tucked into the corner of the portal, the entrance to the apartment building. It was getting harder to breathe. The air was gone; it was all dust. He started coughing, then she did as well. They had to move. *Where?* Jonathan's mind raced. He raised his head. His eyes stung. He could see nothing. For all he knew, there *was* nothing, just never-ending dust and darkness.

Jonathan reached up blindly with his hand, feeling around. Buttons. Call buttons to the apartments. He began pressing them all. A voice crackled on the intercom, a scared elderly voice saying something in Italian that Jonathan could not hear. Jonathan yelled out, he didn't know what, just a cry for help. The disembodied voice said something unintelligible over the small speaker and the door buzzed, vibrating the door with its electric lock.

Jonathan rose, holding Leigh in his right arm, and tackled the door like a linebacker with his left shoulder. The door flew open and they spilled in, Jonathan landing on his back. He kicked the door closed and it slammed shut, sealing them off from the dust and smoke storm outside.

He raised himself up, leaning back on his elbows. He looked around with his stinging eyes. Leigh was beside him, sprawled face down and covered by his coat.

"Are you okay?" Jonathan yelled out. His ears rang and he could barely hear himself.

No response. He shook Leigh. Nothing. He rose, kneeling over her, and uncovered her, tossing the coat aside. He scanned her and she seemed to be in one piece. He carefully turned her over. Her shirtsleeve had rolled up a bit and he saw part of the tattoo on her arm. The tail of a snake wrapped around a tree was visible. For a crazy moment he considered rolling her sleeve up and seeing the rest of it. He shook the thought away.

Leigh's face was still, angelic. Her fine features were covered with a thin layer of dust. She looked like a Michelangelo sculpture, he thought. Jonathan gingerly wiped the dust from her eyelids. He felt her pulse, which was strong, but her breathing was very shallow. He slapped her lightly on the cheek, seeing if she would revive. A little cloud of dust rose up, but she did not move. He wiped his thumb clean on the inside of his shirt then ran it over her lips, cleaning them. He parted them, then leaned over to give her mouth-to-mouth. Just as he was leaning over, she took in a quick inhalation and slowly opened her eyes.

"I'm not that kind of girl," Leigh said in a slow drawl.

Jonathan sat back on his feet and slumped his shoulders. He saw her talk, but couldn't make out the words. His ears still rang like someone had boxed them.

"Jesus, you scared the hell out of me," he said.

Leigh blinked, slowly moving her head. She leaned up on her elbows and looked around. "What happened?" she asked, putting a hand to her ear in confusion.

Jonathan could not hear her at all. He pointed at his ears and shook his head. Then he pointed at her, gave a thumbs up, and shrugged his shoulders. *Are you okay?*

She nodded. Leigh wiped a hand across her face, leaving a streak of grey from all the dust. She looked down at her hands and arms, caked with the dust, and glanced around, wild-eyed and disoriented. She sat up, went dizzy, and leaned forward.

Jonathan put his hand gently on the top of her head. She looked up at him. Her light jade eyes were the only things that sparkled clean through the dust. She gave a weak smile.

He stood up and leaned against the wall, dizzy. *An explosion,* he thought. *A big explosion.* The shockwave had hit them, probably giving them both a concussion. He hoped their insides were okay. The concussive force of an explosion did hell to internal organs, he remembered from somewhere. He poked at his belly but there was no pain.

Leigh, seeing him do this, understood immediately. Her years of training at medical school flooded back through the fog in her head. Even after years of test tubes and computers, she still remembered the basics. She poked and prodded at herself and, satisfied that everything was fine, slowly stood up. She was shaky but recovering quickly.

They both looked at each other and exchanged a troubled look. The ringing was dying down in their ears.

"What happened?" Leigh asked loudly.

"Don't know," Jonathan said. He leaned down to her ear. "Explosion I think. Something blew up."

"Car bomb?" she asked.

"Don't know."

"Where's my bag?" Leigh asked, suddenly aware it was no longer slung over her shoulder. She hunted around for her precious tablet computer. The cool marble entrance hall to the apartments was covered in a fine layer of dust. She spotted her bag in a corner, ran and picked it up, and brought the tablet out of the bag. The computer turned on, though the screen read "Signal Lost."

Leigh breathed a sigh of relief. "It's okay." She looked up at Jonathan and nodded her head.

"We're almost blown up in an explosion and almost choke to death on dust and smoke, and you're concerned about a computer?" Jonathan shook his head. "Why do you care so much about that thing?"

"It's got all my data. All my sampling so far. The computers back at the church do too, but I like having it on me."

Jonathan nodded. "Let's find out what happened," he said. "You up for it?"

Leigh nodded, slinging the bag over her shoulder.

With some trepidation, Jonathan buzzed open the door to the outside. He cracked it open. Dust and smoke roared in and he quickly shut it. He bit his lip, thinking.

"Up," he said, pointing at the stairs.

Leigh nodded and they went to the stairwell.

"That old elevator doesn't look like the safest bet on a good day, much less after all this," Jonathan said.

They climbed the stairs. Leigh kicked off her heels and went barefoot. A few residents began to come out of the apartments and congregate in the halls, asking questions. A burly man came bounding down the stairs and spat some rapid fire Italian at them. Between the ringing in their ears and the man's excited and nervous fast talking, they understood not a word. The man pushed past them and hurried down the stairs.

They made their way up another set of stairs, then down a long hall towards the next staircase. Some doors were open and neighbors were excitedly asking questions of each other. Finally, they crested the fifth floor.

"Look for a door for the stairs to the roof," Jonathan said.

"There," Leigh said, pointing at a big metal door at the end of the hall.

Jonathan went to it and pulled at the handle. "Locked," he said and pounded on the door. It clanged loudly and echoed down the hall.

Dejected, they made their way back to the stairs, when an old woman opened the door to her apartment.

"*Che cosa era quell grande rumore?*" she asked, then stared at Jonathan and Leigh with surprise. They were covered in dust and dirt, their faces grey and ashen. They looked like ghosts. "*Che cosa sta accadendo?*" she asked.

Jonathan shrugged his shoulders. He could barely hear her, much less understand her.

The old woman gazed on them with pity. "*Entrare, entrare,*" the old woman said and motioned them into her apartment.

Leigh and Jonathan looked at each other but did not move. The old woman came to Leigh, took her by the hand, and led her into the apartment. Jonathan followed.

"*Un momento,*" the old woman said, holding up a finger, and went off, leaving them standing in the foyer. She came back with towels and led them to the bathroom.

Jonathan took the towels. They were stiff and sun dried and smelled of the outdoors. He handed one to Leigh, then wet his towel in the sink, wiping his face clean. Soon they had wiped most of the dust from their faces. The old woman, who was looking on, showed relief. *Maybe she thought we were burned,* Jonathan thought. "*Grazi, grazi,*" Jonathan thanked the old woman, putting his hands together and giving a little bow.

They went back to the foyer. The old woman asked something in Italian. Jonathan stood shaking his head, not understanding, when he stopped cold. He looked past the old woman, over her shoulder, to the window. He stepped past her even as she was talking, and walked towards the window, mouth open. Leigh stared outside and followed.

"My God," Leigh whispered.

They stood at the window. Outside, the view looked out onto the Cathedral. Only it wasn't there. A cloud of black and orange billowed from where the Cathedral once stood, lit by the fires within. The whole scene looked like some Hieronymus Bosch landscape of hell.

"What happened here?" Leigh asked, staring open mouthed out the window.

"The Cathedral is gone," Jonathan said. "The whole thing."

"Sally," Leigh said in a low voice, her shoulders dropping. "The Shroud. All those people—" she trailed off and stared, numb.

Jonathan put a comforting hand on her shoulder. "Maybe they're okay," Jonathan said, but that was a lie. He was sure enough looking at the fire that raged beneath them.

CHAPTER 4

Piazza San Carlo
Turin, Italy
May 21, 2025   11:17 a.m.

Asad Hasan sat at an outside table at the Torino Café on Piazza San
Carlo, sipping a Moroccan tea he had spotted on the menu. His big body
barely fit in the seat. He had heard the explosion and smiled. Around him,
people started to get up, the first stages of panic beginning to set in as they
received news of what had happened. A uniformed policewoman ran past
him down the arcade in the direction of the Cathedral.

The mission was most likely a success. Asad would go over after the dust
settled and make sure. Only then would he phone the Lawyer. For now,
Asad sipped his tea and listened to the growing sounds of sirens gathering in
the distance. He smiled to himself and tried not to think of the money, tried
to keep it professional until it was all over. It would be soon.

Turin, Italy
May 21, 2025   11:18 a.m.

Jonathan and Leigh stood and stared at the scene, hypnotized. The cloud
of dust was dispersing but the fire raged on. The smoke wafted away for a
second and, suddenly, the tail section of an airplane was revealed. A great
cloud of black billowed and covered it again.

"Good heavens," Leigh said.

Jonathan stared speechless. Through the smoke, he could see that there
was nothing left of the Cathedral but a couple of ruined walls. The dome had
collapsed completely.

The old woman came up to the window now and said something in Italian
and started crossing herself. She was visibly upset and crying. Leigh put an
arm around her. They all stared out the window at the devastation below.

"Maybe they got out," Leigh said after a bit of silence, but there was no hope in her voice.

"Maybe," Jonathan said. "The room was way in the back, behind the chapel. Those walls were thick. Maybe." He spoke weakly, without hope.

They could hear sirens now. Below them, the thinning cloud of dust flashed blue like some unearthly lightning storm.

"Let's go," Jonathan said, "I feel like a putz sitting up here. Let's get down there. Maybe we can help."

Leigh nodded silently. She took the hands of the old woman and thanked her, looking deep into her eyes. Jonathan thanked her too. The woman gave them the towels and they thanked her again.

Jonathan made his way quickly down the stairs, with Leigh following close behind. He was glad to be moving. Most of the residents were out now, talking in the hall or gathered at windows with their front apartment doors wide open. The couple rounded the last stairs and reached the lobby. Leigh put her shoes back on, leaning on the wall as she slipped them on. They stepped to the front door.

Jonathan hesitated for a moment, then opened the front door. There was heavy haze in the air and clouds of black smoke wafted by. The smell of burning jet fuel was acrid and pungent. Jonathan put the wet towel to his mouth and nose and Leigh saw and did the same. They went right, towards the Cathedral, hugging the wall. Ambulances and police cars filed slowly past them through the smoke, sirens blaring. The lights flashed, turning the smoky street into some demonic nightclub.

They arrived at the Piazza Reale, the open plaza at the end of the street that led to the Cathedral. In the center, tilted to one side and enveloped by smoke, was the plane's tail section. Even from this distance they could feel the intense heat from the ruined Cathedral.

Leigh tripped on something. A pair of pants on the ground. *Why would someone leave a pair of pants on the ground?* she thought. Then she saw a foot sticking out of the leg of the pants. It slowly dawned on her, her mind not wanting to comprehend, that this was a person. A part of a person. She felt ice water pour down her spine and froze, staring down.

Jonathan turned around to see why Leigh had stopped. She stood slump-shouldered, staring at the ground. He looked down and saw the torn torso, registered it, looked over at the raging fire, and decided. He grabbed Leigh by the hand and turned around, going back the way they came.

"We can't do anything here, not now. We need to wait for this to die down," he yelled over the sirens.

"I want to go back to the hotel," Leigh yelled back.

Jonathan looked back at the raging flames and nodded.

They hurried down the street, Jonathan still holding Leigh by the hand. They went past the apartment building they had been in, walking hurriedly down the long block. Fine dust swirled in the air as the smoke began to clear.

Leigh rubbed her eyes. Through the haze she saw the neon red sign of the Chelsea hotel. She pulled at Jonathan, leading him towards it. "Come on," she said urgently.

They crossed the street and went in, past a crowd that had gathered in the lobby. Everyone was talking at once in a Babel of languages.

Leigh went to the front desk but it was unattended. The clerk was at the front of the lobby talking with someone and gesturing outside. She circled around the desk and grabbed her key from a hook on the wall. "Let's go," she said.

They took the stairs up two flights to the second floor and walked down the hall towards Leigh's room. Leigh hurried, the big keychain dangling in her hand. She unlocked the door and they entered the suddenly silent room.

"You okay?" Jonathan asked, staring at Leigh.

"Yeah," she said absently.

Leigh placed the computer bag on the desk and went straight to the bathroom. She washed her hands and came back out and grabbed clothes from the closet.

"I need to get cleaned up, if you don't mind," she told Jonathan.

"Not at all."

She went in the bathroom and closed the door, the tears already welling up. She quickly peeled off her ruined clothes; they fell in a heap around her. She ran the shower hot and strong and looked at herself in the mirror, naked, while the room steamed up. Her wrists and neck were ringed in black from the soot. She rubbed the tattoo that covered her left arm like a tapestry. Leigh tested the water with her foot and stepped in. The black dust washed away, inking the water at her feet. She let the shower run over her, and tried not to think about the awful scene she had witnessed. She closed her eyes, then leaned against the wall and cried in earnest. Her tears mixed with the water and washed down the drain as she continued weeping for a good minute.

"Enough of that," she said to herself at last, trying to regain her composure.

She began scrubbing her body, washing the dirt and grime off and, she hoped, the memory.

Jonathan stood awkwardly in the quiet room. He did not want to sit and filth up the place. Leigh had left the armoire open and he nosed around in it, feeling like a voyeur. Her clothes were hung up neatly; almost all of them were black skirts and long-sleeved blouses or sweaters, with one bright flowered dress that stood out. Her nightstand held an iPod and wireless headphones. A black leather-lined journal with a silver pen resting on top sat to the side of the table. He resisted the urge to thumb through it.

The shower stopped. Jonathan quickly got back near the door and waited, acting casual. Leigh came out of the bathroom dressed in a long sleeve thin black pullover and long black skirt, toweling off her short hair.

"You okay?" Jonathan asked, concerned.

"Much better," Leigh said, as the memory receded. "Your turn, cowboy, if you want," she added. "I'll see if I can rustle up some clothes that'll fit you."

"I don't think I'll look too good in that dress," Jonathan said, trying to lighten the mood.

Leigh raised an eyebrow. "Go get cleaned up," she said.

Jonathan went in the bathroom. He stripped and jumped in the shower. The room was already steamy and warm and the water felt great. The stream washed the dust from his hair, returning it from ashen gray to sandy brown. He laid his hands on the wall, letting the water wash over him, and stared at the soot spiraling down the drain.

He lost himself in thought. The adrenaline and shock were wearing off and the reality was beginning to set in. Almost all his colleagues were dead. He should be dead too, by all accounts. And Leigh also. But they were not.

And the Shroud — what? Destroyed? It could not be. He thought of all the close calls, all the miraculous escapes of the Shroud through history. For two thousand years, assuming it was real, the Shroud had escaped destruction. What about the plane? Was it an accident? Not likely. The water poured over his head and ran down the drain. He had to see, he decided. He had to get to what was left of the Cathedral and see for himself. History repeats itself. The Shroud had to have survived. Somehow.

Jonathan shut the water off and toweled dry. He looked at his dusty clothes lying in a heap on the ground. He wrapped the towel around his waist and opened the door a bit. "You gonna make me wear that skirt?" he called out.

Leigh smiled. "I should. But you're not my size. All I've got is this shirt," she said, and handed it to him through the cracked open door.

He closed the door and shook his pants and socks out in the shower. They rained gray dust. He dressed, thankful at least for the clean shirt. He came out of the bathroom, wearing dusty jeans and a black Armani T-shirt that was one size too small.

"Thanks for the shirt," he said.

"You're welcome," Leigh said and looked him up and down. "It's a little tight," she said, eyeing him.

"A little."

"You keep in shape," Leigh said, blushing a little.

"I try." *Not bad for 45,* Jonathan thought. "Is it a present? For someone else I mean."

"Yes, but I can buy another."

"Boyfriend?"

"Tony's a friend and he's a boy, but no. There's no boyfriend."

"Really?" Jonathan raised an eyebrow.

"Really. He'd find you attractive, though. He likes that rugged cowboy type."

Jonathan laughed. "I don't know how to take that. And you keep calling me cowboy. I don't know my way around a horse, by the way."

"Well, it looks good on you. The shirt. It's Armani."

"So I saw."

There was an awkward silence. Leigh looked at him, then looked away at the window. It had a light dusting of ash.

"You okay?" Jonathan asked her again.

"Yeah." Leigh nodded. "I'm a doctor, I see stuff like that all the time," she lied. "Don't worry about me."

Jonathan looked at her skeptically. "If you say so."

"So — what now?" she asked.

"We need to go back. Back to the Cathedral. I don't know about you, but I need to see it for myself. See what happened."

Leigh looked away nervously, the memory of that torso lying on the ground still fresh. "We should call the Old Man first," she said in a soft voice.

"And tell him what? That the team's all dead and burned? That the Shroud is destroyed?"

Leigh's eyes started to water and her lips quivered.

"Aw, hell, I'm sorry," Jonathan apologized.

"You don't know," Leigh said, her lips trembling. "Maybe they're alive. Maybe they lived. Maybe—" she trailed off and wiped away a tear that had broken loose and streamed down her cheek.

Jonathan stepped to her and put a hand on her shoulder. "Look, I'm sorry," Jonathan said. "And you're right. We don't know. So what are we going to do? Call the Old Man and tell him what? Tell him we don't know anything?"

Leigh nodded, composing herself.

"Let's go to the Cathedral. The dust's settled by now, surely. Maybe they made it somehow. Maybe the Shroud made it. History repeats itself, after all," Jonathan said. "It's made it through more than one fire. Maybe it somehow made it through this one."

Leigh nodded again, wiping her tears away. "Thanks," Leigh said, putting her hand on his, which was still at her shoulder. "I hate being such a girly girl."

"And I hate being an insensitive jerk, but it's who you're stuck with."

Leigh gave a short laugh. "You're not such a jerk."

"You don't know me yet," Jonathan said and gave her a big grin. "Give me time."

Leigh smiled. "Come, let's go."

She grabbed her bag with her tablet computer. They walked down the stairs, through the lobby, and through the crowd that had gathered outside the hotel. They turned, and began the walk towards the foreboding gloom at the end of the street.

Piazza Reale
Turin, Italy
May 21, 2025   12:21 p.m.

Asad Hasan finished his second tea, paid, and rose gracefully for a man his size. He walked calmly down the arcade, past designer shops with their decadent advertising, towards the billowing smoke of the Cathedral. The streets were starting to fill with police and curious people edging closer to see what happened. He got to the corner of the Piazza Reale, jostling his big body through the crowd. He could see the smoke, black and poison like death itself, billowing from the ruins of the Cathedral. Military police, with their strange feathered caps, were setting up a perimeter and blocking the gathering crowd from going further.

It did not matter to Asad. The most important thing was what he could not see. The dome of the Cathedral. It was gone. Through the smoke he could occasionally see the two ruined walls that still stood and the big tail section of the plane. He could also feel the heat even from this distance. There was no way anything survived in there, of that he was sure.

He smiled. Saleem, that gullible bastard, had been spot on, crashing the jet right where he needed to. Asad stood, towering above the crowd, and looked at the mesmerizing fire and the wreckage. *Nothing could have survived,* he thought.

It was time to make the call. Asad moved away from the crowd, away from the noise and commotion, down Piazza Castello. He went inside an Art Nouveau shopping arcade. The glass and steel dome rose above him and expensive shops lined the marble halls. Here, the outside noise was drowned out by the expensive silence.

Asad brought out his phone and called the Lawyer. That is all he knew of him; the Lawyer refused to give his name, much less the name of his client. Asad suspected who that was, though. It was Sheik Al-Khaifa's plane, after all.

The phone rang and rang. It was normal. The Lawyer always took a long time to answer. Asad passed the time looking at the two-hundred euro T-shirts and five-hundred euro shoes.

At last, the Lawyer answered the phone. "Is it finished?" he asked without preamble.

"It is finished," Asad said.

"Any loose ends?"

"The Portuguese. He was sick in the hotel. And Smith is in Milan as you know."

"You'll take care of the Portuguese?"

"Yes. I am going there now."

"Good. Let me know when you are done. I will send you the location of Smith."

"And the rest of the money?" Asad asked.

"When you finish the job," the Lawyer said, annoyed.

"The job is done. Check the news."

"The whole job. That includes the scientists. All of them. And the Spain job too."

"It will be taken care of, don't worry."

"And when it is, you'll get your money."

The Lawyer hung up. Asad bit his lip and checked his temper. He disliked the Lawyer intensely. But fifteen million euros for what had been a fairly simple and very well-funded operation was worth the animosity. Only a little bit of cleanup work and he would be done. And wealthy.

Asad clenched his fist. It was a nervous habit he had acquired after an unpleasant time that he struggled to forget. He did not mind killing. Everyone had to die. It was only a question of when. And he was comfortable choosing that. Especially when it came to furthering his cause for the common good. And he was sure this was.

Asad turned and walked towards the hotel. He tapped on his phone and checked his notes again to make sure. The Chelsea. He knew it. He cut across the square, past the crowds, and walked there. He looked forward to the kill, to finishing the job.

CHAPTER 5

Piazza Reale
Turin, Italy
May 21, 2025 12:35 p.m.

The street ahead was a war zone. Jonathan looked back at Leigh and she gave a weak smile, trying to soften the apprehensive look on her face. They continued towards what was left of the Cathedral. Thick black smoke rose in great plumes from the Cathedral, darkening the sky. As they neared, darkness and dust started filling the air again, although nowhere near as bad as before.

The Piazza Reale, dominated now by the huge tail section of the plane, loomed ahead. Firefighters were scrambling everywhere, dousing the flames licking out from dozens of spots. A police line had been set up and the blue and white cars filled the street.

Jonathan shouldered his way past the gathering throng of the curious, to the police line. He started to cross the barricade with Leigh.

"*Arresto*," a military policeman called out to them to stop.

Jonathan brought out his security badge that allowed him access to the Cathedral. "We're on the Shroud team," he explained and tried to pass him.

The policeman grabbed Jonathan by the arm.

"Hey, our friends were in there," Jonathan insisted, and tried to twist away from the policeman, showing the security badge again.

The policeman, looking harried, studied the badge. He looked on at the crowd trying to get close and, out of frustration, waved Jonathan and Leigh through.

They approached what was left of the dome. Boulders and rubble lay all around them and emergency personnel ran in every direction. Through the chaos and the rubble and the ruins, a great red fire burned, like the mouth of a furnace had opened up at the center of the Cathedral. Even at this distance, the heat kept them at bay.

Jonathan glanced around, trying to orient himself in the destruction and confusion. "I think the chapel was over there," he told Leigh, pointing over to a cloud of billowing black smoke.

They skirted the plaza, stepping over the debris and huge chunks of marble ripped from the Cathedral. A group of firefighters ran past them and one of them stopped, calling out to them. He quickly closed in.

"*Non potete passare. Molto pericoloso*," he said, then added, "very dangerous," shaking his head.

"We need to see," Jonathan told him, his voice loud and rising over the chaos around him. "I need to see."

The firefighter shrugged and moved on, catching up with the rest of his team.

Jonathan turned to Leigh. "Stay here. It doesn't look too safe up there, but I need to see it myself."

Leigh shook her head. "I'm coming with you, mister."

A slight smile played over Jonathan's otherwise grim expression. "Let's go. And stay close."

They arrived at the back of the plaza, where one wall still stood. They followed this, avoiding small pockets of fire and stepping over the great stones flung down from the collapsed roof.

Jonathan turned to look at the plaza from his vantage point at the back. It was a surreal scene. To his right, flames and thick black smoke rose into the air from the rubble where the dome of the Cathedral once stood. The huge tail section of the plane, tilted off kilter, lay in the middle of the plaza. What looked like the remains of one of the huge engines was spread out over and around the other remaining wall. To his left stood the apartment building they had been in before. He looked up, through the haze and smoke, to the old woman's apartment that overlooked the plaza. The sun shone in a pale silvery disc as its light struggled to penetrate the haze. There were emergency vehicles everywhere, with more being added by the minute. Huge fire trucks spewed streams of water over the heart of the fires, and bellows of white steam rushed to the sky like primeval geysers.

Leigh nudged him from behind. "Let's get moving," she said. They walked on. "I think this is the long hall leading to the Sacristy," she said. "*Was* the long hall," she corrected herself.

The long hall, which ran the length of the plaza, was unrecognizable. Now, it was nothing more than a single standing wall. A mountain of collapsed stone stood between them and where the Sacristy should be standing on the far end. Beyond it, from what they could see, was nothing but smoke and fire. They began to climb over the rubble at the head of the hall, when Leigh caught sight of a hand, grey and dusty, sticking out from the stones.

"Jonathan!" she cried out, and pointed at it. She stepped over to it, careful to keep her footing, and started clearing the rubble. She felt for a pulse. "He's alive," she said, looking up at Jonathan who was making his way over to her. Her face was a mask of determination, though her eyes hid an old grief.

Without a word, they started clearing the rocks from the person underneath. Leigh cleared away the rubble around the face, which revealed the visage of Elisio, the young security guard. He appeared unconscious.

"Help me with this," Jonathan said as he tried to lift a huge block pinning the man's arm.

Leigh changed her footing and helped hoist up the square block, sending it tumbling down the pile of rubble. She looked on detachedly as the arm, free of the weight of the stone, suddenly started bleeding from several wounds. "Give me your belt," she told Jonathan.

He quickly undid his belt and handed it to her. She looped it around the man's arm, cinching it tight and staunching the flow of blood.

"We've got to get him out of here," Jonathan said, looking up with a troubled look on his face. The wind had shifted and it was now blowing the acrid black smoke towards them. He coughed, eyes stinging.

Working hurriedly, they cleared the remaining rubble from the guard's legs.

"Help me with him," Leigh said, coughing and trying to breath shallowly. "Easy," she warned as they eased the man out and gingerly moved him to the flat ground, away from the billowing smoke. Leigh knelt beside him, her eyes teary and nose runny from the smoke.

"I've got him. You go see if there's anyone else," she said as she examined him. She started giving him mouth to mouth.

Jonathan rubbed his eyes, glanced forward and sprinted back towards the mound of rubble. He climbed it, landing on the other side of what was once the long hall leading to the Sacristy. Even at this distance, the heat was intense, like standing in front of an open oven. Jonathan shielded his face with his arm and pushed forward. *There's no way anything there could have survived*, he thought grimly. The place was unrecognizable, just wall of fire. He looked in vain for any sign of life, or any sign of the Shroud. Hell, any sign of anything, he thought. There was nothing but flames. He coughed as the black smoke washed over him.

Crestfallen and barely able to breathe, Jonathan turned and hurried over the mound of rubble. He landed on the other side and looked on at Leigh, who was kneeling over the now conscious security guard. She turned to him.

"Anything?" she yelled out.

Jonathan shook his head dejectedly. He wiped his eyes and walked to her. "How is he?"

"He's lost a lot of blood. Looks like a broken arm, concussion, but otherwise he's fine," she said, and was silent a moment. "Nothing?" she asked, her voice low. "You didn't see anything?"

Jonathan's mouth turned down bleakly. He shook his head again. "It's gone. It's all gone," he said.

A group of firefighters ran towards them. They descended upon the injured guard, placing him in a back brace and readying him for transport.

"*Avete ferita?*" one of them asked Jonathan. Jonathan shrugged, and the firefighter repeated himself in English, "Are you injured?"

Jonathan shook his head. "We're fine. Right?" he said, turning to Leigh.

Leigh, satisfied that the guard was properly being treated, rose up, wiping the dust from her clothes. "Yes, we're okay." She walked to Jonathan. "Come, let's get out of here," she said, and tenderly put her hand on his arm.

They walked back towards the police barricade, crossing it.

"Let's get back to the hotel," Leigh said quietly.

"Good idea," Jonathan said. "You okay?" he added, looking over at her.

Leigh's eyes were moist and she was almost crying, both from the acrid smoke and the loss of her colleagues. "Yeah, I'll be okay," she almost whispered.

"Let's go," Jonathan said, eager to get away from the grim scene and back to the hotel.

Turin, Italy
May 21, 2025 12:39 p.m.

Asad walked through the crowd that had gathered at the Chelsea Hotel. He stepped to the side, away from the crowd, into the shadow of the building. He brought out his phone and scrolled through the pictures. There. Giuseppe Marcos. He studied the picture, committing it to memory, then tapped it. His file came up. *Textile expert. Specialty in ancient linens. Has done pioneering work dating Egyptian Mummy linens for the Egyptian Museum in Turin. May have samples or data in his possession.*

Asad thought it over. He would make it look like a robbery. He went into the lobby of the Chelsea. It would be easy, he immediately saw. In the confusion of that morning, the front desk was unmanned. The staff and half of the hotel guests stood outside looking at the billowing smoke rising over the buildings and the emergency vehicles driving by. Asad went to the front desk. The guest book lay open. He glanced at it and found the Portuguese's name. A few years ago Asad had trained himself to read upside-down. It was a good skill, and he practiced whenever he could. Marcos, Giuseppe, Room 10. He smiled. He liked it when it was this easy.

Asad walked up the stairs and followed the signs towards the room. He walked down the quiet red-carpeted hall. He kept an eye out for any other guests or staff, but there were none. He arrived at Room 10. Asad fished a pair of leather gloves out of his pocket and put them on. He clenched his fists. The leather creaked in the stillness of the hall. The light from a sconce behind him cast his shadow onto the door. He readied himself, tensing his muscles and picturing the move in his mind twice. He knocked on the door.

"Room service," he said in Italian.

Footsteps on the wood floor. The click of a lock. The door cracked open.

"I didn't order any—"

Before Giuseppe could react, Asad burst in, pouncing on him and putting him in a headlock. Asad twisted and the old man's neck snapped like a dry chicken bone. He went heavy in Asad's arms. Asad gently lowered him to the ground and shut the door quietly. The whole thing had taken less than five seconds.

Asad locked the door and looked at the old man crumpled pitifully on the ground, still wearing his pyjamas. Asad felt nothing, only a slightly quickened pulse from the burst of energy. The old man was going to die. That was not Asad's decision. It was Allah's. Asad thought of it as mercy. The man was dead before he knew it. No pain, no fear, no months of lingering disease. When it came time for him to give his life, Asad prayed it would be as fast and painless.

He stepped over the dead man and scanned the room. He went to the wallet first, looked through it, past a smiling picture of a silver-haired woman, the man's wife no doubt. Even then Asad felt nothing. There would be pain for her, yes, but pain was inevitable. Better that she should curse the killer of her husband than Allah for taking him through disease or accident.

Asad thumbed through the wallet. A little over two-hundred euros. He pocketed this. He would give it to the first real beggar he saw. He had no need for it. He tossed the wallet aside. Asad opened the suitcase and methodically went through every pocket, tossing everything to the floor to make it look right. There was nothing but clothing in the suitcase.

He scanned the room again. *There.* A silver Rimowa suitcase, a nice one. He clicked the latch open. Inside there were journals and Pyrex sealed test tubes. He held one up to the light and looked at a piece of string. A fabric sample from the Shroud, no doubt. He thought of taking the suitcase, but it was very nice and would attract attention. He scanned the room again. *There.* A black computer case. *Perfect.* He stuffed the journals and samples in the outside pockets of the case. He had to take the computer back to the Lawyer anyway. He searched the room carefully but there was nothing more of interest.

Asad shouldered the bag, listened at the door, opened it and went out into the hall. It was empty. He walked casually towards the stairs, taking his gloves off and pocketing them. He crossed the lobby and opened the front door, pushing it open with his foot so as not to touch it, and walked out into the crowd in front of the hotel. It had grown. People milled about, looking, pointing and talking excitedly. Asad put his sunglasses on and walked through the crowd, towards the train station, and towards Milan.

Turin, Italy
May 21, 2025 12:40 p.m.

Jonathan and Leigh pushed through the crowd, slowly making their way down the Via XX Settembre and leaving the devastation of the Cathedral behind. Sirens blared and the thumping of helicopters sounded overhead as they walked in silence the short way to the Chelsea. As they were nearing it, Leigh turned to Jonathan.

"I can't believe they're gone. That the Shroud is gone, just burned up and gone forever," she said, starting to cry in earnest now.

Jonathan nodded his head. Words of comfort weren't his strong suit and he was not sure there were any. He was about to say something, then stopped himself. With trepidation, he put a hand on Leigh's shoulder to comfort her. She leaned in close and rested her head against his chest. Jonathan put his arm around her. He could feel her warm tears seeping through the shirt as she cried quietly. She wiped her eyes with her hand and looked up at him.

"Thanks," she said.

"Anytime."

"Careful. I might take you up on that," she said.

Jonathan smiled at her.

"Oh look, I messed up your shirt," she said, dabbing at the wet spot at his chest.

"It's your shirt. And don't worry, it'll dry," Jonathan said. "How are you doing?" he asked.

"Better," she said and smiled weakly.

They continued walking down the street.

"You know," Leigh said, "we should go find the Portuguese, tell him what happened. He was out sick, lucky bastard."

"What's his name again?" Jonathan asked.

"I don't remember. Giuseppe something, the textiles guy. I thought you were the one with the photographic memory."

"It doesn't work that way, I told you. Besides, I'm terrible with names."

"No," Leigh said, incredulous.

"Yes, I am."

"I don't believe it."

"You're lucky I remember yours. You just happen to have the same name as a high school crush of mine."

"Now you're pulling my leg," she said.

"Would I do that?" Jonathan asked, smiling.

Leigh smirked at him. "I think you would," she said.

"Hmm, you're catching on to me already," he said, broadening his smile.

They approached the Chelsea Hotel. The red neon sign shone through the haze in the air. The elegant stone façade of the hotel was decorated with carved stone balconies spilling over with plants. The crowd in front of the hotel had grown and people talked and milled about outside excitedly, discussing the tragedy.

"You know we really should—" Jonathan began to say and trailed off. Something like a high-pitched whine was going off in his head. It was happening. His vision clouded for a moment then burst into crystal clear focus for an instant. The Shutter had gone off. Everything in front of him, the crowd gathered in front of the Chelsea hotel, the rising smoke, the acrid smell of jet fuel, the reflection of the blue lights against the panes of glass of the storefronts, everything imprinted onto his brain.

"You alright?" Leigh shook his arm, concerned.

"Yeah, give me a sec," Jonathan said, leaning down and resting his hands on his knees. He thought he'd be used to it by now, but the explosion of information and feelings took him by surprise every time.

"Is that the," Leigh searched for the word, "the memory thing?"

"The Shutter. Yeah, it's that. Just give me a sec. Old brain takes a while to reboot sometimes," he said, tapping the side of his head.

They stopped and got off the street, going in the entranceway of a kebab shop. Jonathan leaned against the wall. Leigh looked on, concerned.

He hated this part. Being weak, even for just a moment. By now, he had trained himself not to dwell on the flood of information, to just let it wash past him and into memory. He could never forget, but he could lay a blanket over it. A drink would help. *Not the time right now, my friend,* he thought and he was right. He felt a hand on his back, gently rubbing it.

"You okay?"

"Yeah," he said, meaning it. "Thanks."

"Anytime," Leigh said.

"Careful. I might take you up on that," Jonathan said. He saw Leigh smile. He straightened up and tugged down on his shirt. "Let's get going."

They walked towards the Chelsea.

Asad crossed the street, striding quickly away from the hotel and the billowing clouds of smoke at the end of the street. The biggest part of the job was done, the one with the most opportunity for failure. The rest he could handle himself. Smith in Milan would be easy.

The business in Spain was trickier. The Lawyer had a good plan, though he hadn't investigated the particulars himself. Asad also had a backup plan, though he hoped not to use it. If he did, he would not be around to see the results. It was a price he was willing to pay, though he'd rather not. He could wait for his 72 virgins. He'd be able to buy them anyway as soon as the mission was done. He walked down the street towards the train station. In two hours, he would be in Milan.

Jonathan and Leigh pushed through the crowd at the front of the hotel. He opened the door and watched as Leigh stepped through. The lobby was busy with people as well.

"What room is he in? Do you know?" Jonathan asked.

"Room 10 I think. He's a floor below me," Leigh said.

"Let's stop by and tell him, then go get cleaned up again and figure out what to do," he said.

They climbed the stairs rather than take the slow elevator.

"We should phone the Old Man after this," Leigh said.

"I guess," he said. "We probably know as much as we're going to know right now."

They walked down the red-carpeted hallway, illuminated with a golden light from the sconces on the wall. They got to the door of room 10. Jonathan knocked. No answer. He knocked again, rapping his knuckles hard.

"Maybe he went outside," Leigh suggested.

"I thought he was sick? Like, couldn't-get-to-work sick," Jonathan said.

"He *said* he was sick," Leigh said.

Jonathan knocked on the door again, then jiggled the handle.

"Jonathan—" Leigh said in a disapproving voice.

"What? I'm just checking if—"

The door swung open a couple of inches.

"Hello?" Jonathan called out into the room. He turned to Leigh. "How do you say hello in Portuguese?"

"*Hola*? I don't know," she responded.

Jonathan finished swinging open the door. There, in the middle of the room, lay the crumpled body of Giuseppe Marco.

Leigh gasped and ran towards him, thinking he had fainted or collapsed. Her medical training kicked in. She knelt at his side and felt for a pulse. Leigh went white.

"He's dead," she said, looking up at Jonathan.

He scanned the room. His senses were on high alert, using up whatever was left of his adrenaline. The emptied suitcases, the clothes strewn on the floor, the unlocked door.

"Someone's been in here," he said.

"Yes, and killed Giuseppe," Leigh said gravely, noting the unnatural angle of the man's neck. "This didn't happen from just a fall." Leigh stood quickly, her concern being replaced by fear.

"Killed?" Jonathan walked over to Giuseppe, knelt, and laid the back of his hand across the man's neck. "He's still warm," Jonathan said, looking at Leigh.

"This just happened, no more than twenty minutes given his temperature," Leigh said. "Jonathan, let's get out of here," Leigh said, nervously looking around.

"Good idea."

"Up to my room?"

"Let's go," he said, rising. "Like right the hell now. And not up to your room, but far away."

Leigh looked down at Giuseppe again. She closed her eyes a moment, then opened them up again. She stared glassy eyed at the body, fear and exhaustion mingling in her green eyes.

"Come on," Jonathan gently shook her shoulder.

She looked up and nodded absently. They walked out of the room, closing the door behind them, and went down the long red-carpeted hall to the stairs.

"We should say something to someone, call the police or something," Leigh said.

Jonathan shook his head. "If you do, it'll be hours of questions and Italian police," Jonathan said, "and it'll matter not a bit. He'll still be dead."

"But," Leigh started to protest.

"But nothing," Jonathan interrupted. "Let's just regroup and get a clear head around everything, then we'll contact someone and figure out what to do," Jonathan said firmly.

Leigh nodded glumly. He was right, but she didn't like it. "Okay. Lead on," she said.

They exited the hotel, walking silently away from the sirens and smoke at the end of the street. They crossed onto a side street, took it to the end, and mixed into the crowd on Via Roma, the wide arcaded street lined with shops that ran the length of central Turin.

Jonathan looked over at Leigh. "You okay?" he asked.

Leigh nodded without looking at him.

They strode in silence past designer shops, walking the opposite way of the curious crowd flocking to the Cathedral.

"Over here," Jonathan said and crossed the street.

He walked towards the Paradiso, a big Art Nouveau café and gelato place tucked under the imposing arched arcades of the Via Roma. A dozen or more small round tables lined the marble sidewalk. Jonathan pulled out a chair and motioned to Leigh.

"Come on, let's sit a bit. Gelato makes it all better," he said, trying to force a grin on his face.

Leigh followed and sat down, slinging her bag off her shoulder and looping the strap around the chair. Jonathan sat beside her.

"Gelato?" she asked, dubious.

"It helps me think. Hell, it'll help you think."

The waiter, wearing a starched white shirt and black bowtie, came over.

"*Duo gelato*," Jonathan told the waiter and turned to Leigh. "What flavor you want?"

"I don't know. I don't care," she said, sat back in her chair and crossed her arms.

"*Duo pistachio*. And two macchiatos too," he said. Jonathan resisted the temptation to order a whiskey. He had to stay sharp.

The waiter left with the order.

They sat in awkward silence. Leigh stared at Jonathan, fuming.

"What's the matter?" he asked.

"You mean besides being almost killed, losing your friends and colleagues, all your equipment, not to mention the most priceless artifact in all of Christendom? And now sitting here having ice cream? Nothing. Not a damn thing."

"It's not ice cream, it's gelato. And it'll make everything better. You'll see."

Leigh balled up a napkin and threw it at him.

Jonathan tried using his big winning smile but it did not work on her.

"Look," he said, turning serious, "I know you've been through a lot. We've been through a lot. But we need to process it. Something is bothering me, niggling at me, and I'm not sure what to do. My dad always said if you don't know your next move, don't move."

"Your dad?" Leigh asked. "What is he, a chess player?"

"Close," Jonathan said, "a marine. Was a marine. Career man, sergeant. Patriotic sort. He called me Johnny as a joke." Jonathan shook his head sadly. "He's been gone, what? Twenty-four years now? Christ, it goes by fast."

"What happened?" Leigh asked, softening.

"Afghanistan happened. I was twenty-one, he was forty. He reenlisted, and got a bullet for his troubles. It seemed right at the time. Probably was right, at the beginning at least," Jonathan looked absently at the people bustling by on the sidewalk. "I never did enlist; he never wanted me to. Talked me out of it, actually." Jonathan fiddled with a napkin, tearing little bits from the corners.

"So don't move unless you know where you're going?" Leigh asked, shifting the subject.

"Right. And, if something don't smell right, it ain't, he used to say. And this don't smell right."

"Agreed."

The waiter arrived with the gelato, carrying two small bright green scoops resting on top of sugary cones, and two macchiatos. They each took a cone and the waiter placed the macchiatos on the table.

Leigh tasted her gelato and her green eyes lit up. "Mmmmm."

"Told you," Jonathan said. "And it matches the color of your eyes."

"Cute." She took another lick of the gelato.

"See? Better?"

"Yes," Leigh admitted. "It's yummy."

So is watching you eat it, he thought, but didn't say.

"Good," he said. "Now, let's put that scientist mind of yours to work."

"Okay," she said around the gelato.

"First, we've got a plane crashing into the Cathedral, most likely on purpose since planes just don't do that," Jonathan said, counting one on his free hand while continuing to nibble on the melting gelato held in his other.

"Second?"

"Second, we've got the Shroud destroyed, barring a miracle. And there have been miracles, keep in mind," Jonathan continued. "Three, we have everyone in the building, most of the team, dead. And four, we have the Portuguese dead. Murdered, rather, at the same time." Jonathan rubbed his face. "The one guy that wasn't there ends up dead," he added.

"Smith," Leigh said.

"What?"

"Smith is in Milan, taking a couple of days off," she said. "He wanted to go see the Duomo."

"Do you know where he's staying?"

"No."

"Do you have his number?"

"No. Never did get too friendly with him. He isn't the friendly type. He's kind of a jerk."

"Yeah. I dealt with him the first day. He's the one that drove me to drink," Jonathan joked. "Nevertheless, we need to warn him. How can we get his number?"

"The Old Man will have it," Leigh said.

Jonathan nodded. "Good. Well, that just leaves—"

"Us," Leigh finished his sentence.

"Us. But we were supposed to be in there, in the Cathedral," Jonathan said, then paused. "We should be dead."

They were both silent a while, letting the realization sink in. They finished their gelato and stirred the macchiato.

"I think we should call the Old Man," Leigh said.

"I think you're right. And I don't think we should go back to our hotels. Do you have your passport on you?"

"Always," Leigh tapped her bag.

"The Old Man's credit cards?" Jonathan asked, meaning the expense account cards.

"Yep."

"Good. Lets call the Old Man then hole up somewhere, preferably not here," he said, glancing around.

"What should we say?" Leigh asked.

"Just tell him what we know. And get Smith's number."

"What about the samples?" Leigh asked.

"What samples?"

"The data. From the sequencers."

"What do you mean?"

"Remember? I had it all streaming from the sequencers to the tablet," she tapped her bag. "It's not complete by any means, but we have something. Quite a bit, actually."

"Well, that's one bit of good news. Was there anything interesting?" Jonathan asked.

"It's just raw data right now. It has to be processed, stitched together. I should start sending it to my lab in Manchester, actually."

"We can worry about that later."

Leigh nodded.

"Well, make the call," Jonathan said. "I think he likes you better."

"Don't all old men?" Leigh asked and smirked.

"Watch it," Jonathan glared at her playfully.

"Okay. I'll call."

"From here?"

"Why not?" Leigh asked.

She brought out the silver and chrome iTablet and swiped it on, the Apple logo glowing white on the backside of it. In a second it had a signal and was connected. She gestured at the screen, brought out the phone app and scrolled down to Rudolph Lahmbrecht, billionaire captain of industry, philanthropist, puller of strings, and financier of this whole mission.

Leigh took a breath. "I hate talking to him," she whispered to Jonathan.

She tapped the screen. The window opened and rang twice. Mr. Lahmbrecht's assistant, George Valenti, answered on voice only.

"Yes, Dr. Lancaster. One moment."

Leigh waited, tapping nervously on the table. The empty macchiato cups rattled.

"Doctor Lancaster." The image of Rudolph Lahmbrecht materialized on the screen. He had a creased, impassive face with sparkling blue eyes that shone like a much younger man's. "So good to hear from you," he said in his slow and deliberate voice. "I take it you are unharmed?"

"Hello, Mr. Lahmbrecht, yes," Leigh said, almost calling him Old Man.

"What do you know?" Lahmbrecht asked, always right to the point.

"Well," Leigh started, "I take it you've heard."

"CNN is saying it was a plane crash. It came on a few minutes ago."

Leigh looked over at Jonathan. "If it was a crash, it was a very accurate crash," Leigh said to Lahmbrecht.

"Indeed. The plane belonged to a Bahraini Sheik. There's talk of terrorism." Lahmbrecht betrayed no emotion. He seldom did.

Leigh and Jonathan looked at each other, wide eyed.

"We went to the Chapel. It was — in ruins," Leigh said, thinking of the scene of devastation. "Everything was destroyed. Everyone," she said, tightening her lips.

Lahmbrecht nodded but said nothing.

"There's more," Leigh said after a moment.

"Yes?"

Leigh thought for a moment, deciding how to phrase it. "Dr. Marcos is dead."

"He was in the Chapel as well?"

"No. We found him at the hotel. He was dead. He was killed, sir." Leigh let the words sink in.

Again, Lahmbrecht's old creased face was impassive. He scowled as he always did. "That is most troubling," Lahmbrecht said, then paused. He often paused for a long time when talking.

Leigh waited patiently even as Jonathan peered on beside her, out of camera range.

"But you are unharmed?" he finally asked.

"Yes. Me and Dr. Tremaine," Leigh said, looking at Jonathan. "We were outside when the fire — when the plane hit."

"Glad to hear about Dr. Tremaine." Lahmbrecht's face was stone.

"Thanks," Leigh said, awkwardly.

"It is most unfortunate about the Shroud," Lahmbrecht said. "All that research, all that investment, all that lost data."

"There is some data," Leigh said.

It was almost imperceptible, but Lahmbrecht's eyes narrowed ever so slightly and his brow added a furrow, if only for a moment. It was hard to see through the video feed of the phone, but Leigh noticed.

"Some data?" Lahmbrecht asked.

"Yes. I'd sampled many of the bloodstains the past two days. As you know, it is," she corrected herself, "was badly degraded, as you would expect from a sample that old."

"Of course."

"But we were starting to piece it together, stitching all the broken fragments. Given enough samples, I think we would have had a very good picture of the entire genome. We may even have enough now."

"You mentioned data?" Lahmbrecht said, a trace of annoyance creeping into his voice.

"Yes. I had it streaming from the sequencers to my tablet."

"Have you found anything?" Lahmbrecht asked. He leaned forward towards the camera ever so slightly.

Leigh shook her head. "It's just raw data right now. I need to process it, and the only computers around here to do it were in the Chapel. The other ones are back in the lab. When I get back to my lab in Manchester I'll be able to process what I have."

Lahmbrecht stared out of the screen, an uncomfortably long pause even for him. "I see. Are you going there now?" he finally asked.

"I think so," Leigh looked over at Jonathan and shrugged slightly. Jonathan nodded. "I'll have a better idea of what data we were able to salvage once the computers in Manchester process it all."

"Good," Lahmbrecht paused. "There is very little reason to stay in Turin. Make your way back to Manchester."

"Yes, sir," Leigh said.

"Ask for Smith's number," Jonathan whispered to Leigh.

"Oh, Mr. Lahmbrecht," Leigh said.

"Yes?"

"Smith, the microbiologist. He's in Milan for the weekend. We need to contact him and tell him what's happened."

Lahmbrecht nodded slowly. "I will see to it he is contacted," he said.

"Yes, Mr. Lahmbrecht, thank—" Leigh was cut short as he ended the call.

She swiped at the tablet and turned it off. She looked at Jonathan and let out a big sigh. "Well that was fun."

"I'm glad I didn't have to talk to him," Jonathan said. "Between you and me, I have an intense dislike of the man, no matter how many charities he contributes to or little orphan kids he saves."

"You don't like him, but you'll take his money, is that it?" Leigh asked.

"All day long," Jonathan said with a grin. He leaned forward, continuing, "I know you don't know this, but college professors don't make as much as hot-shot genetic engineers and future Nobel Prize winners."

"Stop it. Don't butter me up."

"No, you'll get the Nobel sometime. I'm sure."

"When I'm old."

"Old and happy and rich," he said.

"I'd settle for happy," Leigh said.

"May it be so," Jonathan said and sipped his macchiato.

"So, to Manchester. Are you coming?" Leigh asked.

"Of course. I've got to see the lady to her door like a gentleman, after all," Jonathan said with a smile.

Leigh blushed. "Hush, you. And thank you," she said with sincerity.

"For what?" Jonathan asked, fishing for a compliment.

"You know. For taking care of me. Thanks, cowboy," she said.

Jonathan grinned back. "Anytime," he said.

Leigh started tapping away at the iTablet.

"What are you doing there?" Jonathan asked.

"Plane tickets. There is a RyanAir out of Milan in four hours. If we hurry, we can make it," she said, reading the screen.

"Let's get going, then."

Jonathan paid. They got up and hurried towards the train station, keeping an eye out for anyone suspicious. In a short time, the ornate façade of Turin's Porta Nuova station loomed in front of them. They entered.

Leigh stared up at the large departures board. "Darn it, we just missed one. Next one is there, track one," she said pointing up. "Milan high-speed in an hour."

They stepped to the machine and bought two tickets.

"Well, we've got an hour, what do you want to do?" Jonathan asked.

Leigh stared past Jonathan and pointed. "Shop."

He turned to look at a large Prada store in the station. "Shop?"

Leigh nodded. "Hey, I left all my clothes at the hotel. Besides, those pants you're wearing have seen better days."

Jonathan slapped his hands on his jeans, sending up little clouds of dust. "Good idea. Plus, I'm minus one belt," he said, hitching up his pants.

For the first time in a while, Leigh smiled.

CHAPTER 6

Milan, Italy
May 21, 2025 3:55 p.m.

Asad Hasan grew impatient in the lobby of the Park Hyatt Milan hotel. He had hurried to Milan on the fast train for nothing. Smith had not been at the hotel all day. Asad could no longer afford to loiter there; he would be noticed. He did not like this hotel for the act anyway. This was a grand establishment, full of security cameras, keyed elevators and guards. *No, not here,* he thought.

Asad left the hotel, walking out of the lobby and across the Via Tommaso Grossi to a small café. He selected an appropriate table with good sightlines to the hotel's front door, sat, ordered a tea and waited. He brought out his phone, scrolled through his files to Smith's picture, and tapped it. He read the file to pass the time.

Christopher P. Smith, PhD, microbiologist, expert in pollens and plants. Brought on team to sample and study the many pollen grains the Shroud had acquired during its history. Previous sampling in 1978 had revealed pollen from plants indigenous to Jerusalem, indicating the cloth had spent at least some of its history there. Most controversially, the previous sampling had revealed heavy concentration of Gundelia tournefortii, *a plant that only exists in the Jerusalem area and only flowers around Easter. High concentrations of the pollen were found in the head area of the Shroud, the so-called crown of thorns area. Previous sampling was suspect due to less than rigorous methodologies. It is hoped Smith's sampling will be more scientifically rigorous and well documented.*

Asad stared at the information on the phone. *Could it be true? Could the Shroud have been real?* Asad thought. If it was, what would that mean? He shook the thought away and swore at himself for thinking these heretical thoughts. It did not matter. The Shroud was destroyed, and that was one less idol to worship. Only Smith remained, then the matter in Spain. Then Asad could rest and live like a sheik.

He sipped his tea and waited. *There.* A tall lone man walked through the crowded street into the lobby of the hotel. It was Smith. Asad paid for the tea and readied himself. All he had to do now was wait then follow him when he came back out.

The late afternoon sun still beat down on the buildings around him, giving everything a crisp, hard edge. Asad shifted in his chair under the parasol of the café. The streets were crowded here. Picking off Smith would be a job requiring patience.

Less than fifteen minutes later, Smith walked out of the hotel, now carrying a camera bag. Asad rose casually and followed, far enough to not be easily noticed. Smith crossed the street into the famous Galleria Vittorio Emanuele II, a huge nineteenth-century enclosed shopping arcade. He melted into the thousands of people milling inside, but Asad kept an eye on him. Asad followed, passing dozens of designer shops. Smith would occasionally stop and look at a window display and Asad would stop a few stores down, pretending to look as well. The Galleria was amazing, Asad though, with intricate marble floors and a huge glass and steel dome sheltering it all from the outdoors. Expensive restaurants were scattered here and there, their white tablecloths and gleaming glassware holding the promise of a fine meal.

Smith window-shopped his way through the length of the Galleria and finally came out at the Piazza Duomo. The vast open space was filled with people enjoying the late spring afternoon. At the end of the Piazza, the Duomo stood, huge and majestic. The cathedral, one of the biggest in the world, gleamed white like a giant wedding cake. Asad came out of the Galleria and looked in awe at the Duomo, momentarily losing track of Smith. He was astounded at its size and the hundreds of ornate spires rising to the sky. He picked Smith back up as he walked towards the Duomo. Asad prayed that Smith would not go in. He did not want to enter a Christian temple. He would be forgiven if he had to, just as he had been forgiven for shaving his beard. It was allowed in *jihad*, but still he did not want to go in.

Smith strolled leisurely through the plaza, stopping here and there to take pictures with his Leica M11. The gleaming white Candoglia marble of the huge cathedral reflected the sun and bathed the square in golden white light. Innumerable statues ringed the façade, staring down at the plaza from their perch high above. Smith walked past the front entrance to the side of the cathedral. There was a door and ticket booth with a sign in four languages posted above. *Rooftop viewing terrace. Warning: 240 steps: Admission 10 Euros.*

Smith paid for a ticket and disappeared into the small door. Asad hurried and followed, paying the ticket and going up the many stairs. He had to pace himself to not catch up with Smith, who labored up the stairs as he climbed further.

Finally, sunlight started trickling into the dark stairwell. Asad walked through a door of light and came out onto the beautiful white marble roof of the Duomo. This was no mere viewing terrace, but the entire roof of the cathedral that one could walk on. It was even more beautiful from up here, Asad thought, as now he saw the intricate detail of the hundreds of spires. The closer he looked, the more details emerged. Some spires were delicate flowers with blooming petals, and there were designs carved into the petals as well. Some were carved into the shapes of animals, each finely featured. The great plaza below served as backdrop, with hundreds of people moving around like tiny ants. For a moment Asad was overwhelmed at the sight and he lost track of Smith again.

Asad quickly checked himself, focusing back to the task at hand. He easily found Smith at the edge, taking pictures of the square far below. He followed at a distance. Smith would not get lost up here. There was only one way down.

Well, two, Asad thought.

It was late afternoon and the roof was not crowded. Asad examined the situation carefully. There were CCTV cameras at intervals, some of them set quite low and within his reach. He quickly formulated a plan, seeing it unfold in his head. He would have to wait for exactly the right moment, which might not even come up. But if the right moment came, he would be ready.

Asad stalked Smith, who was near the edge taking pictures of the view. *Not yet.* He could see a CCTV camera mounted high, pointed at the area. Asad followed Smith around the roof of the vast cathedral as the scientist stopped here and there to take pictures.

The next opportunity came and it was nearly perfect, with no cameras in the area. Asad readied himself to pounce. Suddenly, a gaggle of schoolchildren noisily filled the area. Asad cursed silently, but then reminded himself to be patient. Smith moved away from the noisy children to a small forgotten gable, hidden from the main expanse of roof by a flying buttress.

There. The spot felt right to Asad. It was hidden and no one would see them. Asad scanned for CCTV cameras. There was only one, mounted low at the corner facing away from him, about head high. The situation felt right. Asad saw the move in his head even as he walked forward towards Smith, who was at the edge of the roof taking a picture of the plaza below. He wanted to review the move again but there was no time.

Asad moved quickly. He took big strides on his long legs, moving with surprising speed for such a big man. As he neared the camera, he reached up and twisted it, snapping the neck of the mount. It cracked but remained on its mount, now facing the wall.

Without breaking his stride he reached Smith, grabbed him by the collar and belt, and heaved him over the safety railing.

Smith did not even hear anyone was on him until he found himself, in horror, plunging down the side of the Duomo in one last confused gasp of life.

Asad kept right on walking, resisting the temptation to look over the side. He got to the stairs quickly. He thought he had heard Smith land, a wet meaty thump, but it could have been his imagination. In either case, Smith was dead and the job was done. As he hurried down the stairs, he thought about the business in Spain. It was a good plan. It would work.

Asad came out at the ground floor of the cathedral. He could not resist the temptation to walk around the Duomo to the other side, where Smith had landed. He could not see Smith, but only the crowd that had gathered around his broken mangled body. It was enough. Asad strolled away through the plaza, towards his train at Milano Central. He would walk rather than take the subway and enjoy the beautiful day.

CHAPTER 7

Turin — Milan ETR-500 Line, Italy
May 21, 2025 4:45 p.m.

"You look nice," Jonathan told Leigh, who was sitting across from him on the high-speed train.

The scenery blurred past them, one long Monet-like streak of greens, yellows and reds.

"Thanks."

She wore a long black skirt, long sleeved black top and black boots.

"I think it looks just like what you had on before, though," he said.

"Yes, but the cut is nicer," she said.

"Well, you looked good before too." Jonathan gave her a big grin.

Leigh looked down, embarrassed, then met his gaze.

"You know, Dr. Tremaine, people in high adrenaline situations tend to develop an intense bond. It's documented. It's all chemicals."

"Are you saying we have an intense bond, Dr. Lancaster?" he asked in his best professor voice.

"I'm saying we should focus on the business at hand," Leigh said, slightly embarrassed.

"All work and no play, is that it?"

"It's not that," Leigh said and looked out the window at the blurred landscape. "I just don't want to get involved with anyone right now."

"Good, neither do I."

"That's what I'm afraid of."

"Crap." Jonathan shook his head. "I walked right into that one."

"I just," Leigh paused, "I know your type." She narrowed her eyes.

"Type?" Jonathan asked, indignant.

"Yeah. Smart, handsome, a player. Lots of girlfriends. Dangerous type."

Jonathan chuckled. "No one's called me dangerous before."

"Am I right about the girlfriends?"

"I wouldn't say lots," Jonathan said. "Well, maybe lots, but none right now."

"See?" Leigh said, arching an eyebrow.

"Maybe I just haven't found the right one," he said and looked into Leigh's eyes and gave her his best smile.

"You are a charming bastard, you," she said and shook her head.

"Now, that I've been called before, and more than once," he said with a laugh.

A trace of a smile crept on Leigh's face.

"Show me the rest of your tattoo," Jonathan said.

"No!" Leigh tensed her face, but her smile spread a bit.

"Then have a drink with me when we get to Milan."

Leigh rolled her eyes. "Let's get to work," she said, taking out her computer.

"All chemicals, huh?" Jonathan asked.

Leigh swiped the computer awake and tapped at it. "Yep. Look up the bridge experiment sometime," she said distractedly as she fiddled with the computer.

"Bridge?"

"An attractive lady interviews several subjects, guys, some on a high bridge, some on a flat street. At the end of the interviews she gives each subject her phone number. The ones on the bridge were six times more likely to call," Leigh said, without looking up, tapping at her computer. "The adrenaline from the high bridge was the factor," she added.

"I think the pretty lady was the factor," Jonathan said.

Leigh smirked, still tapping away at the computer. "All chemicals," she said, absently.

She dialed up her lab.

"Tabor Applied Genetics," the receptionist answered.

"Hi Nicole, is Tony around?" Leigh asked.

"Dr. L, thank goodness. We heard about Turin on the news. We've been worried sick. Are you alright?" the receptionist's voice came through the tiny speaker.

"Yes, fine, thanks," Leigh said, glancing at Jonathan.

"I'll put you through," she said, and there was a click and a pause.

"Leigh? Thank God," Tony's voice sounded out of the tablet's speakers. "We've been worried to death. How's Sally?"

Leigh cast her eyes down, and a tear started to well up. She shook her head. "She was — inside when it happened."

There was silence on the other end. "I — I don't know what to say," Tony said at last.

"I know. Listen. I was able to salvage the data from the sampling we'd done. I'm streaming it to you now."

"Okay," Tony said absently.

"Start processing it, we're flying in. We'll be there late this afternoon, God willing."

"We?" Tony asked.

"Dr. Tremaine," she said. "He was with me."

"Oh, Jonathan? The good-looking guy you were telling me about yesterday?" Tony asked.

"Yes," Leigh said, blushing. "He's — sitting in front of me," she said quickly.

"Ah, I understand."

"Get to work on the samples when you get them."

"Will do," he said. "And I'm glad you're okay."

"See you soon, Tony. And thanks," Leigh said and hung up.

"Good-looking?" Jonathan asked with a smirk on his face.

"I was telling him how insufferable you were," she said, blushing.

"I bet," Jonathan said and grinned.

Embarrassed, Leigh started poking at the computer, setting up the transmission to Tony. She worked on it as the train rocketed down the tracks.

Jonathan looked out the window and fidgeted. He turned back to Leigh. "How the hell does all this work, anyway," he said and pointed at the computer.

Leigh looked up and brightened. She loved talking about her baby. "Well, this is all the data from the sequencers," she said, showing him the tablet. The screen was full of letters, A, C, G, and T's.

"And the sequencer was the big black box back at the church?"

"Yes. It's a nanotube extraction system. Much, much faster than old extractors, like four orders of magnitude faster."

"Okay, you already lost me."

"Really?"

"Yes. I'm a history teacher. Dates and battles I can deal with."

"I failed history. Well, not failed, but came close."

"Talk to me like I'm five," he said.

"You *are* five."

"Cute. Maturity is overrated anyway."

"Okay. Five," Leigh took in a breath. "Our DNA controls everything in our body. It's our blueprint, like our instruction manual."

"Talk to me like I'm twelve."

Leigh smiled. "Everything is coded with four bases, let's just call them A, C, G, and T."

"That I know."

"Years ago, the best way to read the code was through Polymerase Chain Reaction Sequencing."

"Twelve years old, remember."

"Okay, you added a magic chemical and your DNA multiplied, then you added another magic chemical and it all unrolled. You took a picture of it all rolled out, like a barcode. The problem with all this is that it took time. Thirty days to read a whole genome."

"Genome?"

"Your whole instruction manual. And with ancient samples, it was nearly impossible. Old DNA degrades, like everything else. It's like someone put your instruction manual in a shredder. You'd have to take hundreds, even thousands, of samples just to have enough of the shredded bits to put back together again."

"And that's what this little computer does?" Jonathan asked.

"No. This one just is storing the information temporarily. Only the big ones back in Manchester are fast enough to process the data. Five petaflops fast."

"I take it that is very fast."

"Very. Once you have enough samples, the computers read the code and recognize the patterns. The computer then overlays them and pieces them together."

Jonathan nodded. "Now, what part of that makes you the rock-star?" he asked.

Leigh blushed. "I'm not a rock-star. I just stood on the shoulders of giants and all that."

"Yeah, but you came up with nano . . . nanostraws or whatever it is."

"Nanotubes. And I didn't come up with them. I just figured out how to use them effectively for sequencing."

"How's that?"

"Well, the basic premise is that if you could unroll the DNA and force it all through a tiny little tube — straw is actually a good analogy — you could read each base as it came through. You would shine a light through the straw and read the shadow. It would be a different shade of color depending on whether it is an A, C, G, or T. That's a greatly simplified version."

"Thanks for greatly simplifying it for me."

"The problem was it was difficult to unroll the DNA and force it through one hole. It kept breaking up. Imagine trying to force a strip of wet paper through a straw."

"I can't."

"And that's the problem," Leigh said. "We couldn't do it. Not well."

"And then you solved the problem overnight?"

"Overnight over five years. But yes."

"What did you do different?"

"We had it wrong, trying to fit the unrolled DNA through one pipe. We needed it to funnel down into the pipe. Into many pipes. I actually go the idea from work I did on water filters back in Haiti."

"Haiti?"

Leigh nodded but said nothing.

"You'll have to tell me about that sometime," Jonathan said.

"Sometime," Leigh said quietly, as if nursing a great wound.

"So, go on, filters," he said, sensing her discomfort.

"Yes. Filters," she livened up again. "Biosand filters. The way the filters work is the water goes through a diffuser plate, then through one medium, sand usually, which removes a layer of crud."

"Crud? Is that a scientific term?" Jonathan asked with a smirk.

"You want to know about positively charged extraction matrices? I wrote a paper on it."

"Crud is good. Go on," he said.

"So you have one layer of sand, then another layer of finer sand, then gravel, and so on, until you get clean water. That's what gave me the idea. Instead of having one tube to force all the DNA through, you have hundreds of tubes of different thickness. Mind you, thickness is relative. The smallest ones are mere molecules across, more than ten thousand times narrower than a human hair. So the DNA is diffused biologically, broken up, and it goes through hundreds of tubes, filtering its way down. The computers read each chunk and reassemble it virtually, putting together all the shredded bits of that instruction manual back in the right order by overlapping them."

Jonathan nodded, seeming to understand.

"Right now we are pushing over four thousand times the speed of the old way of reading the genome. But the machines are expensive. Not to mention one of them is destroyed. And the neat thing is this system works great for ancient DNA, too, since all that is bits and pieces anyways. I just needed more time, more pages from that instruction manual in the Shroud. And now it's gone forever."

Leigh looked out the window, dejected, as the train slowed. They were coming into Milan Central, past rail junctions and dilapidated outbuildings.

"Well, maybe not gone forever," Jonathan said.

Leigh turned to him.

"What do you mean?"

Jonathan gave a knowing grin.

"What do you mean?" she repeated, staring intently at him.

Milan, Italy
May 21, 2025   4:57 p.m.

Asad Hasan enjoyed the afternoon sun as he entered the palatial front entrance of Milan Central. It had been a productive day. The main mission accomplished, the cleanup work done. He would go to Spain on the train, even though it would take longer. Less paper trail, and the gun was a concern. Air travel was so messy nowadays. Too much security and documentation for even a short flight across the Mediterranean. He would travel in short stretches, making his way through Italy and the south of France to Barcelona, then to Oviedo.

Milan Central was a hive of activity. He went through the crowd and bought a ticket to Genoa from the machine using cash. From there, he would go to Nice.

Asad's phone vibrated in his pocket. It was the Lawyer. This was a burn phone and the Lawyer was the only one with the number.

"You missed two, dammit," the Lawyer barked without preamble.

"What do you mean?" Asad said, keeping his calm. He would not mind dispatching the Lawyer. The man was crass and had no respect for the game, or for life. *A fine thing to say, coming from a killer,* Asad thought.

"I mean," the Lawyer snarled, "that there are two still alive."

"The Portuguese and Smith are complete," Asad said. "I saw to it myself."

"Not them, you idiot."

Asad closed his eyes a moment and counted to three. "I do not see how anyone could have survived the fire," Asad said, trying to keep calm.

"They weren't in there. You should have been watching."

Asad cursed to himself. He disliked the Lawyer intensely, but the man was right. "I told you I needed more men," Asad said. *I didn't want to be too close to the Cathedral in case the pilot missed,* he didn't say.

"You know the orders, minimal personnel."

"Yes, I know. So, who are they?" Asad asked.

"Leigh Lancaster and Jonathan Tremaine. Their file is in your phone. And they have a computer which I require."

"Where are they now?"

"Milan."

"I'm in Milan."

"Where?" the Lawyer asked.

"Milan Central. The train station."

"Hold on. Let me check something."

The Lawyer paused and Asad could hear keys clicking in the background.

"Jesus, they're right there! Milan Central. They're moving slowly," the lawyer exclaimed.

Asad instantly went on high alert. "They must be coming in from Turin. Are they traveling together?" he asked.

"That is the information I have. Hold on one second," the Lawyer said. Asad heard the clicking of a keyboard. "Looks like the east end of the train station."

"I will see what I can do. I will contact you," Asad said and hung up, not bothering to wait for a response.

He scanned the incoming trains on the big board. There. Turin, track 12, at the east end of the station. It had to be that. He briskly walked there, bringing up their files on the phone to familiarize himself with their pictures. Lancaster was pretty, dark haired, pale, with delicate features and big almond-shaped almost Arabic eyes. Asad cringed. He disliked killing women. But it had to be done. He would do it quick. But he had to kill the man first, the greatest threat. He scrolled through the list to Jonathan Tremaine and tapped. The man looked to be well-built. But Tremaine was a college professor, and Asad had done more than his share of killing. Still, he would have to be careful.

Asad thought about it. He had the element of surprise. It would be nice to have an extra man, but he should be able to dispatch two unsuspecting scientists. He went to track twelve and waited at the platform.

Milan, Italy
May 21, 2025   4:58 p.m.

"What do you mean it's not gone forever?" Leigh asked again.

"There may be a way to get our hands on more samples."

"How?" Leigh asked, sitting up straight now as the train slowed to a crawl and pulled into the station.

"Helps to know your history," Jonathan teased her now, dragging out her suspense. "Maybe if you hadn't flunked—"

"Why you—" she said and slugged him on the arm. "Tell me already."

Jonathan laughed. "Ow. You're adorable when you're angry, you know."

Leigh started to slug him again.

"Okay, okay," he stopped her. "You want the five-year-old version or the twelve-year-old version?"

"Just give me the grownup and fast version."

"You got it. Back in the in eighth century in Spain—" Jonathan began to say, and stopped. His eyes glazed over, staring out the window as the train pulled into its track. He stared with a wide empty look out the train's window. Some great hidden synapse fired in his brain.

"Jonathan?" Leigh asked. "Are you kidding around?"

No response.

"Are you okay? Is it the Shutter?" she asked him.

"I know that man," Jonathan said, looking out at the platform where Asad Hasan stood waiting, scanning the crowd.

"Who?"

Jonathan pointed out the window. "The big Arab-looking guy."

"Who is he?" she said, looking. The man was intently observing the passengers as they exited the train.

"I don't know. But I know him. I've seen him."

"Where?"

"I don't know. Hold on," Jonathan said, closing his eyes.

Jonathan forced himself to remember. He was back at the last Shutter, back in Turin walking towards the cathedral, walking past the Chelsea, and could see and feel everything.

The acrid smell of jet fuel belching out of the Cathedral. The black plume of smoke darkening the end of the street. A woman holding her daughter close at the entrance to a store, her reflection in the pane of the glass door. Leigh, beautiful even through the concern and worry on her face, looking at the smoke, distant. A jet's contrail overhead barely visible through the haze in the blue sky beyond. His sorrow for the dead in the Cathedral as it battled his craving for another drink and, somewhere below all that, a small growing desire for Leigh herself. And in front of him, the crowd at the entrance to the Chelsea. Twenty-seven people looking out at the smoke, talking with each other, and one man walking out the door, looking away from the Cathedral. One big man, dark-skinned, his face hard and expressionless. That man. The man on the platform below.

Jonathan took a quick inhale of breath and opened his eyes.

"You okay?" Leigh asked again.

"Remembering is hard," he said, rubbing his eyes. "And I'm sure. That man. He was at the Chelsea when I had my last Shutter. That's where I saw him."

"You sure?"

"More than sure. Positive."

"How can you be sure?"

"Babe, I can tell anything you want. The clothes he was wearing are the same, same height, same features, same everything, though he was wearing sunglasses before and he isn't now. Trust me, it's the same guy."

"Who is he?"

"I don't know. But we shouldn't get off the train."

"Why not?"

"That man, who is waiting for our train here in Milan, walked out of the Chelsea right after the Portuguese was killed."

Leigh's eyes widened as she finally put it together.

"Oh," she let it sink in. "Oh. Sorry, I'm not used to this cloak and dagger stuff."

"Neither am I, but we better get used to it quick. That big Arab, or whatever he is, is waiting for us right there. And I doubt the sincerity of his intentions."

"I don't. I think he sincerely intends to hurt us."

"Yep."

"So what do we do?" Leigh looked around nervously.

"Let's stay on the train, keep an eye on him. If he gets on, we'll try to get off or find the conductor."

Leigh nodded.

They sat in silence, waiting impatiently for the train to get going again and watching the man, careful to not be seen themselves.

"Who is he?" Leigh asked, almost whispering it.

"No clue. But I'm starting to get an idea of what's going on."

"What do you think?"

"Big Arab guy, Sheik's plane crashes into the Cathedral. Connect the dots," Jonathan whispered.

"Terrorists?"

"Terrorists, *jihadists*, call it what you want." He eyed the big man outside, who had not moved.

"But why us? Why the Shroud?" Leigh asked.

"I don't know why us. The Shroud I can see."

"What do you mean?"

"Think about it," Jonathan said, "All through history people, Christians, have venerated it as the most holy relic. The actual cloth that covered Jesus at death. And, more importantly, that covered him at the moment of resurrection, if you believe that. Actual imprinted evidence of a miracle. *The* miracle."

"But why destroy it now?"

"What if science proved it real? Authentic?" Jonathan let the question linger.

Leigh nodded slowly.

"Besides," he went on, "people have been trying to destroy it for hundreds if not thousands of years, probably since Peter and John took it from the tomb," he said, and added, "if you believe that."

"I do," Leigh said earnestly. "Do you?"

Jonathan waved his hands. "I don't know. Historically, I can only trace it back to about the Tenth century, and even that is a stretch. Besides, I have other reasons not to believe."

Jonathan went quiet and continued looking out the window at Asad, who paced slowly up and down the platform. The crowd of people was thinning. A few stragglers ran, boarding the train.

"He's not getting on," Leigh said, peeking out the window. She turned to Jonathan. "What other reasons?"

"Some other time," Jonathan said quietly.

"I'll buy you a drink," Leigh offered.

Jonathan smiled, but it only rose halfway.

A buzzer sounded and the train doors sealed shut. They started moving.

"We're safe," Leigh said, relieved.

"I doubt that," Jonathan said, shaking his head, glancing around nervously. He spoke quietly. "Why? Why was that big Arab waiting for us there? I don't like it. Like my dad used to say, it don't smell right."

"He had to have known we'd be here," Leigh said.

"He must have followed us from the hotel," he said.

"If he followed us, how was he here waiting?" Leigh asked. She brushed a stray lock from her face and tucked it behind her ear.

"Good point." Jonathan concentrated, going over it in his head as the train silently gathered speed out of the station. "Maybe he has a partner," Jonathan suggested. "Maybe he had someone else watching. Maybe they're watching us now."

They both looked around, every person in the car suddenly suspicious. Leigh thought. "It still doesn't explain how he beat us here. He would have had to be on the train before us to get here first. Unless."

"Unless what?"

"Well, unless you're wrong. About him."

"I'm not wrong."

"Maybe it was someone that looked like him."

"I'm not wrong. It was him," Jonathan protested, but now doubt had begun to creep into his mind.

"Maybe he has a twin."

"Now you're grasping at straws. It was him. And he was here, which means he came to Milan right after the hotel, while we were talking to the Old Man and waiting for the train."

"Right after he killed the Portuguese."

"He came here right after. For Smith. He came to Milan for Smith," Jonathan concluded, finally putting all the pieces together.

"And we're next?" Leigh said, the worry shining through her eyes.

"Over my dead body," Jonathan said, then corrected himself. "Sorry, poor choice of words."

Leigh gave a small chuckle. "He somehow still knew that we would come to Milan," she said.

"Somehow," Jonathan said, staring out the window as the railroad yard gave way to the city and then thinned into countryside.

They sat quietly as the train picked up speed.

"So where does this train go, anyway?" Leigh asked.

Jonathan looked up at the screen behind Leigh.

"Venice," Jonathan responded, smiling.

Milan, Italy
May 21, 2025 5:05 p.m.

Asad Hasan stood virtually alone on the platform. *They did not get off the train. Why?* Asad thought it out. Either the Lawyer's information was wrong or they did not get off for a reason. What could that be? There was no way they knew him.

He called the Lawyer, who answered on the second ring but said nothing.

"This is Leon," Asad said, pronouncing it in Spanish. Lion. The name fit him and sounded better in Spanish.

"That was quick. You're a beast," the Lawyer said. "Did you get the computer?"

"They weren't on the train. If they were, they did not get off," Asad said, then added, annoyed, "is your information correct?"

"Of course," the Lawyer said, defensive.

"Why did they not get off?" Asad asked.

"I don't know," the Lawyer said. "Maybe they spotted you."

"Impossible. They've never seen me. I've never seen them. I'd remember."

"I don't know then." The Lawyer exhaled loudly. "What now?"

"The train goes to Venice," Asad said, looking up at the board.

"Venice — hmm," he said and paused. "Hold on. I'll call you back," the Lawyer said and hung up.

Asad looked at his phone and shook his head. He silently hoped that the mission ended with killing the Lawyer.

It's either him or me at the end of the day, Asad thought. He was sure of it.

Asad left the platform and crossed the sea of people to a small noisy café. Hurried travelers leaned on the stainless steel bar, quickly downing espressos and running off for their trains. He paid two euros and got a macchiato from a harried surly waiter who practically threw the tiny cup at him. Asad drank the rich coffee slowly at the bar, contemplating the change in situation.

I need another. Especially if they know me now. I need another person. A good one.

He had someone in mind, someone he had worked with before that he knew to be good and loyal. *There are many good, but few loyal,* he thought.

The phone vibrated in his pocket. He downed the macchiato and went out of the noisy café to a quieter alcove off to the side of the station.

"This is Leon."

"Okay, it looks like they did stay on the train. They are moving. They must have seen you. They must know you somehow," the Lawyer said in his grating voice.

"I doubt it."

"Or they suddenly decided to vacation in Venice, one of the two. Either way, they're headed there now."

"I need another man, especially if they know me."

"I was thinking that. I have someone lined up," the Lawyer said.

"I already have someone in mind. He is good, loyal—" Asad said.

"No," the Lawyer interrupted. "I have someone lined up. I've worked with her before."

"Her?"

"Yes, her. She's good. Very good."

Asad frowned. He did not like it one bit. And not only because she was a woman. That was secondary and he was prepared to accept it. It was that she was the Lawyer's idea. The beginning to the setup. Finish the mission, kill the staff to cover your tracks. Same old story. But they could do nothing until after the Spain business was finished. They needed him for that.

"Very well," Asad said, guarded. "Where's the meet?"

"You were going to Genoa anyway, right?"

"Yes," Asad said. *Did I tell him that?* He didn't think so. He made a mental note to review their conversations.

"Good. She's there. I'm messaging you the contact information. It is near the station. Meet her there and go to Venice, or wherever these bastards end up. With the two of you, you should be able to dispatch them. I'll keep you updated on their position."

The Lawyer hung up.

Asad shook his head. He did not like it, but it was the job. The job paid very well, so he would do it. He pocketed the phone and walked towards the train to Genoa. He had five minutes to make it and would be there in a little over an hour.

CHAPTER 8

Milan — Venice ETR-500 Line, Italy.
May 21, 2025 5:11 p.m.

The high-speed train barreled down the tracks, whistling like a bullet through the green Italian landscape on its way to Venice. Inside, Jonathan and Leigh relaxed in their seats.

"I've never been to Venice," Jonathan said.

"I was there, once," Leigh said. "I was fourteen and on a dreadful family vacation."

"Any brothers or sisters?"

"Nope. Only child. It was me and my mum and dad and my insufferable grandfather and my poor decrepit grandmother. We were only there two days."

"How'd you like it?"

"I liked it better afterwards, once the bad memories had gone away."

"Memory's a funny thing like that," Jonathan said, a mournful look creeping across his face. He quickly smiled to cover it up.

"It is that," she said, noticing the change of expression.

"What was bad?" he asked.

Leigh looked out the window at the flattening landscape flying past, remembering.

"The family. The way everyone would talk about each other behind their back. Everything was right and proper and cordial and dull, then Granddad would get up to go to the bathroom and my parents would launch into a diatribe, tearing him apart and complaining about his complaining."

Jonathan nodded, understanding.

"Then dad would get up and mom did the same thing with Granddad. They talked like I wasn't even there. Made me wonder if they did the same when I got up. If they talked about me the same."

"It must have been hard."

"Yeah. Made me hold it in a lot," Leigh let out a short unhappy laugh. "Anyway, we were there two days, on a cruise. Poor Grandmummy stayed on the ship the whole time. She was too feeble to walk around and no one felt like wheeling her around."

"So anything good you remember?"

"The food was wonderful. So much better than England. And the quiet and the canals and the gondolas. I wanted to ride in one, but they were too dear. Must watch our pence and all that. Though we didn't watch the pounds. I always imagined riding in one, with a cute boy."

Leigh looked out the window, then looked at Jonathan and smiled. He smiled back.

"I've been meaning to ask you about your accent. Can't quite place it," he said.

"Baltimore, Maryland, cowboy," Leigh said.

Jonathan laughed. "Now *you're* pulling my leg," he said.

"No, really. By way of Manchester."

"Explain please."

"I grew up in Baltimore, but my mum was British. We ended up moving there, to Manchester, right after I finished high school. Which was sixteen."

"Early finisher, huh?"

"Yes. But a bad time to move somewhere completely different. I didn't stay in Manchester long and ended up going to Cambridge. I think I was about the youngest student there. One of them, anyway."

"Were you always like," Jonathan chose his words carefully, "like the rebel, the vampire girl?" He gestured with his hand at her outfit.

Leigh laughed. "No, that came much later. I rebelled late and in many different ways."

"You'll have to tell me about them."

"Perhaps I will," she said, arching an eyebrow.

"Over wine at the edge of a canal?"

"That actually sounds rather lovely." Leigh smiled at him. For a moment they regarded each other, their eyes locking together.

"And after school?" Jonathan asked, breaking the spell.

"After school, I went right to work for one of my professors, Dr. Barnette. He owned a genetics research lab. Tabor Applied Genetics Company. It was his idea of a joke," she said, laughing to herself and remembering back with a wistful expression.

"I don't get it."

"T.A.G.C., the four bases of DNA?"

"Ah, yes," Jonathan understood.

"Anyway, I worked there for a few years and got burned out. My boss, Pete, Dr. Barnette, was the religious sort and suggested that I go do something I'd always wanted but had been scared of. And I did."

"What did you do?"

"I ended up in Haiti, doing humanitarian work. It was a great time, but—" Leigh's voice trailed off and her eyes moistened. "Well, that's another story for another time. I left there when I got a call that Dr. Barnette had died in an accident. Died and left me in charge of the lab. So I came back, and the rest, as they say in your field, is history," she said with a melancholic smile on her face. She stared at Jonathan, their eyes locking once again.

The train sped relentlessly through the now flat Italian countryside on rails direct to Venice. The conductor entered the car, asking the passengers for tickets, breaking Jonathan and Leigh from their trance.

"Crap," Leigh hissed under her breath, "what do we do?"

"I'll handle it."

The conductor made his way through the car to them. A conversation ensued with Jonathan playing the dumb tourist and offering to pay the difference in cash, which the conductor gladly took and probably pocketed.

"Cash." Jonathan looked at Leigh and grinned. "Fixes everything."

"Some people can't be bought," she said.

Jonathan shrugged. "We all have a price."

"Yes, but to some it's virtue."

"Ah, an idealist."

"I'd like to say I'm a realist idealist," Leigh said.

"How's that work?" he asked, tilting his head.

"I know people fail. I'm a realist about that. But I also know they are capable of great, good and selfless acts. So I'm an idealist about that."

"I'd say you're half right," Jonathan said and smirked.

"Cynic," Leigh said, but playfully.

"I'll prove it to you. Why did you take this project?"

Leigh looked up, thinking. "I—"

"Money," Jonathan interrupted before she could answer.

"No. Wrong," Leigh said.

Jonathan gave a short laugh. "So the Old Man's millions had nothing to do with it?"

"No, they didn't," Leigh said, straight-faced.

"So why do it? Why take a month or more of your life and devote it to this project? What are you trying to prove?"

Leigh closed her eyes and opened them, moist now. "To hold in my hand the blood, the actual blood of Christ, if it is real, would mean something. Not just for me but for the world," she said.

"What? What could it mean?"

"That this is real blood. That it has real DNA. It's human. I don't know," Leigh shook her head. "I thought it would make it more real to people. Make it more real to me. I mean, it doesn't have much scientific merit. I know that. It's just another genome. It's not like we can clone Jesus or anything."

"Why not?" Jonathan asked.

"That's science fiction. You saw that business in Korea, how exquisitely difficult it is to clone a living human. And that's someone that is alive and in front of you with real fresh blood and stem cells. With ancient blood? Impossible. Anyone that tells you different is trying to sell you the script to a very cheap movie."

"Okay, so why do it then? Why go through all the trouble of gluing together all those DNA pieces?"

"I think," Leigh said, "to have a better view of the man. To show that he was human and like us and still accomplished all these wonderful things. Isn't that why you're doing it?"

"Honey, I'm in it for the money. Was in it. You think we'll still get paid?" Jonathan furrowed his brow.

"Don't change the subject," Leigh chastised. "Why do you do it? And not just this project, but history. Why study it?"

"To know the future," he said, not missing a beat. Jonathan sat up straighter and leaned forward. "We all keep repeating it. History I mean. It's a fact."

"Now that is a cynical view. We're just doomed to repeat ourselves, is that it?" Leigh asked.

"That's realism, babe. Historic Recurrence, all the way back to Polybius. That's the way it is. Always has been."

"So why do it? Why do anything if you can't change anything?"

Jonathan sat back. "That's a good point." He paused. "I study history because it tells me all I need to know about people. It's helpful."

"What do you mean?"

"Take the Shroud for instance. Looking back through history, you can see how people have treated it. Some have revered it, some have been skeptical, some have tried to destroy it. That hasn't changed. It really tells you everything you need to know about ourselves."

"How so?" Leigh asked, brushing a hair back from her eye.

"Some people believe, some don't, some just destroy."

"Which one are you?"

Jonathan rubbed his face. "I think I fall into the not believe camp. Just by default."

"Whose fault?" Leigh joked.

"Cute."

"You know," Leigh said, "you're a last-worder."

"A what?"

"A last-worder. You always have to have the last word."

"I do?" Jonathan asked.

"Not in a mean way or anything. You just always have to have the last word in a conversation," Leigh said.

"If you say so."

"See?"

"What?"

"You're doing it."

"I suppose you're right."

"Stop it," Leigh said, narrowing her eyes.

"Okay," Jonathan said, the trace of a smile creeping over his mouth.

"Why you! Stop," Leigh said and socked him on the arm.

"Fine, I will."

"Stop it!" Leigh socked him again, hard this time.

"Ow. That one hurt."

Leigh let out a little mock growl and Jonathan laughed, then Leigh's face broke from exasperated to smiling to laughter.

Jonathan grinned. "It's good to see you smiling," he said.

She looked at him, blushing a little, then turned and stared out the window. They sat in silence as green fields blazed by at speed.

"What are we going to do, Jonathan?" Leigh said after a time in a burdened voice.

Jonathan turned serious. "Hide, I suppose," he said, "and try to figure out our next move." He stared out the window as well. "I can think of worse places to hide."

Leigh turned to him and smiled again. Jonathan put his hand on hers.

"Everything will be alright," he reassured her.

"Promise?"

"Promise."

CHAPTER 9

Genoa, Italy
May 21, 2025 6:15 p.m.

Asad Hasan looked again at the Lawyer's text message, which simply read: *Lady in Black, 32 Vico del San Sepulcro.*

He mapped it out. It was near the train station, less than 400 meters, down Via San Luca. He memorized the map and set out, walking out of the big station.

The streets turned seedy quickly. There were prostitutes plying their trade openly down small alleys despite it being only late afternoon. Shifty characters were everywhere, and they cast guarded glances at him. Asad was imposing, and he walked confidently, fearlessly. They should fear him.

Asad glanced around. It was this, he thought, the perfect example of the decadence of the West, that he fought against. And that was a fight he would give his life to win.

Asad went over the events of the day again in his head, questioning himself. *Why did the scientists not get off the train? Why does the lawyer want me to work with this woman?* He shook his head. Something was off and he did not understand what. And he did not like it.

He turned down a narrow street with garbage gathered at the curb. Prostitutes propositioned him and he ignored them, walking quickly past. One more corner and he would be at the meet point. He turned into a tight little alley and spotted someone in black at the other end.

There. That has to be her, he thought. Asad stood from afar, watching her, unseen.

She was tall and lithe, leaning against the corner in the relaxed but taut manner that cats have. The woman was indeed dressed in black, wearing tight black pants, leather boots and an elaborate black leather top, which almost looked like a corset. A small, expensive-looking purse hung over one shoulder. Asad studied her face, committing it to memory. She had short black hair and seductive, almost oriental eyes. Venetian eyes, he noted. She was beautiful, or rather, should have been, but there was a cruelness and hardness in her that gave her an air of menace.

She caught Asad looking and gave a twisted half-smile. He nodded and went to her. She walked to him, the heels from her boots clicking loudly in the silent alley. They met in the middle.

"My, you're a big one," she said in Italian and looked him up and down.

"I don't speak Italian," he said, in Italian, though he understood enough and could get by. "French, Spanish or English, please," he said, again in Italian.

"Or Arabic?" she asked with disdain.

"That too."

"Spanish is best," she said.

"Good," he continued in Spanish.

"You are Asad? The lion?" she asked with a smirk. There was a trace of contempt in her voice.

"Yes," Asad said, annoyed that the Lawyer had given her his name. "And what is your name? Or shall I call you the woman in black?"

She considered this. "I do like it. But no. My name is Adriana. Adriana Nyx."

She offered her hand and Asad automatically shook it. She held it for a moment.

"You can tell much about a man from shaking his hand," she said, still holding it and observing it.

Asad let go first. "And what can you tell about me?"

Adriana eyed him. "You are good in your work and a thinker. You have done your time with heavy manual labor, but have not done it in years. You were injured in the past ten years. The scar still shows. And — you do not like me."

"You are right on all counts," he said, impressed. Pretense would be lost on her, he thought.

Adriana smiled a small, amused smile that did nothing to soften her expression. "Good. I do not like false flattery. It angers me."

"Do you know the job?" Asad asked.

"Straight to business, too. I like that." She turned serious. "No. The Lawyer only told me there were two lost sheep and they were in Venice, or getting there at any rate."

"I do not know much more than that," Asad said. "Only that they somehow spotted me."

"How?"

"I am not sure," Asad said, rubbing a hand across his face. "They were on the train in Milan and did not exit. I do not know why. Either that or the Lawyer was wrong about their position."

"How is he tracking them?" Adriana asked.

"I do not know," Asad admitted. "By cell phone, surely." He thought about his own phone, suddenly heavy in his pocket.

"Good. They should be easy to track down," she said.

"Can you handle them alone?" Asad asked, hopeful. He did not want to be partners with this woman.

"I think so. Venice is a quiet town. You have to do it either in the daytime in a crowd or at night in a dark alley, and quietly. Or in the hotel, if you can get in." Adriana thought. "Yes, with two of them, in the hotel, cornered." She licked her full lips.

"Good," Asad said, relieved. "It would not be good for me to come. I'd be a handicap," he said, trying to get out of the job.

"You are hard to miss, my big burly man," Adriana agreed.

Asad motioned to her, just a quick look with his eyes. Someone was coming down the alley. Adriana turned casually to look.

It was a young man, scruffy beard, curly hair, muscular. He walked up to Asad.

"How much?" he asked in Italian, and tilted his head at Adriana.

Asad thought he understood, but was unsure of his Italian. He cast a questioning glance at Adriana.

"What did you say?" Adriana asked the young man, in Italian.

"How much? For just a quick one," the young man said. His eyes roamed freely over Adriana's striking body.

Adriana turned to Asad. "He is propositioning me," she said, in Spanish. Adriana gave a light laugh, but there was no humor in it.

The young man looked at both of them and gave a quick nervous laugh.

Asad looked at the young man and felt the tension in the air thicken. By instinct, he cleared his mind and prepared for trouble, tensing his muscles.

Adriana moved, catlike, to the young man.

"Well, that depends on what you want to do," she told him in Italian, her voice silken and sensual. She walked around the young man, running a finger over his hard chest and around his broad back until she was in front of him again. In her calf-high leather boots, she stood a full two inches taller than him.

"What — what do you like," the young man stammered out, his confidence being replaced by lust.

Adriana slowly, teasingly, brought her left hand around to the back of his head, playfully running her fingers through his hair. She took a big fistful of his hair and tightened her grip. She brought up a leg and coiled it around him. She pulled his head back and went to kiss him, then stopped, bringing herself to his neck and inhaling his scent.

"This is what I like," she hissed in his ear.

Quickly, with her right hand, she slid a stiletto from its hidden sheath in her boot. She brought it around and plunged it slowly into the young man, right under his armpit.

His eyes went wide with surprise, then his pupils dilated with slowly dawning fear as death bloomed inside of him. His body went stiff for a second, then limp. Adriana held him tight, easing him down to the alley floor.

"Sleep, *bambino*," she whispered softly, and laid him on the ground as tenderly as a mother would lay an infant down in a crib. She stared into his eyes and watched the life slowly ebb away from them. She brought the blade out and he gave a little jump. Adriana cleaned the blade on his white shirt, leaving streaks of blood. The young man coughed, sputtering up blood. The wound bled profusely, slowly dyeing the shirt crimson. A tiny sound, like a small clogged fountain gurgling sickly, was the only sound audible in the silence of the alley.

Asad looked on in disgust. It was not the killing that bothered him. He had done that and worse. It was the sheer needlessness of it. The man could have been shooed away easily. Now, there was a body to deal with.

Adriana rose from cleaning her stiletto. She slid it into the sheath, which was expertly hidden at her calf in her black leather boots. She let out a small moan of pleasure.

Liquid steel filled her eyes. Her pupils were huge and dilated and she wore an expression of sensual contentment. She gazed at Asad and, saying nothing, walked past him and down the alley, leaving the dying man on the ground.

Asad glanced down at the man, shook his head and followed her, catching up quickly. They came out of the alley onto a bigger street and both walked away casually but quickly.

Asad started to ask her why she did that, but he stopped himself, fearing the answer. Adriana turned to him.

"See, quiet and quick," she said with a smile, and it was a sincere and fearsome smile.

After they were some distance from the alley, Asad spoke up. "I need to get going," he said, more anxious than ever to leave. "Here," he handed her the cell phone. "This has all of the files on the targets."

"Don't you need it?"

"I have another." And, he thought to himself, if the Lawyer *was* tracking him via the phone, it would not hurt to lose it. Asad took a deep breath. He wanted to finish the Spain business and get his money and never have to deal with the Lawyer or his minions again.

"Anything else, then?" Adriana asked.

"Just a favor."

"Yes?"

"Make it quick for the woman."

"I will," Adriana said.

"Good luck," Asad told her and split off, eager to hop the train to Nice and get some distance between them.

Adriana paused and made a call to the Lawyer. Asad could barely hear her as he walked away.

"No, he's gone. Yes. Yes. I understand," she spoke into the phone, and then Asad was too far away to hear.

Milan — Venice ETR-500 Line, Italy.
May 21, 2025 6:15 p.m.

Leigh woke up from her nap, momentarily disoriented.

"Boy, you were out like a light," Jonathan said. "I almost nodded off myself."

"Trains put me to sleep," she said, yawning. "How much longer?"

"Not long, maybe ten minutes."

Leigh stretched and rubbed her eyes. She looked out the window at the passing landscape. "What's the plan when we get there?" she asked.

"Get a place, get as much cash as we can from the Old Man's credit cards, then, I don't know. Get to the lab, to Manchester tomorrow, I suppose."

"Sounds good."

"Say, that thing get a signal here?" Jonathan pointed at Leigh's tablet computer, which she had in her bag slung across her chest.

"It should."

"Let me see it."

She handed it to him. Jonathan swiped it on and brought up the browser, tapped out an address and scrolled through some pages.

"Whatya doing there, cowboy?"

"Getting us a room. A nice one."

He spun the screen around, showing her the picture.

"Nice."

"Almost everything is booked for tonight, so I had to get us a suite."

"That will do nicely."

"I love spending someone else's money." Jonathan grinned, tapping out the credit card information.

"When you're done, I want to call Tony in the lab. After we settle in, maybe call the Old Man, then food. I'm starving."

"Done. Say, what's that there?" Jonathan pointed at a small window on the corner of the screen.

"That's the processed data of the blood samples I'm getting back from Tony. The tablet has been emailing him the raw data. Looks like he's already started in on it."

"It's pretty," Jonathan said, looking at the gentle scrolling of colors. "What exactly am I looking at?"

"Each slice of color you see is essentially a virtual photograph of each molecule as it passed through one of the nanotubes. The white colored one is an 'A' molecule, the purple one a 'C', the gold a 'G', and the red is a 'T'. The black ones are missing sections, parts that couldn't be read. Here, give me that."

Leigh took the computer and opened the window completely, filling the screen.

"See how there is a band of gaps in this one?" Leigh pointed at the screen, "then it picks back up, here." She scrolled down to a kaleidoscope of colored squares and bars. "The computer reads the data, interprets the signals from the nanotubes, and figures out the order of everything based on the position in the sequence and the time stamp of the sampling."

"I can't say that I understand it all, so I'll just have to go on faith," Jonathan said, shaking his head.

"See? At the end of the day it's all about that. Whether you're talking the Shroud or the science."

"Very funny, doctor. Don't you have some work you should be doing?"

"As a matter of fact, yes."

Leigh tapped on the computer and rang up Tony. His blurry image came up in a window.

"Tony, how's it going?" Leigh asked.

"Hey girl," Tony's tinny voice emerged from the speaker. "Coming along nicely. I started uploading the results from some of the samples you sent."

"I saw. Thanks."

"There are a lot of anomalies in some of the samples you sent. I've got the computer trying to piece it all together."

"What kind of anomalies?" Leigh asked, narrowing her eyes. "Gaps?"

"There are gaps yes, but also just big stretches of one base. Huge stretches. Not normal, even for junk DNA. I'm not sure if the samples were bad or if the sequencers glitched."

"Run them again, then compare those sections to the same sections in other samples," Leigh said.

"I already thought of that. As soon HAL finishes processing the last batch, I'll run it again."

"How long?"

"About four hours. I just put them in."

"Good. Keep me updated," Leigh said.

"Will do."

"Listen, Tony, we've had — a little delay. We probably won't make it in tonight."

"Oh? Is everything alright?"

"Yes. I'll let you know as soon as we get a flight," Leigh said.

"Good. Stay safe out there," Tony said, and hung up.

Leigh swiped the computer to sleep and looked up. Jonathan was staring at her.

"You should have told him," Jonathan said.

"Told him what? That we're possibly being chased by a killer? What good will that do? It'll just worry him. He's worried enough that we were almost killed at the Cathedral."

"Have it your way," Jonathan shrugged. "And, HAL?" Jonathan asked.

"Our little joke. The big computer is, well, pretty big. We call him HAL," Leigh said.

"Very cute."

"I rather thought so."

The train started to cross water.

"We're near," Jonathan said.

CHAPTER 10

Venice, Italy
May 21, 2025 6:23 p.m.

The train sped over the *Ponte della Libertà*. The emerald-green water below glistened with flecks of gold from the late afternoon sun. There was a palpable change in the quality of light, as if everything were lit by the reflections of a golden sea. Even the air felt different, cleaner, more nautical somehow. The train slowed, and they pulled into Santa Lucia station.

"Keep your eyes peeled," Jonathan said as they gathered their possessions, which consisted of Leigh's laptop bag and a small Louis Vuitton suitcase containing all their purchases.

The doors slid open and they stepped onto the platform, losing themselves in the anonymity of the hundreds of people exiting the train. They glanced around, looking for anyone suspicious, and carefully made their way down the long track to the concourse. After taking turns withdrawing the maximum amount from the ATM, they stepped out of the station.

"Wow," Leigh said.

They stood at the steps of the station, looking across to the *Canalasso*, the Grand Canal that snaked its way through the city. On the other side, the Canal was lined with row after row of *palazzos*. The water displaced by *vaporettos* gently lapped at the *palazzos'* beautiful and ornate façades. The broad plaza was filled with tourists going in every direction.

"This doesn't look real. It looks like a theme park," Jonathan said.

"It sure does," Leigh said, glancing around at all the buildings.

"So how do we get to the hotel, Ms. Been-here-before?"

"I was fourteen, cowboy," Leigh said, adding, "and I stayed on a cruise ship."

They looked at the commotion in front of them. People hurried along, going every which way. There were several stations for the *vaporettos*, the bus-like ships that plied the waters of the Grand Canal. Each was marked with a letter for the different lines. It was all hopelessly confusing.

"How about we take a cab," Jonathan said. He pointed over at a dock reading *Taxi Acquei*. Sleek wooden motorboats lined the dock, waiting for passengers.

"Sounds nice. We have the money."

"Done," he said and began walking towards them. Leigh followed.

They walked down the wooden steps of the dock to the first boat, which gleamed with polished wood and brass fittings. Jonathan stepped into the boat first and offered Leigh his hand.

"The San Cassianno, please," Jonathan told the taxi captain and he nodded.

Leigh and Jonathan settled in, preferring to stand up front with the captain rather than in the elegant curtained compartment aft. The captain eased the boat off the dock, spun around easily and throttled it down the Grand Canal.

It was heart stopping. Achingly beautiful. Gorgeous *palazzos* lined the waterway to either side of them. Boats of every sort plied the waters of the Canal. *Vaporettos*, other taxi boats, delivery barges, locals on all manner of small craft and, always, gondolas, crisscrossed and danced around each other and somehow managed to not crash.

"I always wanted to go on one of those," Leigh said, pointing at a gondola gliding down the other side.

"Tonight, your wish shall be fulfilled," Jonathan said confidently.

Leigh looked at him and smiled a beautiful smile as the Grand Canal scrolled past them and her short black hair flapped in the wind. Her eyes were the same light sea-green of the canals. Jonathan wished for a Shutter moment right then, so he could remember every single detail. Instead, he had to rely on his regular memory and hope it would not fade. He closed his eyes a moment and tried to burn the beautiful scene onto his mind.

The taxi motored its way through the Grand Canal that undulated the length of Venice and, after ten minutes, arrived at the San Cassianno, pulling alongside the small dock at the water entrance of the hotel. It was a small but magnificently restored *doge's*, or duke's, palace. They stepped out of the boat and on to the dock.

They entered the hotel and were greeted by a porter. The lobby was filled with oriental rugs and antiques and Murano glass chandeliers and beautiful original art on the walls. Still, it was small and cozy enough to not be ostentatious.

"Now this is a classy place," Jonathan whispered to Leigh as they checked in with the friendly desk clerk.

The porter showed them to their room on the third and top floor. It was magnificent. A large, canopied bed dominated the room, with a couch off to the side. Big Murano glass windows lined either side of the large glass French doors. These opened onto a small balcony overlooking the Grand Canal. Leigh opened them and looked outside.

Jonathan tipped the porter even though there was nothing really to carry.

"It's brilliant," Leigh said, turning around to look at Jonathan.

She looked so happy, Jonathan thought, so different from the worried look she had been wearing the last few hours, as if she could sense this was a safe place. He could scarcely believe only a few hours ago they'd been standing in the smoldering ruin of Turin's cathedral. Everything still felt surreal to him, the way it often does when something horrible and monumental happens.

"It's really nice," Jonathan agreed. He looked around, realizing there was only one bed, although it was a big one. "I'll take the couch," he said.

"Nonsense," Leigh said, "you can sleep on the floor." She smiled coyly at him.

Jonathan raised an eyebrow. "Watch it, miss. There's lots of canals around here you can accidentally on purpose be knocked into," Jonathan joked.

"The couch it is for you, then," she said.

"Hmmm. I wonder if there is anything I can do to improve my station."

"Oh really?" Leigh said, narrowing her eyes and crossing her arms.

"There's hope. I just worked my way up from floor to couch with a few words," he said, grinning broadly.

"Watch it, cowboy."

"Yes, Doctor." Jonathan looked at her, still grinning.

"Good," she said. "Now about that food—"

"It's a bit early," Jonathan looked at his phone. He never wore a watch. "Only seven. It'll be just tourists eating."

"We *are* tourists."

"Good point. Let's go, then."

"Let me freshen up," she said.

"You sounded plenty fresh before."

"I said watch it, cowboy," she said, playfully.

"I am," Jonathan said and stared at her. "Go, go," he added.

Leigh went to the spacious bathroom as Jonathan explored the room. He set the suitcase down on a chair and opened it up.

"You ready yet?" he called out.

"Just making myself beautiful. Or at least presentable."

"It shouldn't take long."

"I'm on to you, cowboy, you and your lines."

"They may be lines, but they're the truth."

Leigh came out of the bathroom. "There," she presented herself.

"See?" Jonathan said. "Lovely."

"Flatterer."

"Only when it's true."

Leigh smiled. "Let's go."

They went out of the hotel into the maze of streets that was Venice.

Genoa, Italy
May 21, 2025   6:45 p.m.

Adriana Nyx sat under the awning of the café across from Genoa's ornate Piazza Principe train station, sipping a macchiato, waiting for the Lawyer to call. She pulled a long slender cigarette from her purse, lit it, and smoked it slowly, savoring it. She thought of Venice and how lovely it was this time of year. She thought of the girl and the man, of stalking them unseen through the narrow Venice streets at night. She smiled to herself.

"Another?" the waiter interrupted her thoughts.

Adriana nodded. The waiter left and returned with a small cup. He set it down and left. Adriana took another pull from her cigarette and started fidgeting with her phone.

"Where are you?" she hissed in a low voice to herself.

She hated the Lawyer. But he wrote the checks, and they were large checks. She had known him for years. He had certain desires, needs really, which she was only too happy to satisfy. And he paid dearly for these, both in coin and in the flesh. But one day she longed to do more than cause him the temporary pain which he enjoyed anyway. One day she longed to see his life ebb away as the young man's had that afternoon. That day would come soon, she hoped. Until then, she was glad to take his money, acceding to his miserable and insistent demands or tolerating his hapless groveling, depending on what mood he was in.

The phone vibrated in her hand. She put the cigarette out. With an uneasy feeling of revulsion, she swiped the talk button.

"*Pronto*," she answered in a curt tone.

"Hello, Miss Nyx," the Lawyer said in an oily voice.

"Stop your useless groveling. This is business."

Business is business and pleasure is business as well, she thought.

"Of course," the Lawyer said, his tone hardening.

"Do you have their position?" she asked.

"Not accurately. I lost the signal shortly after the train station. I'm not sure why."

"Do you have an idea where at least?"

"Somewhere between the Modern Art Museum and the Ca' d'Oro."

Adriana thought back, trying to picture the location. It had been years since she had lived in Venice. "Aren't those on different banks?" she asked.

"Yes," the Lawyer said. "They were probably on a boat in the Canal when we lost signal. As soon as I get more information I will contact you."

"Please do. I do not want to hunt through half of Venice for them."

"Did the Moor leave?" the Lawyer asked.

"Yes. He took the train to Nice."

"Let me know if you need another man."

"You know I work better alone, *mio pulce*," Adriana breathed into the phone. "But I think I can handle two scientists. Don't you agree?"

"Yes, of course. Just let me know if you need anything at all."

"Yes, a hotel. A nice one," she said.

"I'll get you the best. Happy hunting."

Adriana smiled and hung up.

She glanced at the time on the phone, threw some coins down on the table, and left. She hurried across the street to the station and looked up at the departures board. She cursed. All the high-speed trains had left for the day and there was only the Express, which was anything but. She bought the ticket and settled in for the four-hour ride.

There will be no hunting tonight, she thought. She hoped that by tomorrow the Lawyer had better information, otherwise it would be a long hunt indeed.

Venice, Italy
May 21, 2025 7:31 p.m.

"This place is confusing," Leigh said, fiddling with a hopelessly inaccurate tourist map.

"The only way not to get lost is to not have anywhere to be," Jonathan said.

The narrow streets suddenly opened up into beautiful open squares, or just as often dead-ended into steps leading down into a side canal. They stood at one of these dead ends now. The waves gently lapped at the algae covered stairs. It was quiet. The occasional muted engine of a boat and the afternoon singing of birds were the only other sounds.

"I'm fairly sure it's the other way," Leigh said.

"Yeah, that way looks wet."

They backtracked and were soon at a larger *calle*, crossing a small bridge. The late spring sun hung low and fiery orange in the sky, as if wanting to take one last look at the beautiful city.

"This is fairly amazing," Jonathan said, pausing at the top of the bridge and looking at the buildings painted with orange sunlight reflecting from the waters.

"And to think, this was all swamp. It boggles the mind," Leigh said, pausing as well.

"You know, I've read about this city and know a lot of the history, but nothing can prepare you for this."

"It's like talking about being in love, and being in love. No comparison," Leigh said.

"Very well put, Ms. Lancaster."

"That's Doctor Lancaster to you, sir."

"Show me the rest of your tattoo."

"No," Leigh said, and brushed a stray lock back.

"I want to see it."

"I know. That's why I'm not showing it to you." Leigh gave him a small smile and walked on.

Jonathan followed.

"You will," he said, catching up to her.

Leigh laughed and shook her head.

"Ah dammit," Jonathan cursed.

"What?"

"We've been here before," he said as he looked at the name of the plaza.

"It does look familiar."

"That's because we were here about fifteen minutes ago."

"No problem. Let's just make a left instead of a right up here," Leigh said, pointing.

They walked past the San Cassiano church and turned left onto Calle del Campanile.

"This looks more promising," Jonathan said, spotting the Grand Canal ahead.

They walked towards the water and turned right and were at the fish market, which was deserted and scrubbed clean of the day's catch. It smelled of fish, but not unpleasantly so.

"I vote for the first restaurant we come to," Leigh said.

"Okay, but it better be a good one."

They turned off the first side street they came to and found a place, nicely tucked back, not too obvious, with tables set outside on the narrow street.

"This looks like the place," Jonathan said. "Off the beaten track, two exits down either side of the street, and it's a fish place a block from the fish market."

Leigh nodded. "I applaud your instincts."

Jonathan asked for a table for two and a friendly heavy-set waiter seated them at an outdoor table.

"*Uno botella de tu mejore vino*," Jonathan told the waiter before he left to fetch menus.

"That wasn't even Italian," Leigh said, "you just spoke Spanish with an Italian accent."

"How nice of you to notice, Doctor," Jonathan said, adding, "and I think he understood me."

"Let's see what he comes back with."

"If it is wine I'll drink it and you'll drink it."

"I will?" Leigh raised an eyebrow.

"Yes. You promised me a drink."

"You're right. And you promised to share some things about yourself," Leigh said.

"Once you get me drunk."

Leigh took a deep breath. "We should both get drunk. It's been a long day," she said.

"But not too drunk. We want our wits," Jonathan said.

"Not all our wits." Leigh brushed a stray lock back from her face.

"Not all of them," Jonathan agreed, "just enough."

They looked at each other again and said nothing, but it was a comfortable silence and it lasted until the waiter came back with a very good bottle of white.

"Silvio Jermann Capo Martino 2024, sir. Is this acceptable?" the waiter asked in perfect English, presenting the bottle on a white cloth draped across his arm.

"As long as you have more, yes," Jonathan said.

"We do."

"Then pour it, sir. And you can dispense with the pleasantries."

"By all means." The waiter uncorked it and smelled the cork, then poured Leigh's glass half full then Jonathan's, forgoing the tasting ritual as Jonathan had requested.

Jonathan felt the bottle. "No need for ice. It will die soon." He said this last part in Spanish, as it sounded more poetic and less macabre. The waiter withdrew.

Jonathan raised his glass and Leigh followed. "To Venice, to us," he toasted.

"To being alive," Leigh added.

"To being alive," Jonathan repeated.

They ever so lightly clicked the thin crystal wine glasses.

"Did you know that the Swiss always look each other in the eye when toasting?" Jonathan asked.

"I did not."

"Americans, and most others, look at the glass. But the Swiss look each other in the eye."

"How do you know this?"

"I am a depository of useless knowledge," Jonathan said.

"Not so useless if you are in Switzerland," she said with a smile. "Have you traveled much?" Leigh asked.

"Some. All through Europe, mostly to conferences and on research. Jerusalem, too," he said. "Tell me about Haiti."

"No," Leigh said, and looked away down the street with a melancholic smile.

"Okay. Maybe later?" he asked, noting her expression and dropping the matter.

"Maybe. Pour me more wine," she said, downing what she had.

"And I thought I was the drunk," he said, pouring.

"Why do you drink?" she asked.

"Because I'm thirsty," Jonathan said and smiled.

"Really. Tell me."

"To forget," he said, turning more serious.

"Truly?"

"Yes. The problem with my — gift," he said, tapping the side of his head, "is that I remember everything after one of my episodes."

"Everything?"

"Yes. Even how I felt. If I could pick and choose which moments to remember it would be bearable. But you can't pick it. I can't pick it."

"It's hard for me to understand," Leigh said.

"Imagine a time in your past that was a great hurt."

"Okay." Leigh's eyes misted a little, though it was hardly noticeable in the waning light of dusk.

"Now, it doesn't hurt as much because time's gone by, right? Time heals all wounds and all that, right?"

"Yes. I suppose you're right."

"For me, that time never passes. It's always fresh. All those old hurts, they aren't old. It's like they happened yesterday."

Leigh nodded. "Isn't there anything you can do?"

"I can drink," Jonathan said, grinned, and raised his glass and took a healthy pull, "and I can keep a happy face. What the hell is bitching and complaining going to get me anyway?"

"Not a thing."

"You're damn right. Now, show me your tattoo."

"No!" Leigh gave a half-smile.

"Pretty please with sugar on top?"

"Maybe later."

"Maybe after this," Jonathan said and refilled her glass, then his. He held the bottle up to the streetlight to see how much was left.

"Maybe I'll give you a little peek," she said.

"Tease."

"You want it or not?"

"I want it."

Leigh rolled back the sleeve on her right arm, revealing the beginning of her tattoo, the tree roots that Jonathan had already seen.

"I've seen that already. Give me more."

"No." She smiled.

"Please?"

"Is that the best you can do?"

"It is right now."

"It's pitiful, so I'll have pity and show you a bit more."

She raised the sleeve a couple of inches, revealing a snake, green with tiny well-inked scales, wrapped around the tree. To either side of the tree there were two pairs of legs. She rolled her sleeve back down.

"Thank you for your pity," Jonathan said. "I'll take that if nothing else."

"You're welcome," Leigh said. "The wine's good," she added, and took another sip.

"The wine is very good. I'll order another bottle."

"We still haven't ordered dinner."

"No, we haven't."

"I don't know what I want," Leigh said.

"For dinner? Or in life?"

"For now, dinner."

"I'll order for you."

"Oh?" Leigh exclaimed with a smirk. She considered, then said, "I don't like bones. Fish bones, or even bones in meat."

"I'll take that into account."

"I like you ordering for me. It makes me feel like a woman."

"You are a woman. An amazing woman."

"Is that the wine talking?"

"It's me talking. When I'm drunk, the wine will say worse things."

"Will you tell me your great hurt when you're drunk?"

"No. I don't have a great hurt," Jonathan said, and turned his gaze away from Leigh's eyes for the first time and into his wine.

"I can see you do, though I don't know what it is."

"Then get me drunk," he said.

The waiter came by and Jonathan ordered another bottle of wine, a seafood risotto, and mixed shellfish for himself and swordfish for Leigh. The waiter left with the order.

"I didn't know your feelings on shellfish. There's no bones, technically, but there's peeling and work to be done," he said.

"I liked your order. I like swordfish. No bones. Though I'd like a taste of your lobster."

"Sure thing," Jonathan said with a smile, and Leigh smiled back.

They killed the bottle and the attentive waiter brought out its replacement.

"The wine feels good," Leigh said.

"It's good wine. Be careful of good wine. Bad wine is rude and you can see and hear it coming from a mile off. But good wine," Jonathan raised his glass, letting it sparkle in the candlelight, "good wine is a seductress. It'll let you take and take of it and hit you later. When you can barely feel it."

"You know a lot about wine?" Leigh asked.

"I know a lot about a great many things."

Leigh cast a smirking look at him. Their gaze locked.

The risotto came, breaking the moment. The waiter set the small bowls of the creamy rice in front of each of them.

Leigh looked it over, smelled it, and took a spoonful and tasted it. "Mmmm."

"I agree," Jonathan said, tasting it as well. "Risotto makes just about everything better."

They ate silently for a time.

"That was yummy," Leigh said, polishing off the rest of the risotto.

They sat and drank wine, looking around at the quiet street, the weathered brick of the buildings, and each other.

"Ah, our main dishes," Jonathan said as the waiter approached with the shellfish and swordfish.

The waiter graciously set the dishes down and departed, leaving the couple alone at their candlelit table in the narrow street. The candle flickered softly, casting delicate shadows on the ancient brick walls.

"I'd like some of your lobster," Leigh said, eyeing Jonathan's plate.

"I know you would. I'd like to see more of your tattoo."

"Is that the price I must pay?"

"It is."

"So be it," she said, and raised the sleeve another inch, revealing more of the legs and the tree and the snake.

"That doesn't help at all. Give me another inch." Jonathan said.

"Later. Maybe. If you're good. Now stop stalling and let me taste your lobster."

"I'll taste it first, as a servant would for a queen."

"Don't," Leigh said, "I want to form my own opinion."

"Then we'll taste it together."

Jonathan cut two pieces of the tail and Leigh pierced one with her fork. They both ate it at the same time. Leigh tried to keep a poker face but had the barest trace of a smile.

"You first. What do you think?" Jonathan asked.

"No," she said, "I made my mind up. I want to hear what you think."

"Not bad, but it's overcooked. It's difficult to cook lobster properly. I've only had it cooked properly once." Jonathan's eyes went distant, remembering the moment to the minutest detail. His eyes misted over and for a moment he was not there.

"Jonathan?" Leigh asked, then asked again.

"Yes?" he said. He blinked twice, a tear welling up at the corner of his eye.

"You look like you went away for a moment."

"I was away. I was remembering. About the lobster."

"Was it a good memory? Leigh asked.

"It was," Jonathan said, staring away into the dark, "though it's bittersweet now."

"Is it part of the great hurt?"

"It is, but a happy part. Sometimes the Shutter goes off in a happy part, and I can remember perfectly cooked lobster and the warm feeling of a good wine and the blossoming of a new love and it is so deep and intense that it brings tears to my eyes despite myself."

"I think we all have moments like that," Leigh said.

"I hope you do. Good remains good forever. It's only the bad that's supposed to fade away, to be swallowed by time. Usually."

Leigh smiled and tilted her head. "I think the lobster is overcooked, too. But only slightly," she said.

Jonathan smiled.

"Where did you grow up?" Leigh asked.

"Everywhere. I was a military brat. We moved constantly. Spent time in Germany, South Carolina, California. Though if you were to call anywhere home, it would be Florida. Do you want one of my shrimp?"

"No, thank you," Leigh declined.

"I'll peel one for you. They're sublime. Much better than the lobster." He peeled carefully with his knife with the skill of a surgeon. He pierced the flesh with his fork and offered it to Leigh.

She ate it and her eyes went wide.

"See? I told you," Jonathan said.

"I've never had shrimp like that — so sweet."

"It's a night of firsts."

"What firsts?" Leigh asked.

"First time in Venice, for me. First date, if you want to call it that, for us. First lovely delicious shrimp, for you. First time being chased by killers."

"Stop joking like that."

"For tonight, I will."

They looked around. The night was quiet and peaceful and all theirs. It was plainly evident that, whoever was chasing them, they had given him the slip. It was hard to imagine anyone stalking them; in fact, it was hard to imagine any of it had happened at all.

They finished their meals in silence, exchanging shrimp for swordfish. The waiter cleared the plates.

"The dessert is next. We need a different wine," Jonathan said.

"Now I know you're trying to get me drunk, mister."

"I'm not trying very hard. You're doing a good job all on your own." Jonathan smiled at her.

He ordered a *dolcetto*, a sweet red wine that went perfectly with the strawberry mousse the waiter set before them.

"This is really good," Leigh said with her mouth full.

"It is."

"Will you tell me of the great hurt now?"

"No. Let dessert linger a while. I'll tell you soon, but enjoy dessert first."

They drank the rest of the *dolcetto*, looking at each other and enjoying the cool quiet night. People around them finished with their meals and started to leave.

"Two more," Jonathan ordered more wine from the waiter, who brought it promptly.

"I'm drunk," Leigh said. "I'm not going to remember what you tell me."

"That's for the best," Jonathan said, "but you will remember some of it. I have to remember all of it. Always."

"So tell me, cowboy."

"I was married, once," Jonathan began, then paused.

Leigh nodded, waiting for him to go on.

"I married my high school sweetheart," he continued. "I was young, stupid, and didn't know half the things I know now." Jonathan looked off into the darkened end of the street. "But Christ did I love that woman," he said and shook his head.

"What's her name?" Leigh asked gently.

"Was. Julie," he said, looking in the distance. "Was—" he repeated, trailing off.

"I'm sorry," Leigh said.

"Don't be. You didn't kill her. God took care of that." Jonathan stared into his wine. "I guess I should be grateful," he continued. "We had a good four years. Some people never even have that. But four years is enough to know what you're missing. To know it in your bones."

Leigh nodded but said nothing.

"But the worst part, the great hurt as you call it, is this damned gift I have. You see, she died, just like that," Jonathan said and snapped his fingers. "Brain aneurysm. One day I kissed her goodbye in the morning, and later that day she was dead. One second here, one second gone. The worst part is this damned Shutter went off right at her funeral. Right at the viewing."

Jonathan looked away, past everything, as if seeing it all right in front of him. Leigh put her hand on his.

"Right in the middle of the thing," he continued. "Right when I was looking at her lying in the casket. People will tell you that you are peaceful in your casket, but you are not. You're not even you. You're artificial, created. Every bit of life she had was taken from her. Her face, her beautiful life-filled face was a mask, an approximation of what some embalmer who had never met her thought she looked like. I'm sure you know, Doctor, that the aneurysm causes your face to contort. I could have gone on thinking of her alive and with joy on her face. But God, the powers that be, fate, whatever, chose that very moment for my Shutter to go off. Right when I looked at that mask. It was crushing. All that moment's pain is there for me, anytime I want it, and even when I don't want it."

Jonathan drank the rest of his wine, and closed his eyes. He opened them and shook his head, as if clearing images away.

"I'm sorry," Leigh said, solemnly.

"Don't be, you didn't do it."

"Just allow me to be sorry. No one else can, but I can."

"I will allow you," Jonathan said. "And thank you."

"No need to thank me."

"Please allow me to thank you," he said.

"I will allow you," she said, solemnly again.

"So that's it. That's the great hurt. It's there and if I close my eyes I can see her death mask all the time."

"Don't close your eyes. Keep them open. Look at this great city, the beauty around you," Leigh said, squeezing his hand.

"Let's get out of here," Jonathan said. "I think we've eaten everything in the restaurant."

Jonathan asked for the check and paid it with the Old Man's money.

They set off towards the fish market and the Grand Canal and walked along the quay, looking at the various boats moored on ancient timbers sunk into the water. The tide was rising and covering up the first few steps of the quay, the water gently lapping at the old stones.

"This is nice," Leigh said, getting close to Jonathan and hooking her arm around his, leaning on him.

"It's so quiet. No cars," Jonathan noted.

The boats rocked back and forth, rubbing against their moorings. The hemp rope tethering them stretched taut and added its own nautical sound to the night. An occasional *vaporetto* steamed slowly past, carrying its freight of tourists down the Canal.

They strolled past the Rialto Market, Leigh holding on to Jonathan for balance. The empty stalls awaited the next day's produce. Though the market was desolate, there was a low hum in the air. Past the market, the street opened to a lively square with hundreds of young people gathering at various bars, drinking and filling the air with excited talk in a dozen languages.

"Looks like they're having a good time," Leigh said.

"Ah, to be young again," Jonathan sighed.

"Hey, we're not that old."

"Maybe you. You could fit in there, punk girl."

Leigh punched him in the arm, playfully. "I'm not a punk girl. I am a respected scientist," she said, then added, "I *was* a punk girl."

"Show me the rest of your tattoo."

"No." She punched him harder, but still playfully, on his big arm.

"Are you drunk?" Jonathan asked, looking at her.

"No. Maybe a little. Yes."

Jonathan chuckled. "I hope you're not a mean drunk."

"Not at all. Just a clumsy one. Don't let me fall into a canal."

"I'll keep you safe," Jonathan said, wrapping an arm around her waist and keeping himself between her and the canal.

They rounded the bend, still walking along the quay past the rows of closed tourist shops and open restaurants, and came to the Rialto Bridge.

"Wow," Leigh said, and they both stopped.

The famous bridge was painted a golden white from the floodlights and the reflections of the buildings around. It straddled the Grand Canal magnificently. Rows and rows of stores lined both sides of the bridge. There were hundreds of people leaning over the railing looking out at the moonlight reflecting on the water.

"Isn't it lovely?" Leigh said, turning around to look at Jonathan. The moonlight kissed her skin and made it glow like ivory lit from within.

"It is lovely," Jonathan said. "The bridge isn't bad either."

"Hush, you flirt. Be serious."

"I am."

Leigh blushed a little. "Well, don't be serious then," she said.

Jonathan leaned down to kiss her. She smiled and turned away, walking and holding onto his hand, dragging him forward. "Come on, let's get a drink or a café or both," she said turning back to look at him.

Jonathan shook his head, the target for his kiss gone, and grinned. "Okay, but only one more for you."

They walked over the bridge, pausing at the top to see the city's reflection dancing on the water. Leigh's black hair blew in the wind and she looked lovely, wild, Jonathan thought.

"Come on," Leigh said.

They crossed the bridge and walked right along the bank, and then turned left where it ended into a gift-shop lined street filled with tourists. Little trinkets of Murano glass, *Carnevale* masks, and T-shirts filled the stores, and throngs of people stopped to look at the window displays. The streets twisted and turned, gradually giving way to lonely narrow alleys, and they were alone. The plaster peeled from the walls, exposing the weathered brick beneath. Huge iron bars covered the windows of seemingly abandoned buildings. Overhead, empty shirts hung on clotheslines and flapped in the breeze.

Leigh hooked her arm around Jonathan's again. It was very quiet, with only their footsteps echoing off the walls keeping them company.

"Hmm, that's funny." Jonathan pointed at a trash bag on the ground, attached to a clip and a string, which led upwards to the fourth floor balcony. "They lowered it from that pulley," Jonathan said, pointing up.

"That's one way to take out the trash," Leigh said.

"Beats walking down four flights," he said.

They passed the garbage bag and continued to the end of the narrow street, turning onto a busier street lined with restaurants. They followed this and came suddenly to a huge rectangular plaza. It was impressively large and busy after the maze of narrow streets. Cafés lined the side and hundreds of people milled about.

"*Campo* Santo Stefano," Jonathan read the ceramic street sign on the wall of a building.

"This looks like the perfect place for that café," Leigh said.

"I agree."

They sat at a café well off to the side, and, over macchiatos, watched the parade of people go by.

"To Venice," Jonathan raised his tiny coffee cup.

"To Venice," Leigh repeated, and they clinked cups.

Jonathan alternated between watching the crowd and looking at Leigh. Occasionally, she would catch him looking and she smiled at him. They sat in a comfortable silence.

"There's a well dressed couple," Jonathan said, pointing out a tuxedo clad man and a stunning beauty in a long red dress.

"Wow, " Leigh said. "They're probably going to the opera or something."

"We should go. I've never been to an opera."

"Me neither. But some other time. Unless this coffee starts to kick in, I'm going to crash here soon." Leigh stifled a yawn.

"Yeah, we need to keep moving or call it. It's been a long day," Jonathan said.

"Do you know the way back to the hotel?" she asked.

"I have not a clue. Let's go that way. It looks promising."

They finished the macchiatos and strolled down the *Campo*. Leigh hooked her arm around his.

"Listen to that," Leigh said, smiling.

They were passing the San Vidal church on their right. Out of the church poured forth the most exquisite music. A concerto was in full swing inside. They went up the steps to better hear.

"It's Vivaldi, I think," Jonathan said. He went up the steps to the marquee advertising the concert. "Nope," he said, "Tommaso Albinoni, if the poster is right."

"Vivaldi I've heard of," Leigh said, "Albinoni, never."

"Me neither. It's beautiful, though."

They stood outside the door to the church and listened, letting the music wash over them. Leigh closed her eyes and she looked angelic as she listened. After a silent time, they both walked on together. The music receded into the background, following them softly for a time.

The *Campo* narrowed and they came out onto the Accademia Bridge. The wooden bridge arched gracefully over the Grand Canal.

Leigh brought out her tiny tourist map and fiddled with it, turning it this way and that. "Well, I suppose we should cross, then veer to the right," Leigh said.

"I have a better idea," Jonathan said. "Come with me."

He grabbed her hand without thinking. It was a natural thing and only after they were halfway over the bridge did they both realize it. Neither let go, and they settled into the hand holding easily, Leigh giving him a little squeeze. As they crested the bridge, they both stopped.

"Wow," Leigh said. "Look at that."

To their left was a heart-stopping view. The Grand Canal, lined with palace after palace, opened up to become the Canal de San Marco. The broad waterway was filled with ships crisscrossing it. The huge dome of Santa Maria della Saluto stood like a massive beacon at the end of the right bank. Beyond that, on the left bank, they could see the huge Campanile di San Marco, the bell tower that dominated the skyline.

They both stood and stared speechless, for a time. The wind came in from the Lagoon and blew the day's warmth away.

"It's getting chilly," Leigh said.

Jonathan put his arm around her and they both stood, watching the lights dance and play on the waters.

"So, where were you taking me?" Leigh asked.

"Ah, yes. Sorry, got distracted."

"I can see why," Leigh said, turning to face him.

"Over here. It's a surprise."

They crossed the bridge, holding hands easily now. Jonathan led her around the bridge to a dock. Striped poles, like big barber poles, rose out of the water, and three gondolas were moored there.

"For real?" Leigh's face lit up like a girl at Christmas.

"For real," Jonathan said and grinned.

Jonathan went over and conversed with one of the gondoliers, who was standing at the dock wearing the typical white and blue striped shirt and blue pants. They settled on a price, and Jonathan came back to Leigh.

"Our carriage awaits, miss," he said.

He took her by the hand down to the dock. She boarded, taking the gondolier's hand. The gondola rocked back and forth, finally settling down once she was seated. Jonathan stepped on and sat next to her on a richly upholstered chair fit for royalty. Under their feet were oriental rugs, and pillows lined with Venetian cloth cosseted them. Even Jonathan felt a giddy thrill when the gondolier gracefully cast off with one foot, pushing against the mooring pole as he leaned into and balanced on his oar. Suddenly, they were gliding forward into the busy Grand Canal.

Jonathan watched as the gondolier deftly avoided the *vaporettos* and other boats and picked up speed with surprisingly short strokes of the oar. It was an interesting stroke, Jonathan thought. He had rowed a little, in college, and this stroke was like nothing he'd done. The gondolier pushed forward with the main stroke, and kept the oar in the water on the return, twisting and leaning on it at the same time.

The gondolier stroked, and used the oar as a rudder to rotate the gondola into a side canal. Free from the wake of *vaporettos*, the gondola glided silkily down the narrow canal. They went under a bridge.

Jonathan and Leigh relaxed in their seats. Leigh drew herself close to him, settling into the nook of his arm, resting her head on his chest.

"This has been the craziest day ever," she said without looking up.

"It takes the cake," he agreed.

"Jonathan, what are we going to do?" she asked.

"Tomorrow. Whatever it is we're going to do, we'll do it tomorrow. For tonight, let's enjoy the night."

"You're right," she said, and snuggled closer.

He held her tight, held her so he could remember that moment as best he could, wishing for the Shutter to go off then. To remember that moment in perfect clarity. To remember the soft lapping of the waves against the side of the gondola, the smell of Leigh, like jasmine and candy, and the soft feel of her hair against his cheek. To remember the little temporary private place they had each time they went under a bridge. He was falling hard for her and it worried him. In a way, he hoped she felt the same. But for tonight, everything was right and he held her tight. She felt small and vulnerable in his arms and he felt the responsibility and duty to protect her.

They glided down silent canals, past floodlit *palazzos* and down darkened narrow ways. Occasionally they would pass another gondola and the tiny wake would rock them ever so slightly in a comforting side-to-side bob.

They were quiet sitting in their royal chair, and had reached the point when words only spoiled a moment. At some point, Jonathan thought, words cease to matter and it is the act, the experience, that mattered. Even to think of the experience ruined it. It was a hard trick to live in that present, he thought. His whole trade was dealing with the past, and, in that way, with the future. The present was an unknown country, but one he welcomed to explore with Leigh.

She was falling asleep, he was sure, but when he craned his neck to check he saw she was wide eyed and staring out at the dark green water.

"What are you thinking of?" he asked.

"Nothing. Everything. When I start thinking of everything it washes over me like a wave, drowning me."

"Then don't think, not tonight."

"This is incredible. Thank you," she said earnestly.

"Thank you," Jonathan said. "I would be a right silly bastard riding this thing alone without a beautiful woman in my arms."

Leigh chuckled but said nothing, hugging him tighter.

They glided silently down the canal. Occasionally, the gondolier would duck to go under a bridge, then push off the wall or a post with his leg. Not once did he hit or rub up against another gondola or wall, even when they were inches apart. Slowly, they wound their way around the San Polo *sistieri* until they came to a side canal near the hotel.

The gondolier leaned down and asked Jonathan, "Would you like to go to the hotel now, or would you like to go on?"

"What would you like, Doctor?" Jonathan asked Leigh.

"The hotel is good. I want to go on, but sometimes it's better to be left with some want or desire rather than quench it all."

"That is sound advice, Doctor, even if I do not follow it myself," Jonathan said, then added, to the gondolier, "To the hotel, *signore*."

They glided out of the side canal onto the majestic openness of the Grand Canal. They had come out just north of the Ca' d'Oro, and the gondolier pivoted and brought the stately palace and the other elegant buildings into view. The *palazzos* were floodlight and beautiful, contrasting against the darkest sapphire of the sky.

Jonathan recognized the San Cassianno hotel on the right. Its small but ornate façade of deepest coral was detailed with white stone-carved balconies holding flowerboxes gloriously spilling over with spring flowers.

With skill, and in silence, the gondolier docked. He tied off the gondola to a pole with a small black rope and a quick hitch knot. Jonathan rose and helped Leigh out, alighting first so he could take her hand from a stable position. She got out, unsteadily. They both thanked the gondolier, who untied the rope with a flick of his wrist and shoved off noiselessly. They stood on the dock and watched him go as the gondola disappeared into the night. They turned and walked into the hotel.

At the front desk was the night clerk, who they had not yet met.

"Room 207, please," Jonathan said.

The man turned and fished the key from a row of tiny cubicles behind him. Without a word, he handed the key to Jonathan.

They walked up the stairs to their room.

"Not the friendliest fellow, is he?" Leigh said.

"Not quite. Not like the guy before."

Something bothered Jonathan. A small uneasy feeling grew inside him.

The man, who we've never met, gave us the keys without asking for any identification, he thought. He knew this was common procedure in hotels, but things looked different when they were being chased. *If* they were being chased. There had certainly been no sign of anything abnormal that night. It had been a wonderful evening. He decided not to spoil it by saying anything to Leigh.

They rounded the corner and came to their room. Jonathan opened the door carefully. It was dark. All the lights turned off unless the key card was inserted in a slot, which Jonathan now did. The room lit up, the glow from the Murano glass chandelier casting soft colored light on everything.

"Wait here," Jonathan said.

"What's wrong?" Leigh asked.

"Nothing. I think. I hope. I just want to check the room."

Leigh hung back, a slight worried look coming over her face.

"Sorry to be a buzzkill, just want to be safe," he said as he walked in.

He looked around, opening the bathroom and checking inside. He walked to the closet and swung the doors open. Nothing. Just extra blankets and the safe.

"Don't forget to check under the bed," Leigh joked, poking her head inside.

"Don't think I have to," Jonathan called out.

The bed was a wonderful big affair on an ornate solid wood pedestal. There was no room for anything under there.

"Can I come in now?"

"Yes." Jonathan locked the door behind her.

"Check the balcony too."

"Good idea," he said.

He swung open the doors to the tiny balcony. The fresh night air, smelling faintly of salt and the sea, filled the room.

"Hardly room for more than two out here," Leigh said, coming up behind him.

They both stepped out.

"It's beautiful," she said, looking out at the gentle ripple of water that reflected the *palazzos* and the Ca' d'Oro to their right.

"It is that," he said, looking at her.

Leigh turned to Jonathan and they exchanged something serious and wonderful with only a look. He leaned down and she rose to meet him and they kissed the way new lovers do, haltingly, exploring at first and then with a hard passion. He took her head fully in his hand and pressed himself to her and kissed her again hard. Below them, boats plied the waters and time marched on, even as it stood still for them.

CHAPTER 11

Santa Lucia Train Station
Venice, Italy
May 22, 2025 12:31 a.m.

Adriana Nyx arrived in the dark. The floodlit *palazzos* reflected off the Grand Canal in front of the train station, casting a golden glow to the plaza. She carried her small backpack past the late arriving tourists, weaving between them as a tiger does through high savannah grass. She stopped at the ticket machine and bought a one-day *vaporetto* ticket.

I should be done by then, she thought.

She swiped her card and boarded the *vaporetto* towards Rialto. As she waited for the nearly empty vessel to depart, she swiped on her phone and dialed.

"Yes?" the Lawyer answered at once.

"I'm here. Any updates on their position?"

"Nothing yet. I should have something exact by morning."

Adriana rolled her eyes. "See that you do, otherwise it will be a long time tracking them down here."

"I understand," the Lawyer said. He added, sheepishly, "It'll be done."

"How about my hotel?" Adriana asked. "Something near the Mercado like I asked?" It was a central place, she thought, the logical place to start.

"Yes. I've got you booked at the Rialto Palace, right by the Mercado."

"It had better be nice."

"I hope so," he said.

"Call me tomorrow morning as soon as you have a location."

Adriana hung up, and the *vaporetto* started to move. The cool night breeze blew down the canal and she turned to face the wind. She brought out a map and studied it in the shifting lights, reacquainting herself with the maze of streets she had known so well many years ago. The *vaporetto* steamed its way down the canal, pausing at various stops. *Riva de Biaso, San Marcuola, San Stae.* The names brought back memories of her year here with Pietto. She looked out at the water, remembering that time fondly. It had been a good time, at least until Pietto's money ran out.

The boat rounded the bend and the Ca' d'Oro came into view. She looked at the beautiful building, oblivious to the small deep-coral colored *palazzo* across the canal.

On the balcony of the *palazzo*, two lovers kissed in the Venice night. Adriana, facing the other way, sailed past.

The *vaporetto* arrived at the *Rialto Mercado* stop. Adriana alighted and strolled down the empty market looking for her hotel. *There.* A sign for the Rialto Palace. She followed it down a small side street and looked at the entrance. This was no palace, but a small *pensione.* She cursed the Lawyer's name and rang the doorbell, pressing a button inside a bronze lion's mouth. The door buzzed open.

Adriana checked in, using her false passport. No need giving away information. She went to her small room and settled in.

Damn that cheap bastard, she silently cursed the Lawyer again. She would take it out on him next time he craved her abuse. She would also take it out on his expense account tomorrow.

Adriana sat back on a threadbare chair and stared at the wall, thinking about tomorrow. Thinking of how to hunt them, of the best way of doing the act. She wished she had a partner with her. It made surveillance so much easier, not to mention the act itself. But she could do it alone, do the first one quickly, and then take her time with the other. She'd need a disguise to blend in. A rich tourist, a photographer maybe. Tomorrow, she would shop for the appropriate clothes and get the right camera. Something expensive, high end. You were treated better if you looked like you had money, whether you had it or not.

And she would have it soon. Already she had confirmed her upfront payment for the job and moved it to a different account. Tomorrow she would be rich. Well, maybe not rich, but very comfortable for a while. She still had not decided whether to take the Lawyer's other job of killing the big Moor. The Moor was good, and could smell the trouble and would be defensive and ready. Still, she thought she could do it, if the circumstances were right. Two defenseless unsuspecting scientists were child's play. But taking out a trained assassin, that would be difficult. The price would have to go up. For the right price, she would do anything.

Adriana took out a long cigarette and lit it, blowing smoke at the "No Smoking" sign in the room. It was the least of her sins. She opened the window and sat on the ledge, staring at the wall of the next building over. She was almost close enough to touch it.

Who is financing this mission? she asked herself. The Lawyer had money, but not this kind of money. Someone very wealthy was behind this. Someone to whom a million euros was nothing. And someone willing to kill for little to no reason. Whoever it was, she hoped to meet him. He was her type.

San Cassianno Hotel, Venice
May 22, 2025 12:43 a.m.

Jonathan and Leigh kissed one more time on the balcony, a long lingering kiss. They took one more look at the moonlit Grand Canal, seeing a *vaporetto* steaming by below them, before stepping back into the room.

"Wow, that was," Leigh said and searched for the word, "unexpected."

"Unexpected?" Jonathan asked in mock indignation. "After a romantic dinner and gondola ride through Venice ending at our suite on the Grand Canal? Unexpected?"

"Unexpected is the wrong word. Nice, then. Unexpectedly nice," Leigh stammered. She added, "I'm a bit tipsy."

"It's off to bed with you then, miss."

"You still get the couch, cowboy. I'm not a first-date type of girl."

"I'll be a perfect gentleman," Jonathan said. "Unless I'm not," he added, grinning.

"I'm keeping an eye on you, mister," she said, and walked over to the Louis Vuitton bag, fishing around inside it for something to wear. She brought out the silk pyjama top from Jonathan's purchase back in Turin. "I'm going to change," she said and went towards the bathroom.

"Don't change too much," Jonathan said.

"Cute." She smiled at him and closed the door.

Jonathan changed, putting on the pair of Armani pyjama bottoms and folding his new and expensive clothing carefully. He brought out the extra bedclothes from the closet and arranged them on the couch. It was a bit short for his 6'2" height. He thought about calling down for a cot, but was not in a mood to deal with the night clerk and the commotion and time it would take. He finished with the couch and, on impulse, turned down the corner of Leigh's bed. He crawled into his cocoon on the couch, bending his knees to fit.

Leigh came out of the bathroom, dressed in the large pyjama top, which draped long over her and covered her arms.

"You look adorable," Jonathan said from the couch.

"And you look pitiful, you poor thing," she said.

"It's alright. I can sleep standing up. A couple of whiskeys from that minibar and I could sleep out on the balcony."

Leigh padded over to the bed and saw that he had turned down the corner. She smiled and her heart gave a little falling feeling, a pleasant fall like on a roller coaster.

"Thank you," she said.

"It's all part of my M.O."

"Just take the thanks."

"Taken," he said.

Leigh slipped into the huge bed and gave a little moan of contentment. "This feels *so* good," she said, looking at Jonathan who was curled up miserably on the couch.

"Watch it, miss, don't rub it in."

"Quiet, you. I was feeling pity on you. Don't spoil it." She was silent a moment, then said, "And get over here."

"For real?"

"Yes. Before I change my mind."

Jonathan uncurled himself from the couch and went to the other side of the bed. He slipped in.

"No touching, or you get the floor," Leigh said, playfully.

"I will do my best, but, I must warn you, it's not the first time I've ended up on the floor."

Leigh flipped around and turned to him. She smiled, then turned serious.

"Thank you, Jonathan, for everything."

"Thank you too. We're going to be okay."

"Goodnight," she said sleepily.

"Goodnight."

Leigh flipped off the light. Through the slightly open balcony door, a soft sea breeze drifted in. Waves gently lapped against the building. Their heat built up under the sheets.

It felt to Jonathan as if they were great magnets turned to opposite poles, with a pleasing and delicious resistance keeping them apart, but also with a strong and fundamental need to flip around and lock into one. These thoughts soon gave way to sleep and wonderful darkness. There were no memories in that darkness, and it was good.

PART 2

Joseph hurried through the crowded Jerusalem streets to the city gate. He ran back to Gulgalta, and could see now that they were taking Him down already. Joseph approached slowly, careful not to get too near, and watched as the limp and naked body was placed on a pallet. The rabbi's head was already covered with a blood-soaked cloth, and now one of the women draped a blanket on top of Him. Joseph looked on from afar, then motioned to the centurion. "Pilate has given permission. I am to take His body," Joseph told the guard, who nodded. Joseph waved to young John, who stood white with shock alongside his dead Master and friend. "I have brought the burial Shroud," Joseph said, showing him the fine linen cloth. John walked to him and nodded absently. Joseph looked on him with pity, then spoke. "Come, I will show you where the tomb is."

CHAPTER 1

Oviedo, Spain
May 22, 2025 8:31 a.m.

Asad did not like it. It had been a long train journey to Oviedo. He sat on a bench in the plaza outside the San Salvador Cathedral, contemplating it. Now that he surveyed the site in person, he did not like it one bit. He needed another plane, he thought. The surest way to do it was with another plane. But it was a luxury he did not have. Later that day he would meet his contact for the supplies. He feared he would need much more. This Cathedral was well fortified with massive stone walls, much more so than the one in Turin. And the target lay in the very center of it.

Asad began to think that the only way to do it was from inside. To get a bomb in there, right beside it and close. The suicide option he considered and would do if necessary, but he would try any other way first. The only way to find out was to go in.

He closed his eyes and prayed for forgiveness. He rose from the bench and walked across the plaza, practically empty of tourists at this early hour. He strode towards the Cathedral. Asad thought he looked ridiculous. He was dressed in his best tourist gear, with a SLR camera in one hand, a fanny pack around his waist, a t-shirt he wouldn't be caught dead in, and a backpack. He felt like an idiot, and tried to carry that feeling to the look on his face, but his eyes and mind were racing, assessing the situation.

Asad would have to have a talk with the Lawyer. His intelligence was worthless. The plan had been for a truck bomb, to make it look like ETA separatists had committed the act. He could see now that it was a worthless plan. A truck bomb would not scratch the surface of these old stones. He would call the Lawyer and tell him so, but only after he had formulated a plan of his own.

Asad came to the huge wooden door of the Cathedral. He prayed again and walked through a smaller door cut into the huge door. He had never been in a Cathedral and was immediately impressed by its size. Thick stone columns soared into a majestic vaulted ceiling that took his gaze heavenwards. It was dark inside and his eyes took time to adjust. A solitary priest, thin and wiry, busied himself at a side alcove. There was a "No Pictures" sign up and he decided to test this by taking some. No one approached him. In fact, there appeared to be no security of any sort.

Asad walked slowly through the Cathedral. He could appreciate the artistry and skill, but was aghast at the icons and attempted representations of God. Also, he abhorred the infidel worship of the woman, Mary. He walked past richly decorated side altars devoted to one saint or another, and followed the signs towards the back of the Cathedral to the *Camara Santa*, the Holy Chamber where it was kept.

He purchased a ticket from the attendant, the first person other than the priest he'd seen, handing over five euros. Asad asked the attendant about the *Camara Santa*, which was off to the right of the Cathedral proper, where the relic was kept.

"This section here is the oldest part of the Cathedral. It was built as the keep for the fortress of King Alfonso the Second, over 1,300 years ago," the ticket attendant enthusiastically told him. "Have a look around. The *Arca Santa* is upstairs. And there is a museum after."

Asad thanked him and went through a door, entering inside. He went up a wooden spiral staircase of modern construction to the *Camara Santa* itself, the Holy Chamber where it was kept. Asad thought it interesting that it was on the second floor. He filed this away and made sure to see what was under it.

Asad entered the outside room, probably what once was a reception room in the castle. The walls here were massive. Meters upon meters of thick stone. He doubted that even a plane could penetrate them. He would have to do it from inside, no doubt about it. Through an arch at the end of the room lay the innermost chamber, the place where it was kept. Asad walked in, noting every detail and taking pictures. The inner chamber here was a vaulted stone room, relatively small, no more than ten by twenty meters. There was a substantial iron gate splitting the room in two. Behind the gate, locked with a massive ancient lock, was a treasure trove.

Ornate and bejeweled gold crosses and small treasure boxes filled with some type of relic or another lined the sides and back of the room. And in the center, under a spotlight, was the *Arca Santa*, the huge silver chest containing it. His target. What was in there had to be destroyed, but how?

Asad's mind raced. The walls were so thick. Behind the relics and gold crosses, up high, was a window carved into the back wall. There was a sliver of daylight visible through the carved stone, thick iron bars, and Plexiglas that comprised the window. Asad made a mental note of the size and shape of the window.

He looked around the room. There did not seem to be any security cameras, but they were probably there, hidden. They had to be. So far, security had been almost non-existent. His backpack was not searched, and there were no guards in here.

He heard a noise, footsteps, outside. Two tourists, pilgrims from the look of them, walked in. They smiled at him and went to the iron bars, getting as close as possible to the silver chest. The couple had on huge backpacks and carried walking staves. They set the staves and backpacks against the wall at the side, crossed themselves and knelt, praying. Asad observed them, trying to be inconspicuous and respectful. There were little scallop shells dangling from their backpack, designating them as pilgrims on the road to Santiago.

They too have a pilgrimage, he thought, and remembered back fondly to his own pilgrimage to Mecca.

He waited for them to leave, studying the details of the Chamber in the meantime. The *Arca Santa*, or Holy Arc, sat on a broad stone base and was surrounded by thick bulletproof glass. Behind it, below the window, was a framed replica of the cloth inside the chest. The cloth, he knew, rested safely inside the chest and was only brought out on special holy days.

The two pilgrims finally left. Asad brought out the SLR camera and started taking pictures, both for later study and to test security. Again, nothing. No one came to admonish him. Satisfied, he walked out, leaving the silver chest where it had sat for 1,300 years with its precious relic safely inside.

Asad continued the rest of the visit. Upstairs, in a newer wing of the ancient building, was a museum of other holy relics and gold trinkets. These held no interest to him. However, here, finally, was a security guard. Asad casually worked his way around to the guard's desk, pretending to look at the paintings lining the wall. The guard's desk had two banks of four monitors, eight in total, showing different camera views. He scanned them quickly and efficiently. All eight cameras were trained on different museum exhibits. None were of the *Camara Santa* and its holiest of relics. If the Chamber was monitored, he hadn't seen it.

Asad walked through the museum and took a picture. Here, at last, the guard admonished him. It did not matter. These treasures and trinkets were useless. He walked on through the museum, hurrying past gold plates and chalices of gold and wooden crucified Christ after Christ. He went down a stone spiral staircase to the ground floor and came out to the pretty inner courtyard of a former monastery. He walked around, orienting himself. To his right should be the *Camara Santa*, one floor up. He consulted a detailed diagram of the Cathedral that was etched onto a plaque by the wall. He was right. The *Camara Santa* was there, the left thick side wall visible from the courtyard. According to the map, there was a graveyard just beyond the courtyard, on the other side of the *Camara Santa*. A huge outer castle wall encircled the entire complex.

He walked towards the graveyard. He stood in the center of the graveyard and could see, on the second floor of the building in front of him, the same small stone carved window with the thick iron bars that he had seen from inside the *Camara Santa*. Asad walked to the side of the graveyard, around to the right side of the building. There was an opening on the ground floor. He read the plaque on the wall. *Crypt of St. Leocadia, martyred ca. 304 in the Diocletian persecution.* He ducked through the low entrance and found himself standing in the crypt.

It's right under the Camara Santa, Asad thought, scarcely believing his luck. He walked through the crypt. Inside, several weathered tombs lined the floor. The floor plan mirrored exactly the *Camara Santa* above. Asad's heart raced, his mind already calculating and weaving out a plan even as he continued looking. At the far end of the crypt, exactly under the spot where the silver chest and the target lay, was the raised tomb of the martyr, lit from behind with a golden light which bounced off the vaulted ceiling. It looked like a sacrificial table, Asad thought, and he was reminded of the story of Abraham sacrificing, or almost sacrificing, Isaac. That was a faith he admired, and a story they all had in common, he thought.

Asad sat on the ground, contemplating it. He sat there in that forgotten corner over an hour and no one came by. No tourists, and certainly no security. He measured the huge stones and distances with the span of his hand, noting them all carefully. He would calculate exact distances later. Above the raised tomb was the target, separated from him by five feet of stone at the highest point of the arch, he estimated. The plan was coming together in his head. He took dozens more pictures of the crypt, then exited and walked back through the graveyard to the courtyard, admiring the stone architecture.

A sign pointed to the exit and he went to it, satisfied he had enough information. The exit was unguarded. It was a simple large door leading out to the *Corrada del Obispo*, the square to the south side of the Cathedral. He stepped through. No one was in sight as he left the complex. Asad's confidence in the plan swelled.

He walked back to the hotel to make calculations. He needed to talk to the Lawyer, meet with the supplier, and see about getting one more person. He needed one more person. One more good and dependable person with practice in explosives. He would call Samir. He was good, if young, and could be there within the day, most likely. Asad saw the entire plan in his mind. He went over it and over it, refining it, and seeing it all end in very satisfactory flames.

CHAPTER 2

Venice, Italy
May 22, 2025 8:45 a.m.

Jonathan awoke in the early morning light, disoriented. *Where am I?* he asked himself.

He lay on his side, right arm draped over Leigh. Their bodies were pressed tight and warm, warding off the early morning chill. He looked around without moving, observing the ornate room and the dawning day outside the window. As the sleep left him, he remembered the previous night. The wine, the gondola, Leigh inviting him to bed. He smiled to himself and drew ever closer.

"I thought I said no touching, cowboy," Leigh said in a sleepy voice.

Jonathan lifted his arm.

"I didn't say move either," Leigh said.

Women are so confusing, Jonathan thought, but did not say. Instead, he whispered, "Good morning." He kissed the back of her head, inhaling deeply and savoring her sweet scent.

"Good morning to you, cowboy," Leigh said. She brought her hand up to meet his and squeezed. "You know this means the floor for you, mister," she joked.

"It was worth it," he said. "And besides, how do you know that you didn't start it?"

"Hush, you," she said, and flipped around to face him. He brushed back a stray lock from her head, tucking it behind her ear.

"Good morning," Jonathan said, and caressed her cheek.

"You already said that."

"I was stating a fact this time. It is a good morning."

"Hey, any morning you wake up alive is, right?" she asked.

"Alive and next to you, yes. How you feeling?"

"Better than I should," she said.

"Good wine doesn't give you much of a hangover."

She touched his cheek, feeling the roughness of his stubble. "You need a shave, cowboy."

"Can't. Left my razor in Turin."

"Then grow a glorious beard. None of this in-between stuff."

"I like the in-between," he said, whispering the words in the quiet of the room.

"I'll let you off easy," Leigh said with a smile.

"For what?"

"For the beard. And the touching. Just buy this girl breakfast."

"Done."

"I'll go change," Leigh said and got out of bed, wearing Jonathan's large pyjama top.

"Don't change too much."

"You already used that one."

"So I did," he said as he sat up on the bed. "Show me the rest of your tattoo."

"No," Leigh said, flashed a mischievous grin, and disappeared into the bathroom.

Jonathan got up and ran his hand through his hair. He stretched and did a few pushups. "I need a quick shower," he called out to Leigh in the bathroom.

"I'm hungry," she said through the door.

"It's for your benefit as well."

"Okay," Leigh said, opening the door and coming out, dressed. "But be quick about it," she added.

He was. In a minute Jonathan was done and came out of the bathroom, a towel wrapped around his waist. He dried his hair with a hand towel.

"Forgot my clothes out here," he said, and fished a black Armani shirt and underwear from the bag and grabbed his jeans, which were folded and lying on the table from the night before. Leigh's eyes lingered on him a moment.

He disappeared into the bathroom and came out a moment later and finished dressing. "Let's go," he said.

They went downstairs to the breakfast room, a long light-filled and splendidly decorated affair with a large window facing the Grand Canal. They sat at a table by the window and ordered two cappuccinos and a basket of pastries and breads from the waitress. The view out the window was magnificent, with the morning sun making the canal sparkle with white gold.

They sat in silence staring out at the beauty outside and were interrupted only when the waitress came back with their breakfast.

"Well, tomorrow is here, I suppose, and we've got to figure out what to do," Leigh said, stirring her coffee.

"Grab a plane to Manchester, no?" Jonathan asked. He took a bite of a croissant.

"I don't know," Leigh said hesitantly. Something was bothering her, some unresolved detail. "Yesterday, when you said that there may be more samples, what did you mean?" Leigh asked.

"Ah yes, we got off track."

"Yes, so what did you mean?"

"Didn't you read up on the Shroud's history at all?"

"Not much. Look — I'm all test tubes and centrifuges, not history, remember?"

"Yes, but—"

"But nothing. Quit stalling and tell me," Leigh said impatiently.

"Yes, Doctor."

"Thank you."

"Well, the Shroud you know about. But there is another cloth. The Oviedo cloth."

"I heard something about that when I arrived to Turin. I think one of the others from the team was talking about it. Peter, I think, the forensics guy." Leigh bit her lip, suddenly remembering that he and everyone else was dead. She composed herself quickly, so that Jonathan would not notice.

"Yes. Do you want the five-year-old version or the twelve-year-old version?" Jonathan asked.

"Cute. We've got all breakfast. How about the clueless adult version?"

"You asked for it," he said with a smile, shifting into his professorial tone. "In Oviedo, in Spain, in the Cathedral there, they have a relic called the Sudarium of Oviedo, also called the Holy Cloth of Oviedo. Now, Sudarium is just a fancy Latin word for sweat cloth."

Leigh chuckled.

"What's funny?"

"You. You struggle with the Italian, but you know Latin."

"Latin and ancient Greek and Hebrew. And I know how to read them, not how to speak them. But that's beside the point."

"Sorry to interrupt, teacher," Leigh said with a smile.

"I'll continue. The Sudarium is a very ancient piece of blood-stained cloth. It's documented as being in Oviedo since about the year 1075, probably much earlier even. There is very reliable historical evidence placing it in Toledo around 718, and even further back than that, of it coming out of Palestine around 614. That's about where we lose it to history. If you want to go back further, you have to read the Bible."

"It's in the Bible?" Leigh asked.

"Oh yes. The apostle John mentions it and the Shroud in his Gospel. Historically speaking, it is a very convincing document. But many so-called serious historians don't even see the Bible as a source. Too much baggage."

"So John mentions it?" Leigh asked, trying to recall the passage.

"Yes, almost offhand. John goes into the empty tomb after the resurrection and sees the burial cloth, that is, the Shroud, and the other cloth, the Sudarium, lying to the side."

"You know," Leigh said, "it's funny. I've read John a few times and never noticed it."

Jonathan nodded. "Like I said, it's almost an off-hand mention. That sort of small detail, to me, has the ring of truth to it." Jonathan took a sip of his cappuccino. "This next part is the graphic part. You want to hear it?"

"Cowboy, I'm a doctor. I can out-gross you any day of the week," Leigh said, arching an eyebrow.

"Alright, cowgirl. So, history lesson. Starting from the top, which is to say, the beginning. The Jews then, as now, believed that everyone's blood is holy and is needed for the resurrection. Even now, you'll see devout Jews mopping up after a suicide bombing. They're not being tidy. They are being religious, saving the blood."

Leigh nodded.

"So, two thousand years ago it was no different. Jesus of Nazareth, a Jew, is crucified. It's about the most horrible way to die, and I won't go into it."

"I know all about it," Leigh said.

"Good. So, the thinking goes that when Jesus died on the cross, they wrapped a cloth around his head. Much like we cover the face of the dead today, no different. This cloth soaked up the blood and, when they took him off the cross, soaked up even more blood that seeped out his nose and mouth. In fact, there is a thumbprint on the cloth, like someone was holding the cloth to his face to soak up all the blood and pulmonary fluid. You see, when you're crucified a lot of water builds up in your lungs and—"

"Yes, I know that," Leigh interrupted. "Doctor, remember?"

"Yes, of course. You know better than me, then. So here's something you don't know, Miss I-Flunked-History."

Leigh kicked him under the table. "C. I got a C," she said.

"Ow," Jonathan rubbed his shin. "Okay, Miss Average-in-History."

Leigh pursed her lips and glared at him, but playfully.

"The Sudarium soaks up the blood as the body is carried to the tomb. Then, Jesus is laid on the linen cloth we think is the Shroud. Was the Shroud," Jonathan corrected himself. "He is wrapped up in the Shroud and the Sudarium is taken off and entombed with him, off to the side, in the tomb. And it stays there until John finds it, three days later on Sunday."

"Then what?"

"Then nothing. It's lost to history. There is a legend that Peter took the Shroud and Paul took the Sudarium, but it's just legend. Nothing accurate or reliable. The only thing we know for sure is that the Sudarium surfaces in Spain around 616 A.D. along with other relics carried by people fleeing the Persians. It makes its way up north in Spain as they flee the Muslims, and ends up in Oviedo, where it's been ever since."

Leigh sat in deep thought. "So why aren't we studying the Sudarium?" she asked at last.

"We should be. Historically, it is much more impressive than the Shroud. But there is no image or anything. I just looks, if you pardon my sacrilege, like a dirty rag. No curb appeal."

Leigh's eyes sparkled as her mind raced. "You know, if we can get a sample of the blood on the Sudarium, we should be able to match it up to the blood samples from the Shroud in my tablet." Leigh tapped the side of the bag slung over her shoulder.

"If you could prove they are from the same man," Jonathan nodded his head, "well, that would be monumental. For historians, anyway."

"But how can we get a sample?" Leigh thought out loud.

"Maybe the Old Man can pull some strings, get us in there. Maybe he's friendly with the Spaniards."

"If anyone can talk the Spanish into it, it would be the Old Man," Leigh agreed. "Let's call him."

Jonathan glanced at a clock on the wall at the far end of the room. "It's still early over there."

"Well, we'll call in a couple of hours," Leigh offered.

"In the meantime, lets book a plane ticket back to Manchester, just in case," Jonathan suggested. He brought out his phone.

Jonathan poked and prodded at it while Leigh sipped her coffee. He sighed.

"What is it?" Leigh asked.

"Everything is booked until tonight," Jonathan said. "I've got us on the RyanAir at 9:20 p.m., direct."

"Well, that will have to do."

Jonathan pocketed the phone. "What do you want to do till then?" he asked, smiling a coy smile.

"We're in Venice. Let's see the town," Leigh said, excited.

"Sounds lovely," Jonathan said.

CHAPTER 3

Venice, Italy
May 22, 2025 9:15 a.m.

Adriana Nyx sat by her window and dialed the Lawyer's number. It rang and rang and at last he picked up.

"Where are they?" Adriana asked, not waiting for a hello.

"You've any idea what time it is over here?" he said blearily.

"Yes. Early. Now, do you have their position or not?"

She heard him set the phone down and fumble about, tapping something out. At last he came back to the phone.

"The last report I have is that they withdrew money at the train station, then, nothing. No activity on the card. They must be paying for everything cash."

"What about the tracker?" she asked, growing more annoyed.

"We lost the signal sometime after the train station yesterday. Don't know why. These old buildings, they can block the signal. Maybe her batteries ran out. Who knows?"

"When after the train station?"

"Not sure."

"Idiot," she spat out, in Italian.

The Lawyer cringed. Adriana angry was stressful. She was a handful on a good day. "Let me check." There was more shuffling and tapping. "Last known position was on the Grand Canal. Right across from a place called Ca' d'Oro." He pronounced this *kay door*.

"I know it. I'll start there."

"If I pick up their position, I will call you at once."

"Let me talk to the man tracking them directly," she said.

"I can't do that, I'm sorry," he said almost sheepishly.

"You can tell me," she whispered into the phone, her voice suddenly sultry and seductive.

The Lawyer closed his eyes and took a deep breath. "I can't, Miss Nyx. I really can't. I'm sorry," he said, his voice turning softer and softer.

"When will I see you next?" Adriana asked, still sultry and seductive.

"I hope to get to Italy soon," he said, his words almost a breath now. "It's been too long," he added.

Adriana smiled. Men were so easy. "Let me know when you pick up their position," she said, harshly now. "And when you come over, I have some special things planned for you." The tone of her voice was equal parts threat and promise.

She hung up before he could respond.

Adriana cursed again to the empty room. She hated dealing with him, but he paid the bills, and paid very well. He was a depraved sorry excuse for a human. She would be glad when they met again. She would plan an interrogation session, just some not-so-harmless role-play. But it would turn very real very quick. Adriana licked her lips, picturing it all in her mind. She lit a cigarette and smoked it slowly by the window, looking at the maze of streets outside and hoping she would be able to find them.

Venice, Italy
May 22, 2025 9:45 a.m.

"Wow, this is confusing," Leigh said.

Jonathan flipped the map around and looked up at the street sign. Now they looked like any one of the hundreds of hapless lost tourists they'd seen. Getting to the hotel by boat had been easy. Getting out on foot was confusing. They turned left and dead-ended into a canal. A turn right and they dead-ended into a wall. Another turn and they circled back around to where they'd started.

Jonathan scratched his head. "Okay, we've tried three out of four ways. The fourth must be right."

They made their way out of the den of alleys out into the plaza surrounding the Chiesa di San Cassiano, a relatively modest neighborhood church.

"Ah, better," Leigh said, walking to the center of the wide plaza. She shifted her bag to the other shoulder.

"This is pleasant," Jonathan said, turning in a circle to look at the whole beautiful plaza.

They walked on without destination, enjoying the cool morning air and the play of early light on the walls of the old buildings and the shimmering canals.

"So let's say we get a sample," Leigh said as they walked, continuing the conversation from breakfast.

"Yes?"

"And let's say it's a match to the blood on the Shroud. What does it matter? What does it prove?" she asked.

"Well, historically, it would push the dating of the Shroud back to the year 700," Jonathan responded.

"But the Shroud is gone," Leigh noted.

"Yes. It's still hard to believe," Jonathan said and shook his head. "But we have much information on it. Videos, countless photographs, your blood samples, even threads of it still stored in a couple of labs. I think if we were to match the blood, it would prove the authenticity of the two, personally."

"How so?"

"You've got two relics with very distinct paths through history. Two very divergent paths. If the blood comes from the same man, the most logical explanation is that they are both real, as they have been treated through history. The skeptic argument would make no sense."

"Why not?" Leigh asked. They walked over a small footbridge and into a narrow street.

"You'd have to believe that someone with advanced skills in forensics, microbiology, DNA, photography, etcetera, would fake all this before the year 700, then send both of these relics through wildly different paths through history. It makes no sense."

"No it doesn't," Leigh said. "But you only answered half my question."

"What's that?" Jonathan asked.

"You answered what does it prove. I asked what does it matter."

"Ahh, now you sound like me," Jonathan said and grinned.

"So what's your answer?"

"In the end, I think nothing, to tell you the truth." Jonathan shook his head, a resigned expression settling over his face. "I think Jesus could put on a show at Carnegie Hall and people would still either believe or not believe."

"I still say that's cynical," Leigh said.

"I think it's realistic."

"Can it be both?" Leigh asked.

"I don't know. I'd love to be wrong about people, but I don't think I am," Jonathan said, pensive.

"I think your problem is you look at people, not the person. The individual," Leigh said, "can be persuaded. Can be made to believe through rational scientific evidence."

Jonathan gave a short laugh. "I don't think you have the right diagnosis of the human condition there, Doctor."

"How about you?" Leigh asked turning serious.

They walked over another bridge and paused on top, looking out at the blue-green water kissed with gold from the sun.

"What about me what?" Jonathan responded.

"Why don't you believe? Is it because of the great hurt that you told me of?" she asked.

"That's part of it," he said.

"What's the other part?"

"I don't want to say." Jonathan looked out at the far end of the canal, to the distant buildings on the other side.

"I'll kiss you," Leigh offered.

Jonathan smiled. "Show me the rest of your tattoo."

"Not yet. A girl's gotta have some secrets."

"Okay. I'll take that kiss, though," he said.

Leigh stood on tiptoe and met his lips as Jonathan slipped his arm around her waist, pulling her to him. The kiss lingered on as the sun peeked over a building to light the water under the bridge.

"Mmm, that was nice," Leigh whispered.

"Yes it was," Jonathan agreed.

"So tell me."

"Not now."

"You promised," Leigh protested.

"I didn't. I just said I'd take the kiss." Jonathan grinned.

Leigh socked him on the arm.

"You're getting to have a hell of a right hook," he said, rubbing his arm. "And I'll tell you," he added, "just not right now. I'm happy and I don't want to spoil the moment."

"Okay," Leigh said. "I'll wait until we're miserable."

Jonathan chuckled. "It won't take long. You'll be sick of me in two days."

"We may be dead in two days."

"You're awfully cavalier about it," he said.

"What am I going to do, worry?" Leigh shrugged.

"I am."

"And what's that getting you?" she asked.

"Good point. Not a damn thing."

"Anyway," Leigh said, "I haven't seen any big Moors or other suspicious characters."

"Me neither," Jonathan said.

"If there was anyone after us, I think we gave them the slip."

"I hope you're right."

CHAPTER 4

Venice, Italy
May 22, 2025 10:30 a.m.

Adrianna Nyx lingered over her coffee at the hotel's breakfast, picturing various scenarios for the kill. She would have to improvise, but it still helped to be prepared. She scrolled through the pictures and biographies of the two targets on her phone. The girl was cute. Adriana distractedly licked her lips. She would love to take her time with the girl and started picturing her in different predicaments.

"More coffee?" a waitress asked, appearing at her table while Adriana was distracted.

"No," Adriana replied curtly, regaining her composure quickly.

She finished the coffee and rose from the table and passed the lobby. She walked out of the hotel and down the alley and headed towards the shops.

The first store she entered was a camera store run by a handsome young man.

"I want something big and expensive," she said in Italian to the young clerk.

The clerk saw her striding in, wearing black boots and tight black pants, and an obviously expensive blouse and waistcoat. He immediately perked up. His day normally consisted of tourists buying memory cards or batteries, and big sales were few and far in between. Especially big sales to beautiful women.

"Of course. What kind of photography are you going to do?" the clerk asked.

"I don't care. Something professional. And a camera bag too," she replied curtly.

"Certainly. If I were to buy one myself, it would be this one." The clerk took a camera body out of a glass case. "The Leica 7," he presented the camera. "And to start, these lenses." He brought out a short 28 millimeter lens and a longer 50 — 200 millimeter zoom.

"Just the big lens," Adriana said. "And that camera bag too," she pointed at a black unadorned bag that looked serious and expensive.

"Don't you want to know how much?" the clerk asked.

"No. Here." She handed him the Lawyer's credit card, the expense account as she liked to call it. The clerk rang it up, verified the card against her false identification and everything checked out.

"Load it all for me, get it all ready," she said impatiently.

"Of course," the clerk said and hurried to comply. He loaded the memory card and clicked the lens into place. He began to box it all up.

"Don't," Adriana stopped him. "I'll wear it out."

She walked out of the store already half looking the part, with the big serious camera slung over her neck and the bag over her shoulder. But she needed more conservative clothes.

Next she walked over the Rialto Bridge towards San Marco to Vogini, a store she had frequented in the past during her time in Venice. It was mostly leather goods and casual but stylish clothing. She walked in and savored the aroma of the leather. In a short time, she was dressed like a well-heeled tourist, wearing a white blouse and khakis. Casual but expensive, a sort of safari-chic. A lady of means. The helpful clerk at Vogini had her other clothing and a couple of additional purchases sent back to her hotel. She thanked the clerk and stepped out into the perfect weather outside.

Now she completely looked the part. The huntress in her gear, ready to stalk her prey through the maze of Venice's streets. She smiled and headed towards Ca' d'Oro and their last known position.

Venice, Italy
May 22, 2025 10:55 a.m.

Jonathan and Leigh strolled down a small street that opened into a large plaza. They passed by a kiosk selling trinkets and newspapers, and Jonathan froze. The newspaper headline read "Turin Terrorism" and showed video of the chaotic scene in front of the ruined Cathedral with people running this way and that. Jonathan picked up the ePaper, a cheap plastic electronic reader, and scrolled down the page. Leigh came up behind him, peeking at the newspaper.

"What's it say?" she asked.

"It was a brand-new private plane belonging to Sheik Abdul Rhaman Al-something, highjacked on its maiden voyage on the way to Bahrain. He denies any wrongdoing, will not leave Bahrain to answer questions but is otherwise cooperating, blah, blah. The typical."

"Any word on survivors?" Leigh asked softly.

"None," Jonathan said.

"Sir, you want to buy, yes? Ten euros." A voice in accented English interrupted them. It was the kiosk clerk.

"No, thanks," Leigh answered. "Let's go to a café, we can read it on my tablet," she said to Jonathan.

Jonathan put the ePaper back on the rack.

"Thanks," he said and they walked away.

"Let's sit there," Leigh said, pointing at a café across the plaza.

"Looks nice," Jonathan agreed.

They sat outside at the café at a table facing the *Campo* s. Aponal, a small pretty square tucked away in the middle of the city and surrounded by modest buildings. What looked like an ancient large well, now capped, stood in the middle of the square. Tourists walked up and down and children played in the middle of the square. Jonathan ordered two cappuccinos from the waiter and Leigh added an order of a croissant with crème. Jonathan gave her a sideways glance.

"Second breakfast," Leigh explained.

Jonathan arched a skeptical eyebrow. "Okay. Just let me have a bite?"

"If you behave yourself."

"Have I not been?"

"You have. For the most part," Leigh agreed.

"For the whole part," he corrected her.

Leigh smiled at him, and they gazed at each other, not saying anything, letting their eyes speak.

The waiter came with the cappuccinos and the croissant, breaking their spell.

"Cheers," Leigh said, and they sipped the strong coffee.

"Let's see about that newspaper, yes?" Jonathan asked her.

"Certainly." Leigh unsnapped her bag and brought out her tablet computer. She swiped at it and frowned. She swiped at it again, then pressed the reset button at its base. "Ah darn it," she exclaimed.

"What's wrong?" Jonathan asked.

"It's dead. I forgot to charge it last night."

"You had other things on your mind," Jonathan told her with a half-smile.

"See? It's your fault."

"Mine?" he asked indignantly.

"Yes, yours. You got me drunk," Leigh pouted.

"If it makes you happy, blame me."

"It does. A small part of me likes it," Leigh said. She had a playful smile on her face, like she was trying to be serious but not being very good at it.

Jonathan laughed.

"But," Leigh said, "I came prepared." She brought out a power cord from her bag with a flourish. "Now where do I plug in," she mumbled to herself.

"Behind you," Jonathan pointed at the power outlet by the wall.

"Ah, thanks."

Leigh plugged in the tablet and the little white light softly came to life, pulsing and receiving power.

Venice, Italy
May 22, 2025 11:11 a.m.

Adriana's phone buzzed inside her pocket. She fumbled, looking for it in her unfamiliar many-pocketed clothing. She found it and glanced at the display. It was the Lawyer.

"*Pronto*?" she answered the phone.

"We have a signal."

"Where?"

"In a plaza. Looks like Aponal Plaza on the map. Sound familiar?"

"I know it. I am near," she said.

"Remember, get the computer. It is important."

"Of course, you fool," Adriana hissed into the phone.

The Lawyer paused. "How are you going to do it?" he asked at last.

"I don't know yet. I will find a way, don't worry," she assured him. The Lawyer wanted to hear the grisly details, but she would not indulge his habit, not this time.

"Good. Call me when you're done. We'll celebrate soon," he said.

"*Ciao*," she said and hung up on him.

Adriana turned and strode quickly towards the *Campo* s. Aponal. She tapped on her phone and brought up a map to make sure she knew where she was going. Having lived in Venice for a couple of years, she was familiar with the city. But even the lifelong residents still got lost. She confirmed her destination and hurried there. She willed her excitement down, trying to stay calm and reminding herself that it was only observation for now. She would track them at a distance until the opportunity presented itself. Then, she would have her fun.

Venice, Italy
May 22, 2025 11:15 a.m.

"Is it going to live?" Jonathan asked Leigh, pointing at her tablet computer.

"It's fine. The battery must have run out yesterday with all that uploading of the DNA samples to Manchester," she said.

"How is that going?"

"It's done. Looks like Tony's sent me more files of the processed samples, all stitched together." Leigh pointed at the screen. Jonathan scooted closer to see.

She scrolled down the page. Thousand upon thousands of A, C, G, and T's, all coded in different colors, filled the screen like a kaleidoscope. "You know, this is amazing to me," Leigh said quietly with awe.

"What?"

"This. The amount of information that is packed into each cell of our body. It's always fascinated me," she said, staring intently at the screen, scrolling casually down the thousands of lines of code.

"It is amazing," Jonathan agreed. He took a sip of the cappuccino.

"I mean, look at this," she held up the tablet. "This is a very advanced and large computer, especially compared to a strand of DNA, and still, it can only hold about as much information as three or four cells. Amazing." She continued scrolling down, then paused. "Hmm, that's strange."

The screen had turned mostly red, filled with the "T" base almost exclusively. Leigh frowned and zoomed in and out. There were solitary squares of white, the "A" base, at intervals, but mostly the screen was filled with red.

"What is it?"

"I'm not sure. See this?" She flipped the tablet around, showing Jonathan the screen full of red T's. "It shouldn't be like that. It's probably a glitch from when the battery died, or a transmission error or something."

"Could it be just gaps like you talked about before?"

"It's possible, but unlikely. Gaps would show up as black squares. To show up in any color as a base, the computer checks itself against five other samples," she explained. Leigh bit her lip, thinking. "No, this is strange, even for junk DNA."

"Whoa. What's junk DNA?" he asked.

Leigh smiled. "Well, it's a misnomer, actually. It's not really junk. Formally, it's called noncoding DNA. It can consist of transposons, retrotransposons, telomeres—" Leigh stopped, reading the blank look on Jonathan's face.

"Five-year-old version, please."

"Right. Sorry. The DNA that actually makes your body, the genes, the DNA with the written instructions, is only about two percent of your total DNA. The rest serves, for the most part, no known purpose. There are exceptions, like telomeres and such, but I won't go into them. It's all just filler material, seemingly random. But this," she turned her attention to the red screen, "well, this is just odd. It has to be a mistake."

"How can you know? If it's a mistake or not, I mean?"

"We'll figure it out when we get to Manchester. I'll need the big computers to run some tests, and we'll get it sorted."

"Good. Now," Jonathan said and gave Leigh a serious look. "I have an important question for you."

"Yes? What is it?" she asked, concerned.

"Are you going to eat that croissant or not?"

Leigh laughed. "Yes. But here is the bite I promised you." She tore off a little bit of the pastry and handed it to him.

"Thank you, lady," he said. "Now, about that newspaper."

"Oh yes, here you go." Leigh minimized the DNA viewer and tapped the International Herald Tribune button. She handed the iTablet to Jonathan.

"Good coffee, my newspaper, a beautiful woman, all in a sidewalk café in Venice." Jonathan exhaled, contented. "It doesn't get any better than this."

Venice, Italy
May 22, 2025 11:19 a.m.

Adriana Nyx tried to soften her expression as she rounded the corner to the *Campo* s. Aponal. She changed her stride from a fast purposeful walk to a casual stroll. Behind her Prada sunglasses, she scanned the crowd in the plaza. There were tourists everywhere, children playing a makeshift game of soccer in the middle of the plaza, lovers sitting on benches. She methodically searched the crowded plaza, looking through the viewfinder of her new and expensive camera.

There. Finally.

Sitting against the back wall outside the café, were Jonathan Tremaine and Leigh Lancaster, her targets. Her eyes immediately fell on Leigh. *Bellisima*, she thought.

Adriana took pictures of the square and, casually, the couple. She ambled around, waiting for them to leave, but they were taking their time. Not wanting to be noticed, she went to another sidewalk café across the square where she had a clear view. She ordered an espresso and paid for it. She relaxed, sitting back in her chair, playing with her camera, but keeping her predatory eye on them.

Leigh leaned forward in her chair. "Alright, mister, enough news. That stuff only gives you an ulcer, don't you know?" she said. "Let's do some Venetian things."

"You're right. And there's nothing in here about us that we don't know." Jonathan handed the tablet back.

Leigh swiped it off, unplugged it and put it back in her bag. "Where to?" she asked.

"What are you in the mood for? Churches or art?"

"No churches," Leigh said quickly.

"Right. Art then. No flying babies, though," Jonathan said.

"The Guggenheim? It's modern art."

"Whatever you say. I'm in your hands," he smiled.

"I remember wanting to go there when I was a girl. My dad didn't like modern art, so we never went."

Jonathan unfolded his tourist map. "Let's see." He scanned the map. "Here we are," he traced his finger to their current position, "and we have to get here," he pointed at the museum. "I think I have it. Make our way back to the Market, then the No. 1 line to *Accademia*, unless you want to take a taxi again."

"No, we can travel with the great unwashed masses," Leigh said.

Jonathan laughed.

"Do you always plan these museum outings like a military mission?" Leigh asked playfully.

Jonathan laughed again. "Yeah. Habit. Dad being a Marine, everything was a mission. We had to be ready for the big bad world and all."

"Is that such a bad thing?"

"It is when you're six. We didn't exactly play catch in the backyard." Jonathan smiled wistfully, remembering back.

"It must have been difficult," Leigh said tenderly.

Jonathan shrugged. "It had its good side. There were camping trips, long talks about military history, survival training. Once I got older, I appreciated it more, appreciated what he was trying to do." Jonathan got up from the table. "You ready?"

"Yep." Leigh got up and slung her bag over her shoulder. They paid and walked towards the Museum.

Across the plaza, Adriana Nyx saw them rise from the table. She downed the rest of her espresso and got up, following them at a distance. They were not hard to miss; the man was tall and broad shouldered and the woman dressed all in tailored black clothes. *At least she has good taste in fashion,* Adriana thought.

Adriana followed them through the maze of streets as they passed right by her hotel and arrived at the Rialto Market. She kept a sharp eye on them through the crowded market, passing the cornucopia of fruits and vegetables brought here from all over Italy and beyond. Occasionally, they stopped to look at some stand, and once they stopped and bought a pint of tiny strawberries. She kept her distance and watched them intently in the reflection of a storefront window.

Jonathan and Leigh arrived at the *vaporetto* stop, bought tickets from the machine, and waited at the floating dock on the Grand Canal. They stood there, eating the tiny berries. Adriana hung back, blending into the gathering crowd of tourists waiting for the boat. At last, the *vaporetto*, essentially a big floating bus, pulled up to the floating dock. The boat bumped up against the rubrail and the first mate, standing at starboard and ready, quickly tied a clove hitch to the big black iron cleat on the dock. The captain feathered the throttle and held the boat steady and flush to the dock. The rope groaned and the knot tightened. They did this in seconds, with quick, practiced moves.

The first mate slid aside the metal guardrail and a rush of people got off even as the crowd at the dock tried to get on. Jonathan and Leigh were carried by the wave onboard, and Adriana followed behind.

"There," Jonathan pointed to the bow where there were two recently vacated chairs. They jostled their way up and sat at the front of the boat.

Adriana stood back, right behind the captain's control cabin at midships. There were only about ten seats on the boat at the front, and these quickly filled. Most people stood and tourists with unwieldy luggage struggled to settle in. The first mate closed the guardrail and undid the clove hitch with a quick flick of the wrist. The captain throttled the engines and they were underway.

The Grand Canal unfurled majestically in front of them. They passed under the Rialto Bridge. Hundreds of tourists stood at the wide stone railings, peering down at the Canal and the boats. Some waved at them. Leigh waved back and looked at Jonathan and smiled. For the third time since they'd been to Venice, Jonathan wished to remember that moment in perfect clarity, but the Shutter remained quiet.

The *vaporetto* stopped at the next station and the crew repeated the docking and loading ritual. Dozens of people got on and dozens got off. They traveled leisurely down the Canal, stopping along the way, until they reached the *Accademia* stop, right near where they had boarded the gondola the night before.

"This is us," Jonathan said, and they quickly got up. They made their way past the crowd of people on the boat, right past Adriana.

Adriana stood perfectly still and savored the feeling as they brushed by. *Too many people to do anything here*, she thought. *If it was only one, maybe, and escape in the confusion. But not two.* She inhaled, leaning forward ever so slightly when Leigh walked past, smelling her sweet scent. It was thrilling, this part of the hunt.

Jonathan and Leigh stepped off the *vaporetto* and onto the floating dock. Adriana followed, getting off at the last second. She followed them at a discreet distance as they worked their way around the streets. The couple made one more turn and walked into the pretty, walled garden of the Guggenheim museum, an old Canal-front *palazzo*-turned-repository for some of the greatest works of modern art. The couple bought two tickets and entered, and Adriana followed. She relaxed a little. There was only one way in and one way out, unless they decided to swim. Adriana chose to linger in the sculpture garden outside and keep an eye on the door rather than follow them from gallery to gallery, where she could be noticed. She waited as they lingered in the garden, and took more pictures of them when they weren't looking.

"Wow, this is lovely," Leigh said.

"This is a nice pad," Jonathan agreed. A sculpture caught his eye. "Look, a Henry Moore." He walked over to the sculpture. Leigh followed. "I love Henry Moore," Jonathan said as he regarded the sculpture of three elongated abstract figures.

"What do you like about it?" Leigh asked, curious.

"I'm not sure, to be honest. It's like he captured something inside the figures, some life force. I don't know. I just like it."

"I never pegged you for an art lover, cowboy."

"I'm telling you, you've got the wrong impression of me. I'm not a cowboy, more the strong sensitive type. Except when I'm not," Jonathan said, smirking.

"Not what? Strong? Or sensitive?"

Jonathan chuckled. "Sensitive. I tend to be a jerk sometimes." Then he added, "Remind me to show you."

Leigh socked him on the arm, playfully.

"I'm going to get a bruise there," he said teasingly. "You better switch."

"Oh, I'll switch," Leigh raised her hand to hit him in the other arm.

In a flash, Jonathan caught her hand and brought it down, not roughly, but the speed startled her. He brought it quickly behind her back, being careful and gentle, but quick, and pressed her close to him.

"Did your dad teach you that?" she asked, after she'd processed what happened.

"Yes," Jonathan said. "But this next part is all my own."

With his other hand, he cradled the back of her head and leaned down and kissed her hard. She stood on her tiptoes to meet him and brought her free hand around his broad back.

"Mmm, that was nice," she said when he'd finished the kiss.

"I'm not done."

Adriana looked at the two kissing in the sculpture garden. *They should get a room,* she thought, then considered this. *Room.* She began to think that the hotel room would afford the best opportunity. Venice in May was too crowded, even at night. *Yes.* She would follow them back to the hotel, sneak into the room, and do it there. In the meantime, she would stay close and out of sight. She smiled malevolently and took another picture of the two kissing by the sculpture.

Jonathan and Leigh finished kissing.

"Well, are we actually going to see some art here, cowboy? Or did you just want to come here to make out?" Leigh asked coyly.

"After you," Jonathan extended a hand, leading her up towards the entrance to the galleries.

The two strolled through the morning shade of the garden and into the gallery.

"This is pretty cool," he whispered as they walked through the front room. The museum was mercifully empty at the time, as it was still relatively early. They walked from gallery to gallery, stopping here and there as a particular painting grabbed their attention.

Leigh ambled on ahead and entered a room full of Jackson Pollock canvases.

"Wow," Leigh gasped in wonder.

Jonathan came up behind her. "Wow is right. Look at all these," he said in hushed tones.

"I've seen these in books and on the computer, but never in real life," Leigh said. "They're incredible."

"Yes," Jonathan agreed. "He's one of my favorites."

"It always looked like just paint splotches and squiggles in the pictures. Look at this texture, though." Leigh got up to the wall-sized painting, inches away. Layers upon layers of paint rose and fell and intersected with each other. "It's like ten paintings, one on top of another," she said, turning to look at Jonathan with an expression of wonder on her pretty face.

"An interviewer once asked Pollock how he knew when he was done with a painting," Jonathan whispered in the gallery. "You know what Pollock said?"

"What?"

"He asked the interviewer, 'How do you know when you're done making love?'"

Leigh smiled, then blushed a bit, her ivory skin turning the barest shade of pink.

"That's what I like about these," Jonathan continued, studying the painting, *Enchanted Forest*. "It's passion that's frozen but somehow still alive and speaking, even now."

Jonathan came up right behind Leigh, who was standing in front of the painting, and kissed the top of her head. They stood in front of *Enchanted Forest*, his arms around her, and contemplated it silently for a time that seemed to last forever.

CHAPTER 5

Oviedo, Spain
May 22, 2025 11:45 a.m.

Asad stood at his hotel window, staring out at the Cathedral's spire in the distance. He pressed a button, and waited for his new cell phone to connect. It rang and rang, and, at last, a man picked up.

"Yes?" the voice answered, in Spanish.

"Samir?"

"Yes."

"It's Leon," Asad said, giving his codename.

"Good to hear from you, my brother," Samir said, recognizing him now. It was about the last person he'd expected to call right then. "It has been too long."

"Yes it has," Asad agreed. "I may have a job for you."

"Yes?" Samir said, interested.

"A restaurant in Oviedo. We need a cook for a great feast." Asad always used code on the phones. One could never be too careful.

"A cook?" Samir's voice turned hard and sharpened.

"Yes. It will be a big feast. If you could get forty kilos of meat, it would be great," Asad said, meaning explosives.

"What kind of meat?"

"The best kind. Top grade." *Semtex.*

"Will I have to clean up as well?" Samir asked with a trace of hesitation in his voice. *Will it be a suicide job?*

"No, no. Just cooking. No cleanup. Just setting the oven on a timer and supervising. Very easy," Asad reassured him.

"Good," Samir said, the relief palpable in his voice. "The meat may be a problem. I only have twenty kilos in the freezer."

"I will see about making up the difference."

"When is the feast?" Samir asked.

"The clients want it soon. Tomorrow if possible."

"I could be there this afternoon. It is about a four hour drive." Samir paused, then asked, "What is the pay?"

"They are wealthy, these clients," Asad said. "I can probably get fifty euros for the job."

"Fifty?" Samir asked.

"Yes. I may be able to get more."

"Good. I will be there tonight. Where shall I meet you?"

"I am at the Melia Reconquista," Asad said. "Call me on this number when you get in. You will stay at the Ovedense hotel nearby. I will have a room reserved for you. We will meet at the restaurant of the same name on the ground floor."

"Ovedense. Very well," Samir confirmed.

"Go in God's protection," Asad said, and hung up.

He looked out the window of his richly appointed room and contemplated the spire of the Cathedral rising up over the rooftops of the ancient city. He thought out the Lawyer's plan, and the changes that had to be made. He needed to talk to the Lawyer, an event he always hated. But it was part of the job. He dialed his secure line and waited as the filters scanned for anyone listening. At last, the Lawyer answered.

"Hello, this is Leon," Asad said, switching to English.

"Are you done over there yet?" the Lawyer barked out impatiently.

"I arrived recently." Asad remained calm. "And your report was wrong. The plan is wrong. It will have to be reworked."

"What do you mean wrong?" the Lawyer spat out.

"I mean that whoever wrote the report did not study the area. Not well," Asad said.

"What are you saying?"

"Send a wise man and do not advise him," Asad said, quoting the proverb.

"What the hell does that mean?" the Lawyer asked.

"What I'm saying is I've studied it, and the initial plan will not work. It was ill-conceived." Asad explained to him about the layout of the Cathedral and the thickness of the walls.

The Lawyer cursed silently. It had been his own plan, after all. But he knew better than to contradict Asad. The man was good and a professional and the Lawyer trusted him in these matters.

"What do you suggest?" the Lawyer asked, swallowing his pride.

"I have a good plan. The details are unimportant. But I will need a second person to assist, and he will cost one-hundred."

"Euros?"

"Yes."

"Fine," the Lawyer said. He was in no mood to dicker. "What about the Basque? Have you been in contact with him for the supplies?"

"Not yet. I will not need a carload as you had planned. But I will need to meet with him for part of the supplies."

The Lawyer was silent, mulling things over. "Tell me your plan," he said at last. "Just the outline," he added.

"There is a point of weakness below the target. I can hit it there and destroy it surgically."

"Hmm." The Lawyer thought about this for some time. At last, he spoke. "Sounds good. Do that, but go ahead with the original plan as well."

"Why? If you don't mind me asking," Asad said.

"If it is too surgical it will not look right. We need a big show to make it look right. And the truck will make a big show. Plus it'll wipe away evidence."

Asad thought about it. "You are right," he admitted. "I will assure the target is destroyed, then cover it up."

"Good," the Lawyer said. "I will contact the Basque and let him know to expect your call."

The Lawyer hung up.

Asad set the phone down and rubbed his eyes. That had gone relatively well, but the man's voice still grated on his nerves. He drew the curtains, and sat down at the small desk, barely fitting in the chair. He got to work on refining the calculations, remembering the dimensions and layout of the crypt as if he were there. To be safe and ensure the demolition of the structure, at least forty kilos of Semtex were needed. Less would probably work due to the concave shape of the crypt's ceiling under the *Camara Santa*, but Asad wanted to err on the side of caution. An additional four kilos of ANFO or ANNM would ensure the incineration of everything in the chamber. He saw it all in his mind's eye: the explosion concentrated upwards, the collapse of the crypt's ceiling and the floor of the *Camara Santa*, the secondary flash of the ANFO as the contents of the chamber, and the target, dropped and were consumed by fire. Asad went over the rest of the materials he would need from the Basque, creating a mental checklist. TOVEX and blasting caps, two old cell phones, wire. The rest he could get himself at a store.

Satisfied, Asad got up from the desk and retrieved his jacket from the closet. He left the hotel and walked towards a nearby park. Oviedo was surrounded by mountains, and the wind blowing down from the peaks gave the air a chill even at this noon hour. Asad consulted his phone for a camping supply store. He pulled up the nearest one and mapped it out. He walked there, thinking about the plan, refining it, working out the details.

On his way there, he walked by a store selling religious trinkets. He entered it with trepidation, looking at all the unfamiliar statues of saints and hundreds of crucifixes on the wall. They seemed to stare at him. The tiny crucified Christs gazed at him patiently, as if waiting for an answer to a question he'd not heard. Asad shook these thoughts away and focused on the task at hand.

At the front of the store, on the counter by the cash register, was a display of many scallop shells hanging from strings. He picked one up, turning it over in his hand.

"Oh, you are doing the pilgrimage?" the friendly older clerk asked, in Spanish, as he finished arranging some boxes.

"Yes," Asad replied. "Me and a friend." He picked up another shell.

"I did it years ago, in my youth," the clerk said, smiling and remembering.

Asad nodded. He did not know much about this pilgrimage, only the basics. "How was it?" he asked.

"It was a long walk to Santiago. Much rough terrain. But God gave me strength," the clerk said.

"I hope He will do the same for me," Asad said. "Thank you," he added, paid for the shells and left.

At the camping store, Asad bought two of the biggest backpacks available and two walking staves. He saw they sold the scallop shells here as well. *This city must get many pilgrims*, he thought.

Asad also bought hiking boots, shorts, and a T-shirt to complete the uniform. He bought some for Samir as well, guessing at his size and buying slightly bigger. He carried it all back to the hotel.

In his room, he laid his purchases out carefully on the floor. Stepping over by the window, he gazed out for a moment at the Cathedral spire rising over the rooftops of the city. He brought out his phone and made the call to the Basque.

"Yes?" a man answered in Spanish.

"This is Leon," Asad said.

"Good. I was expecting you. Take this address down," the voice on the phone said.

"Go on."

"National Road 231, Kilometer 14. There is a restaurant called *El Horno de Eustacio*. Meet there at six today. We will go from there."

"Very well." Asad repeated the meet point and time.

"Good. I will see you then," the man said and hung up.

Asad sat on the chair by the desk and leaned back, still looking out the window. He took a deep breath. Tonight would be a busy night. He allowed himself to relax until Samir showed up later that afternoon, and contemplated the Cathedral spire in the distance.

CHAPTER 6

Venice, Italy
May 22, 2025 12:15 p.m.

Leigh and Jonathan walked out the back door of the art gallery onto the landing on the Grand Canal. The big stone and marble porch of the *palazzo* contained more sculptures and, to the side, large mature trees, a rare sight in Venice.

"That's an interesting one," Leigh said, pointing at the huge sculpture in the middle. The sculpture, a stylized naked man riding a horse with arms and legs outstretched in joyous ecstasy, dominated the landing.

"It's called the Angel of the City by Marino Marini," Jonathan said.

"Well, he's a very happy angel," Leigh said, smirking and pointing at the naked figure's erection.

Jonathan laughed. "I'll say. Peggy Guggenheim got a lot of crap for putting this out here for everyone to see from the Grand Canal. For pointing this thing," he gestured at the sculpture, "at the city. The old money saw it as a kind of insult."

"How do you know all this?" Leigh asked, fascinated.

"Not sure. I must have read it somewhere or had it flash onto my brain during one of my episodes. If I think about it, I can remember when and where, but it takes a lot out of me."

"You know," Leigh said as they strolled out by the water, "in a way that memory of yours is like one of these works of art."

"How so?" Jonathan asked, curious.

"Here, let's sit," Leigh said, pointing to a shady spot on the low stone wall ringing the dock. "All this art," she continued, "is emotion frozen in time, like you said back there. So is your gift."

Jonathan nodded. "I see where you're going with that, but I'd hardly call it a gift."

"I'd call it a gift," Leigh said.

"What? Remembering the worst part of your life over and over?" he asked and looked across the trees and into the water.

"And the best. You remember the best, too, right?" Leigh asked, and added, "I hope."

"Not as much, it seems," he said gazing at the ripples in the water.

"I hope I make it in there," Leigh said, "to your permanent file."

Jonathan turned to her and smiled, but it was a melancholic smile. "I hope so too. And I hope it's a beautiful memory in Venice," he said after a pause.

Leigh cast down her eyes, then looked in his eyes again. They gazed at each other in a comfortable silence, not needing to say anything.

Jonathan grinned. "Show me the rest of your tattoo," he said, lightening the mood.

Leigh laughed. "Okay." She started rolling up her sleeve.

"Really?" he asked, incredulous.

"No," she said with a smile and pulled the sleeve back down. Her green eyes sparkled in the clear Venetian sun.

"Tease." Jonathan narrowed his eyes.

"You love it," she said.

"I must admit I do," he said and chuckled.

"Come, let's go grab a café and call the Old Man," Leigh said.

Adriana Nyx ambled around the sculpture garden, keeping an eye on the gallery door. She took pictures of the sculptures and the *palazzo* to keep herself occupied and looking like a tourist. *This really was a nice place*, she thought to herself. It would be good to have a villa like this, not in Venice, but in the country, with privacy. Maybe she would take the job of the big Moor, if the price went up. Maybe she could hold the woman's computer the Lawyer wanted for ransom. A large ransom.

The couple walked out of the gallery. Adriana saw them and stopped her daydreaming, locking on to them. She tailed them discreetly.

Jonathan and Leigh walked through the sculpture garden and out of the museum. They made their way through the maze of streets to the *vaporetto* stop they had been at earlier. They waited for the boat to arrive as the dock filled with tourists.

"Where to?" Leigh asked.

"Well, we can't leave Venice without seeing St. Marks. Let's get over there and sit and have a coffee. And a drink," he said.

"Coffee," Leigh said, glaring at him.

"What? It's past noon."

"Coffee," Leigh repeated firmly. "And a pastry," she added, with a smile.

"Okay, coffee," Jonathan relented. "And a pastry," he said in a teasing tone. "And later, a bottle of white wine on our terrace."

"Are you trying to get me drunk again, cowboy?" Leigh asked, playfully.

"Yes," he said, straight-faced.

Leigh shook her head. "You've got an uphill battle there. I'm a reformed alcoholic after last night."

Jonathan laughed. "We'll see."

They looked at the *vaporetto* approaching in the distance plying the emerald green waters of the Grand Canal.

"I think whoever was following us is long gone," Jonathan said, studying his surroundings.

"I think you're right," Leigh said. "I haven't seen anyone suspicious since we got here."

"I'm starting to think it was just me being paranoid," he said, but it was just wishful thinking.

"Told you," Leigh said, smiling and stroking his arm.

On the dock with them, in the crowd of tourists, Adriana Nyx stood almost close enough to hear.

The *vaporetto* pulled alongside the floating dock and bumped it slightly, jostling the crowd of tourists. The first mate slid the exit gate open and half the passengers emptied out of the boat. He slid the entrance gate open. Everyone on the dock rushed to get on. Jonathan and Leigh, and Adriana, were carried onboard by the crowd.

"Let's just stand," Jonathan said to Leigh. "It's just a couple of stops."

He stood, planted solidly on the deck, and Leigh shifted her computer bag and hugged his side. Behind them, Adriana watched.

The *vaporetto* pulled out and navigated through the Grand Canal, avoiding the many boats and gondolas that shared the waterway. The sun shone intensely, making the canal sparkle a vivid green kissed with flecks of gold. As they moved forward, the Basilica di Santa Maria Della Salute came into view. The huge majestic dome of the church rose from the corner of the

Dorsoduro, the huge bulk seemingly floating on the small sliver of land. The *vaporetto* stopped and more tourists got on and off.

The *vaporetto* crossed the Grand Canal, here at its widest point where it merged into the open waters of the San Marco Canal. The water was rougher with the wake of many ships, and Leigh held on tight. Jonathan smiled, content, smelled the sea air and imagined himself sailing. In the approaching distance, they could see the iconic *campanile* of the Piazza San Marco. The tall bell tower dominated the skyline.

The *vaporetto* docked at the next stop, Vallaresso. Most of the people on boat disembarked.

"Is this the stop?" Leigh asked.

"I think so," Jonathan said, and they got off.

Adriana trailed them, blending in easily among the crush of tourists.

Jonathan and Leigh walked alongside the water on the quay, past Harry's Bar and other touristy stores and stands full of trinkets and t-shirts. The quay opened up into a broad esplanade, which in turn opened up into the majestic Piazza San Marco.

Leigh and Jonathan stood still and gazed up and around at the hundreds of columns and arches of the Palazzo Ducale, the ornate Byzantine domes of the Basilica di San Marco, and the huge bell tower standing guard over all.

"Wow, this is amazing," Leigh said as they stood still, letting the sea of tourists flow around them.

"It sure is," Jonathan agreed.

They stood there, holding hands, and let the world flow by for a bit while they took it all in.

"This I want to remember forever," he said.

"Me too."

Jonathan leaned closer to Leigh and kissed her, a small gentle kiss on the lips. She stood on tiptoe to meet him.

Wordlessly, they walked hand in hand to a café on the side of the giant arcade-encircled plaza and sat at a table overlooking the whole incredible spectacle. People from all over the world filled the broad plaza and large groups of tourists followed tiny flags. A long line of people waiting to get in the *Basilica* butted up against another long line of people waiting to get in the *Palazzo*.

Adriana, her keen eyes on the couple, moved to the side of the arcade that surrounded the plaza. She leaned against a column and hid in the shadows, watching them place their order with a sharply dressed waiter.

Jonathan sat back. "Now this is the life," he said.

"We should call the Old Man," Leigh said.

"All business, huh?"

Leigh nodded. "All business," she agreed. She unsnapped her bag and brought out her tablet and swiped it on.

The computer came to life.

"He's available," she said, looking at his green icon.

"Call him up," Jonathan said reluctantly. Talking to him always made him edgy, as if the Old Man were examining him under a microscope.

Leigh tapped out her code and the video call went through. "It's ringing," she said.

Jonathan scooted his chair over so he could see the screen.

"Yes, Doctor Lancaster," George Valenti, the Old Man's assistant, answered on voice only. "We have been waiting for your call. One moment."

The screen flickered and the image of Rudolph Lahmbrecht materialized.

"Good morning, Doctor Lancaster. Or afternoon, I should say," Lahmbrecht said. He was in England, an hour behind.

"Good morning, sir," Leigh said, looking into the camera at the top of the tablet.

"Where are you? That does not look like Milan, or Manchester," he said, looking past her at the background of the busy plaza.

"No sir, we had a problem."

"Problem." Lahmbrecht let the word linger, not really asking a question with it so much as making a statement.

"We," Leigh paused, thinking of how to phrase it, "we thought we were being followed. From Turin to Milan. We're in Venice now."

"I see." Lahmbrecht paused. "Is anyone following you now?"

"No. I don't think so."

Jonathan gestured to Leigh. "Let me talk to him," he whispered.

Leigh handed him the tablet.

"Yes, Mr. Lahmbrecht," Jonathan said.

"Ah, Dr. Tremaine."

"Hello. Look," Jonathan said with a directness Lahmbrecht was not accustomed to, "we've got a problem here. Surely you can see that. Something is going on and someone is out to get us, I think."

"Why?" Lahmbrecht asked, tilting his head ever so slightly.

"I'm not sure. The Sheik and the plane and that big Moor," Jonathan paused, "it's got to be some kind of *jihad*."

"*Jihad*. That sounds logical," Lahmbrecht agreed with him.

"I'm just thinking out loud," Jonathan admitted. "But it makes sense. And it all has to do with the Shroud and the samples that we have. The samples that Dr. Lancaster took of the blood."

"How are those samples?" Lahmbrecht asked, leaning forward slightly.

"They're safe," Leigh said, leaning into camera range. "I've got them here with me, but I need to get them to the lab, directly, and start analyzing them."

"I see," Lahmbrecht said, mulling this over.

"We need to get out of here," Jonathan said. "Either back to Manchester, or to Spain."

"Spain?" Lahmbrecht asked, the word lingering in his slow speech.

"Yes, Spain. Oviedo, specifically. We were thinking that if you could get us permission, we could sample the Sudarium. Hell, if you managed to get access to the Shroud, you've got to be able to pull some strings and get us in there to the Sudarium."

"I have been considering the Sudarium," Lahmbrecht said in his slow voice. "The last historically viable possible sample of the blood of Jesus is on that Sudarium, if it is authentic."

Leigh leaned into the camera and tilted the tablet to her. "Mr. Lahmbrecht, I think I have enough data to test if the DNA of the Sudarium and the DNA of the Shroud are from the same man. Once I get samples from the Sudarium, I'll be able to tell you to a 99% certainty, maybe more."

Lahmbrecht was silent and still for a long time, his face carved out of stone. He sat, framed by his big leather chair and the rich tapestry that hung on the wall behind him. Finally, he spoke. "Yes. Make your way to Oviedo. I will personally see to getting a sample of the Sudarium for testing. I have some contacts in Spain's government. I will make calls. With luck, you will have it ready to test by tomorrow."

Leigh looked at Jonathan and smiled. "Thank you, Mr. Lahmbrecht," she said.

"Call me when you get there," Lahmbrecht said, and hung up, the screen turning dark.

"Well, I suppose we have to leave Venice behind," Jonathan pouted.

"Duty calls," Leigh said, already tapping away at the tablet for plane tickets.

Jonathan sipped his espresso and picked at the pastry that Leigh, in her excitement, had forgotten about.

"Bah. All booked for today." Leigh exhaled.

"No worries. Nothing wrong with one more night in Venice," Jonathan said, smiling.

"Well, I cancelled our Manchester flight and got us on the first flight to Madrid tomorrow morning. We'll change planes and get into Oviedo," Leigh paused, scrolling down the screen, "at one in the afternoon."

"Good. Let's get to the bank, get some more cash out from these cards, maybe have that drink on the terrace at the hotel?" Jonathan asked, with a hopeful lift of an eyebrow.

Leigh pursed her lips. It did sound pleasant. "Sounds like a plan," she said.

"Excellent," he beamed.

They paid and left, strolling through the plaza and scaring up pigeons as they went.

"Let's walk back to the hotel," Leigh said, "see some of the city on the way to the bank."

"Lead on," Jonathan said with a smile.

CHAPTER 7

Venice, Italy
May 22, 2025 12:45 p.m.

Jonathan and Leigh walked through the Piazza San Marco, past the islands of tourists. They left the plaza behind, walking through the narrow bottlenecked streets, through a jostling throng of tourists. Adriana followed, trying not to lose them in the crowd. The street was so full of people they were practically standing still.

"Ugh, I can barely walk," Leigh said.

"Let's go this way," Jonathan said and ducked into a small alley. Leigh followed.

"Where does this go?" she asked, stepping into the practically deserted alley.

"I have no idea," Jonathan admitted, "but there are no tourists."

Adriana, standing back, saw Jonathan, who was taller than the rest of the crowd, slide into an alley. She fought through the crowd and arrived at the entrance to the alley and looked in. The alley was empty except for her two targets. Adriana considered doing it now. She looked up to the small windows lining the buildings. A woman was hanging laundry from a line stretching across the narrow alley. *Too many eyes*, she thought. Adriana decided it would be better to stick to her plan. She stood at the entrance to the alley, out of sight, and waited for them to finish traversing it. She hurried down once they were clear, careful to not be noticed.

Jonathan and Leigh emerged at another street lined with craft shops selling *Carnevale* masks. This street was not nearly as crowded as the prior one. They turned and went in the general direction of the hotel, following the little yellow signs reading *"Per Rialto"* that appeared at intervals and pointed them towards the Rialto Bridge. Adriana prowled behind them.

They came to an opening in the street where it met a larger street and formed a little plaza. At the corner was a bank. Jonathan pointed to it.

"Let's see about that money," he said. "I'd like to have a good amount on me before setting off to Spain. Just in case."

They stepped inside. After waiting their turn, they handed their cards and passports to the teller.

"I need a cash advance on these, please," Jonathan asked him.

The teller swiped the cards. "Maximum withdrawal is five-thousand euros," he said in a thick Venetian accent. "Are you sure?" he asked.

"Yes," Jonathan said.

"Wait here, please," the clerk said, and went away with the cards and passports. After confirming and clearing the transaction, he returned.

The teller handed them back the passports and cards and counted out the money in a combination of fifty-euro notes and five-hundred-euro notes. He slid the wad of cash across the counter.

"*Grazie mille,*" Jonathan said, taking the cash. He pocketed his share and Leigh stuffed hers in an inside pocket of her computer bag.

"See? I know some Italian," Jonathan said to Leigh as they walked out of the bank.

Adriana waited outside near the bank, and immediately saw them. She blended into the crowds of tourists, observing. "*Fretta, fretta,*" she whispered under her breath. She was getting anxious and wanted to get on with it. She eyed Leigh adjusting the bag on her shoulder. The two set off walking. Adriana tailed them, gazing at the back of Leigh's raven-black hair, and hoping that she would be able to take her time with the pretty girl.

Jonathan and Leigh walked down the street and it led them to the Rialto Bridge. The iconic bridge was lined with shops running along its spine and edged with a broad sidewalk and balustrade on both sides. They crossed and stopped at the top, gazing out at the Grand Canal alongside the throngs of tourists. Jonathan put his arm around Leigh and they stood quietly watching the boats and gondolas go up and down the canal. After a few moments, they made their way down the bridge and over to the Rialto Market.

They walked through the fish market, which was in full swing now. Sardines, shrimp, tuna, every kind of shellfish, all the fruits of the sea lined hundreds of stands. One stand had a big swordfish head for sale.

"You want to buy that?" Jonathan asked, pointing at it.

"Eww." Leigh grimaced, turning her face away from the swordfish head.

"You know, for self-defense," Jonathan went on.

Leigh chuckled. "I thought all a cowboy needed was his fists?"

Jonathan laughed. They passed the market and crossed a bridge back to Piazza San Cassiano, where they had begun their morning.

"It was this way, right?" Jonathan asked. The streets here were hopelessly confusing.

"I think so," Leigh said.

Adriana saw them crossing the square and ducking into a little *soportorgo*, the narrow covered alleys that connected certain streets. They entered the dark alley. Adriana trailed behind, entering after them. It was quiet. A small water fountain trickled at the far end. She considered pouncing on them in the alley, but a group of people entered at that moment. She hung back, keeping an eye on them, not daring to get too close in these small streets.

There were signs now to the hotel, pointing the way down the narrow streets. A right, a right, and a left and then they were walking down a street which dead ended at the water, with the hotel entrance on the right. They turned into the hotel's courtyard entrance.

The San Cassianno. Adriana smiled a cruel smile. Her blood pumped as it always did when she anticipated the kill.

Jonathan and Leigh walked through the richly appointed lobby.

"You go up to the room, I'll go see about that wine," Jonathan said.

"Okay. Don't be long," Leigh said. She asked for the key from the front desk clerk. The clerk turned to the wall of tiny cubicles behind him, all labeled with the room numbers. He picked the key from 207, and handed it to her.

Jonathan walked down the lobby to the bar and Leigh went up the stairs to the room.

"I'll be right there, sir," the front desk clerk called out to Jonathan. "The bartender is not in yet," he added.

"Very well," Jonathan said. He walked to the bar and waited.

The clerk got out from behind the front desk and walked through the lobby to meet him. "What would you like, sir?" the clerk, settling in behind the bar, asked Jonathan.

Jonathan thought about it. *A whiskey would be nice.* He decided to wait on that.

"Let's see," he paused, thinking. "Something light and fruity. Something chilled."

"I have just the thing, a Bracchetto," the clerk, now bartender, said.

Adriana walked into the lobby of the hotel cautiously, but it was deserted. She walked to the front desk. There was no one there. She shook her head. *This will be easier than I thought.*

She looked at the tiny cubicles of keys behind the front desk. Most of the keys were stashed safely in their cubicles, all of the guests out sightseeing or the rooms empty.

There. 207. Adriana saw that the key was missing. *That has to be it,* she thought. Adriana went up the stairs, unslinging the bag off her shoulder. She arrived at the second floor and set the camera bag down at an antique table in the stair's landing, freeing her hands. Adriana reached down with her left hand and unsheathed a long stiletto from the sheath built into the side of her boot. As she walked down the hall towards the room, face set in a hard expression, she brought out a small curved blade from a hidden sheath in her belt. She gripped the small blade with her right hand. She arrived at the door.

Adriana took a deep breath and tried to calm herself. She had to do the man quickly and get to the girl before she escaped. With luck, she'd be able to incapacitate the girl silently and take her time. Adriana closed her eyes and pictured the girl writhing, the dark red of her blood painting her ivory skin. She cleared this from her mind and readied herself. She knocked on the door.

"Well, that was quick, cowboy. I was—" Leigh did not finish the sentence.

Adriana kicked the door open, knocking Leigh to the floor. She sprang into the room and scanned it for the man. *Not here.* She jumped on Leigh in an instant, straddling her as she lay dazed from the blow of the door. Adriana brought the stiletto to Leigh's cheek. Leigh's eyes went wide with shock and horror as the knife edge pressed to her cheek.

"Where's the man?" Adriana asked in her thick Italian accent. She slowly pressed the stiletto into Leigh's cheek, almost, but not quite, to the point of breaking the skin.

Leigh was paralyzed by fear.

"Where is he?" Adriana asked again, and pressed harder. A trickle of blood welled up on Leigh's cheek and she cried out.

"*Fessa!*" Adriana, still straddling Leigh, cursed in Italian. She leaned down like she was going to kiss Leigh on her bloodied cheek. Adriana hovered close over her for a second, savoring the look of fear in her eyes. She darted her tongue out and licked the blood on Leigh's cheek, then bit down on it.

Leigh tried to scream as Adriana bit down on her cheek, but managed only a frightened moan.

Adriana let go.

"Next time I bite it off. Now, where is the man?" Adriana asked again, her mouth twisted in a cruel red smile.

"Here I am," Jonathan said from behind her.

He swung the bottle of Bracchetto, cracking Adriana hard on the side of the head. It landed with a sickening crystalline thud against Adriana's skull. The ruby-red wine splashed out of the open bottle, which did not break. It slipped out of Jonathan's hands and fell to the floor, spraying wine everywhere.

Adriana was knocked to the side. As she fell, she twisted towards her attacker and swung her right hand out, meaning to eviscerate Jonathan with the small curved dagger. Jonathan arched back, trying to avoid the blade. It snagged his shirt, slicing a clean seam into it and catching him in the abdomen.

Jonathan recoiled and brought his hands to his abdomen. With the adrenaline coursing though him, he could not even feel anything yet. He looked down at his bloodied hands, and a part of his brain told him it was not serious. *If it was, I'd be holding my guts*, he thought.

As Adriana fell and rolled to the side, Leigh scooted back like a crab, away from the knife-wielding woman. She sat in the corner in shock clutching her computer bag, staring intently forward at Adriana. *Nice boots*, some crazy part of her brain thought amidst all the chaos, as she stared, frozen in fear, at the woman who had tried to kill her.

Adriana got up on one knee, dazed, and tried to shake off the blow. She stared at the man who had hit her and sneered.

Jonathan looked over at Leigh, who was by now bleeding quite a lot from her cheek. "Leigh!" he said with sick dread. He stepped quickly to her.

With catlike speed, Adriana sprung up, shaking her head clear and brandishing the big stiletto. She cornered Jonathan and Leigh against the back of the room, against the Murano glass doors leading to the balcony. Adriana spat on the ground.

"Now I have to do you both quick," she said in disgust.

Jonathan helped Leigh up and shielded her. He looked around, assessing the situation. In front of them, between them and the door, Adriana closed in with her knives. Behind them was the balcony overlooking the Grand Canal. *Only one way out*, he thought.

"Leigh. Balcony, now," Jonathan told her.

"What?" Leigh asked, still disoriented.

"Get on the balcony now," he repeated, insistent.

Leigh opened the doors and scrambled out to the balcony, Jonathan still shielding her from Adriana.

"Now what?" Leigh yelled out.

"Jump."

"Are you serious?" Leigh peeked over the railing at the canal far below and glanced back at Jonathan.

Adriana came at them. Instead of turning away, Jonathan blasted forward like a track runner, avoiding the stiletto and charging his right shoulder into Adriana's torso. They tangled together as Adriana was pushed back several paces.

"Go!" Jonathan yelled out.

"Oh, goodness," Leigh said as she nervously hooked her legs over the railing. She slung the computer bag over her head so the strap ran diagonally across her chest. Leigh looked down at the blue-green waters of the Grand Canal, three stories below.

Adriana recovered from the charge and swung the small curved blade, trying to embrace Jonathan with it and plunge it into his back. He saw her arm move from the corner of his eye and pushed her down hard. She landed on the ground, sliding back on the floor. Jonathan stole a glance back at Leigh.

"Jump!" he yelled out again.

Leigh took a deep breath and jumped.

Her arms flailed in space as she dropped through the air. She landed with a big splash feet-first in the canal. The water was shockingly cold and she almost breathed in a lungful of the canal. She kicked and swam to the surface, which seemed impossibly far away. She kicked and kicked, swimming towards the golden shimmering disc of the sun above her. At last, Leigh broke the surface, gasping for air.

Jonathan, seeing her jump, glanced at Adriana. She sprang up, ready to charge at him again. He did not hesitate. Jonathan turned and ran to the balcony and launched off the railing, diving headfirst into the Grand Canal.

He crashed into the water, landing awkwardly. He came to the surface spitting up water and looked around wildly for Leigh, who was bobbing off to the side. Jonathan looked up at the balcony, at Adriana, who glared at them but did not jump.

"Swim across!" Jonathan yelled out.

Leigh, kicking in the water just to keep afloat, started to swim slowly. She kicked but it was awkward in her long skirt and boots, not to mention the computer case wrapped around her chest like a small anchor. Jonathan swam alongside her, helping her with his left arm and stroking with his right. They swam across the Grand Canal, watching on either side of them for boats. People across the canal watched and pointed, and a small crowd was gathering at a gondolier's dock across from them, watching the whole strange sight.

Adriana, still dizzy from the blow to the head, stood at the balcony watching them swim away. She cursed out loud to no one, furious. She took a breath and calmed herself down and thought of her options. She couldn't jump in after them. Though she could easily catch them, it was a spectacle now, with people staring from both sides of the canal.

Thinking of what to do, she went back in the room. It was a disaster. She hurriedly closed the door. Furniture was upended; the bottle of wine lay on its side, still weeping. The light red wine covered the floor, mixing, Adriana noticed, with dark red rivulets of blood.

I did cut him, she thought. She took some small satisfaction from this. She stepped to the mirror and examined herself. The side of her head had a nasty bruise, skin split, and was swelling fast. She went to the bathroom, wet a towel, and pressed it to her wound. She cursed again and stared at herself in the mirror.

"I'm going to cut you open like a fish," she said in Italian, imagining Jonathan in front of her.

She went back to the balcony and stared at the two still swimming in the canal.

Leigh and Jonathan were halfway across the canal. A taxi boat, appearing huge from their position in the water, was coming at them. The captain, concern etched on his face, waved at them and slowed, gently pulling alongside. Jonathan and Leigh treaded water. The captain threw a life preserver over. It landed right by Leigh, who hooked her arm around it.

The captain ran back through the cabin of the boat to the stern where the side tapered down and it would be easier to pull them aboard. He motioned to Jonathan and yelled something in Italian. Jonathan reached up and took the captain's hand. He kicked his legs and, with the help of the captain, was able to grab hold of the side with his free hand. Jonathan pulled himself onto the boat with a loud grunt and grimaced in pain. He ignored it and turned immediately to Leigh.

"Give me your hand," he said, reaching out with his right hand as he held his left to his abdomen.

The captain also yelled something in Italian and reached down as well. Leigh grabbed Jonathan's hand, then the captain's. They pulled and fished her out of the water, her petite body rising easily over the side of the boat. She landed with a wet plop on the polished teak decking of the boat, her arm still holding the life preserver in one hand. She sat there a moment, dazed, then said, "Thanks."

"Don't mention it," Jonathan said, looking at her and catching his breath.

"You are hurt!" the captain said in heavily accented English when he saw Leigh. He rushed off and entered the cabin.

Leigh, in her adrenaline rush, had forgotten about the cut on her cheek, which bled insistently, sending a little stream of blood sliding down her wet cheek like a weeping virgin statue. She reached up and touched it, looking at the blood on her finger. She looked over at Jonathan, who wore a look of concern on his face.

"It's nothing, don't worry," she said.

The captain rushed back with towels and a first-aid kit. He handed Leigh and Jonathan the towels and Leigh took the first-aid kit from him. Leigh thanked him.

Jonathan looked up at the balcony from which they had jumped. Adriana Nyx stood there, hands on the railing, staring down at them with unbridled malice.

"We need to get out of here," Jonathan said to Leigh.

"Where to?" Leigh asked.

Jonathan thought a second. "To the train station," Jonathan said to the taxi captain.

"Not back to the hotel?" the captain asked.

"No!" Jonathan and Leigh said simultaneously.

"The train station. *Ferrovia*, and fast. *Molto rapido*," Jonathan said, exhausting his Italian. He pulled out his wallet and fished out two soggy one-hundred euro notes and put them in the captain's hand.

"*Naturalmente*," the captain said and gladly took the money. He ran back through the cabin to the helm.

The taxi boat, which had been adrift in the middle of the canal, now drifted perilously close to an oncoming *vaporetto*. The captain thrust the engines and spun the boat around, avoiding the *vaporetto* and surging forward towards the train station. Jonathan and Leigh held on, almost flying back and out of the boat. The boat sped ahead up the Grand Canal, past the *palazzos*, going as fast as the captain dared in the busy canal.

They settled in the back, Leigh sitting on the padded bench built into the side and Jonathan almost lying down opposite her. In a matter of seconds, Leigh had gauze out and was pressing it to her cheek.

"What the heck just happened back there?" she asked Jonathan. It had all happened so fast, her mind still reeled. "Who was that woman?"

"I don't know, but I think there's more than just big Moors after us," Jonathan said, then grimaced and pressed the towel to his belly.

"You're hurt?" Leigh asked with surprise and concern.

"A bit," Jonathan downplayed it. Despite his bravado, he winced again as the boat bounced along the water.

"Did she cut you?"

"Yes."

"Let me have a look." She kneeled on the boat deck at his side.

"Yes, Doctor," he said, trying to smile.

He lifted up the towel he'd been pressing to his belly. His shirt was cut open. Leigh carefully lifted his wet shirt out of the way, revealing a long bleeding wound. Leigh carefully inspected it, dabbing at it with fresh gauze she'd unwrapped from the first-aid kit.

"We're going to have to take care of this," she said.

"Is it bad?" Jonathan asked.

"It's not good. It's not deep, though. Nothing vital. But you'll need stitches. And we need to douse this with alcohol. This canal water might be pretty but you don't want it in your system. We should get to a hospital," Leigh said.

Jonathan shook his head. "No hospital."

"Don't be daft. This isn't time for macho hour," she chided him.

"It's not that," Jonathan said and shook his head again. "Whoever that was back at the hotel knew exactly where we were. If we go to the hospital, we'll be there a long time, have to answer questions, the whole of it. We'll be sitting ducks." He looked at her skeptical face, trying to convince her. "No, we should keep moving. Get out of town fast," he added.

Leigh thought about it. "I suppose you're right, but I don't like it," she said at last. The boat bumped up against the wake of a passing *vaporetto* and Jonathan grimaced again.

"Can you take care of this?" he asked.

"Let me see." Leigh looked through the first-aid kit. "Yes, but not on the boat."

"Good. We'll get to the station, get this taken care of, and hop on the first train out."

Leigh nodded quietly, not fully sold on Jonathan's plan. "Keep pressure on it. I'll butterfly it as soon as it's dry until I can sew you up."

"I'm not looking forward to that," Jonathan admitted.

"Me neither. It's been a long time since medical school. And I never was very good at it."

Leigh sat by Jonathan and they toweled themselves off as best they could. Leigh continued to press gauze on the cut on her face. The blood had almost stopped. She dabbed alcohol on it and put a band-aid on as Jonathan looked on, worried.

"It's not deep. It'll heal right up," Leigh said, reading the concern on his face. She stared away absently at the passing buildings. "She was asking where you were," she went on, remembering. "She just wanted to scare me." A tear, then two, welled up in Leigh's eyes and rolled down her cheeks. "It worked," she said, and sobbed.

Jonathan reached up with his free hand and gently stroked her short wet hair, comforting her. "It'll be alright," he said, and put his arm around her. "And all this time I thought I'd be the one getting drunk and falling into a canal," he joked, trying to take her mind off of the memory. It was something he knew quite a bit about.

Leigh gave a short, wet laugh and kept crying even as a smile fought to establish itself on her face. She leaned over and put her head on Jonathan's chest.

"We'll be alright," Jonathan whispered to her as the boat plowed through the water on the way to the station.

CHAPTER 8

Venice, Italy
May 22, 2025 1:05 p.m.

Adriana Nyx looked on from the balcony as her two targets were fished out of the water by the taxi boat. The boat turned and powered up the canal to the left. *They have to be going to the train station*, she thought. The hospital, she knew, was the opposite way. It was the only place they could be headed. It's where she would be going if she were in their shoes.

She left the room quietly, closing the door and putting on the Do Not Disturb sign. She walked down the stairs, picking up her camera bag along the way, and then walked casually through the lobby. She put her phone to her ear to conceal the bruise and pretended she was in the middle of a conversation. The front desk clerk did not pay her any mind; she was just another guest.

As soon as she was out of sight of the front door, she started running. She raced down the alley and onto the streets, weaving around tourists and following the *"Per Ferrovia"* signs leading to the station. It was a twenty or so minute walk; she could make it in ten or less.

She was still dizzy from the blow to the head, but shrugged this off. She vowed herself to repay the man for what he had done. And to finish with the girl. Adriana could still taste the girl on her lips, and she craved more.

Jonathan rose slowly as the station neared. He stood up on the back deck of the boat and watched as the captain deftly docked and tied off. The captain went through the cabin and to the back and asked again if they were okay. Jonathan grinned through gritted teeth.

"Just fine. We'll try to not be so clumsy next time," he said with a forced smile, adding, "Thank you very much for your help."

"I'll be taking this and the towels," Leigh said, holding up the first-aid kit.

Jonathan fished out another wet one-hundred euro note and gave it to the taxi captain, who was as happy as he was perplexed.

Leigh got out of the boat first, giving Jonathan a hand as they stepped up to the dock. They both glanced around nervously and hurried through the plaza to the station. Every once in a while the waterlogged couple would catch the eye of someone who stood and stared at them.

"You're a sight," Jonathan said to Leigh, who was still soaked despite her best efforts with the towel. Her hair clung limply against her head and her black skirt refused to flow.

"You too, cowboy," Leigh said. "You look like you've been bucked, and into a river."

"I feel very bucked over," Jonathan said with a smile.

As they walked into the station from a side entrance, Jonathan spotted a unisex handicap bathroom down a small hall. "In here," he said, walking towards it.

"You're so romantic," Leigh kidded.

They went into the big bathroom. "How's this for an operating room?" he asked.

"It'll have to do," she said, looking around dubiously. "Now, you. Strip and dry off."

"Just what I've always wanted to hear from you," Jonathan said with an amused smile.

"Quiet, you," Leigh told him, and started heading out the door.

"Whoa. Where are you going?" Jonathan asked.

"I need a couple of things," Leigh said.

"I don't like you going out there alone," Jonathan said, shaking his head.

"I'll be okay. I won't be long."

"Be careful."

"I will," Leigh said. "And, you, start washing that," she said, pointing at the wound. "Use lots of soap." She went out.

Jonathan locked the door behind her. He waited impatiently in the bathroom, gingerly taking this shirt off, and hitching down his wet jeans a bit. He looked at the wound in the mirror. It was about three inches of neatly sliced skin. He could see the layer of fat, the subcutaneous layer he remembered from somewhere, underneath the skin. He ran water over it, soaping it up and cleaning it as best he could, and winced.

"Ouch," he said out loud to no one.

There was a knock at the door. "It's me," Leigh said through it.

Jonathan opened the door and Leigh walked in with a bottle of Jack Daniels in one hand and a bag from Burberry's in the other.

"Now that looks like a party," Jonathan said.

"Not for you, cowboy," Leigh said and locked the door. She set down the Burberry's bag and the bottle and meticulously washed her hands.

Jonathan stood shirtless, holding the towel to his abdomen.

"I need to clean the wound, and it's too big for these little swabs. I need to soak it," Leigh said, drying off. "It's going to hurt," she added, and picked up the bottle.

Jonathan leaned back against the sink.

"Be gentle," he pleaded.

She uncapped the bottle of Jack Daniels, tearing the paper wrapper and unscrewing the cap. Jonathan looked at it.

"Say, before you do this, you think I can have a swig?" Jonathan asked.

"You shouldn't have any booze," Leigh said, and saw the scared look in his eyes that he was valiantly trying to hide. "But it *is* going to hurt."

She handed him the bottle and Jonathan took a long pull. He handed it back.

"Thanks."

"Don't thank me yet. You ready?" she asked.

"As I'll ever be," Jonathan said and gripped the sink.

Leigh poured the alcohol liberally over the wound, the booze running over his belly and soaking his pants. Jonathan gave out a short yelp, which he quickly stifled. He winced, sucking in air through clenched teeth. She cleaned the wound with gauze from the kit, and then took a small rubbing alcohol swab from the kit and dabbed it on the wound. Jonathan took another quick inhalation.

"Okay, that hurts," he said, gasping.

"Not as much as this will," Leigh said.

She took thread and needle from the first-aid kit. Leigh took a big breath, placed the needle against Jonathan's flesh and started.

Jonathan looked into the distance and tried to block the pain out as Leigh stitched the wound shut. He went a little lightheaded and looked over at the bottle of Jack Daniels just out of his reach. He looked down at the top of Leigh's head and her small hands steadily fixing him.

"That hurts," he said.

"Quiet. It's supposed to hurt," Leigh said curtly.

The Blood

"Thanks, Nurse Ratched."

"Shh," Leigh said, concentrating. "I haven't done this in a very long time. And it's Doctor Ratched, thank you."

Jonathan tried to smile but instead just gritted his teeth as Leigh methodically stitched the wound shut.

"There," she said at last. "Finished. That wasn't so bad, was it?"

"Speak for yourself."

"It'll leave a scar, but it shouldn't be too bad," Leigh said, and absently rubbed her arm.

"That's okay. You girls like scars, right?" Jonathan said, looking at the stitches in the mirror.

"This one looks like you had a c-section," Leigh said with a smirk.

"Ouch. That cuts deep," Jonathan said, in jest.

"Don't move too much," Leigh said, dabbing at the stitched wound with an alcohol swab.

"We *need* to move," Jonathan said. "We need to get out of here."

"Hold still and let me bandage this," Leigh said. "Hold here," she told him, and he held a strip of gauze against the wound.

She wrapped it with even more gauze, going around his back to loop it around, almost hugging him. She looked at his chest and strong midsection and blushed a little but kept her professional game face on.

"What's in the bag," Jonathan asked, pointing to the Burberry's bag.

"Clothes. Can't walk around in soaking wet clothes. Plus now you smell like a bum with all that whiskey," she said. "All done," she added, tying off the bandage and tucking it in.

Jonathan looked in the mirror, examining it. "Looks good."

Leigh pulled the clothes out of the bag and handed them to him. "Get dressed," she said.

"Yes, Doctor," Jonathan said and smirked. He held up the checkered shirt in the traditional Burberry colors. "Very preppy," he said.

"Hey, it's dry. It's the first thing I saw. Go ahead and change. I'll turn around."

Leigh turned around and Jonathan stripped down, drying off with the towel.

"I say we get the first train out of here, wherever it goes," he said as he dressed.

"Then what? Make our way to Spain still?"

"I think so, but—" Jonathan trailed off. Something was bothering him. "This crazy bitch found us at the hotel. How did she find us?"

"Maybe she was following us too?" Leigh suggested.

"Maybe. I doubt it, though. All the way from Turin?"

"Maybe the credit cards?"

"Maybe. How hard would that be to do, to trace them? Isn't that government spy stuff?" Jonathan asked.

"Not really. A moderately talented hacker could do it," Leigh said.

"Maybe that was it. Okay, no more cards. All cash." Jonathan finished dressing. "All done."

Leigh turned around. "Very preppy," she said, looking at the khaki pants and checkered shirt.

Jonathan looked in the mirror. "Hmm, not my style. I'm more of a jeans and t-shirt type guy. And my shoes are soaked."

"I didn't have time for shoes," Leigh said.

"I'll live. Your turn."

"You mind stepping out?" Leigh asked him sheepishly.

"I promise I won't look," Jonathan said and gave her a half-smile.

"I don't have anything to blindfold you with," Leigh said and smirked.

"Kinky," he said, raising an eyebrow.

"Hush. Go. Guard the door."

Jonathan stepped out into the hallway of the station. He stood at the door, watching up and down the hall. The side hall connected the station's side entrance with the main hall. He could see the beehive of travelers going this way and that in the main hall. If he craned his neck he could see the big departures board, though he could barely make out the letters at this distance. He paced nervously, waiting.

"You done in there yet?" he called through the door.

"Almost."

Jonathan scanned the crowd nervously, shifting in his still wet shoes, half expecting that crazy woman to jump out at him. His mind raced, trying to figure out their next move.

Adriana came to the *Ponte degli Scalzi*, the bridge that crossed the Grand Canal and led to the plaza in front of the Santa Lucia train station. She bounded up the stairs of the bridge two at a time, breathing hard now despite her conditioning. It had been a full on sprint through half the streets of Venice to get here. She slowed as she reached the station, still walking fast but blending in among the hurried travelers. She caught her breath and walked through the front doors into the main hall. Adriana made her way to the middle of the huge hall and stood in front of the big departures and arrivals board. Her eyes scanned the hundreds of people going every which way, looking for the man and woman.

"Let's go, girl, we're not going on a date," Jonathan said to Leigh through the door.

"Don't ever hurry a girl, mister," Leigh said. "We'll just take twice as long. And besides, these boots are soaked and hard to put on."

"We'll get you new ones. I'll take you shoe shopping and you can take as long as you want but only if—"

Jonathan's words trailed off. His blood went cold. There, in the middle of the crowd, standing in front of the departures board, was the woman. The woman who'd tried to gut him.

With his back to the door, standing as still as possible, he pounded on the door.

"Let's go," he said.

"I'm almost ready," Leigh replied.

"Now."

Leigh heard the urgency in his voice and opened the door. She was dressed in a flowery skirt and a long-sleeve white top. Her computer bag was slung across her body.

"Just have to put on these boots. They don't match but I'm sure I can—"

"She's here," Jonathan interrupted her.

"What?"

"The woman. She's here. Over there under the departures board."

Leigh looked over. "Oh goodness. What are we going to do?"

Jonathan scanned the area. The hallway they were in led off to a side exit, with access to the tracks.

"This way," he said and grabbed Leigh's hand.

He pulled her down the hall. She followed, her boots in her hands, padding along barefoot. They came out to the far side of the tracks, where the local trains departed.

Frantically, Jonathan looked at the smaller departure screens at the end of each track, trying to see which one was about to depart. "First one that moves we get on," he said.

Adriana moved through the station. She was sure they were here. She could feel it. She walked under the departures board and out to the tracks, looking everywhere for them.

Jonathan and Leigh stood at the tail end of track number 12, at the end of the train. The train was a far cry from the sleek intercity trains at the other end of the station. This train was old and had seen better days; its sides were well-marked with layers of graffiti. A conductor stood far down the track at the head of the train, consulting his watch.

"This should be the next one, but you never know with these local trains. Let's go," Jonathan said and started walking.

Leigh froze. "She's over there," Leigh whispered, staring straight at her across the station.

Jonathan turned to look at the exact moment that Adriana turned her head their way.

Their eyes met.

Adriana smiled a cruel half-smile and ran, sprinting towards them with surprising speed.

"Run!" Jonathan yelled to Leigh.

They both started running down the platform by the side of the train. The conductor, half hanging out of one of the doors at the head of the train, blew his whistle and went inside. Leigh and Jonathan ran straight towards the nearest door of the train.

"Get on!" Jonathan called out.

Leigh sprinted ahead, faster, as Jonathan clutched at the wound on his abdomen. She threw the boots she was carrying on the ground and ran fast towards the old train, pumping her arms.

Adriana rounded the bend at the track 12 platform and closed in fast on them. Her face wore the determined intense look of a predator closing in on its prey.

Leigh reached the door of the train, which was beginning to move ever so slightly. It was closed. Leigh grasped a silver handle, which looked like a big old-fashioned metal window crank, and yanked sideways on it. The door sprung open. She ran faster, almost falling, as the train began to move in earnest now. Holding onto a metal bar, Leigh pulled herself up and into the train.

"Come on!" she yelled and waved her hands at Jonathan.

He reached for the bar as the train picked up speed. He stumbled, almost fell, but regained his balance and grasped at the metal bar. With one last jump he vaulted onto the step and pulled himself onboard, spilling into the train on his belly. He lay on the ground and flipped over onto his back, breathing hard. He leaned up, propping himself up on his elbows.

Adriana saw them jump into the train, which slowly picked up even more speed. She ran as hard as she could and neared the door. She grasped for the bar of the briskly moving train.

There. She had it.

She swung with amazing dexterity up and into the train's car, only to be met by a solid kick from Jonathan. Adriana staggered back, nearly falling off the train, but hung on to the bar. Her boots scraped along the ground for an instant. She soon regained her footing on the train's step. She took a moment to recover and sprung once again into the train's car.

Jonathan, still half-sitting on the ground, propped up on his elbows, pumped his leg at her again. Adriana dodged and grabbed at him, latching on to his leg and pulling herself towards him. With his other leg, Jonathan kicked at her, hitting her in the shoulder and nearly kicking her loose. Adriana regained her balance and pulled on Jonathan's leg with one hand and brought out the little curved knife with the other. She lunged at him.

"I'm going to gut you," she sneered.

"No you're not!" Leigh declared, standing over her.

She swung her computer bag as hard as she could, hitting Adriana in the face, stunning her momentarily. Jonathan took advantage and again kicked at her and this time did knock her loose. She lost her hold on Jonathan and went flying back, tumbling out of the train onto the platform.

Adriana twisted and rolled as she landed, springing right back up. She growled and ran towards the train again but it was picking up speed out of the station. The train outpaced her and she could not grab on. Adriana slammed her hand on the side of the moving train and yelled curses in Italian at them, at the train and at herself.

CHAPTER 9

Outside Venice, Italy
May 22, 2025 1:28 p.m.

Jonathan looked at Leigh, let out a long breath, then collapsed back, lying down on the floor of the car.

"I don't want to do that again today," he said, catching his breath.

"Me neither," Leigh said, half-stunned still.

"Good thing you carry that darn bag with you everywhere," he told her, turning his head to look at her as she stood above him.

She still held the strap of the bag, which swung back and forth from the motion of the train. Leigh then clutched the bag to her chest, not looking at Jonathan and instead gazing absently out the open door at the railroad yard going by quicker and quicker.

Jonathan rose slowly to his feet, holding a hand to his wound. He put an arm around Leigh. "Hey, you okay?"

Leigh paused. "Yeah. I will be," she said, still dazed by all that had happened.

Jonathan moved to the door and shut it. "Come, let's sit," he said, guiding her over towards the seats.

The train was virtually empty, and they were completely alone in the cabin. No one had seen the fight with Adriana. They shuffled towards a seat. Jonathan tried to smooth out his too-big rumpled checkered shirt. His khaki pants were now dusty and stained from the scuffle on the floor and his shoes, still wet, squished when he walked. Leigh did not fare much better, walking along barefoot with her flowered dress and white cardigan covered in dust from her spill on the dirty floor.

"We're a sad sight, aren't we?" Leigh asked, gave Jonathan a weak smile.

"Hey, you did good back there," Jonathan said, comforting her.

They sat, slumping down into the first seat they came to. Jonathan put his arm around her and she laid her head on his chest. Together, they stared out the window. The old train continued picking up speed in fits and starts as it left the rail yard. Soon they were cruising over the *Ponte della Libertà*, the long bridge connecting Venice to the mainland. They sped over the blue-green waters and watched the magic city of Venice recede.

"Where are we going, anyway?" Leigh asked without looking up, breaking the silence.

"I'm not sure," Jonathan admitted.

The inside door to the car opened and the conductor came in. "Tickets, please," he said to them automatically, then eyed them suspiciously. They looked like bums, albeit designer bums.

"Hmm, about that," Jonathan said. He explained to the conductor that they did not have any and asked if they could buy some now. He took out some of his soggy money.

"Please, we lost our luggage," Leigh pleaded with the man.

The conductor relented and allowed them to pay for the cost of the ticket and did not charge them the customary one-hundred euro fine for boarding without a pass.

"Where's the first stop?" Jonathan asked him.

"Mira-Mirano, *signore*, twenty minutes," the conductor replied.

"And when does the next train arrive there?"

"Only the local train goes there. It is a very small town. One train every hour," the conductor said in accented English.

"Thank you," Jonathan said.

The conductor moved on to the next passenger car, leaving the two strange travelers alone.

"So, what are we going to do?" Leigh asked Jonathan after the man had left.

"I don't know. I'm just making this up as I go along," he said.

Leigh frowned. "Well, we better think of something."

Jonathan thought it over. "I think the next stop will be best. We'll have an hour head start for sure. If we go to the bigger cities, she can catch up on the faster trains."

Leigh mulled over the plan. "We should rent a car, get more mobile. I've had enough of trains," Leigh said.

"That makes sense. Drive the hell away from here, and get to Spain. And let's take the batteries out of our cell phones, in case that's how they're tracking us," he suggested.

Leigh brought out her still wet computer bag and took her small phone she barely used from it. She took the batteries out, then brought out her tablet computer. She poked at the darkened and now cracked screen.

"How is it?" Jonathan said as he took the batteries from his own cell phone.

"Dead. Soaked," she frowned. "Maybe once it dries it'll work. The data should still be there in the memory regardless. I'm sure I can get it fixed."

"It'll be okay, I'm sure," Jonathan reassured her.

"Thanks," she said, looking up to him and smiling. "And thanks," she said again. "For saving my butt back there, mister."

"Hey, you too," Jonathan said. "We make a good team, you and I."

Leigh rested her head on Jonathan's chest. He wrapped his arm around her and stroked her hair lightly with his hand. They gazed out the window as the train sped through the green Italian countryside.

CHAPTER 10

Venice, Italy
May 22, 2025 1:41 p.m.

Adriana hurried away from the train station, her phone pressed to her ear.

"They got away," Adriana Nyx told the Lawyer on her cell phone.

"They what?" he asked, incredulous.

"You heard me," Adriana said, her voice on the edge of anger.

The Lawyer cursed. "Where are they?" he asked, getting irate now.

"On a local train, headed to Chioggia," she said. "But they can get off anywhere before then," she added. She turned down a side street and walked over a small bridge.

The Lawyer cursed again. "Anywhere? How the hell are we going to find them?"

"Use your tracker. Tell me at what town they stop," Adriana told him impatiently.

"I can't track them," he said.

"What?" she barked out at him.

"The signal went dead. About forty minutes ago. I don't know what happened," he said.

"Water," Adriana said, rolling her eyes.

"What?"

"The water. They jumped into the water in a canal to get away."

"They jumped into a canal?" the Lawyer asked, disbelieving.

"*Porca miseria*," Adriana cursed. "Do not make me repeat myself again," she said in a sudden flash of anger.

"I'm sorry," the Lawyer quickly apologized.

"So you have no idea where they are?" Adriana asked him.

"Not right now. But I have it on good authority they are going to Oviedo, Spain," the Lawyer said in a conspiratorial tone.

"Are you sure?"

"Yes," he said. "That is what my sources tell me."

Adriana nodded, mulling this over. "I will make my way there. Call me if you pick up the signal," she said.

She hung up, not waiting for a response. She rubbed her temple and hurried back to the hotel to change and take care of the wound. As she walked through the Venice streets, she thought of nothing but how she would kill them next time they met.

Mira, Italy
May 22, 2025 2:05 p.m.

The old train pulled into the small station, squeaking and grinding to a halt. Jonathan and Leigh looked out the window at the weed-strewn ground.

"You sure about this?" Leigh looked at him dubiously.

"No," Jonathan admitted, "but it's the last thing you would expect. Anyone in their right minds would go to Milan."

"That doesn't fill me with confidence," Leigh said. "But, if we're going to do it, lets do it."

They got up and stepped out of the train. The doors closed behind them and the train pulled away, leaving them virtually alone on the platform of the small station.

"I hope you have a plan, mister," Leigh said in the sudden silence.

"I told you, I'm just making it up as I go along," Jonathan said.

They walked out of the station into a virtually deserted small town. Far off the tourist track, they could see only the occasional local walking down the street. Here, without the Venetian sea breeze, the hot afternoon sun beat down hard.

"Not much of a nightlife here, I bet," Jonathan said, observing the desolate streets. This was beginning to seem like a bad idea.

Leigh walked barefoot down the old and dusty streets. "You're going to make good on taking me shoe shopping, mister, and soon," she said.

"As soon as I find an open store," Jonathan said.

The streets were lined with shuttered shops and apartments, as if the whole town had closed down. The street stretched on desolate before them. A single lonely bar was the only thing open.

"Let's go in here and ask for a car rental place," Jonathan suggested.

They walked towards it and arrived to the entrance of the Bar DaConte. Jonathan opened the door to the place, which looked like it had not been decorated since the year 2000.

A young bartender with a shock of blonde hair stood behind the bar, absently polishing the granite countertop. He looked up in surprise at the customers walking through the door, then squinted at them. They were dressed like bums, in dirty clothing, and the woman was barefoot. Hippies, perhaps, he thought.

"How about a drink?" Jonathan asked Leigh as he took a look at the bottles arranged behind the bar.

Leigh frowned, then relented. "Okay. One. It'll help settle my nerves," she said.

"Two whiskeys," Jonathan said to the bartender.

The bartender, hearing them speak English, perked up. "Yes, of course," he said.

"We need to rent a car," Jonathan said to the young man. "Is there anywhere that rents them around here?" he asked.

The bartender shook his head as he poured the whiskey. "No rental car here," he said.

"Bus?" Leigh asked.

The bartender hitched his thumb to the right. "Bus to Venice, every hour," he said.

"Not Venice," Jonathan and Leigh practically said at the same time. "Milan?" Jonathan asked.

The bartender furrowed his brow, thinking. "Every four or five hours. I am not sure," he said in his heavily accented English. He set the whiskeys in front of them. "How do you say? Cheers?"

"Cheers, indeed," Leigh said.

Jonathan took a pull of his whiskey.

Leigh sipped at it tentatively and grimaced. "Wow, that's strong," she said.

"Put some water in it. It'll be good," Jonathan suggested. He motioned to the bartender, who brought over a small cold bottle of water.

Leigh poured some water in, fixing her drink. She took another sip. "Better," she said. She just about drained the glass.

"Thirsty?" Jonathan asked.

"Nerves," she responded. "I'm not used to jumping out of three-story windows into freezing water, running for my life, and performing surgery in a bathroom."

"Me neither. But you're doing just fine," Jonathan comforted her.

"How's the wound?" Leigh asked.

Jonathan pressed against his abdomen, testing it. "It's okay. We'll probably need to re-dress it soon. It itches."

"Good. Itching is good, means it's healing. Don't scratch it," she said.

Jonathan drained his drink. "Let's keep moving. I don't want to lose any more time here."

Leigh finished what was left of her drink and Jonathan paid. They walked out to the warm afternoon streets of the empty town, walking in the direction of the bus station.

"So we take a bus to Milan?" Leigh asked.

"Or Padua, maybe. I'd like to rent a car, be more mobile. Not have to sit around waiting," he said.

They walked and turned at the next street, following the bus icon on a sign.

Jonathan stopped, staring at something.

"What is it? Leigh asked, worried.

"I've got a better idea," he said, pointing at a vintage small green Fiat 500 with a "For Sale" sign in Italian in the window.

Venice, Italy
May 22, 2025 2:45 p.m.

Adriana finished packing her bag. She took one more look in the mirror, gingerly touching the slight bump on her temple. With the makeup, and her hair combed to the side, the bruise was not visible. She stared into her own eyes in the mirror and swore vengeance again on the man and woman that had bruised her. Her face grew hard as the anger in her eyes burned. Then, like someone had thrown a switch, she softened her face and smiled at the mirror, readying herself to check out of the hotel.

She checked out, paying in cash, and made her way to the *vaporetto* stop. In twenty minutes, she was once again at the train station, once again standing under the big departures board.

She bought a ticket at the machine and walked towards the Milan high-speed train. Once there, she would get to Barcelona, then onto Oviedo. As she settled into her first-class seat, she tried to force herself to relax and rest. She would need all her energy once she caught them.

CHAPTER 11

SR11 Road, 65 km. from Verona, Italy
May 22, 2025 4:25 p.m.

"Slow it down, mister," Leigh called out.

"Never. This little girl likes to run. Besides, we're not going *that* fast," Jonathan said, smiling, and reaching for the gearshift.

The little Fiat 500 reached the bend in the road. Jonathan downshifted, matching revs, and bent the little car through the turn.

"Okay, you're going to make me ill driving like that. It's not like—"

"Like we're trying to get away from assassins hell-bent on killing us?" Jonathan finished her sentence.

"Yes, but they're not bloody well right behind us," Leigh reminded him.

"Okay, okay. I'll slow it down," he said, adding, "a little."

Jonathan upshifted and settled into a gentler speed on the country road.

"I still can't believe you up and bought an auto, cowboy," Leigh said.

"It was the best solution. We needed to be mobile, and it was in the budget. Besides, I always wanted one," he said, then grinned.

"Boys and their toys," Leigh said, rolling her eyes.

"How much money you got left, by the way?" he asked.

"Three-thousand, give or take," she said.

"Good. Plenty to get us to Oviedo, and Manchester."

"And buy me shoes, cowboy."

"And buy you shoes."

They cruised down the road at a good clip, passing cars.

"I guess we're not making that plane tomorrow, huh? How far is Oviedo, anyway?" Leigh asked.

"Not sure. I'm not used to driving without a nav. It's a good long ways," he said.

"And you're sure about this? About this cloth? The Sudarium, was it?"

"Yes. And I'm not one-hundred percent sure, but yes."

Jonathan hit a straight and accelerated the little car, revving the engine and hustling it down the country road.

"And the cloth in Oviedo, it's not some medieval forgery?" Leigh asked, still skeptical.

"Not likely. It was there 800 years before the medieval forgery of relics really took off," Jonathan explained.

"It's just surprising, you don't really hear much about it," she said.

"Well, it doesn't get much press. It doesn't look like much, actually. Just a stained cloth."

"A blood stain. Of Jesus' blood?" Leigh asked.

"That's what some people believe," Jonathan said.

Jonathan downshifted as they approached a hill.

"Well, we should be able to see if there is a DNA match with the Shroud samples. See if they came from the same man. That's assuming we can get samples," Leigh said as she grabbed the handle over the door and held her breath.

The car crested a hill and ahead of them on the road was a slow moving tractor, practically standing still. Jonathan calmly accelerated and veered into the other lane, passing the tractor and upshifting. "We should be able to get the samples," Jonathan said, not missing a beat. "I think the Old Man will come through."

"Well, we'll find out soon enough," Leigh said, turning back to look at the tractor. She took a breath.

The car sped down the road, passing a sign reading "*Autostrada.*"

Jonathan downshifted. "We're getting on the highway. It'll take forever on these little roads. Hold on," he warned Leigh.

Jonathan took the turn into a traffic circle. He bent the little car around smoothly, pointing it to the highway entrance and flooring it.

"Geez, mister," Leigh called out as she braced herself. "You a race car driver in your spare time?"

Jonathan laughed. "No, but I did race, a long time ago. Strictly amateur stuff. Autocross, timed rallies, that type thing. Once, we went on a vintage rally tour of Wales," Jonathan recounted, smiling sadly.

"With your wife?" Leigh asked quietly.

"Yes. Julie hated it. Driving top-down in an old Jaguar through half of Wales wasn't her idea of fun." He shook his head, remembering it. "It was a good time. For me, anyway."

"Where did you go?" Leigh asked.

"Southern Wales, mainly. Around Cardiff. I can't even pronounce the names of all the little towns," he said.

Leigh laughed, knowing exactly what he meant.

They merged onto the highway, settling in among all the trucks and cars speeding down the smooth ribbon of road.

"I hope you can drive stick, because this is going to be a long drive for me if you can't," Jonathan said as he relaxed back into his seat.

Leigh looked away, out the window to the green countryside flying past, and shifted in her seat uncomfortably. "Stick. Yes, well — not so much. You'll have to give me a crash course," she said sheepishly.

"I can do that," Jonathan said with a smile.

They passed a sign that read "Verona 49 KM."

"When we pass through Verona, we'll stop for gas and a map," he said.

"And shoes," Leigh reminded him.

"Of course, Doctor," Jonathan said.

Leigh settled into her seat. "You mind if I nap a little until we get there? I feel like I'm going to pass out."

"Not at all," he said.

Leigh curled up on her seat and shut her eyes. The adrenaline of the day was long gone and exhaustion was settling in. Jonathan pointed the car at the horizon and sped up. Something inside him told him that the sooner they could get to Oviedo, the better.

CHAPTER 12

Outside of Oviedo, Spain
May 22, 2025 7:05 p.m.

Asad Hasan sipped a *cortado* at the roadside restaurant, waiting. He added more sugar to the small strong coffee, his third, and stared out the window at the late afternoon sun reflecting on the restaurant's sign, *El Horno de Eustacio*. He looked over at Samir, who had arrived two hours before and now sat across from him, nervously fidgeting with his empty cup of coffee.

"They are late. How much longer will they be?" Samir asked impatiently.

"Not long, I hope," Asad said. "You know how these things are. They have probably been watching us for the past hour."

Samir glanced around, suspicious of everyone. He ran his thin, almost delicate, hand over his fine-featured face. "Well I am tired of waiting," he said. "It was a long drive for me."

"Patience is the key to joy, brother," Asad counseled the younger man

"Waiter!" Samir called out in Spanish and ordered another *cortado*, his fourth.

"Let us go over the plan again," Asad said to Samir, trying to distract and calm him.

"We've already gone over it."

"We will go over it again," Asad said firmly, then added, "my young friend."

Samir took the hint, and nodded his head in respect to the older Asad. "Yes, let us review it again," he said.

"This evening, if the meet goes well, we will get the supplies from the Basques. We will do the rigging tonight. I have been watching the church and it starts getting busy around eleven. We will do it earlier, at nine," Asad explained. "You will drive the van," he continued, "and I will drive in your car, leaving it parked nearby. You will park at the designated spot, which is what?" Asad asked, testing him.

"*Calle* San Vincente," Samir said.

"Yes. You will park and leave the van locked, with the hazards on, as if you are making a delivery. Remember to arm it before you leave it. Make your way around the corner to the plaza, and don't forget the backpack," Asad told Samir.

"Yes, yes. You will go in dressed as a pilgrim with the other backpack and let me in the back door," Samir said, his impatience returning.

"What is the name of the plaza at the back door?" Asad asked, testing him again.

Samir thought. "What does it matter? I know where it is," he said, unable to think of it.

"Details matter," Asad said patiently. "You will learn this. Details keep you alive."

Samir nodded. "You are right. I am sorry."

"*Corrada del Obispo*," Asad told him. "After I let you in," he continued, "we will go through the courtyard to the left side, where the entrance to the crypt is. We will go slowly, as tourists, looking at the architecture and such. Once inside we plant the charges as we discussed. What then?" Asad asked him.

Samir thought. "Then, out through the exit to the car in the parking garage." Samir looked up, trying to remember the name. "Parking Jovellanos," he continued, "down the street and around the corner. We drive out, trigger the first device, then the van. Then we drive to Madrid."

"And if we get separated?" Asad asked.

"We meet at the RV point. The hotel Melia Reconquista."

"Good," Asad said, approving. "Now, for this meeting, I will talk. You stay back. They will have more men, and there will be someone behind you. Stay close to one of them; if there is trouble, they will be afraid to shoot their own. I do not anticipate trouble, but I like being prepared."

Samir nodded gravely.

They both took a sip of the strong coffee. Asad nodded towards the window.

"They are here," he said, watching a black Mercedes CLS followed by a blue Citroën C7 pull into the parking lot.

"How do you know it's them?" Samir asked.

"I know."

"Yes, but how? I want to learn," Samir asked him.

Asad gave the barest trace of a smile, glad for the younger man's inquisitiveness. "They are traveling together, both are expensive cars, the

Mercedes more so. That will be the principal's. Look around the restaurant," Asad told him. "It is all tourists and truck drivers stopping for a coffee. Those two cars are neither. It has to be them."

Samir nodded, taking note of Asad's wisdom.

"Let's go," Asad said. He paid for the coffees and got up.

They walked outside into what was beginning to be a chilly late afternoon. The sun was still peeking over the mountains, but soon it would be gone and the coolness would wash over the land. The gravel of the parking lot crunched under Asad's feet as he walked to the black Mercedes, which had parked by Samir's car. The tinted window of the Mercedes lowered and a man, bald and with a scowling, square face, leaned out.

"Follow us," he said in Spanish, and they started pulling out.

"You heard them," Asad said to Samir.

The young man slipped into the driver's seat of his Audi RS4 and fired up the big engine. Asad crowded into the passenger's seat and put his seatbelt on.

The gravel crunched under the Audi's wide tires and they followed the black Mercedes out of the parking lot. The blue Citroën pulled in behind them. They drove down the A231, going east, for several kilometers. The Mercedes pulled off to a smaller side road, then to a small dirt road. They followed them, the dirt now kicking up and dusting Samir's immaculate silver Audi with a fine layer of dust.

The dirt road led to a remote farm. Several buildings, all in a state of disrepair, dotted the property. An ancient stone cottage sat at the end of the drive. The Mercedes pulled up to it, and Samir turned and parked nose out. The Citroën pulled in alongside.

Four thick and sullen-looking men exited the Citroën.

"Remember," Asad said to Samir in the car, "if there is trouble, get close to one of them. And watch my back."

Samir tapped the gun on his belt. "Do not worry," he said.

Asad got out first. It was very quiet and peaceful in the remote farm.

A short man, balding and wearing sunglasses despite the fact the sun was now behind the mountains, got out of the Mercedes. He walked up to Asad and extended his hand.

"Hello, I am Benoit Karnera, as I am sure you know," he smiled an unpleasant smile that revealed his crooked teeth.

"I am Leon. Thank you for your help," Asad said, looking at the man but taking in every detail around him.

"It is a pleasure," Karnera said flatly.

"You have been paid, yes?" Asad asked.

"Yes. The payments have been received, plus extra. Do you know why?"

"Good. The extra is for a few more supplies. I hope you have them," Asad said.

"Certainly. What do you need?"

"Twenty kilos Semtex, four kilos ANFO, Tovex and blasting caps."

Karnera nodded. "Yes, of course. It is nothing. That can be supplied," he said, squinting his eyes with suspicion.

"Good," Asad said.

"Doing a side project, are we?" Karnera asked, arching an eyebrow.

"No. It is all part of the same plan."

"Good," Karnera said. "The Lawyer assured us they would not be used for another 25/2," he said, referring to the terrorist bombing in Madrid five years before. "We do not want loss of life. It is not productive to our cause," Karnera said.

"I assure you casualties will be minimal," Asad promised.

Karnera nodded. "Walk with me," he said.

Karnera walked towards a dilapidated farmhouse. The late afternoon sun had left, though the heat radiating from the rocky ground still warmed them. Behind the farmhouse, green mountains dotted with hard rocks rose in the distance. The farmhouse, a once great grey stone building, stood in a state of decrepitude. Asad walked towards it, warily, following Karnera. The four beefy fellows followed. Samir moved with them, keeping close to one of the four.

Karnera fished a key from his pocket and worked the large lock on the farmhouse door. He undid the large iron clasp and swung the heavy wooden door open.

The light flooded the darkened and dusty barn. Inside, standing in the middle of the barn, was a white Ford Sprinter van with a logo reading "*TAV Distribuidores, S.A.*" painted on the side. To the right of the van was a large table lined with meticulously arranged plastic drawers of various electronic components.

"The van is already rigged," Karnera explained. "It is on a phone trigger. The safety is on, of course."

Asad nodded. "If you do not mind," he said, "I would like to see the rigging."

"Not at all," Karnera said. He walked to the rear of the van and opened the panel doors.

The inside of the van was filled with brown cardboard boxes and, at a glance, looked to be set to make its deliveries.

"Here," Karnera stepped inside and gingerly pulled out one of the boxes. He opened it. Inside was a foam cutout with an old cell phone fitted to the center. Wires ran to it.

"The phone is connected to the detonators. There are 800 kilos of Titadyn, compressed dynamite," Karnera pointed out. He moved through the van to the front and Asad leaned in to see. Karnera picked up a small black box with two buttons and red and green lights. "This is the arming trigger. I would suggest arming it when we are away. Far away."

"And the phone number?" Asad asked.

Karnera walked hunched over to the back of the van.

"On the back," he flipped over the box with the phone, showing the neatly stenciled numbers.

Asad nodded. The work looked to be first-rate. Still, he wanted to make sure. He called Samir over, who had been eyeing the scene nervously from the opened door to the barn alongside Karnera's four beefy guards. Samir walked over.

"Check it out," Asad told Samir in Arabic, deferring to the younger man's superior knowledge of explosives.

Samir went to work examining the wiring and charges.

Asad turned to Karnera.

"This is what I need," Asad said, handing Karnera a scrap of paper.

The man took it and read it.

"Of course," he said. "We have all that here."

"Mind if we pack it here?" Asad asked. "It would be more convenient," he added.

"As soon as we leave, the place is yours," Karnera said with a big insincere smile.

"Good," Asad said, satisfied.

Karnera motioned the four guards over. "See he gets this," he said, handing the scrap of paper to one of the men. He turned to Asad and eyed him warily, then handed him the keys to the van. "Do not make too much of a mess," he said.

"We will be careful. The military barracks are abandoned at this time," Asad told him with a straight face.

"Good," Karnera nodded. "We want to send a message, but we do not want to shout it."

Asad kept his face impassive. It was the Lawyer's idea for the cover story, and Asad had to admit it was a good one. Karnera, terrorist or not, might have second thoughts about bombing a Cathedral. But military barracks were not on his conscience.

"Good luck," Karnera told them. He walked out of the barn, his guards following, leaving Asad and Samir in the dusty silence.

CHAPTER 13

A10 Autostrada, Outside of Genoa, Italy
May 22, 2025   7:44 p.m.

The Fiat 500 jerked and bucked forward, then ground to a halt.

"Bloody hell," Leigh said, exasperated.

"No problem, just relax and try again," Jonathan said patiently.

Leigh started the car again. She put it into gear and revved the engine almost to redline, then took her foot off the clutch too fast. The car shuddered then shot forward in the empty and desolate overflow parking lot of the rest area. She tried to shift to second but missed and went into fourth, bogged the engine, and stalled it again.

Leigh let out a growl of frustration. "Ugh, who even buys stick shift anymore?"

"You'll get the hang of it," Jonathan said, though he didn't really believe it. "We can practice more later," he said, eager to get moving again.

Leigh opened the door and got out, the heels of her new Ferragamo boots clicking on the ground as she walked around to the passenger's side. Jonathan got out and they met. Leigh, still frustrated, tried to brush by him, but Jonathan took her by the arm.

"Hey, you, don't worry about it," he said gently.

Leigh huffed, still angry at herself for not getting the hang of it. "I'm not," she said unconvincingly.

"Show me the rest of your tattoo," Jonathan said, giving her a smile.

"No," she said, turning away, but the frustration was already melting away.

"Give me a kiss then," he said, and held her close. She looked up at him and gave a slight smile. Jonathan bent down and they kissed.

"Better?" he asked.

"Yes. Thank you," she said earnestly.

"Good. Now, let's get going. We've got a long way to go."

They got in the car and sped out of the parking lot and merged on the highway. The low sun lit the horizon with orange and yellows, shadowed by the green hills to their right. To their left, the Mediterranean was an unending palette of greens and blues and grays stretching as far as the eye could see. Jonathan accelerated and pushed the little Fiat, getting closer and closer to Oviedo.

Outside of Oviedo, Spain
May 22, 2025 9:15 p.m.

"Are you nervous?" Asad asked Samir.

"No," the younger man lied.

He handed Asad a backpack. Samir took the other backpack from the Audi's trunk and they both walked back towards the farmhouse in the dark. In the desolate compound, the only sounds in the cool night air were far-off insects and their own footsteps on the stony ground.

"A little nervousness is fine. It keeps you sharp. Too much, and you get sloppy, hesitant. The trick is to balance it," Asad counseled the younger man.

Asad paused at the door to the farmhouse and looked around him. The grounds appeared empty, Karnera and his crew long gone. The two entered the farmhouse. Samir turned and began to close the huge door with his free hand.

"Leave it open," Asad said.

"Certainly. Why?" Samir asked.

"It will be easier to hear anyone approaching."

Samir nodded, learning from Asad. They set the backpacks down at a table and Samir began preparing the equipment, eager to do what he'd been brought in to do, to show Asad his specialty. He opened a metal box and gingerly brought out a brick of Semtex, then another, setting them down on the table. He took a deep breath and steadied his hands and cleared his mind.

"Is there anything I can do?" Asad asked.

Samir shook his head. "This is solitary work. Do not worry. It is safe. I have done this before."

Asad nodded. "I will scout the farm, then. Make sure we're alone."

Asad went outside to the dark yard and waited for his eyes to adjust. He eyed everything in the moonlit night. The truth was he was uneasy sitting in the same building with almost a ton of explosives. He walked off the nervousness, running a perimeter around the area.

He went to the rundown cottage, tried the door, and it opened. He entered warily, alert. The place was dilapidated, long abandoned. Dust covered the few scraps of furniture left. He scouted the small cottage but there was nothing and no one.

He pulled up a chair that was upturned in the corner, righted it, and sat in it. He closed his eyes and thought of the long night ahead, and of the job tomorrow. He reviewed each detail in his head carefully. He was glad to have Samir. He was young, but loyal, and talented with the explosives.

Asad reflected on the job so far. It had gone well, for the most part, except for the loose end of the two scientists. He hoped that Adriana had been able to dispatch them, and he hoped she had been professional about it. God willing, tomorrow the job would be done and he would be rich. He allowed himself to rest while Samir finished with the explosives. Tomorrow would be a busy day.

PART 3

Joseph entered the tomb first. Carefully, he laid out the linen cloth on the rectangular stone rising from the earth. John and the women stood outside and the others followed in, carrying the Master. Joseph stepped aside as they hefted the body through the tomb. He turned away as he caught sight of the Master's horribly mangled back. They set the body on the cloth. One of the men removed the cloth wrapped around the Master's head and set the blood-soaked cloth aside in a nook. Joseph folded the Shroud over the Master and bound it. "Nicodemus is here with the myrrh," Joseph heard someone outside say. The women came in now with the oils and herbs. The smell of death and myrrh mingled in the low ceiling of the tomb. After the anointing and the prayers, Joseph and the others stepped outside into the dark and brooding afternoon. The leaden sky was turning ominously dark, as if creation itself had been angered. The crowd outside the tomb, an odd mix of centurions and the Master's followers, stood around nervously glancing up at the heavens. One of the centurions rolled shut the stone to the tomb, and placed a seal on it. The sky cracked with thunder, and then opened up, weeping rain onto the earth.

CHAPTER 1

Oviedo, Spain
May 23, 2025 4:07 a.m.

Father Ernesto Goya awoke startled. He sat straight up on his cot, silhouetted by the pale moonlight that lit the austere room of the Rectory of the Oviedo Cathedral he called home. The thin wiry priest took a deep breath.

"My God," he said, in Spanish. It was not an expression of alarm, but true words of reverence.

The prophetic dream had come to him in a flood, vivid as daylight and with an overwhelming feeling of power. And it called him to action.

He arose even though it was very early. He dressed and walked out of the moonlit room to the hall. Silently, he walked down the hall to the door of Father Paulo Martin. He knocked on the door as quietly as he could so as not to wake everyone. After a couple of knocks, Father Goya heard Martin inside awakening.

"Father Martin," he whispered through the door.

"Yes? What is wrong?" Father Martin asked through the closed door.

"We must speak."

There was a pause. "One moment."

After a few seconds, Father Martin opened the door, tying his robe. "Come in," he said, with a concerned look on his face. Father Goya entered. "What is wrong?" Martin repeated.

"I have had a dream, a vision," he said, grave distress etched on his face.

"A what?" Father Martin asked.

"A dream. But unlike any other dream. I believe it was a prophecy, a message from God."

"Father Goya, it is early," Father Martin said and rubbed his eyes. "Are you sure it was not just a dream?"

"Paulo," Goya said, putting a hand on the priest's shoulder and calling him by his familiar name, which he seldom did. "It was no ordinary dream. It was a vision."

The expression in Father Goya's eyes was unlike anything Father Paulo Martin had ever seen. They seemed to be lit from within. In the years they had known each other, he had never known Father Goya to be anything but loyal and steadfast. Certainly not one given to flights of fancy.

"Go on," Father Martin said, beckoning him to sit down.

Father Goya did not sit, but paced around the room. "It was a message from God, I am sure," he said excitedly.

"Calm down," Martin said gently. "Tell me."

"I was in the *Camara Santa*, in front of the *Arca Santa*, praying at night as I always do," Goya said rapidly.

"Wait, was this last evening or in your dream?"

"In the dream. It was very vivid, as if I was there. I knelt and prayed. Suddenly, there was a great white light, so bright I could not stare at it, though it did not hurt to look at. The light dimmed a little and it seemed to be coming from inside the chest. To be going right through it, making it translucent. I fell on my face but a strong and gentle voice said, 'Rise my good servant.' I stood up, but was trembling. The voice said, 'Take my holy blood to the sacred mountain.'"

Father Goya paused. He was trembling, eyes filling with tears.

"Go on," Father Martin said, putting a comforting hand on the priest's shoulder.

"The voice was," Father Goya paused, "it was unlike any other. Like a rushing stream and the gentlest trickle of water all at once. That is all the voice said. Then the light from inside the box brightened until I could see the Holy Cloth inside. It did not hurt to look at, at first. Then, the light brightened until I had to close my eyes, but it went through my eyelids and I pressed my hands against my eyes but it went through them too. And it became hot, unbearably hot. The *Camara Santa* filled with fire and crackled and flames licked at everything. And then I awoke."

Father Goya seemed calmer now that he had recounted the dream out loud. Father Martin, however, looked visibly shaken. He sat on the edge of his bed, shoulders slumped.

"What is it?" Father Goya asked.

"I too have had dreams of fire in the *Camara Santa*, but no voices as you heard," he said, voice quivering.

"Dreams? More than one?"

"Yes. For three nights now."

"Why did you not say anything?" Father Goya asked.

"They were ordinary dreams, I thought," Father Martin said. "I ignored them." He paused, staring at the ground. "What does this mean?" he asked, looking up at Father Goya.

"I think the church is in trouble. I think the Sudarium is in trouble."

"You think we are being warned of a fire?"

"It is possible," Father Goya said. He paused and thought. "I think it is a warning, yes." He nodded his head.

"What then shall we do?" Father Martin asked.

"The voice. He," Father Goya paused and crossed himself, "said 'Take my holy blood to the sacred mountain.'"

"The Monsacro?" Father Martin asked.

"It can only be that," Father Goya said. "I think He wants me to take the Holy Cloth to Monsacro."

"To the Hermitage?" Martin asked.

"Where else?" Goya responded. "You know the history," he added.

Father Martin nodded. "Yes," he said, thinking about it, then gave a stronger more convincing "yes" as the pieces fit into place. "When? When should we do this?" Martin asked.

"I believe right now," Father Goya answered. "We will open the *Arca Santa* and prepare the Sudarium. I can be ready by dawn."

"It is a long journey to the Monsacro. Do you think you can do it?" Father Martin asked. Father Goya was much older than he, though he was strong and wiry. "Perhaps I should go," he added.

Father Goya shook his head. "I will go. I may be old, but I did the *Camino de Santiago* five years ago," he said, thinking back to his time on the pilgrimage. "Besides, if God wants me to take it to Monsacro, what can stop me?"

"That is true," Father Martin said, nodding his head.

"Very well. I will take it. I will go get my keys," Father Goya said.

"I will dress and meet you there," the other priest responded.

Father Goya left, walked down the hall, and went to his small room. He took a key that hung from a silver chain on his neck and opened a wood coffer. Inside, laying on purple silk, were several ancient keys of various sizes, along with a small, modern key. Most of the locks on the *Arca Santa* required two keys to unlock, and for hundreds of years the two priests that were the designated caretakers of the relics each had possession of one of the two keys. Father Goya rolled up the keys carefully in the silken cloth and walked down the stairs of the rectory.

He opened the door that led to the Cathedral, which was lit only by the moonlight shining through the stained glass windows. Father Goya waited a moment for his eyes to adjust, then crossed the dark, empty Cathedral. His footsteps echoed in the cavernous space. He paused as he walked by the altar, stopping to kneel and cross himself. He walked across the rest of the Cathedral's nave to the side door that led into the most ancient part of the Cathedral, the part built by Alfonso the Second over 1300 years ago. The door creaked open with a loud groan that echoed off the walls, and he walked in. Here the space was smaller, the silence less noticeable. Father Goya passed the small counter where the ticket attendant normally sat and climbed the stairs to the *Camara Santa*, where the Holy Cloth of Oviedo, the Sudarium, had sat, undisturbed, for hundreds of years.

Father Goya knelt in front of the huge iron bars as he had in his dream and as he had every night for over twenty years. He was filled now, as always, with a feeling of peace. But also more, like a gentle electricity that filled the air and coursed through him. He remained kneeling, praying, and waited for Father Martin to arrive.

He heard footsteps and got up. Father Martin walked in, carrying his own bundle of keys.

"Are you ready?" Father Goya asked.

"Yes."

They knew the procedure well. Every Good Friday and on two other Feast Days, they had taken the Sudarium out to be exhibited and venerated. They took out the two biggest keys and inserted them into the top and bottom lock of the iron gate. They turned slowly, scraping and with some effort.

"They should be oiled," Father Goya said.

Father Martin nodded.

The huge door swung open with a groan escaping from its hinges.

The two priests crossed themselves and went inside. They each took out a small modern key from their satchel and inserted them into a small silver box with blinking red lights. This was the control box for the seismic and motion sensors for the clear Lexan box that surrounded the *Arca Santa*. They disabled the sensors. Father Goya went up to the *Arca Santa*. The big silver chest sat on a stone pedestal, surrounded by the clear Lexan box. In a move he'd done three times a year for many years, he swung the top of the clear cover up and behind the chest. They both undid a clasp at each side of the clear box, and swung these out of the way. The remaining Lexan section at the front swung out of the way and now they had access to the *Arca Santa*.

The big silver chest sat a little higher than waist height. The silver was intricately carved with the twelve apostles in groupings of three covering each quadrant, and Christ was, of course, in the middle. To either side of Christ was a Seraph, a fearsome winged lion with the face missing. The places where the faces should have been were the keyholes.

"Are you ready?" Father Goya asked.

"Yes," Father Martin said before doubt could creep into his mind.

They turned the keys and the locks sprang open. Gingerly, for it was over a thousand years old, they both lifted the top of the big chest open. An old but pleasant smell rose from inside, a combination of cedar, old leather, and frankincense. Father Martin held the chest open while Father Goya looked inside. The inside of the chest was lit from the spotlight in the ceiling directly above. Father Goya looked at the different relics inside, each in their own small treasure box. But the main relic, the one Father Goya was convinced was real, was in a jeweled rectangular box, ornate with delicately carved gold reinforcements at the edges and corners. Father Goya lifted the reliquary, which was about the size and shape of an overlarge attaché case, out of the chest. It was thin and not heavy, but it was a bit awkward to carry. Inside the reliquary, Father Goya knew, was the Sudarium, the very cloth used to cover the head of Christ as He was taken down from the cross, the cloth used to soak up His holy blood as He was moved to the tomb. Despite the lightness of the reliquary, it felt heavy in Father Goya's hands, as if the years themselves were stored inside.

"Will you manage alright?" Father Martin asked.

"Yes. I think so. I will prepare a satchel with supplies for the trip and will leave in ten minutes."

A creeping doubt began to enter Father Martin now that the silver chest was open and the Sudarium was out. He kept the doubt to himself. "How will you know when to return?" he asked.

"God will let me know," Father Goya responded.

"I hope you are right. I will close up. You go get ready," Father Martin said.

Father Goya walked out of the *Camara Santa* with the reliquary in one hand, leaving Father Martin closing up the empty chest and reassembling the Lexan shield. Goya walked down the stairs and into the nave of the Cathedral carrying the jeweled reliquary and the holy Sudarium within. Goya readied himself mentally for the long climb. It had been a long five years since the last time he had made it to the top of the Monsacro. As Father Goya prepared a knapsack with water and some bread and fruit, the certainty filled him that he would not be coming down from that mountain. The thought did not scare Goya, however, but filled him with an indescribable peace.

CHAPTER 2

Outside of Oviedo, Spain
May 23, 2025   4:35 a.m.

Samir gently shook Asad awake, being very careful. The last thing he wanted was his neck snapped.

"Your shift, brother," he whispered.

Samir's voice was nearly swallowed by the huge nearly empty barn. Off to the side, a single light shone on the table, which was littered with bits of wire and parts. Leaning against the table were the two backpacks, the bottom filled with Semtex and ANFO and, over this, clothes, in case they were searched.

Asad opened his eyes, not moving. A strange dream of clouds and mountaintops was cut short, and he struggled to wake his body. "What time is it?" he asked.

"A little after four-thirty," Samir replied in a hushed voice.

"Everything well?"

"Yes. Nothing but quiet and a few mice for company."

Asad got up from his makeshift bed, really nothing more than straw with a blanket thrown on top.

"Get some sleep, friend. Two hours. We will do a final check, pack, and set out."

Samir nodded and took Asad's place on the blanket.

Asad stretched, walking the inside of the barn. He went to the door and stepped outside. It was a crisp, clear night. He walked a perimeter around the barn. Above him were stars without number. Far from city lights, the thin mountain air unveiled a tapestry of light, with the Milky Way ever so slightly visible.

A chill went down Asad's spine as he looked up at the splendid sight. For a moment he forgot about the bombing and the killing as the light of creation was revealed before him. For a moment, he thought, he would drop everything, drop the job and the money, just to bask in that feeling of revelation a while longer. He took a breath and shook these thoughts away, focusing on the task at hand. He busied his mind on the details and the stars disappeared from above him. In a few hours his mission would be complete. In a few hours he would be able to enjoy a starry night anywhere in the world. He turned and went back in the darkened barn to wait out the rest of his watch.

A-8 Autopista
Outside of San Sebastian, Spain
May 23, 2025   5:05 a.m.

Jonathan sped through the construction zone. For the last ten kilometers, the highway was in the midst of a widening, and barricades with blue lights lined the side of the road in the dark night. The blue lights merged at speed into one continuous blue streak that Jonathan followed like airport landing lights. He had the distinct feeling that he was flying, just piloting the car through empty space. He rubbed his eyes.

"I'm getting off at the next exit," he said to Leigh, who was fast asleep. "Get me some espresso, some chocolate, it'll be golden," he continued.

He'd been having a one-way conversation with Leigh's sleeping body for the last one hundred kilometers.

"Maybe a cappuccino this time," he continued. "But, back to my last point, which you didn't challenge by the way. The looks. *That* is why the E-Type Jaguar is the greatest car ever. It's sex on wheels, don't you agree?"

Leigh dozed on in the seat.

"I thought so. Hey, look, two kilometers for an exit. Food and gas twenty-four hours, baby," he said out loud, half delirious with exhaustion.

He reached over and gently shook Leigh. "Wake up sleeping beauty," he said.

Leigh rubbed her eyes and slowly rose up. "Mmm, what time is it?" she drawled and yawned sleepily.

"Five or so, don't know," Jonathan said.

"Where are we?"

"No clue. Somewhere near San Sebastian."

"Wow, I was out," she said.

Jonathan chuckled. "That's an understatement. You slept through all of France."

Leigh socked him in the arm. "You dolt," she teased him.

"Ouch, what was that for?"

"You could've let me drive, you know. You could've woken me," she said.

"You looked so peaceful sleeping. I didn't want to wake you. Besides, you were a grand travel partner. I've told you things I haven't told anyone."

Leigh laughed. "You were talking to yourself?"

"Well, talking to you. But yes. Talking to myself, I suppose. I had to stay awake. We're stopping soon, by the way."

They drove down the dark highway a bit longer then took the exit. He pulled into the service station and shut the car off. Jonathan put his hands on the steering wheel, leaned forward, and stretched.

"Tired?" Leigh asked, rubbing his shoulder with one hand.

"No," Jonathan lied. "You can keep doing that all night, though."

"Don't get used to it, mister."

"I'll just have to drive fourteen hours every time I want it, is that it?" he said jokingly.

Leigh smiled. "Thank you for driving."

He smiled back. "Let's get some coffee," Jonathan said and opened the door. They both got out and walked across the deserted service station to the store.

Leigh blinked in the glare of the fluorescents inside and watched sleepily as Jonathan worked the espresso machine. He took two cups from the machine.

"One for now, one for later," he said. "Do you want anything?" he asked her.

"You. We need to go to the bathroom, you and I," she said.

Jonathan raised an eyebrow.

"Don't get excited, mister. I want to check you out. Your wound I mean."

Jonathan set the coffees down and they walked to the bathroom.

Leigh locked the door. "Let's have a look."

She washed her hands meticulously and peeled the bandage off. She bent down, examining it. "Stitches look good. It would still not be a bad idea to get this looked at. I don't want you to have an ugly scar there," Leigh said.

"It'll be fine," Jonathan said, looking in the mirror. "You did a good job."

Leigh cleaned the wound, blotting a couple alcohol swabs on it.

Jonathan hissed.

"Sorry," she said.

"You don't look sorry. You don't have much of a bedside manner, do you?" he asked with a smirk.

"There's a reason why I work with computers and test tubes," she said absently and she peered at the wound. She let the alcohol evaporate off and then she bandaged it again. "All done and clean," she said, putting the first-aid supplies back in her bag.

They walked out of the bathroom towards the clerk and Jonathan picked up his coffees again. The clerk eyed them suspiciously. Jonathan paid for the coffee and some candies, and one-hundred euros worth of gas.

"How much longer to Oviedo?" Jonathan asked the clerk in Spanish.

"Oviedo? In that little car? Five hours," the clerk guessed.

Jonathan thanked the man and they went out into the chilly night, eager to arrive. The faintest trace of dawn was beginning to lighten the eastern horizon. Ahead of them, to the west, the mountains laid shrouded in darkness. Beyond that stood Oviedo and the ancient piece of cloth they hoped to soon see.

Outside of Oviedo, Spain
May 23, 2025   7:00 a.m.

"It is time," Asad said. The big man shook Samir awake. "Relax a moment, clear your head, and we'll begin the checks," he told him.

Samir got up slowly and nodded. They went outside to the clear dawn. The sky was silver, the sun still hiding behind the distant mountains.

"This will be an easy job, yes?" Samir asked with a trace of insecurity.

"If we keep to the plan and are careful, yes," Asad said.

Samir nodded gravely. They gazed at the dawn together for a moment longer and went inside the barn. They dressed in their tourist outfits, looking like hikers on the pilgrimage trail.

Samir tested the detonator circuits carefully while Asad packed the car. Samir turned on the old cell phone and made a call, testing it. The detonator circuit's red light came on. Satisfied, Samir powered down the cell phone and placed the circuit's black box back in the van, connecting it to the system again. Once in position, he would trigger the safety and arm the circuit; until then, it would be safe. He repeated this for the two backpacks. He finished by wiring the black box into each backpack, covering it with clothing. Asad stood behind him now, waiting for him to finish.

"What is the scallop shell for?" Samir asked Asad, pointing at the shell tied on a red ribbon that hung from each backpack.

"It is the symbol of St. James, one of the followers of Jesus that they revere. They say he made it to Spain, to Santiago de Compostela, to preach the gospel. Many pilgrims walk the route there, from all over France and Spain. If anyone asks, you started in San Sebastian," Asad explained to him.

Samir nodded. "Interesting," he said.

"Are you ready?"

"Let me check the circuits on the van again, then I will be."

"Good," Asad said, taking his backpack out to the Audi and gingerly setting it down in the trunk. He strapped it down, securing it, and said a quick prayer under his breath. He closed the trunk and went back to the barn to do one more check.

Samir hoisted the other backpack into the back of the truck and secured it. "Everything is ready," he said.

"You go first, I will follow behind."

Asad squeezed into the Audi and pressed the start button. The big V8 sprung to life, the exhaust note heavy and sonorous. Asad looked in the rearview mirror at the white Ford Sprinter van coming out of the barn. Samir got out of the van and closed up the barn door, then got back in.

They drove down the gravel driveway and then onto the narrow country road. The two vehicles merged onto the main National road, virtually deserted at this hour, and headed towards Oviedo, towards the scrap of cloth they hoped to destroy.

CHAPTER 3

Monsacro, the Sacred Mountain, Spain
May 23, 2025   8:30 a.m.

Father Goya paused, setting down the ornate gold reliquary containing the Sudarium, and leaned with one hand on a rocky outcropping. He breathed in the thin mountain air and wiped the sweat from his brow, there in spite of the chilly morning air. He continued forward on the fog-shrouded path, walking by memory and faith. The path steepened and he struggled to climb. He persevered and continued when, suddenly, he was above the fog and under clear azure skies. He walked a little further then turned and stared at the white clouds that completely blanketed the mountains below him. He set the reliquary down and contemplated the spectacular panorama of the desolate mountain and the world shrouded by clouds below him.

He closed his eyes a moment.

"God, grant me strength for this," he whispered.

Father Goya picked up the reliquary with both hands. It was not heavy, but it was bulky and awkward to carry. This last part of the path, he remembered from so many years ago, was the steepest. Ahead of him, sitting serenely on the hilltop, was the Hermitage, the Capilla de Santiago. The ancient octagonal stone chapel shone in the sun. Its weathered grey stone walls contrasted with the red clay tiles of the roof. The chapel looked both out of place in the desolate wilderness and also like it was growing out of the very rock there.

A cold wind blew through the solitary mountains. Father Goya had not seen a soul since he left Otura, the small town, really only a collection of houses, at the foot of the Monsacro. He continued on now, laboring up the rocky and steep final stretch. Setting the reliquary down, he scrambled up the steepest bit, then leaned down and picked it back up.

He paused again near the top, laboring for breath. Father Goya gazed down at the valley below. The path he had traveled trailed off into a cloud-filled world below. In the distance was another chapel, the Capilla de la Magdalena, similar in construction. A small lake far below reflected the intense blue sky and decorated the valley like an aquamarine in a brooch. Cows and the occasional bull grazed on the green grass far below him. The distant music of their cowbells mingled with the breath of the wind and gave Father Goya an intense feeling of peace and solitude.

He contemplated the serene scene for a few minutes, catching his breath, then finished the short walk to the Capilla de Santiago. He went to the door and set the reliquary down. Father Goya fished in his leather satchel for a large key marked "Capilla."

A large ancient lock held the door shut. Almost no one came up here and there was nothing of value in the spartanly decorated chapel, but still it was locked. Father Goya shook his head and chuckled, marveling at the distrust of man. He unlocked it, hung the lock from a bar and swung the old wooden door open. The creaking was loud in the stillness that surrounded him. He crossed himself, picked up the reliquary, and walked into the chapel.

The inside of the octagonal-shaped room was cold and empty. A simple stone altar sat towards the far wall. Dead flowers lay on the floor from some forgotten offering made who knows how long ago. A small statue of a virgin with a tiny baby Jesus in her arms sat in a niche behind the altar. Red candles, unlit, ringed the room on the floor. The room had a primitive, almost medieval feel. Inside the chapel, with no ties to the outside world, it could be 2025 or 1025.

Father Goya's labored breathing was loud in the silence of the chapel. He took the reliquary to the front of the room, towards the altar. Underneath the altar, hidden by a mantle cloth, was a rectangular cutout in the floor, hewn from the rock the chapel was built upon. Father Goya knew the history of the place. The cutout in the floor, known as the well of Toribio, was the exact place where 1300 years earlier the armies fleeing the Muslim invasion of Spain had brought that same reliquary and hidden it. The remote mountains had protected the most precious relic inside, the Sudarium, for untold years until it was moved to the Oviedo Cathedral.

Father Goya, staring down at the cutout in the floor, marveled that he should be the one to bring it back after all these centuries. He kneeled, working the reliquary under the altar. It slipped into the stone cutout, fitting perfectly. As it slipped in, almost clicking into place, Father Goya felt a tremendous chill go up his spine. He, a modest priest, was a part of the great history of this most holy relic. The thought filled him with awe, even as his humility struggled to accept it. It also filled him with the feeling, again, that he would not be leaving this place. It was a peaceful thought.

Having set the reliquary out of sight and safely in its place, he slowly rose to his feet. He walked over to his pack and brought out matches. One by one, he lit the red candles ringing the room. When he was done, he lit the three candles at the altar. For a moment, he was ten years old and gazing up with awe and reverence at the suffering Christ hanging from the cross at his small town's church. As a child, he would pray that God would give him the strength and wisdom to do His will. He knelt on the hard ground and prayed that same prayer now as the candles ever so slowly warmed the room.

Oviedo, Spain
May 23, 2025   8:52 a.m.

Asad pulled the Audi into the parking garage. The big engine thrummed against the low ceiling. He backed the car up, parking near the exit in a good spot. There was a sudden silence as he shut the car off. He pulled out his phone and dialed.

"Have you made the delivery yet?" Asad asked into his phone.

"I am almost there. Two minutes," Samir said and hung up.

Samir turned right onto the narrow pedestrian road that ran alongside the Cathedral. Though the pedestrian road was closed to normal traffic, it was open to delivery vans and trucks. Already, other vans were making the morning deliveries to the restaurants and bars that lined the surrounding streets. Samir inched the Sprinter van past a large truck delivering crates of cider and kegs of beer to a restaurant. He drove slowly down the cobblestone road to the predetermined point behind the Cathedral, the point that was closest to the *Camara Santa* housing the Sudarium. Samir parked the truck tight against the wall and shut it off. He turned on the hazard lights, and went through the procedure twice in his head before arming the device.

He got out of the truck and glanced nervously around him. An old man, a bum, sitting on steps across the street from the Cathedral smiled a toothless smile at him and shook a plastic cup of change. Samir ignored him. He went to the back of the van and retrieved his backpack. He closed the doors, remembering to lock them, and walked quickly towards the plaza, the *Corrada del Obispo*, he remembered.

Meanwhile, Asad was taking his own backpack out of the Audi's trunk. He hefted it on and headed out of the garage and up the steep street towards the Cathedral. The twenty kilos of Semtex were heavy. Asad, ever mindful of the instant death at his back, stepped quickly across the street and over to the plaza in front of the Cathedral. He regarded the imposing building for a minute before going inside.

It was dark in the gothic Cathedral. The pale morning sun filtered weakly through the reddish stained-glass windows. There was a chill in the air inside and it smelled of frankincense. It was an ancient smell, as intimidating as it was welcoming. Asad stepped as quickly as he could without appearing to hurry. He paused here and there in the vast space to gaze upward at the columns and the vaulted ceiling far above.

He made his way to the side of the Cathedral to the door. The sign read "*Camara Santa*," the holy chamber housing the Sudarium, which would soon join the Shroud of Turin in ashes. He stepped inside.

Asad paid the attendant, who did not glance twice at the big backpack adorned with the scallop shell, and entered. He walked up the stairs, laboring with the heavy backpack despite his conditioning. He went to the outer chamber, down a few steps, and into the inner chamber where the cloth was kept inside its jeweled silver chest. Asad allowed himself a few moments to contemplate the chest and the holy relic he thought was inside. He then walked out of the chamber and through the museum as he had the previous day to the outer courtyard.

He glanced around and made sure there was no one near. At this early hour, he had the courtyard to himself. He went across to the exit door and cracked it open.

"Samir?" he whispered out.

Samir came to the heavy wooden door and opened it. "Ready?" the young man asked nervously.

"Yes," Asad said. "Is the van in position?" he asked.

"Yes. Everything is ready," Samir confirmed.

"Follow me."

Asad led him across the courtyard of the ancient monastery, which was lined with columns and completely and eerily silent. So silent, in fact, that

Asad thought for a crazy moment that anyone would be able to hear his very thoughts. He pushed this notion away and concentrated on the task at hand.

"It's through here," Asad said, leading to the smaller graveyard off to the side. Samir followed with his big backpack. The ancient graveyard was populated by cats, which lounged on the cool marble tombstones. At the side of the building, right below the *Camara Santa*, was the crypt that Asad had scouted the day before. Asad ducked and entered the low-ceilinged crypt and Samir followed. Inside, Asad had to keep his head bowed like a penitent, though Samir could stand up straight.

"This is it. This is directly under the chamber," Asad said, setting his backpack down. "And this tomb is directly under the chest," he added, pointing at the tomb of the martyr at the far end of the crypt.

Samir examined the thick stone walls and the curved ceiling.

"The blast should concentrate and expand upwards, towards the thinnest spot," Samir said and pointed at the ceiling.

"That is what I thought as well."

"Let's do it," Samir said, and set down his own backpack.

They placed the backpacks on the crypt like some kind of apocalyptic death offering. Samir busied himself with the backpacks. For a moment, Asad was reminded of Abraham sacrificing his one and only son. Only, Asad thought, Abraham never went through with it. *God would not be calling this offering back*, Asad thought.

"Is everything armed?" Asad asked.

"It is ready. Let us go," Samir said.

Casually, but quickly, they walked out of the crypt, through the graveyard and past the columns of the courtyard to the exit. They closed the big wooden door behind them, hearing the click of the lock.

"Let's get to the car," Asad said.

They hurried through the early morning streets, past shops and restaurants taking their morning deliveries, towards the parking garage. Asad went straight to the car, to the driver's side. Samir followed hurriedly, looking nervously behind him. They got in.

In the silence of the car, Asad finally breathed a sigh of relief. Samir turned to Asad.

"Shall I do it?" he asked.

"Wait until we are out of the garage," Asad told him.

He fired up the Audi and drove slowly out of the garage. Asad paused at the garage exit, waiting to merge onto the street.

"Make the call," Asad said.

Samir nodded grimly. He brought out the old cell phone and dialed the number. He gave Asad one last look before pressing the send button. Asad nodded, and Samir pressed send.

To their left was a flash of golden light. A moment later they heard the explosion, feeling the shockwave go through them. The garage behind them erupted in a chorus of car alarms. A cloud of dust poured out of the street that led to the Cathedral. A black plume of smoke rose over the top of the nearby buildings. Thirteen hundred years of history collapsed in an instant.

Asad, satisfied, drove out and away from the Cathedral.

CHAPTER 4

Oviedo, Spain
May 23, 2025   9:22 a.m.

J onathan merged onto the ring road surrounding Oviedo. He rubbed his eyes and sat up straighter, energized now that they had reached their destination.

"Doctor Lancaster, I present to you Oviedo," he said, sweeping one hand in front of him.

"Looks nice. Smaller than I thought," Leigh said.

"It's been a while since I've been here, but you'll like it," Jonathan said. "You've gotta try the cider. It's yummy," he added.

"You're just trying to get me drunk again, mister," she said.

Jonathan chuckled. "Hey, you make a cute drunk."

"Oh? And I don't make a cute—" Leigh's words trailed off as she looked out the window at the city spread out before her. A look of alarm spread over her face.

"What is it?" Jonathan asked, concerned.

"Look," she pointed to the side, towards the center of town.

A plume of thick dark smoke rose from the center of the city. For a moment, they were back in Turin, the plume of smoke eerily familiar.

"Nah, you've got to be kidding me," Jonathan called out.

"What's going on, Jonathan?"

"I don't know, but that does not look good."

Jonathan sped up, weaving through the morning rush hour traffic.

"Do you think they destroyed it? Like in Turin?" Leigh asked.

"I don't know," he said softly to himself.

He sped up even more, cutting into the passing lane and revving the engine to redline. A BMW behind him flashed his lights but Jonathan flogged the Fiat and outpaced him. The Fiat cut in and out of traffic as Jonathan rushed to get there.

"City Center," Leigh pointed out the sign to him.

"Right," he said.

He cut over two lanes, threading through the traffic, and just making the off-ramp. They slowed and came into a roundabout with a huge fountain in the middle. The water sparkled like silver in the clear morning air.

Jonathan craned his neck around, trying to get his bearings. He knew that the Cathedral stood, like so many, in the exact center of town. He entered the traffic circle, looking for signs or anything else to guide him. Leigh caught a glimpse of the smoke rising over the buildings.

"There," she pointed to the right.

Jonathan slowed and cut across the circle and into a street lined with apartment buildings. A sign reading *"Centro Cuidad, Catedral, Informacion Turistica"* pointed them ahead. He drove up the street.

"Ah crap," Jonathan hissed.

Ahead of them, the street was blocked off by a police barricade. Flashing lights, red and blue, lit up the street. Fire trucks and ambulances filled the road and clamored to get close. Jonathan pulled the little Fiat into a side street leading into a large apartment building and parked in a no-parking zone, the only space available.

"Let's go," he said to Leigh.

She grabbed her computer bag and slung it over her shoulder. They got out of the car and Jonathan stretched.

"Man, am I sore," he complained.

"Let's go, old man," Leigh kidded him, outpacing him.

"Quiet, you," he said and caught up to her.

They walked up the steep hill towards the Cathedral and the emergency vehicles lining the road. A woman walking a huge Great Dane was ahead of them. They caught up.

"What's happening?" Jonathan asked her in Spanish.

"I don't know," she replied. "I heard a loud explosion about ten minutes ago. I was going to go see."

Jonathan and Leigh hurried past her, running as best they could up the steep hill. The road leveled off as they came to the main street lined with still-closed shops. As they neared the chaotic scene, they were again reminded of Turin. They stood beside a police barricade and looked up at the thick cloud of smoke, though it was nowhere near as thick as the smoke in Turin. The smoke cleared for a moment as the morning winds whipped down from the mountains and cleared the air.

"Look!" Leigh pointed up.

The spire of the Cathedral rose up into the blue sky as it had for a thousand years.

They exchanged a glance, then ran towards the Cathedral. The streets leading up to the plaza in front of the Cathedral were crowded with emergency personnel and bystanders. Jonathan muscled through the crowd and Leigh followed closely as they fought their way up the crowded streets. The crowd thinned out and they came to the large open plaza in front of the Cathedral. A couple of television vans were already parked in the plaza and were setting up their satellite antennas. All around them was chaos as police tried to hold back the curious and firefighters rushed towards the Cathedral.

The Cathedral façade looked largely untouched. The plume of smoke rose from behind it, from the back of the Cathedral.

Jonathan leaned down to Leigh, speaking in her ear to be heard over the noise. "If I remember right, the Sudarium was kept in an older part of the Cathedral, towards the back. Come on," he told her. He took her hand and they stepped through the crowd to a side street, going a block over, away from the crowd. "Up a couple of blocks and we'll be behind the Cathedral," Jonathan said.

They turned a corner and froze.

The street behind the Cathedral was unrecognizable. It looked like a war zone. Debris and rubble were strewn everywhere. Firemen sprayed water cannons mounted on large trucks, throwing water at the great maw that had opened up in the back of the Cathedral. Across from the Cathedral, a building lay in steaming ruins and it too was being sprayed with water by the firefighters. A large crater was gouged out of the earth in the center of the street. Ambulances lined the perimeter, waiting for the injured, but there did not seem to be any.

Jonathan and Leigh stood open-mouthed and watched the surreal scene unfold.

"We need to find out if the Sudarium was destroyed," Jonathan said.

"Where did they keep it?" Leigh asked.

"If I remember right, just about where that big hole is," Jonathan said grimly.

"Oh no," Leigh sighed.

"Come, let's get closer."

They walked around the ambulances and through a crowd that was filling the side street. Here, large chunks of stone that had been ripped from the ancient Cathedral littered the ground.

A policeman stopped them. "You cannot pass," he said in Spanish.

"Please, we have permission," Jonathan lied. "We are scientists that were studying the Sudarium," he explained. Jonathan flashed his security card from Turin. It looked serious and official.

The policeman looked them up and down. Leigh smiled at him. The crowd pressed against them from behind.

"Pass," the policeman waved them on, not paying too much attention in the chaos of the scene.

Leigh and Jonathan glanced at each other. Jonathan almost imperceptibly raised an eyebrow. They passed through a line of policemen, most of who were staring at the fires burning in the collapsed building to the right and the newly opened gash in the Cathedral to the left.

"We need to find someone in charge here," Jonathan said to Leigh, leaning in close to talk over the noise.

"How about that guy?" Leigh pointed at a firefighter standing at the side of a truck yelling instructions into a walkie-talkie.

They approached him.

"What is the situation here?" Jonathan asked him in Spanish, practically yelling over the noise of the trucks.

"Who are you?" the firefighter asked back.

"Dr. Tremaine, head of the Sudarium study team," Jonathan said, inventing it as he went along. He flashed the badge again.

The firefighter shrugged. "Fernandez, chief of this unit," he said. "We don't know too much. Looks like a car bomb from the crater. I saw one like it in San Sebastian five years ago."

"So what is the situation?" Jonathan asked again.

"We've got this building down," Fernandez yelled over the diesel engines of the trucks and the spray of water from the cannons. "Homeless shelter, soup kitchen, church administration. We're looking for survivors, though it was early and there were not many people in there."

"And the Cathedral? What about the inside of the Cathedral? The *Camara Santa*?" Jonathan asked.

"Look for yourself," the firefighter pointed.

Past the smoke and steam, Jonathan could make out the inside walls and a huge iron gate, almost dangling in midair and now leading to empty space. The back wall facing the street was completely gone, as was the floor.

"There are a couple of fires inside the museum, but we've got those under control. The *Camara Santa* itself, though," the firefighter shook his head and the façade of intense professionalism peeled away for a moment. "It's just not there," he finished.

"What do you mean not there?" Jonathan asked.

"It's not there. That's the iron gate leading into it," he pointed again.

Past the iron gate, there was nothing but empty space and rubble. There was no sign of the treasures and relics once held there.

"When the rubble cools, we'll go through it," Fernandez said. "Excuse me," he turned his attention to a firefighter that had come up to him.

Jonathan thanked him and turned to Leigh. "This doesn't look good," Jonathan said.

"What did he say? My Spanish is rusty," Leigh asked.

Jonathan told her, translating what the firefighter had told him.

Leigh shook her head. "So that's it then? There's nothing left?" she asked in resignation, not expecting or wanting an answer.

Jonathan shrugged. "Maybe it's buried under all that rubble. Let's see what else we can find out."

"From who?" she asked.

"The news," Jonathan said with a knowing smile. "Come on."

CHAPTER 5

Oviedo, Spain
May 23, 2025   9:37 a.m.

Jonathan and Leigh threaded through the crowd in front of the Cathedral. Firefighters were coming in and out of the huge main doors, but their unhurried pace gave the impression that things were under control inside. Jonathan headed towards the news trucks, which now had their satellite antennas fully extended and pointed at the sky. Leigh followed through the tunnel of people as Jonathan muscled his way through the crowd.

They arrived at a little circle that had been carved out of the crowd, where the news reporters stood, their backs to the Cathedral. To the side of one of the reporters stood a tall priest in long black robes.

"Come closer," Jonathan told Leigh.

They got as close as they could to the perimeter. Leigh pressed up tight against him and they looked on.

The reporter, a short pretty blonde, spoke in rapid-fire Spanish. Jonathan strained to listen.

"Terror in Oviedo," the reporter said in her most serious voice. "A car bomb has claimed the lives of at least five people and heavily damaged the Cathedral. No one has yet taken responsibility for the bombing, and no advance warning was given. The bomb collapsed a social outreach center, killing five inside. It also heavily damaged the Cathedral and the *Camara Santa*, where one of Christianity's holiest relics, the Sudarium of Oviedo, has historically been housed."

"What is she saying?" Leigh asked impatiently.

"Shh. I'll tell you in a second," Jonathan told her and intently listened to the reporter.

"Some are saying it was a miracle that things were not worse," the reporter went on. "Among those is Father Paulo Martin, the Dean of the Cathedral, who joins us now. Welcome Father," the reporter greeted the priest.

"Good morning," Father Martin said with a slight bow.

"Father Martin, you are saying that things could have been much worse. How is that?" the reporter asked.

"Yes. As you know the explosion occurred very close to where the Sudarium was housed. By a miracle, I can tell you that the Sudarium is safe," he said, hoping that Father Goya had indeed made it up to the Monsacro.

"Safe?" the reporter asked.

"Yes. It was moved last night."

"Where is it now?"

"It is in a safe location. Given all that has occurred, I will leave it at that."

"That is certainly one bit of good news. And what of the damage to the Cathedral?"

"There was extensive damage to the outer wall and the *Camara Santa* was all but destroyed. There was also damage to the San Miguel Tower and part of the main chapel," Father Martin said, shaking his head.

"Any lives lost in the Cathedral?" she asked.

"Thank God, no."

The reporter thanked Father Martin and wrapped up the story, repeating the details back for the newscast.

Jonathan turned to Leigh, wide eyed.

"What is it?" Leigh asked.

Jonathan was speechless.

"Translate, darn you," Leigh said, socking him in the arm.

"The priest said the Sudarium is safe," Jonathan said, scarcely believing it himself.

Leigh let out a big sigh of relief. "That's the first bit of good news I've heard. Where's it at?"

"He didn't say, just that it's safe," Jonathan said, and then translated the gist of the reporter's conversation for Leigh. He kept an eye on the priest, who was now giving the same interview with the other reporter.

"We need to talk to that priest," Leigh said.

"Indeed," Jonathan agreed.

They waited for the priest to be finished with the interview. The priest smiled, thanked the other reporter, and moved out of camera range. He moved down the square towards the Cathedral, the crowd parting to let him through. He walked to the edge of the square where the crowds of bystanders had thinned out.

"Come," Jonathan said, taking Leigh's hand.

They fought through the crowd and caught up to the priest.

"Excuse me, Father," Jonathan called out in Spanish.

The Father Martin looked back but kept walking.

Jonathan let go of Leigh's hand and raced in front of the priest.

"Father, I must speak to you," Jonathan insisted.

The priest stopped, not that he had much choice in the matter with Jonathan blocking the way.

"Yes?" Father Martin asked, visibly annoyed. "What do you want?"

"The Sudarium. You said it was safe?" Jonathan asked.

"It is," Father Martin said nervously, looking past Jonathan to where he wanted to go.

"Where is it at?" Jonathan asked excitedly.

"It is safe. Now excuse me," Father Martin tried to walk past.

Jonathan stepped in front of him again. "I'm sorry Father," he said. "Allow me to explain. My name is Jonathan Tremaine. This is my associate Doctor Leigh Lancaster," he presented Leigh, who gave a little wave and a smile.

"Yes?" Father Martin said, unimpressed.

"We were working on the Shroud, in Turin. We were on the team studying it," Jonathan explained and showed him the security badge.

Father Martin nodded, understanding a little more now but still suspicious. "It was a tragic loss, what happened there," he said guardedly.

"We came to Oviedo to study the Sudarium, to take samples for DNA study. A man named Rudolph Lahmbrecht was supposed to help authorize it. You have not heard?"

Father Martin shook his head. "The name sounds familiar, but no, no one has authorized any studies. And there will not be any, least of all in light of what's happened. Now, if you excuse me," Father Martin tried to walk around Jonathan, who once again stood in his way.

"Father, the Sudarium is under attack. Surely you can see that. How can you be sure it is safe where it is?"

"It is safe. The place where it is being kept has stood the test of time. Now, if you will excuse me," he brushed past Jonathan, leaving him standing there. Jonathan stared as the tall priest walked down the plaza towards the side of the Cathedral.

"I take it that didn't go well?" Leigh, who had been listening to the entire exchange trying to understand with her rudimentary Spanish, asked.

Jonathan shook his head. "He said he hadn't heard from the Old Man, hadn't heard of us or any authorizations for study of the Sudarium."

"And he didn't tell you where it is?" she asked.

"Nope. He wouldn't say. Just that it was safe."

"That's it?"

"Yes." Jonathan put a finger on his chin. "No. He said something else. He said the place it was being kept at had stood the test of time." Jonathan looked up at the sky, as if trying to remember something.

"What do you think that—" Leigh said but was cut off. Jonathan put a finger up to silence her. She narrowed her eyes at him.

"The test of time," he repeated, "which means somewhere old," he went on, to himself, lost in his thought. "A castle or a church. Toledo, maybe? But it wasn't safe in Toledo. That's why they moved it here, when the Moors invaded. No, not here. Not at first."

Jonathan snapped his fingers.

"Of course!" he exclaimed.

Leigh sighed. "You want to tell me what the bloody hell you're talking about, mister?"

"History, baby. Come on. I'll explain on the way."

Jonathan grabbed her by the hand and they headed back towards the car.

"On the way where?" Leigh asked.

"You'll see."

"You sure about this?" she asked, dubious.

"No," he admitted, "but I've got faith," he said and grinned.

A-66 Highway, Outside of Oviedo, Spain
May 23, 2025 9:45 a.m.

"Play it again," Asad told Samir.

Asad gripped the steering wheel, slowing the Audi down as they drove on the highway leading out of town. Already he felt a clenching sensation; the elated feeling he had of the job being done evaporated.

Samir swiped at the phone again, and replayed the newscast he had just watched.

"Here it is," Samir said, holding up the phone so Asad could glance at it as he drove.

On the tiny screen, the pretty blonde reported from the Cathedral plaza. Black smoke rose from the church behind her and a large crowd was gathered there looking on.

"Can you skip ahead to the priest?" Asad asked, keeping one eye on the road and the other on Samir's phone.

"Yes," he said, and fiddled with the controls. "There."

The newscast played on, the camera focusing on Father Martin. His tinny voice came out of the speaker. "By a miracle, I can tell you that the Sudarium is safe," he repeated on the small screen. The newscast went on and Asad listened attentively.

When it was done, Asad cursed in Arabic and slammed his big fist on the steering wheel.

Samir looked at him, concerned about the rare display of emotion from the normally stoic man.

"What are we going to do?" Samir asked after a moment's silence.

"Find him," Asad said curtly. "Get online and look him up. Father Paulo Martin. Oviedo Cathedral. He must live close by." Asad spied an exit coming up and changed lanes, ready to turn around.

"What will we do when we find him?" Samir asked.

"I do not yet know," Asad admitted.

Asad's phone rang. He cursed again. He knew it was the Lawyer before he looked at it. He picked up the phone, took a deep breath to calm himself, and answered it.

"Yes?"

"Leon," the Lawyer, agitated, spat out at him. "Have you seen the news? Because I've seen the news. And the news is not good."

"I am taking care of it," Asad said. He gripped the steering wheel, wishing for a free hand to rub his eyes.

"I know you're going to take care of it. If you don't take care of it, I don't take care of you. The job was to destroy the relic, not the Cathedral."

"I know the job," Asad said, an edge to his voice.

"Then how did you screw it up?" the Lawyer barked.

"I went yesterday. There was no indication they were moving it. I don't understand."

"Well you better start understanding. You better start doing what you need to do," he said.

"What about the scientists?" Asad asked.

"You worry about the relic, Adriana will worry about the scientists," the Lawyer tried to dismiss him.

"Then she hasn't done it yet?" Asad asked, knowing the answer.

"Worry about the relic. Do your job," the Lawyer said and hung up.

Interesting, Asad thought. The woman had not killed the scientists yet. He didn't know whether that was due to her lack of skill, bad luck, or if they were more competent than he gave them credit for. He would not underestimate them.

"That was the handler?" Samir asked, grim faced.

Asad nodded.

"What did he want?"

"To hear himself talk," Asad said.

Samir allowed himself a small smile.

"Find anything?" Asad asked.

Samir poked at the phone. "Father Paulo Martin. Lives in the rectory right to the side of the Cathedral, according to the website. Confessions on Tuesday, Wednesday and Thursday."

Asad chuckled. "Good work."

"It was nothing. It was easy," Samir said with a shake of his head.

Asad saw the exit ahead. He accelerated and easily passed a line of cars. The big Audi barreled past and he changed lanes and took the exit at speed, hauling the car down with the big brakes and sending little puffs of smoke from the tires.

"The car is new, brother. Be gentle," Samir said with concern.

Asad gave a small laugh. "You'll be able to buy three more with the Sheik's money when we finish. Besides, for this next part, you'll drive," he said, already formulating the plan in his head.

He turned and got back on the entrance ramp, accelerating at a blistering pace back towards Oviedo.

"We need to make a stop first to do some shopping," Asad said.

"What do we need?" Samir asked.

"A bag, rope, and duct tape."

CHAPTER 6

Oviedo, Spain
May 23, 2025   10:04 a.m.

Asad looked at the phone, at the frozen image from the newscast of Father Martin. He committed the face to memory. He handed the phone back to Samir.

"So I just wait for your call?" Samir asked.

"Yes. I will find the priest. When I call you, get as close as you can to the road. I will let you know."

"Very well."

Asad stepped out of the car and Samir drove off. He walked back towards the Cathedral, back to the scene of the crime. He let out a deep breath. The streets around the Cathedral were crawling with police and emergency personnel. He rethought the plan. It would be near impossible to drive the Audi up to the rectory door given all the police blocking off the street. It would also not be wise to carry an unconscious bound man through the streets. He would have to draw Father Martin out. He tried to think how he would, then thought of the newscast.

Perfect, he thought.

Asad walked down the street towards where the bomb had gone off. He passed by the door of the rectory the Cathedral priests called home. He continued walking, getting closer to where the fire trucks sat still spraying water into the outreach building. The fire at the Cathedral itself had apparently gone out already. As he neared, going right up to the police lines and blending among the curious, he saw that they had done a good job. It was very surgical, taking out the Camara Santa and very little of the surrounding Cathedral. It was a shame about the other building, and the deaths, but those could not be helped. It was all part of *jihad*. He stood, contemplating his handiwork a bit longer, just another curious bystander gawking at the destruction. He was reminded of Turin. *Disasters do not come one by one*, he thought, the proverb entering his mind.

Asad, his plan firmly in his mind now, walked back to the rectory. He rehearsed the story to himself as he made his slow way there. Arriving at the door, he took a deep breath and knocked.

The locks scraped open and a young man, a priest, not Martin, answered.

"Yes?" the young priest asked through a half open door.

Asad gave him a big smile. "Hello, I am here to interview Father Paulo Martin, from Telesur," Asad gave him the name of the Spanish southern television station.

"Your name?" the young priest asked.

"Roberto. Roberto Gomez."

The priest eyed Asad. "One moment," he said and closed the door and disappeared into the building.

Father Martin opened the door. "Yes?"

"Hello," Asad said, "I am Roberto Gomez," he extended his hand. "I'm the producer for Telesur news. We'd like an interview with the hero who saved the Sudarium."

Father Martin's face reddened a little.

"Well, I am hardly a hero. I didn't—" he said, stopping himself and thinking of Father Goya up in the mountain.

"Nonsense," Asad smiled, "the people of Telesur want an interview. It will only take a few minutes. Will you come?"

"Of course, of course," Father Martin said, then called out inside the rectory to the young priest. "Javier, I will be right back."

He stepped out of the rectory and onto the street alongside Asad.

"We are setting up at the far end of the street," Asad said, pointing down the road. He took out his phone and called Samir. "Sancho?" Asad said. "I've got Father Martin with me. Will you set up the camera?"

Samir, momentarily confused, caught on to the ruse quickly. "Yes. Where would you like me to set up?"

"The end of the street. Be ready in three minutes," Asad said and hung up.

Asad smiled a big television smile at Father Martin, who trustingly followed him down the street. Asad saw the Audi pull up at the far end of the street. The hazards came on and Samir got out and opened the trunk. He got back in the car, hidden behind the tinted windows.

"We'll be setting up at the end of the street so we can have the emergency vehicles in background," Asad said, smiling.

"Very well," Father Martin nodded.

They arrived at the end of the street, where it joined the larger main street. Asad walked beside the Audi, his senses on full alert, studying the street for anyone that might be looking at them. No one was; everyone was distracted by the destruction at the end of the street.

"Where are the cameras?" Father Martin asked.

Asad scratched his head, walking past the open trunk of the Audi.

"I told that camera man to be here," he said in mock exasperation. He walked a little further, trying to get Father Martin to follow him, to get him in position in front of the open trunk.

Father Martin stood on the sidewalk, a few feet from the Audi. Asad walked almost across the street. Father Martin followed, stepping off the curb, right behind the Audi.

Asad saw Father Martin in position out of the corner of his eye. He turned quickly to block his path.

"Ah, there they are," Asad pointed behind Father Martin, who turned to look.

In an instant Asad was on him. Asad wrapped his big arms around the thin man's neck and squeezed like a python. The priest, startled, automatically struggled, but it was of no use against Asad's strength. Father Martin soon lost consciousness as Asad expertly cut the blood flow to the man's brain. Soon, the body went limp and Asad lowered him into the Audi's trunk, glancing around as he did so. Asad folded the priest's long legs into the trunk and shut it. He quickly stepped into the car.

"Go," he said to Samir.

Samir fired up the car and snicked it into gear. He drove off quickly, but not unduly fast.

"We need to stop somewhere private. He will wake up soon," Asad told him.

Samir drove down the main avenue that skirted the south edge of the city, looking at the navigation system.

"Here is a dead end street," he said and pointed. He turned right.

The street was lined with tall apartment buildings and appeared quiet. There was no traffic and no one walking.

Asad shook his head. "It is not ideal, but it will have to do. Turn around and be ready to leave."

Samir did a three-point turn at the end of the street and parked, leaving the engine on. Asad got out and examined the street. Satisfied they were alone, he opened the trunk.

Father Martin, still groggy, looked up, shielding his eyes from the sun. Asad flipped him over, quickly tying the priest's hands behind him and his ankles together. He took out a knife and cut the ends of the rope. He then took the roll of duct tape and quickly wrapped it several times around the priest's mouth. Asad examined the man's bonds, then the inside of the trunk. He pulled and broke off the emergency handle to the trunk's release and, satisfied, shut the trunk.

Asad got back into the car, handing Samir the T-shaped red handle to the trunk release.

"Sorry. I had to make a small modification."

Samir set the handle down in the console and shook his head. He pulled out of the parking spot and back onto the main road. "Where to?" he asked.

"Back to the farmhouse," Asad said. "I have work to do," he added with a grimace.

On the MO-4, La Foz
Outside of Oviedo, Spain
May 23, 2025   10:05 a.m.

"You're going to make me sick," Leigh said as she turned a decidedly pale shade of green.

Jonathan took another switchback, turning almost one hundred eighty degrees and climbing further up the winding mountain road.

"I'm sorry, but it's the road, not me," he said.

"Any idea how much longer?"

"Nope. Open the windows. It'll help."

Leigh did, flooding the car with cool mountain air. The road, dark with overhanging trees, tunneled its way through the thick forest, winding steadily up. Leigh took a deep breath and inhaled the pine-scented air.

"Does it help?" Jonathan asked.

"Yes, thanks."

"Good. You were looking a little green back there."

"So, mister, do you have any idea where you're going?"

"Sort of, according to the tourist map. I'm mostly making this up as I go along. But I have a good feeling about this."

"I haven't seen a village in fifteen minutes. What makes you think the Sudarium is up here?"

"It's what the priest said about it standing the test of time. The Sudarium was moved up north when the Moors threatened Seville. The priests moved it to Toledo, but soon that was threatened too. So they brought it all the way up here and hid it in a cave, eventually building a small chapel on the spot. They kept it there for years, hidden away in the mountains. When the threat died down, they brought it to Oviedo, where it stayed ever since."

Leigh scrunched her face. "And you think that's why it's there now? That's a stretch," she said, shaking her head.

"It's a long shot," Jonathan admitted. "But history repeats itself," he added.

The road straightened out and Jonathan sped up. A sign ahead read "Otura, 1 KM."

"That should be it," he said.

The road curved again, gaining altitude. The chilly mountain air blew in the windows. Jonathan slowed down as they reached the village. The road ended at a collection of buildings perched on the side of the mountain.

"Not exactly a happening place," Leigh said, looking out the window.

There was no one to be seen. A tiny plaza served as a parking lot. A couple of simple brick houses and a large retaining wall surrounded it. There were no restaurants or bars or even stores. Jonathan parked and shut the car off. They got out.

An eerie quiet filled the air. At first, there were no sounds, just the dying echo of the car engine and the buffeting of air. Gradually, as their ears acclimated, they could hear birdsong, the rustling of leaves, distant cowbells and the ever present whistling wind.

A dilapidated sign read *"Ermita de Santiago"* and an arrow pointed to a path.

"This has to be it," Jonathan said. *"Ermita.* The Hermitage of Santiago."

"You sure?" Leigh asked.

"No. You ready?"

"As I'll ever be."

They went up a set of stairs carved into the rock and past the two houses that seemed to comprise the village. They started up the path, which was lined with cow and horse droppings.

"Eww," Leigh said and made a face.

"Watch your step, city girl," Jonathan said to her, smiling.

They walked past a fenced-in field. Two white horses, almost mirror images of each other, stood bright against the lush green grass. Here, the path was lined with trees. An old farmhouse stood to their left. Bales of hay rolled against the side were the only clues of human habitation.

As they walked on, the trees thinned out. The mountains turned rocky and barren. The gravelly path seemed to stretch on into the misty distance infinitely. The wind picked up, sending great billows of clouds through the mountains.

"This looks like it may take a while," Jonathan said, pausing to look at the long path.

"Let's go, cowboy. Only one way to find out if you're right," Leigh said, and stepped in front of him.

She walked up the path and Jonathan caught up to her in a few long strides. There was beautiful desolation around them. The soft crunch of the gravel under their shoes was the loudest sound. They walked side-by-side on the path, sharing the stillness of the mountain, on what they hoped was the right way towards the Sudarium.

CHAPTER 7

Outside of Oviedo, Spain
May 23, 2025 10:15 a.m.

The Audi pulled in front of the barn, the gravel crunching underneath its tires. Samir shut the car off and they were enveloped in silence.

"Still looks like we have the place to ourselves," he noted, craning his head around.

"Make sure," Asad said. "I'll take care of the priest."

"Please do," Samir rubbed his eyes. A thump sounded from the trunk. "There he goes again. I'm sure he has dented the trunk," he added.

The priest had been hitting the inside of the trunk somehow for the past hour, despite his hands being tied behind his back.

"Let's go. Let's do this," Asad said, wanting to get it over with.

Samir exited the car and made sure first that the barn was clear. He gave the all clear to Asad, then started doing a perimeter check.

Asad opened the back door and retrieved the bag of supplies they had bought. He flicked open his knife and cut a length of rope, then examined the canvas bag he'd bought. He closed his eyes a moment and clenched his fist, the old scars there suddenly itching. He took a deep breath and tried to visualize his next move as well as steel and distance himself from what he was about to do. This next part was all clinical, he reminded himself, and he tried to remain dispassionate. He stepped to the trunk and opened it.

Father Martin, locked in the darkness for more than an hour, shut his eyes against the bright morning light. Asad quickly ripped the duct tape from his mouth and put the canvas bag around the priest's head. Father Martin gave a little scream of surprise as Asad tied off the bag with a rope around his neck.

Asad cut the ropes around the priest's ankles and, with a heave, took him out of the trunk. He set him on the ground. Unsteadily, Father Martin tried to stand up, but it was difficult with his hands tied behind his back.

"Let's go," Asad said, helping the priest up and tugging on the rope around his neck.

Asad led him towards the dark emptiness of the barn. They entered, and Asad shut the door.

Monsacro, the Sacred Mountain, Spain
May 23, 10:30 a.m.

"That is the biggest goat I have ever seen," Leigh said.

"I know. I thought it was a bull," Jonathan replied.

The rocky path they were on had cleared out into a sparsely vegetated moonscape. Two-dozen or more goats blocked their way, comfortably sitting in the middle of the path.

"Shoo, goat," Leigh said without much conviction.

Most of the goats ignored her, but one small kid stared at her. The little kid walked up to her, and tensed its haunches, ready to butt its head into Leigh.

"Jonathan!" Leigh called out, and tried to shoo the kid away.

Jonathan bent down and picked up two stones. He walked calmly past Leigh, clicking the stones together. The goats parted, scrabbling up the rocky ground to either side of the path. The little kid ran away to his nanny.

"Showoff," Leigh said to him.

"Nothing to it. Just remember, they're more scared of you."

"They may be scared of *you*, cowboy. That little one looked like he had my number."

Jonathan laughed.

They continued up the steep path past the goats. A misty fog enveloped the mountain, blotting out the sun and blanketing everything in gray. The only sounds were distant cowbells, birdsongs, and the ever-present low hum of flies and insects. They crested the hill and paused.

"Wow," Leigh said in awe.

"That's spectacular," Jonathan agreed.

The fog and clouds suddenly rushed past them at the crest of the hill. The wind opened up the landscape for a moment, showing a never-ending vista of lush green fields on this side of the mountain, then the white curtain of fog covered the world up again and left them swimming in an unearthly grayness.

They watched this cycle repeat for a few moments as the mist kissed their cheeks, then continued down the hill.

"You okay?" Jonathan asked Leigh, who had fallen behind a bit.

"Yeah, it's just steep. These boots aren't helping either." The boots she'd bought back in Italy were stylish, but not made for mountain climbing.

"Here, lets stop and rest a bit," Jonathan said and pointed to a bend in the path.

There was a broad stone there, shielded by a tree growing from the very side of the mountain. The area looked like a little cave. They sat on the broad stone, sheltered from the wind and mist. Jonathan took a water bottle from his jacket and offered it to Leigh.

"Thanks," she said, taking a drink.

"Anytime."

They examined the little cave. One of the walls was painted with a white cross and the words "*Jesus el Nazareno te espera,*" written underneath.

"What does that say?" Leigh asked, pointing at the strange graffiti.

"It says Jesus of Nazareth is waiting for you," Jonathan translated.

"That's what I thought. Sounds a bit ominous, yes?"

Jonathan chuckled. "I thought you were the Christian."

"I am, but I'm not so sure I want to meet him *today.*"

He chuckled again. "I see what you mean. Come, let's get going."

They got up and walked on in the silence of the steel-grey mist, laboring back up the path.

"You really think that the Sudarium is all the way up here?" Leigh asked. In the grey mist, with nothing visible around them, she didn't see much hope.

"I don't know," Jonathan admitted, his confidence faltering the further they walked. "History repeats itself, though."

"I hope you're right."

The path before them suddenly widened into a huge green field carpeted with white and yellow and purple flowers, visible whenever the wind rushed past and blew away the patchy fog.

"Is this the right way?" Leigh asked.

"I think so. I haven't seen any turns on this path," he answered.

They walked down into the valley, then back up the path were it narrowed again. Fog shrouded them, and the path got steep. They labored up, Jonathan helping Leigh scramble up the rocky way. Suddenly, they rose above the fog and they were looking at blue skies and a world blanketed by billowy white clouds. They paused.

"Wow, this is incredible," Leigh said.

The green peaks of mountains in the distance rose up out of an ocean of white. They stood at the top of the peak. Jonathan came up behind her and put his arms around her.

"You warm enough?" he asked. The air was getting colder the further up they walked.

"I'm good, thanks," she said. "But better now," she added, and brought her arm around and squeezed his hand.

They continued on the path, which went back down now, and walked back into the clouds. There was a fork in the path in front of them, the first they'd come to. There were no signs to be seen.

"Left or right?" Jonathan asked.

"I've no idea. I can't see anything," she said.

"Right it is then."

They climbed the path, which was especially steep here. The wind whipped around them and, suddenly, the path ended at a sheer precipice. They paused at the top and gazed around, confused. The wind blew and cleared the fog away for a moment, revealing the fork in path and, beyond it, another peak.

"Look!" Leigh pointed. Across on the other mountain, to the left of the fork and barely visible in the mist, was the Hermitage.

"That's it!" Jonathan exclaimed. "I recognize the octagonal shape."

"That, and the fact it's the only building for miles," Leigh added.

"Smartass," Jonathan kidded her.

"Let's go, Captain Obvious," Leigh ribbed him. "We're almost there."

They hurried on with renewed energy now that their destination was in sight.

Outside of Oviedo, Spain
May 23, 2025   10:43 a.m.

Father Martin stood in the middle of the dimly lit barn, his head covered by the canvas bag and his hands still tied behind his back. Asad stood behind him, threading a thick rope through a pulley then lifting it high above, securing it to a wooden crossbeam. He tied one end of the rope to the side of a post and pulled on the other end, testing the pulley with all his weight. The pulley creaked but held. He let go of the rope, which dangled ominously. Satisfied, he stepped in front of Father Martin.

"Who are you? What are you doing?" Father Martin's muffled voice escaped from the canvas encasing him.

Asad ignored him. "Get on your knees," he said coldly.

"Who are you?" Father Martin repeated.

The priest did not see the blow coming. Asad slapped him on the side of the head, open handed. Not hard, but hard enough to get his attention. Father Martin gave a little yelp then froze in place, mute.

"Kneel," the big man repeated.

The priest slowly knelt.

Asad stepped behind him again and threaded the rope through Father Martin's bound hands behind his back. He tied it off. Asad walked over to a table, picked up a notebook and pen, and took hold of a chair. He dragged the chair back to the kneeling priest, letting it scrape on the ground. It filled the barn with a grating noise calculated to disquiet the prisoner. Asad placed the chair a few feet in front of the priest. He leaned down, untying the rope around the priest's neck. Father Martin flinched at his touch.

Asad yanked the canvas bag off and threw it on the ground.

Father Martin glanced around bewildered. The huge imposing figure of Asad stood in front of him. He was in a dilapidated stone barn, he saw. Sunlight streamed in dusty beams through holes and gaps in the roof and walls. Rusty farm implements, unused for years, hung from the walls.

Asad pulled his chair a little closer and sat down. He pulled out the notebook and clicked the pen.

"I will ask you questions," he said. "You will answer them truthfully. Do you understand?" Asad asked.

Father Martin, frozen with fear, said nothing.

Asad swung his foot, kicking the priest in the ribs, though not hard. Father Martin cowered lower, still kneeling.

"Do you understand?" Asad repeated.

The priest nodded his head automatically. "Yes, yes," he said quickly.

"Good. Let's begin. What is your name?" Asad asked and peered at the man's face, studying it.

"What? You already know," the priest said, confused.

Asad calmly stood up, setting the notepad and pen down on the chair. He stepped over beside the priest and kicked him once, viciously, in the ribs. Father Martin fell to the side, gasping for breath. Asad went to the rope and pulled on it. The rope winched up, pulling on Father Martin's wrists tied behind his back. He scrambled to his knees to take the pressure off.

Asad walked back and calmly sat on the chair, taking the notebook and pen. He clicked the pen again. "What is your name?" he repeated.

"M — M — Martin," the priest said, still catching his breath. "Father Paulo Martin."

"Where do you work?" Asad asked, impassive.

"I'm a priest, the Dean, at the Oviedo Cathedral," he said between labored breaths.

"For how long?"

"Ten, no, eleven years."

Asad scribbled on his pad, not really writing anything down but instead studying the man's face.

"Where did you work before Oviedo?" Asad asked.

"What's this all about?" Father Martin asked, his composure returning to him.

Asad rose, once again setting the pad and pen down on the chair. He walked over by Father Martin, who winced. He paused there a second, then walked to the rope. He untied it from the post and pulled. It rose into the air, making the pulley creak, and pulled the priest's arms up.

Father Martin scrambled to his feet to relieve the pressure, but Asad kept pulling. Soon, Father Martin was standing up, slightly bent at the waist, as his arms were being painfully lifted in the air behind him. Asad tied off the rope, leaving the priest in the uncomfortable position.

"Father Martin," Asad spoke from behind him, "I do not know if you have studied your church history much. In particular, the Inquisition." Asad stepped in front of the priest, who struggled to look up from his humbled position. "The strappado," Asad continued, "such a simple technique, really, with just a length of rope. See, what will happen is the rope will be pulled up until your feet leave the ground. This will put great strain on your shoulders. So much so that they will dislocate, eventually," he continued, clinically. "It is incredibly painful. You see, anyone in the Fifteenth Century would have seen the rope and known this immediately. They would have known and they would have feared. And they would not be asking questions, only answering them."

Asad sat back down.

"So I ask you again," he continued, "Where did you work before Oviedo?"

Father Martin stared at the ground in front of him, straining already against the pull of the rope.

"I was in Toledo," he said through gritted teeth, referring to his years at that largest of Cathedrals.

"When did you come to Oviedo?" Asad asked, intently studying the priest's face.

"Eleven years ago."

"How long have you been entrusted with the Sudarium?" Asad asked, leaning in closer.

Father Martin paused. His mind raced. He closed his eyes, for he knew what was coming. Or thought he knew. He weighed answering these questions, which were harmless, against remaining quiet. He knew there would be questions coming that were not harmless, questions that he prayed he would not answer. A steely resolve filled him, as well as an odd sense of peace that he did not quite understand. He straightened up, which put more strain on his arms.

"May God forgive you for what you are going to do," Father Martin said, peering into Asad's eyes. He slumped back down.

May He indeed, Asad thought.

He rose, walked behind the priest, and untied the rope from the post. Father Martin's arms dropped and he breathed a temporary sigh of relief, even as he steeled himself for what was to come. Asad pulled on the rope. It wound through the pulley and tensed as Father Martin's arms began to lift. Tied behind his back as they were, they soon reached their limit. Father Martin groaned as his arms were pulled unmercifully up, though his feet remained on the floor.

Asad tied off the rope to the pole and sat back down. He waited for the initial shock of the pain to die away and the insistent pain to begin building in the priest.

"I see you want to skip ahead to the hard question," Asad said after a time. He nodded his head. "Very well. But before I ask, I would point out to you that your feet are still very firmly on the ground. It can get much worse, but it does not have to end badly for you. Just answer the question and the pain will stop."

Asad picked up the notebook and clicked the pen. "Where is the Sudarium?" he asked.

Father Martin said nothing. The huge and empty barn echoed with the sound of his labored breathing.

"Where is it?" Asad repeated. He felt a wave of frustration but controlled it. These things required patience, he reminded himself.

Asad rose from the chair. As he passed, Father Martin whispered to him, "May God forgive you."

Asad, impassive, winched the rope up. Father Martin expelled a low guttural groan as his feet left the floor. His breathing sped up and his legs kicked, searching for ground that was not there.

Asad walked back to his chair and watched the man struggle.

"This is not nearly as bad as it can get," Asad told him. "Save yourself and tell me where the Sudarium is."

Father Martin moaned and started sweating profusely despite the cool of the barn.

Asad waited, watching. The priest's feet were now almost touching the ground as the muscles and tendons of the shoulders stretched or were torn.

"Where?" Asad asked. "Where is it? Where did you move it?"

"It is safe," Father Martin croaked out. He repeated it over and over, softly, almost to himself.

Asad rose and winched the rope up another foot. He then pulled on it, lifting the priest even further up, then suddenly let go.

Father Martin screamed, his voice echoing in the barn, as his body fell and the rope went taut and jerked on his arms and shoulders.

Asad walked in front of him, not bothering to sit, and looked in the priest's face which was now about level with his. "Where?" he asked.

Father Martin made an unintelligible noise that ended in his saying "please" softly over and over.

"I will let you down. Just tell me where? Where is it safe?"

"The — the," Father Martin searched for the words, "the museum."

"Which museum?" Asad asked, intently studying the man's face.

"The history museum. In Oviedo," he muttered out. "Please—" he trailed off, his face a mask of pain.

Asad lowered the rope until the priest's toes barely brushed the ground. The big Moor walked past the priest, towards the door of the barn.

"Wait," Father Martin called out. "Don't leave me like this!"

Asad ignored him and stepped outside into the sunlight, closing the door behind him. Birds chirped in the bucolic mountainside. Samir stood outside.

"I heard screaming. I did not want to interrupt," the younger man said.

Asad leaned back on the wall of the barn and closed his eyes. He rubbed his temples.

"Did he tell you? Did he tell you where the Sudarium is?" Samir asked.

Asad shook his head. "No. He said it was at the history museum. He was lying, trying to get me to stop."

"Maybe it is there," Samir said.

"No. I will know when he tells me the truth. He will not do so willingly. Not this one."

"So what do we do?"

"We wait. I will tell him I went to investigate, and that I found nothing. I will continue to break him down. He will break, eventually. Everyone breaks," Asad said, and clenched his fists.

CHAPTER 8

Monsacro, the Sacred Mountain, Spain
May 23, 2025 10:54 a.m.

Jonathan looked up at the Hermitage perched on the hill above them. "Just a little further," he encouraged Leigh, who had fallen behind. He waited for her.

"I'm coming," she said. She stepped around a boulder on the steep trail and climbed up, then lost her balance. She reached out into space and Jonathan grabbed her hand, pulling her up. "Thanks, I owe you one," she said, regaining her footing.

"Don't mention it. Actually, now that you do mention it, show me your tattoo," Jonathan said, smiling.

"Not bloody likely," Leigh said and smiled back, climbing the trail past him.

"One of these days you'll say yes," he said, and climbed after her.

"You'll have to earn it, cowboy."

They went further and stopped at a gnarled old tree at a bend in the path, which provided the only shade on the trail. The sun was shining here above the clouds and, despite the cool mountain air, the exertion of the climb made beads of perspiration glisten on them both.

"Are you sure about this?" Leigh asked. "I haven't seen a single person since, well, since the road."

"I don't know," Jonathan said, looking around him. "I'm beginning to have my doubts. But there's only one way to find out. Come on, we're almost there."

They climbed the last stretch of the trail, which grew mercifully easier as the steep mountain plateaued. The Hermitage loomed in front of them now, larger than it had appeared from a distance. They approached the entrance with a slight trepidation, fearful of finding nothing in there.

"The door's open," Leigh whispered.

As they neared, they could see a reddish flickering glow coming from inside. Cautiously, Jonathan pushed the door the remainder of the way open. The hinges groaned loudly, reverberating in the hollow of the old stone building. Jonathan winced.

He poked his head inside.

The small interior of the Hermitage was bathed in the red glow of candles that ringed the entire room. At one end of the room was the figure of a robed priest kneeling in front of a stone altar. The priest rose up and turned to face them.

"Hello," Jonathan called out in Spanish, then, unthinkingly, knocked on the door.

"I've been expecting you," Father Goya said in accented English.

Jonathan tilted his head, confused, and entered the building. Leigh followed, peering around Jonathan.

"You've been expecting us?" Jonathan asked, confused.

Father Goya nodded. "I knew someone would come. I did not know it would be so soon."

Jonathan approached the priest. "I'm Jonathan Tremaine," he said and put his hand to his chest. "This is my associate Dr. Leigh Lancaster."

"Hi," Leigh greeted the priest and turned to Jonathan. "Associate?" she asked, silently mouthing the word.

Jonathan shrugged.

"I am Father Ernesto Goya. Why are you both here?" the priest asked.

"It's a long story," Jonathan said.

"We have time," the priest replied.

"We've come to see if the Sudarium is here," Jonathan said.

Father Goya straightened up and smiled. He was of medium height, thin and wiry, and looked younger than he probably was.

"The Sudarium is in a safe place," he said with a smile.

"I'm not so sure about that," Jonathan said, shaking his head. "Have you not heard?"

"About the Cathedral?" Father Goya asked, nodding his head. "I knew it was coming. How bad is it?"

"The *Camara Santa* and a building across the street, destroyed. The main part of the Cathedral was spared, mostly," Jonathan said, then, tilting his head quizzically, asked, "Wait, what do you mean you knew it was coming? Did someone warn you?"

"You could say that," the priest said, a sly smile playing across his face. "Please, have a seat. You must be tired after the long climb." He gestured to a row of wooden folding chairs at one end of the octagonal room.

Father Goya went to one chair and sat down. Jonathan turned two chairs to face the priest, offering one to Leigh.

"Who told you where the Sudarium is?" the priest asked them.

"No one. We spoke to a Father Martin. He only said it was in a safe place. A place that had stood the test of time, he said," Jonathan told him and shrugged, adding, "It could only be here."

"How did you know this?" Father Goya asked, perplexed.

"Allow me to explain. I'm an historian. Dr. Lancaster and I were on the Shroud study team in Turin. You've heard what happened there, right?"

Father Goya nodded gravely. "Yes. A tragedy."

"Dr. Lancaster was studying the DNA of the blood of the Shroud. She's found some, well, unusual things."

Leigh interrupted him. "We sampled the blood from the Shroud and found anomalies. We're not done processing everything yet, and we're not sure, frankly, that we had enough samples for a complete picture. We may. We'll have to wait. But we can sample the blood on the Sudarium and see if there is a match. We can take samples without damaging the cloth. We may be able to prove that the Sudarium and the Shroud came from the same man. And we can get a complete sample of the DNA and see what these anomalies are all about."

Father Goya shook his head. "There are procedures for these studies. People that must sign off—" he trailed off.

"I'm sure those procedures do not involve the Sudarium being transported into the mountains by a single priest in the middle of the night," Jonathan said with a skeptical raised eyebrow.

Father Goya smiled but said nothing.

"Look," Jonathan said, "you know the Sudarium is in danger. I don't know how you know, but you know. It's not safe. Someone wants to destroy it. Someone wants to kill us. The best thing to do is to keep it moving," Jonathan tried to persuade the priest.

"You say someone is trying to kill you?" Father Goya asked, frowning.

"Yes. Someone killed one of the scientists working on the Shroud in his hotel room. We saw the killer in Milan. Big fellow. Arab or Moorish. And in Venice, a dark haired woman, an Italian, came damn close. She gave me this," Jonathan said, lifting his shirt and showing his bandage.

Father Goya winced. "Oh my word," he exclaimed.

"She was most unpleasant," Leigh chimed in.

"They, whoever they are, have managed to find us twice," Jonathan said.

"Did you stop to think you might have led them here?" the priest asked.

Jonathan paused. "No one followed us. We made sure. Besides, we would have seen them on the mountain path."

"That is true," Father Goya said, putting a finger to his lips, thinking, "still—"

"Look, we have time," Jonathan said, "but not much. If we figured out where you were, that big Moor will figure it out too, one way or another."

A chill went down Father Goya's spine as he thought of Father Martin. A slowly dawning certitude began to fill him that the Sudarium was not safe here. This battled with the clear command from the dream, though, and Father Goya dared not disobey what he was certain was the word of God.

"Are you okay?" Leigh asked the priest, who had a far away look in his eyes.

"Yes, yes. Sorry. Where would you go with it, with the Sudarium?" the priest asked as he regained his train of thought.

"Manchester," Jonathan said. "To Dr. Lancaster's lab."

Leigh nodded. "It will be safe there. The security is very tight," she said.

The priest closed his eyes, looking very troubled.

"Father Goya, when you said someone warned you, who did you mean?" Jonathan asked.

The priest took a deep breath. "I — I had a dream, a vision, really."

"What kind of vision?" Leigh asked, leaning in closer.

The priest's voice lowered. "Last night, I saw fire and light consuming the *Camara Santa*," he said. "And there's more," he went on, almost whispering. "I heard a voice. A voice unlike anything I've heard. It was—" his voice trailed off, "well, it was like the sound of many waters," he finished, quoting Ezekiel. Father Goya fell silent, lost in the remembrance of that voice, and stared down at the floor.

"What did it say?" Leigh asked, breaking the silence. "What did the voice say?"

Father Goya looked up.

"'Take my holy blood to the sacred mountain,'" Father Goya whispered.

The three visitors to the remote Hermitage sat silently for a moment while the wind whistled outside. A cool breeze blew in through the opened door and the red candles flickered, their light dancing over the ceiling. Suddenly, Leigh opened her eyes wide. Her mouth fell open.

"Tabor!" she exclaimed, her voice ringing out in the silence.

"What?" the priest asked.

"Yeah, what?" Jonathan asked as well.

"My lab. My company. Tabor Applied Genetics Company. Don't you see?"

"Frankly, no," Jonathan said.

"The sacred mountain," Leigh said excitedly. "The voice said take the blood to the sacred mountain."

The priest nodded. "Yes, Tabor," he said.

"Okay, either of you want to tell me what's going on?" Jonathan said, not quite understanding.

"Tabor. Mount Tabor? In Israel," Leigh said. "Mr. Historian, don't you know?" she asked and smirked.

Jonathan searched his memory as a blank expression came over his face.

"The mount of the Transfiguration," Father Goya said reverently.

Jonathan nodded as the memories of some long ago study flooded in. He saw the open book as if it were in front of him. "The mount where Jesus was transfigured, where his countenance was altered, and his raiment was white and glistering," Jonathan said softly, reading from the page in his mind.

"Tabor. Maybe," Leigh picked her words carefully, "the voice meant bring the cloth there. To my lab."

"Maybe," Father Goya thought it out, at least considering the possibility. There was no such thing as coincidence, he knew, and the fact these two made out of Turin alive and unscathed only to show up here weighed heavily on him. "Maybe," he repeated.

"Maybe we should get going," Jonathan said, not wanting to stay in any one place too long.

Father Goya considered the matter. A soft warm feeling came over him, a feeling of peace. This was surely what God wanted. "You give me your word the cloth will not be harmed?" he asked at last.

"Yes," Leigh said. "We'll use the same process as we did for the Shroud."

"And it will be returned?"

"As soon as we can do so safely, yes," Leigh said.

Father Goya nodded. Something inside told him it was the right thing to do. He knew he would not leave this mountain; it was something he was certain of. But the Sudarium must remain safe.

Jonathan and Leigh sat breathless, hanging on his decision.

"Very well," he said at last. "You will take it to your laboratory. It will be safe there."

Leigh smiled and Jonathan breathed a big sigh of relief.

"Good," Jonathan said, impatient. "Let's get going. Where is it?"

"Why, Dr. Tremaine, if you know your history, you should know," the priest said and a slight smile played over his lips.

Outside of Oviedo, Spain
May 23, 11:30 a.m.

"It is time," Asad told Samir.

They had been waiting outside the barn for the better part of half an hour. Every now and then they could hear the muffled pleadings of Father Martin coming from inside the barn.

"Isn't it difficult to do that?" Samir asked and pointed inside the barn.

"Yes. It is unpleasant. Not as unpleasant as when it is done to you," Asad said, clenching his fist without thinking. "Still, it is necessary."

Samir nodded. "It would be difficult for me to do that," he said. "To set off a bomb," he shrugged, "it is nothing. But that—" he peered at the barn door, "that is more personal."

"You know the saying: give the bow to its maker. It is part of the job, a job I know how to do well," Asad said, resigned. "He has something we need to know. And it is my job to find out." Asad straightened and took a big inhale. "Stay out here unless I call you in. Be ready, though," he said, and walked through the door.

Asad took a moment for his eyes to adjust to the dim light of the barn. Father Martin, he saw, hung from the rope, his arms twisted back behind him at an unnatural angle. The big man came close to the priest and stood facing him. He stared intently into his face.

"You disappoint me, Father Martin. I would have expected the truth from you."

The priest's face showed no surprise or shock, but only weary resignation.

Asad nodded. As he thought, the priest had lied, eager to stop the torture. He stepped around him and walked to the rope. Asad began hoisting the priest up in the air.

Father Martin let out a loud groan of pain as the movement reawakened his tortured flesh. As he rose above the ground, he whispered, "Father, forgive him," over and over. Asad pulled on the rope, gathering the slack, then released it.

Father Martin plunged towards the earth and the rope bit down. There was a sickening wet pop, which was immediately drowned out by Father Martin's scream. It rang loud in the emptiness of the barn. Asad waited patiently for the screams to die down to a soft whimper. He stood in front of the priest and looked up at him. The man's face was etched with pain.

"It is safe, priest," Asad said.

"Yes, it is," Father Martin mumbled, almost whispering it.

"I must take you to it, priest," Asad said, his voice calm and soothing.

"Yes."

"Where do I take you?" Asad asked as casually as he could.

Father Martin, delirious from the pain, moaned.

"Mon—," he began to say, then trailed off.

"Where?"

"It is safe," the priest said, some still conscious part of him catching himself.

Asad rose again, shaking his head.

So close, he thought.

He decided to try another tactic. He went and picked up the canvas bag that he had tossed aside earlier. Asad unwinched the rope, lowering Father Martin down. When his feet touched the ground his arms lowered and he groaned anew at the pain. Asad quickly put the canvas bag over the priest's head again and tied it off. He winched the rope back up, bringing with it a new series of screams from the man. He left the barn, leaving the priest in darkness.

Asad squinted as he walked out into the light.

"Any luck?" Samir asked.

"Not yet. He is close, though. I have an idea, and I will need your help."

Monsacro, the Sacred Mountain, Spain
May 23, 2025   11:34 a.m.

Jonathan glanced around the inside of the Hermitage. "So where is it?" he asked again.

"Dr. Tremaine, why, in the Well of San Toribio, of course," Father Goya said with a smile. He rose from the rickety wooden chair and walked to the altar at the other side of the room. He took a cloth off the altar and pointed underneath. "The Well of San Toribio," the priest said, unveiling it.

Jonathan rose from his chair and walked, open-eyed with wonder, towards the altar.

"Who's San Toribio?" Leigh asked.

"Scholars are divided, but he was most likely a bishop in the seventh century," Jonathan said distractedly as he peered under the altar.

"It is said that he was warned in a dream to move the Sudarium in order to save it from Muslim invaders," Father Goya added.

Jonathan rose up and smiled. "See? History repeats itself. San Toribio moved it to this spot here where this altar now stands."

Leigh stepped over and looked under the altar. There was a rectangular cut-out in the stone which held an ornate box.

"This building, this Hermitage, was built later for the pilgrims that would come here, even after the Sudarium was moved to Oviedo," Jonathan explained.

"Almost no one comes here anymore," Father Goya said. "Just a few come for masses on a few feast days, is all."

"So the Sudarium is in that box there?" Leigh asked.

"Yes," the priest said.

"Can we see it?" she asked.

"Of course."

The priest knelt down and scooted his fingers to the side of reliquary, prying it from its stony temporary home. He set it on top of the altar. The reliquary itself, ornate with gold trim at the corners, looked rather like an oversized attaché case. Father Goya unclasped the ancient latches holding it shut and carefully and reverently opened it. The old hinges of the reliquary creaked in the silence of the Hermitage.

Jonathan and Leigh looked on, inching closer. They half-expected rays of light to come streaming out. They held their breath and looked in. Inside, there was a purple satin cloth, which Father Goya gently lifted, revealing the Sudarium.

They both stared at it, transfixed.

Leigh got closer, drawn to it. The Sudarium itself looked exactly like what Jonathan had described earlier — a stained cloth. Only this stain contained the blood of Jesus Christ and, Leigh hoped, a full DNA sample and some answers. A shiver went through her. "It's—" Leigh trailed off, at a loss for words.

"It's a 2000-year-old dirty linen cloth," Jonathan said.

"No, it's more," Leigh said. "I can't describe it, but it feels like the Shroud. I get that same feeling when I see it." She looked up at Jonathan, eyes misting.

"I have seen it many times," Father Goya said, "and I always feel as you do. If anything, the feeling gets stronger."

The three stood in silence, clustered around the small altar and the holy relic upon it. Red lights from the candles danced and flickered over the ancient chapel, giving the scene a surreal and timeless quality.

"Let's get going," Jonathan said, breaking the spell. He was eager to get started on the hike back.

Father Goya carefully closed the box and prayed silently. That peace he'd felt before filled him. The Sudarium would be safe with them. He handed it to Jonathan.

Jonathan thanked him.

"Yes, thank you," Leigh added.

"Take good care of it," Father Goya said.

"We will," Leigh said.

"Let's go," Jonathan said and walked towards the door. Leigh followed, but the priest stood still. Jonathan paused.

"Let's go, Father," he said.

Father Goya smiled and shook his head. "I will not be joining you."

"What?"

"I will be staying here."

"Nonsense," Jonathan said. "Let's go. We'll help you down."

"I did not tell you part of that dream, that vision. I will not leave this mountain alive."

"Now that is total nonsense. Come on," Jonathan insisted.

"Yes, let's go, Father," Leigh pleaded with concern.

"It is fine. It is the way it is supposed to end," the priest said, giving them a kindly smile.

Leigh went over to him. "Are you sure?"

"More sure than I have been of anything. Take the Sudarium, keep it safe. I know, in my heart, that you two will bring a message of hope to millions. Billions, even," Father Goya said.

Leigh, eyes watering, hugged the priest. "Be well," she said.

"You too, my child," the priest said and, to Jonathan, "take care of her."

Jonathan nodded solemnly. "I will," he said with conviction.

Jonathan stepped out the door, carrying the reliquary under his arm and Leigh followed. They stepped out onto the bright mountaintop and began the long walk down, leaving Father Goya at the door of the Hermitage.

The priest took one last look at the sunny blue skies and went back inside. He knelt in front of the altar, looking at the empty rectangular cut-out in the floor, and began to pray for the two travelers. He was convinced they would need all the help they could get.

Outside of Oviedo, Spain
May 23, 2025 12:30 p.m.

Samir checked his semiautomatic again and chambered a round.

"You're sure you understand?" Asad asked him again.

"Yes."

"Give me five minutes, then do as we discussed," the big man said.

He went towards the barn door and opened it. Asad went inside into darkness, and waited for his eyes to adjust.

Father Martin hung from the rope attached to the pulley on the rafters. He swayed slowly. His hands, tied behind him, were two purple claws clutching an unseen object. He was breathing hard and cold sweat dripped onto the dirt-covered floor.

"Priest, you can make this stop at any time," Asad said as he walked near the bound man.

Father Martin's head, still encased in the canvas sack, turned in Asad's direction. He groaned and mumbled a plea for help.

"I am going to give you one more chance, priest," Asad said, glancing down at his watch. "If you think you know pain now, this is nothing compared to what is next."

"I — I can't," Father Martin croaked out.

"You can," Asad said in a caring and understanding tone. "It is inevitable. Don't you see that? The only thing you can control is the pain. Now," Asad said as he pulled on the rope, hoisting the priest higher, "tell me where you moved it to. Do not make me let go of the rope again."

Father Martin felt himself rise into the air. He chased away evil and vengeful thoughts and instead said, "I forgive you."

Asad winced from these words, but let go of the rope nonetheless.

There was a moment of silence as the priest fell. Then, the rope around his wrists bit down and was pulled taut. The air left Father Martin's lungs and he hung there, unable to even scream. Eventually, short ragged breaths came to him and he prayed that he would pass out, but he did not. His whole world was darkness and pain and he wished for it to end.

Asad looked at his watch again. It was almost time.

"The next step is stones. Inquisitors would tie heavy stones to the victim's legs to pull down even harder. Surely you don't want to—"

The barn door burst open. Samir ran in yelling, in Spanish, "Stop! *Guardia Civil!*" he called out, identifying himself as the authority that policed rural Spain.

He pointed his gun towards the rafters and fired off two rounds, which cracked like thunder in the empty barn. Asad let out a grunt and fell to the ground, lying motionless but examining the priest carefully.

The noise and gunshots startled Father Martin. He glanced around in vain and saw only the inside of the canvas bag.

"Help me!" he cried out.

"Are you okay?" Samir asked, running towards him.

"No. Help me down," the priest cried out again.

"Looks like I arrived just in time," Samir said, continuing the ruse. "The others should be here shortly."

Samir went to the rope while Asad, still lying on the ground, looked on. As carefully as he could, Samir brought the priest down, who groaned with every movement the slack allowed.

"An ambulance is on the way, do not worry," Samir said, "but we need to know where the Sudarium was moved to. It is in great danger."

Father Martin, blinded both by pain and the canvas bag still around his head, did not have time to think. "Yes. It is safe," he breathed out, "in Monsacro. Father Goya has it."

"Where in Monsacro?" Samir asked.

"At the Hermitage," Father Martin croaked out. He barely stood on shaky legs, his arms bent upwards still at an unnatural angle.

Asad got up, smiling. He clapped a hand on Samir's back.

"Well done," he complemented the younger man.

At the sound of Asad's voice, Father Martin froze. After a moment of confusion, the realization of what had happened seeped in. Even before the bag was taken off his head, he knew he'd been tricked. He had led these evil men right to the holy Sudarium. Father Martin fell to his knees despite the pain, and prayed for forgiveness.

Asad looked down on the man with something resembling pity. The priest had been a tough one, much tougher than he looked or Asad had expected. He respected the man. Asad took the bag off the priest's head.

Father Martin looked up with defeated eyes. "Make it quick, please," Father Martin pleaded.

Asad nodded. "You deserve that much," he said.

Asad bent down and wrapped his big arm around the priest's neck.

Father Martin closed his eyes and prayed, "Father, into your hands I commit my—"

With a practiced twist, Asad cut the priest's words short and ended his life.

CHAPTER 9

Monsacro, the Sacred Mountain, Spain
May 23, 12:54 p.m.

Leigh walked in front of Jonathan and scrambled down the steep path, sending loose rock flying.

"Careful, it's slippery," she said. "Hand me the box."

"Nah, I can handle it," Jonathan said, and took a step down the path.

The gravel gave way before him and he slipped, falling on his backside. He hugged the reliquary to his chest and slid down the steep path on the seat of his pants, as if he were on a slide at a playground. He came to a stop at Leigh's feet.

She looked down at him and, seeing he was fine, let out a short laugh.

"I suppose you think that was funny?" Jonathan asked from the ground, trying to stand and recover what was left of his dignity.

Leigh started to say something and let out a loud giggle. "No, of course—" her words were cut off as she giggled again. "I'm sorry," she said, trying to compose herself, and laughed again.

Despite himself, Jonathan smiled, then broadened it into a grin. "At least help an old man up," he said, reaching out a hand.

"Certainly," Leigh said. She took the reliquary from him and offered a hand, pulling him up.

"It wasn't that funny," he said, patting down his clothes and sending puffs of dust flying.

"I beg to differ. It was," Leigh said and giggled again.

Jonathan smiled and took the reliquary back, holding it in one hand. With this other hand he made a sweeping gesture. "Ladies first."

Leigh walked past him, patting him on the butt and sending more dust flying. "You missed a spot," she said and coyly smiled and walked on.

"Very cute," Jonathan said and continued down the path.

The noonday sun had chased away most of the clouds and fog. The air was crisp and they could see the long mountain path snaking beneath them, stretching to the green and boulder-strewn valley below. Ahead of them was a dewy green field and a herd of cows placidly grazing. The path went right through the grazing cows.

"Look out for that guy," Jonathan said, pointing out a bull at the far end of the field.

"That's a big bull," Leigh said.

The reddish brown bull turned to them with its big horns gleaming in the sun. It started meandering towards them.

"Um, it's coming towards us," Leigh said.

"Don't worry, just ignore him."

"You're going to tell me you were a bullfighter, too?"

"Actually, I used to — no, I'm just kidding. Just don't spook him," Jonathan said.

The bull stopped a few yards away, eyeing them. They walked past, keeping a wary eye on him.

"See? Nothing to it," Jonathan said confidently. At that moment, the bull broke into a trot. "Crap," Jonathan hissed. "Run!"

They ran down the rocky path, careful to keep their footing. The bull snorted once then stopped and watched the two intruders to his field run away.

Once they were safely down the path, Jonathan stopped and turned to look at the bull. Leigh kept running down the hill, fists and legs pumping.

"Hey, it's okay," Jonathan called out, but Leigh continued to run. "Leigh!" he called out again. She kept running and he yelled after her again.

Leigh finally stopped, one hundred yards down the path, and turned.

"It's okay!" Jonathan called out again, then started to laugh.

"Okay, that was not funny, mister," Leigh yelled across the valley.

Jonathan jogged to her. "Oh yes it was," he said, catching up.

Leigh narrowed her eyes.

"You should have seen yourself run," Jonathan joked with her. "I didn't know you had it in you."

"Hush," Leigh said, then gave him the barest trace of a smile.

"At that rate, we'll be down this mountain in no time," he said. "Though I don't know if I could keep up."

She gave him a look and smiled and said, "Let's go, cowboy."

The two walked side-by-side down the path as the noon sun warmed the rocks around them.

Outside Oviedo, Spain
May 23, 2025 1:19 p.m.

Samir downshifted into third and pressed the accelerator. The Audi's big engine let out a muted roar and the car shot ahead, easily passing the line of cars and the big truck that was slowing the traffic. He got back into his lane with plenty of time before the oncoming traffic rushed past.

"Is this the right way?" he asked.

"Yes," Asad said quietly from the passenger's seat. The time with the priest was weighing on him. The man's composure and pleas for forgiveness for his torturer had affected Asad, he was reluctant to admit. *People are slaves to good deeds*, he thought, remembering the proverb from his childhood. He pushed these thoughts away and concentrated on the job.

Asad focused on his phone. He scrolled through the map and pinched the screen, zooming out.

"According to this, turn off at the MO-4 and go towards the town of Los Llanos. At the end of the road there will be a village named Otura."

"Then what?"

"Then we walk. This website said it was an hour and a half hike up the mountain to the Hermitage." Asad poked at the phone, saving the page for later should they need it.

"Are you sure about this?" Samir asked, and passed another line of cars. The scenic mountains blurred by.

"Yes. You heard the priest. He was not lying. The Sudarium is there," Asad said confidently. At the thought of the priest, that feeling returned again, a feeling he could not quite identify. It was not quite regret, not quite guilt. Whatever it was, it was taking his focus away and he tamped it back down.

They drove down the country road in silence, passing the slower cars easily two and three at a time.

"I cannot wait to destroy this thing and be done," Samir said.

"We will not destroy it," Asad told him.

"What?"

"We will hold on to it until we are paid. Once we are safely away with our money, then we will hand it over or destroy it or do whatever the Lawyer wants."

Samir nodded. "Good thinking."

"Always cover your back and your trail," Asad advised him.

Samir nodded again.

"Here we are," Asad pointed out the road sign to the MO-4.

Samir slowed the Audi and turned onto the narrow steep road, keeping as fast a pace as he could on the snaking road. The mountains here were lush with woods, and the road was canopied with trees, as if the forest itself wanted to grow over the road. The sun shining through the trees painted dapples of light on the steel-gray car as they drove from switchback to switchback, speeding up in the straights and slowing for the sharp corners. A car approached from the opposite direction and Samir slowed as the two passed each other on the narrow road. Gradually, they climbed the mountain and got nearer and nearer to the village of Otura and the Sudarium in the mountains beyond.

Near Otura, on Monsacro, the Sacred Mountain, Spain
May 23, 2025 1:22 p.m.

"Finally!" Leigh exclaimed.

The two rounded a bend in the path where it leveled out and led to the village.

"Look, I can see our car from here," Jonathan said, pointing out the light-green speck of the Fiat in the distance.

"It's about time. First stop is going to have to be food. I'm starving," Leigh said.

They walked down the path, past the horse farm and the two white horses still grazing, and along the small stone wall that ran along the path as it gradually turned to a gravel road. Jonathan shifted the ornate wooden reliquary containing the Sudarium to his other hand.

At last, they reached the stone retaining wall overlooking the tiny plaza where the car was parked. Exhausted after the long hike, they both went towards the wall. Jonathan set the reliquary down.

"Whew," he breathed out. "I'll be glad to stop carrying that."

Leigh sat down and let out a long sigh. "I could sit here for an hour, it feels so good," she said. She leaned her head back and closed her eyes, letting the sun kiss her face.

"We don't have an hour," Jonathan said.

"Aw, come on. Give a girl five minutes at least."

"Okay, five minutes. Then we're gone."

On the MO-4, near Otura, Spain
May 23, 2025 1:33 p.m.

"How much longer?" Samir asked as he skillfully took another turn.

"Five minutes," Asad said, looking at the navigation on his phone while he braced himself against the turns. "Just five more kilometers. Probably quicker as fast as you drive."

A smile appeared on Samir's handsome face. "Hey, I like my new car," he said, and downshifted. The car shot forward, closer and closer.

Otura, Spain
May 23, 2025 1:36 p.m.

"Okay, let's go," Jonathan said.

"That didn't feel like five minutes," Leigh remarked.

"It wasn't. All this silence," Jonathan said and looked around the peaceful deserted village, "it makes me edgy."

Leigh rose, stiff legged, and groaned. "Alright."

Jonathan got up too and picked up the reliquary. They walked on unsteady tired legs down the stairs to the plaza and to the car.

Jonathan set the reliquary down by the Fiat. "I'm going to feel this tomorrow," he said, and stretched. He fished for the keys in his pocket, patting one pocket, then the other. An expression of alarm spread over his face. "Uh-oh," he said.

"What is it?" Leigh asked, worried, standing in front of him.

"The keys."

"The what?"

"The keys to the car," he patted his pockets again. "I must have left them at the Hermitage."

"What?" Leigh asked, her tone a mixture of anger and concern.

"They must be at the Hermitage. You're going to have to go get them," Jonathan said, straight-faced.

Leigh stared at him open-mouthed.

"I'll stay here with the car," Jonathan said. "You just run up there and get the keys."

Leigh narrowed her eyes and almost snarled. "If you think I'm going back up there because you forgot—"

"Wait, what's this?" Jonathan brought his hands to Leigh's ear and, with a flourish, produced the set of keys. "There they are," he said and grinned.

Leigh stared at him dumbly for a second, then the concern left her face, but some of that anger remained.

"Why you!" She hit him in the arm. "You think that's funny?"

"You're cute when you're angry, you know that?" he said, still grinning, and turning his body away from her fists.

Leigh shook her head and despite herself, smiled a little. She hit him again. "You're daft. Let's go before you really do lose the keys."

Jonathan walked to the passenger door and unlocked it. He folded the seat forward and placed the reliquary with the precious relic in the back seat. He folded the seat back again and, with a sweep of his hand, said, "Milady, your carriage."

Leigh smiled and sat. Jonathan ran to the other side and climbed in and started the little Fiat.

"It's a long way to Manchester. Maybe you'll let me drive some this time," Leigh said, her arms folded and a playful pout on her lips as she recalled his refusal to let her drive on the last trip.

"Absolutely. You'll get the hang of it yet," Jonathan said and smiled. He revved the engine twice, slipped it into gear, and scooted forwards.

The Audi rounded the bend. The road straightened out in front of Asad and Samir, and the tiny town of Otura lay ahead of them. A small green Fiat, an older model, came towards them and Samir inched to the right to let the car pass on the narrow road.

Asad looked at the car as it approached, then at the people in it. His eyes went wide.

"Look at this guy, hogging the road," Jonathan said as he scooted to the side, almost to the soft shoulder of the narrow road.

They approached the Audi, slowing down to pass alongside. Jonathan looked at the driver, a handsome young man with darker skin, then turned to look at the passenger. Past the reflections on the windshield from the dappled sun filtering through the canopy of trees overhead, Jonathan saw the face of the big Moor, the man from Milan. His heart dropped.

Asad reached over and grabbed the steering wheel, yanking on it and careening the Audi to the middle of the road.

"What are you doing?" Samir yelled out and corrected the steering to avoid the Fiat passing alongside. Asad renewed his grip on the wheel and the Audi lurched to the side, clipping the little Fiat on the back.

"It's them," Asad almost yelled.

Leigh let out a little scream, which was drowned out by the revving of the little engine as Jonathan floored the accelerator. The car was tossed to the side and the back end was knocked towards the ditch running alongside the road. The back right tire spun in the air and the corner of the car slipped, falling into the ditch. Jonathan snicked the shifter into second and floored it. The front wheels clawed at the ground and took hold, propelling the car forward. Jonathan straightened it and then passed the tail of Audi, shooting forward and out of the ditch.

"What the bloody hell was that?" Leigh asked.

"It's the Moor, the man from Milan," Jonathan said and changed into third.

The Fiat sped down the road and the Audi got smaller and smaller in the rearview mirror.

"What is he doing here?" Leigh asked, looking back at the car, which was trying to turn on the narrow road. They entered the bends and she lost sight.

"Coming to get this," Jonathan said, hitching a thumb at the Sudarium in the backseat. "And to finish the job with us," he added grimly.

"Oh, God," Leigh whispered under her breath.

"Turn around!" Asad yelled out.

Samir tried to turn on the narrow road, but it was difficult. He was sideways, the front and rear of the car almost in the ditches that lined the road. At last, he maneuvered the Audi around. With one final turn, he floored it and the car shot forward.

"What is going on?" Samir asked as he blasted down the straight, then slowed for the corner before flooring it again as he cleared the apex.

"Those are the scientists from Turin, the ones that got away. They must have the Sudarium or a sample; there is no other reason for them being here."

"Are you sure they have it? I thought the other priest had it," Samir said, eyes focused on the road.

"I don't know if they have it, but it doesn't matter. We need them dead. It is part of the job, and there's a nice bonus in it for you."

Samir smiled. "That's all you had to say."

He gripped the steering wheel and stared intently at the road ahead and the rapidly approaching green Fiat.

Leigh was practically turned around in her seat looking out the rear window. "Hurry, he's closing," she warned Jonathan.

The Audi's LED headlights, a slanted and evil gleam in the darkness of the canopied forest, loomed larger and larger.

"I'm wooding it," he said. "This is as fast as she goes."

The Audi closed fast as they approached a sharp turn. Jonathan feathered the accelerator and bent the Fiat into the corner, carrying most of his speed as the tires squealed in protest. Leigh grabbed for the bar above her head and gave a little yelp of surprise. The little car slid through the turn.

Jonathan checked the rearview mirror and the Audi was gone, left behind as the bigger, heavier car had to brake into the turn.

"Speed up," Asad told Samir.

"You don't want to end up in a ditch, do you?" Samir asked.

Asad shook his head.

"We will catch him on the straights. Do not worry," Samir said and floored it out of the bend.

"He's catching up again," Leigh said.

The Audi quickly closed the distance between them. Jonathan tried to nudge the car forward, flogging it as fast as the small engine would spin. He looked up into the rearview mirror. The Audi loomed large.

"Hold on," he said.

The Audi was on his bumper now, trying to get around him. Jonathan swerved to the side to block it. The Audi lunged forward and hit their bumper.

Jonathan kept it under control. "Hold on to your lunch," he said.

"I haven't had lunch."

"Hold on anyway."

Jonathan eyed the long tight turn ahead and went as wide as he dared, painting the outside white line, before bending the Fiat on a textbook racing line through the turn. The Audi fell away behind him, the bigger car's back end stepping out a little as the driver braked too hard. The Fiat slid through the turn on a four-wheel drift, with just enough grip to keep it on the road, and carried most of its speed out.

Asad grabbed at the dash as the Audi hunched forwards on its brakes and the rear stepped out. The tires protested as Samir plowed into the curve. He watched helplessly as the little Fiat slid easily through the curve and got further and further away as he had to scrub off speed to keep the big car on the road. Samir said nothing and focused intently on his driving, both hands gripping the steering wheel hard, and barely keeping the car inside the lines.

"Careful," Asad counseled him.

Jonathan upshifted. Ahead of him was a long straight, which was the last thing he wanted. The trees thinned and here and there the sun shone hard through the gaps. The bends he could dance through, he thought, but the straights were trouble. He tried to build up as much of a lead as he could, revving the engine within an inch of its life. The Audi came out of the turn and into view, catching up again.

"Oh, Jonathan," Leigh called out with concern as she looked at the car closing fast.

"We'll be okay," he said, not really believing it.

The Audi closed fast.

"Hold on," Leigh warned and braced herself.

There was a loud crunch and the Fiat jumped forward as the Audi hit it squarely from behind.

Jonathan sawed at the steering wheel, trying to keep the little car pointed forward. The Audi revved hard, its engine loud, and it lunged forward to try to pass them. Jonathan eyed it in the sideview mirror and slid over, blocking him and receiving another hit as their reward.

"If he gets beside us, we're dead," Jonathan said, fighting with the steering wheel to keep control.

Again the Audi tried to get around, this time on the other side. Jonathan cut him off, dividing his attention between the road ahead and the murderous car behind.

"You're not going to get around him, not like that," Asad said.

"Don't worry, I'll get him," Samir replied.

He accelerated, getting right up to the Fiat's bumper, a little offset, then floored it, pushing the little car forward and diagonally.

"Ah, crap," Jonathan exclaimed.

He felt the Fiat being pushed forward, then starting to drift sideways. Jonathan steered slightly the opposite way to correct it.

"Just a little further," he said as he looked at the road coming up. Ahead, the forest canopy returned and the road turned curvy again.

Metal groaned and plastic broke as the Audi tried to push them off the road. The big car was starting to overpower them and Jonathan knew he had to do something, and quickly. A big switchback approached, the hairpin turn dropping rapidly as it rounded a hill. Jonathan spied a worn footpath cutting from the top of the road, right before the switchback, to somewhere on the bottom. The footpath cut the corner in half.

"This is going to be ugly. Hold on," he warned.

"What's going to be ugl—?" Leigh's words were cut off with a gasp and a scream.

With a sharp tug, Jonathan turned as hard as he could. The Fiat's tires howled as the car got almost sideways and careened off the road and onto the footpath. Gravel and rock flew up and peppered the undercarriage. Jonathan narrowly avoided a tree and bounced down the steep footpath, leaving the Audi and its stunned driver behind on the road. The branches of the trees clawed and scratched at the Fiat. They hit a bump and both of them flew up. Their seatbelts cinched tight, holding them down, but the reliquary in the backseat crashed against the roof of the car and back down.

Jonathan saw the road approaching fast, a large curb ready to destroy the car utterly. He sawed at the wheel and turned towards the very edge of the path where it leveled out with the road. The Fiat's tires hit the curb and the whole car bounced out of the path and back onto the road.

"Holy crap," Leigh breathed out as she looked back to the footpath they had just blazed through.

"You see him back there?" Jonathan asked as he focused on regaining control of the car on the road.

"No," Leigh, turned around in her seat, breathed out a sigh of relief. "Wait, there he is," she said with alarm.

The Audi rounded the bend, forced to take the longer way around the switchback. It sped up, closing again, fast.

Jonathan accelerated as much as he could, but the Audi relentlessly caught up to them and showed no signs of slowing, as if he was going to go right through them.

"Hold on," Leigh said and gripped the grab bar.

The Audi smashed into the back of the Fiat, sending the car bouncing forward. Jonathan slid it to the right, then the left, and tried to keep it on the road. Leigh let out a little scream.

"I've got it," Jonathan assured her as he brought it back under control.

The Audi lunged forward again, taking advantage of Jonathan's distraction. The driver tried to get alongside them, and succeeded. The big car nosed up beside Jonathan, close enough to touch. The two cars blazed down the narrow canopied road side-by-side.

Jonathan glanced out the side window. There, not three feet away, was the big Moor.

Samir gripped the wheel.

"Keep it steady," Asad said, and drew out his semi-automatic. He lowered the window and pointed the muzzle of his Heckler & Koch 45T at Jonathan's head.

Everything happened fast.

Jonathan saw the dark eye of the gun, then a glint on the road ahead from the chrome of an oncoming truck, looming huge and taking up half the road. He slammed the brakes.

Leigh screamed, and the reliquary flew forward and hit the back of the seat. The Audi disappeared as it continued speeding forward towards the big truck. The Fiat's tires grabbed and clawed at the pavement, leaving behind a black smoking streak of rubber.

Asad pulled the trigger and the gunshot cracked the air loudly, but the Fiat had disappeared. The little car braked hard and was now behind them. He looked behind him at his target screeching to a stop, then turned to Samir.

"Stop the car, I—"

Asad did not finish his sentence.

Jonathan saw it all in slow motion.

The Audi, careening in the wrong lane towards the huge truck, turned hard, swerving back into its lane too late. The truck flashed his lights and blew its horn as it grazed the Audi's back bumper. The driver of the Audi, going almost sideways now and skidding, tried to correct the slide but over-steered. The back end of the car pitched to the left then violently to the right and, suddenly, in the blink of an eye, the Audi was gone, crashing through the dense forest lining the road.

Jonathan came to a dead stop, and hunched over the steering wheel. A second later, the truck thundered past them, its brakes squealing and protesting as they tried to bring the huge bulk to a halt.

Jonathan and Leigh turned and looked at each other, speechless. The only sound was the soft purr of the engine.

"Do you think they're dead?" Leigh asked, breaking the silence.

"I don't think we'd be that lucky," Jonathan said, "but we're not going to stick around and find out."

Jonathan put the Fiat into gear and scooted cautiously forward. They passed the place where the Audi had plunged into the woods. The car itself was not visible from the road, and only a few broken branches gave any indication that anything at all had happened. They drove past the spot, half expecting the big Moor to jump out of the woods at them.

Jonathan up-shifted and accelerated down the road. He slumped back in his seat. "I need a drink," he said.

"I think I'll join you on that one, cowboy," Leigh said and sighed.

CHAPTER 10

Outside of the Monsacro, Spain
May 23, 2025 2:07 p.m.

Asad rubbed his eyes. Fine dust and bits of broken glass covered him. The airbag oozed out from the dash like a dead jellyfish. He quickly regained his composure and assessed the situation.

The Audi was resting on a steep hillside, leaning forward at a sharp angle. The hood of the car was accordioned against the trunk of a large tree, the windshield smashed by a branch. Samir was slumped forward against his seatbelt, a rivulet of blood flowing from a gash on his forehead. Asad took stock of his own body and, satisfied, reached across and put two fingers on Samir's neck, checking the unconscious man's pulse. He was alive, probably suffering from a concussion.

Asad observed his surroundings. Trees and foliage enveloped them. He tried the door but it was wedged tight against a tree. Asad peered behind them and he could see the tunnel they had carved through the forest to land here.

"Samir?" he said and shook the unconscious man.

Samir groaned and brought a hand to his head.

"You are bleeding, but it is fine. It is not bad," Asad told him. "Is anything broken?" he asked.

"I don't think so," Samir said as he wiggled his arms and legs.

Asad reached up and pressed a button on the headliner, opening the sunroof. He grabbed his gun, which had fallen to the floor, holstered it, and unbuckled himself, bracing with his hands as he slumped forward. The big man pulled himself out of the sunroof with surprising ease. Carefully, he scooted off the car and onto the damp forest floor. He gazed again at the tunnel they had carved and up to the road. They had landed twenty meters or so, by his estimation, from the road, in a steep and densely forested ravine. The ravine inclined upward at a good angle, and disappeared below them into dark impenetrable forest. Without that big tree, Asad saw, they would likely be dead.

Asad struggled for footing on the leafy wet ground. He went to the driver's side of the car and tried to open the door but could only crack it a few inches.

"You're going to have to crawl out," he told Samir, pointing at the sunroof.

Samir nodded and slowly and unsteadily made his way out, landing with a thud on the ground and breathing hard. He contemplated his ruined car and shook his head. Asad clapped a hand on his back.

"Do not worry, you can buy another. Let us go."

The two climbed up the ravine, aiding their ascent with the small saplings that covered the mountainside. Asad climbed ahead. As he cleared the forest and stepped onto the road, the truck driver ran towards him.

"Oh, you're alive. Thank God," the truck driver, a short thick-set man with a large mustache, said in Spanish. Then, with a twinge of anger, he added, "What the hell were you doing on my side of the road?"

Asad looked at the man, then at the truck, which was sitting further up the road stopped with its hazards flashing. Asad decided his next move in an instant.

"Please help me with my friend," Asad said. "He is still down there."

Asad went to the edge of the forest, a couple of feet off the road. The truck driver came near.

"Where?"

"Right over there," Asad said, pointing.

In a flash, Asad wrapped his big arms around the truck driver's neck and twisted. The man slumped into Asad's embrace, dead. He lowered the truck driver to the ground as Samir, still somewhat dazed, emerged from the trees and looked on. Asad searched the man's pockets, drawing out a set of keys. He then unceremoniously shoved the body down the ravine with his foot. The truck driver's body tumbled down and landed with a thump against the trunk of a tree, well out of sight of the road.

Asad looked at the body impassively for a second. He clenched his fists, the old scars itching. He cleared his mind.

"Let's go," he said, and started walking towards the truck.

"Where?" Samir asked, following.

"To the Hermitage, to where the priest said the Sudarium was. It is our only choice now. We will not be catching the scientists in that," he pointed at the truck as they neared it, "and, besides, I have to see for myself whether the Sudarium is there or not."

Samir nodded. The two walked up to the big truck.

"I'll drive," Asad said as he thought of what to do next.

"Be my guest," Samir said, holding his head. He climbed into the passenger's seat.

Asad started the truck and put it into gear, inching forward up the mountain and picking up speed.

"Check in the glove box. There should be a first-aid kit there, or behind the seat. Take care of that gash," Asad advised the younger man.

Samir looked in the mirror and winced. He rooted in the glove box and brought out a rudimentary first-aid kit.

"When we get to the top, I want you to take the truck," Asad said as he put a plan together. "Get to the airport and rent a car, something fast. Lose the truck, park it somewhere inconspicuous, then meet me back here," Asad told him, then added, "Are you good to drive?"

"Yes, I will be fine."

"I will take two or three hours to get to the Hermitage and back," Asad said.

Samir nodded, then winced as he cleaned the gash with an alcohol swab. He bandaged the wound as best he could.

"What will you do up there?" Samir said.

"I will see if the Sudarium is up there, and get it. If it is not, then the scientists have it and we will go after them. Hopefully the Lawyer can find them again. He has been tracking them somehow."

Asad changed gears and the truck rounded the sharp bend and labored up the mountain. He thought of the unpleasant task awaiting him on top of the mountain, and of calling the Lawyer, and wondered which was worse.

CHAPTER 11

On the A-8, Spain
May 23, 2025 2:47 p.m.

Jonathan slowed the car, stopping to pay the toll, and accelerated away. A nasty rattling noise came from underneath the car.

"That does not sound good," he told Leigh.

"What do you think it is?" she asked.

"Don't know. Let's stop at the next service station and check."

"You're a mechanic?" Leigh asked with a skeptical raised eyebrow.

"Not really. Old cars like this, I can muddle through the basics. The new stuff," he shrugged, "I can't do anything with all that electrical stuff."

They sped down the highway as fast as they could go, the car protesting with that insistent rattle.

Leigh brought the tablet out of her bag and poked at the screen.

"Anything?" Jonathan asked.

"Nothing. Still dead. I'll have to wait until Manchester I suppose."

A red light lit up on the car's dash.

"Crap," Jonathan hissed, looking at the brake warning light. "Brake problem," he said.

He continued driving, a little slower, and passed a sign reading *"Area de Servicios."*

"There we go," Jonathan said and he pulled off the highway and down a long exit ramp to a large service station. There was a large restaurant and store, a few gas pumps, and multiple Hi-Volt charging stations. The place was busy, with cars coming and going and those people with the electric cars milling around waiting for them to charge.

Jonathan pulled up to a gas pump and shut the car off. The rattling finally stopped and left them in silence.

"I'm going to look at this," he said, turning to Leigh.

"I'll go get us food," she said, and got out of the car.

Jonathan stepped out and popped the hood, then went to the back of the car. He took a moment to gaze at Leigh's petite figure as she crossed the station and walked towards the store. "Back to business," he whispered to himself, and opened the hatchback and searched inside, looking for the jack. *Nice,* he thought to himself as he found not only the jack, but a small toolkit and a bunch of rags. Soon, he had the car jacked up and was crawling under it, rag in hand. He examined the undercarriage for a time.

Leigh came back and kicked at Jonathan's legs, which were sticking out from under the car.

"Hey mister, find anything?" she asked.

Jonathan crawled out, wiping his hands on one of the rags.

"Actually, I did. That horrible rattling noise is nothing. Just a heat shield from the exhaust that's come loose. Now this, though," he held up a stained rag, "this is more serious."

"What is it?" Leigh asked, looking at the rag covered with reddish brown stains.

"Brake fluid. Got a bit of a leak under there," he said, wiping his hands with a rag. "It should be okay as long as we keep it filled. I'll go buy us a few bottles."

"Before you go," Leigh stopped him, "I need the phone to call the lab and let Tony know we have the Sudarium and have him get everything ready. And I should call the Old Man too," she said.

"Very well, but don't be too long," he said, and handed her his phone and the battery. "Need anything from inside?"

Leigh held up a bag with her purchases. "Got it sorted," she said, smiling.

"Be right back," Jonathan said and went off towards the store.

Leigh inserted the battery and swiped on the phone. She scrolled through the names. Jonathan had Lahmbrecht's number filed under "Old Man." She smiled and pressed the send key.

"Mr. Lahmbrecht's office," his assistant answered.

"Hi, this is Doctor Leigh Lancaster, is he in?"

"One moment," the voice said and put her on hold.

Leigh waited, leaning against the little Fiat. The distant highway droned like the low purr of a giant cat from behind a stand of trees. Leigh nervously kept an eye on the cars pulling into the service station, half expecting the big Moor to come leaping out of one of them.

"Doctor Lancaster," Lahmbrecht's unmistakable slow and deliberate voice sounded out.

"Hello, sir," Leigh said, getting into the car where it was quieter.

"Where are you?" he asked.

"Spain, sir, leaving Oviedo. There's been some," she paused, searching for the word, "developments."

"What kind of developments?"

"Well, I'm sure you've heard of the terrorist bombing in Spain."

"Yes, of course. There was a man, a priest, on the news that said the Sudarium was safe."

"It is," Leigh said.

"The priest would not say where though. No one I have contacted knows where it is."

"Actually, I do," Leigh said, glancing in the back seat at the reliquary.

"You do?" Lahmbrecht asked. She could swear she heard an edge of surprise in his voice.

"Yes."

"Where is it?" he asked, his voice again uncharacteristically tinged with a trace of agitation.

"My back seat," Leigh said, and winced. A small part of her thought the less people that knew they had the Sudarium, the better. Even if that meant the head of the project, Rudolph Lahmbrecht.

"Your what?" Lahmbrecht asked.

Leigh was sure she heard disbelief or surprise in his voice. She wished she'd been on a vid-phone to see his face.

"My back seat," she repeated. "We have it with us."

"I will send someone for it," he said immediately.

"No. We're taking it to Manchester ourselves, to my lab. We'll be able to run the tests there, before the Spanish catch wind and ask for it back," she said with conviction.

There was a long pause from Lahmbrecht as he considered this. "Very well. Keep me informed of any changes. And call me when you get to Manchester."

"Yes, sir."

Lahmbrecht hung up. Leigh looked at the phone a moment, and looked up to the store. She could see Jonathan still in there past the plate glass windows. She dialed the lab.

"Tabor Applied Genetics," a pert female voice answered.

"Hi, Nicole, it's me. Can you put me through to Tony?"

"Sure thing, Dr. L," she said and put her on hold.

"Leigh!" Tony Subramanium answered with his slight Hindi accent. "What a relief. I've been trying to reach you, but it keeps saying your number is out of service."

"Hi, Tony," Leigh said and smiled. "Yes, I kind of," she hesitated, "messed up the iTablet. I got it — well, a little wet. Soaked, really."

"Oh my," Tony thought a moment. "Well, the memory should be okay. We can get the data out when you get here."

"Good. That's what I thought," Leigh said, relieved.

"Listen," Tony said, "about that data, I've been analyzing the samples you sent. There are," he paused, "well, there's something strange there."

"Strange? Is that your scientific assessment?" Leigh asked lightheartedly.

"Quite. I've run the samples through four times. I keep finding huge swaths of the same base over and over. Pages and pages of Thymine. I've never seen anything like it."

"That is strange," Leigh said, pursing her lips.

"I thought it may be a transmission error, so I was hoping to get a direct reading from the data you have," he said.

"We'll be able to do better than that," Leigh said, looking at the reliquary in the backseat.

"How's that?"

"I'm," she paused, taking a breath. "I'm bringing in a sample."

"An actual sample?" Tony asked.

"Yes. A piece of cloth with the blood. Get everything ready for it. We'll be there in a day or less."

"Leigh, this is all," he searched for the word, "highly irregular."

"You have no idea," she said and smiled a weary smile.

"What's going on?" he asked.

"I'll fill you in when we get there."

"Be careful," Tony said, concerned.

"I will," she said and looked out the windshield to Jonathan who was walking back, juggling three bottles of brake fluid and a couple of bottles of some drink in his hands. "I'm in good hands," she added.

"See you soon," Tony said.

"Take care," she said and hung up.

Jonathan returned to the car and set down the bottles on the roof. He filled the brake reservoir, closed the hood, and put the rest of the bottles and the rags in the trunk. He lowered the car and put the jack back and closed the hatch.

"Ready?" he asked, getting in.

"Ready," Leigh said and smiled.

"What did you get us to eat?" he asked.

"Cookies. Lots of cookies."

PART 4

John sat in the crowded room, full of sullen and scared faces. There was a cry outside, and he rose up. The women burst in. "They have taken him," they all said at once. The room erupted in arguments, the men disbelieving the women and chastising them. Mary took John and Peter aside. "They have taken away the Lord out of the tomb," she told them, her face lined with grief and sincerity. John and Peter glanced at each other, and Peter ran out the door. John followed, running fast, the wind in his face. He passed Peter, and arrived at the tomb first, breathless. The stone was rolled away. John cautiously put his head in the tomb and saw the linen Shroud, lying flat against the stone, and the strips of linen that had bound it tight still tied together. The blood-soaked Sudarium was still in the nook. Peter charged into the entrance of the tomb, rushing in. John followed him, and stared in disbelief at the empty tomb and the Shroud lying there. He approached it, reaching out his hand, as if to touch it would make him believe. He got close and saw the bloodstains and the faint outline of the Master's face etched somehow onto the cloth. He and Peter exchanged a look of confusion and bewilderment, and ran back out to tell the others.

CHAPTER 1

Miami, Florida
May 23, 2025 8:47 a.m. EST

Mildred Johnston walked down the richly carpeted hall with the file in her hand. She opened the thick solid mahogany door into her office and walked past her desk, checking the message light to see if anyone had called while she was down at the archives. She didn't understand why her boss asked for the archived original of the file rather than just accessing the copy on the computer, but, then again, she did not understand many of the things he did. She did her job, didn't ask questions, and took home a very sizable paycheck.

She paused at his door and, after taking a moment to collect herself, knocked. "It's me, Mr. Caine," she called out, as was the procedure.

"Yeah, get in here," he called out.

She took a deep breath, steeled herself, and opened the door into his richly appointed office. Inside, the office looked like a Venetian palace, with the exception of the floor-to-ceiling windows looking out on downtown Miami and Biscayne Bay beyond, gloriously lit with golden morning sunlight.

"Here is the file you requested, sir," Mildred said, laying down the tablet on the desk.

Robert Bale Caine, attorney-at-law, looked up from his gilded antique desk. He cast a glance at the archive tablet, then turned his attention back to his work.

"Is there anything else, sir?" she asked.

Before he could answer, a cell phone, sitting off to the side of his desk, began to vibrate. It buzzed and danced on the red leather surface of the antique desk.

"Get out," Caine spat out with his characteristic unpleasantness.

"Yes, sir," Mildred tightened her mouth and backed out of the room.

Caine waited for his secretary to leave, then picked up the phone. "Leon," he said, turning in his big leather chair to face the window. "I hope you have some good news. I really hope so for your sake."

Asad, half a world away, sighed, his distaste palpable over the phone.

"It is bad news," he said. "Your woman in black," he half spat out the words, "she did not take care of the scientists. I suspect they have the Sudarium, though I will not know for certain for an hour or so."

Caine grew alarmed at this new bit of news. If the scientists had the Sudarium, they could get to the lab and run more tests. That would be bad. That would be the worst-case scenario.

"Where are they?" Caine asked.

"They are leaving the Oviedo area now. I do not know for certain."

"How did you find out?"

Asad gave him a shortened version of the car chase.

"Dammit," Caine gritted his teeth.

"You will let me know their destination, yes?" Asad asked.

"Of course. As soon as I know it, I'll call you. Let me know what you find out with the Sudarium," Caine said. He stared out the window for a moment. "And don't screw up again," he added, and hung up.

Caine looked out the window at the silent Miami traffic far below and the emerald-green waters of the bay. He gripped the phone tight in his hand and resisted the urge to smash it against the plate glass window.

He sighed loudly. *There are so many balls in the air now,* he thought. These scientists that should be dead were mucking up the works. There was nothing he could do about it now, so he focused back to the task at hand.

Caine picked up the file that his secretary had brought. He swiped on the archive tablet and typed in his partner's code, unlocking it. He scrolled through the file. Sheik Abdul Rhaman Al-Khaifa's file contained many sub-menus, each representing a small part of the vast affairs that the firm of Harris, Bradford and Caine, P.A. managed for the Sheik. As big a client as the Sheik was, though, he was not the biggest.

Caine scrolled through the file. He accessed the sub-menu for Europe, and brought up the Sheik's European subsidiaries. He looked at the long list of the businesses the Sheik owned in Europe.

Caine poked at the screen, pressing buttons. "Accept incoming data?" read the pop-up page on the screen. Caine pressed "Yes" and swung around on his chair to his desktop computer, bringing up the files he had been working on that morning. With a few keystrokes, the Sheik had a new corporation in his archived file, blending into the many assets he already owned. Any search of the Sheik's files would now show Arbar Consolidated, SA, a corporation that recently made a number of large wire-transfers to one Asad Hasan, as well as certain other unsavory characters in Spain. Caine followed the instructions, typing out the sequence of commands that would cover his tracks, then locked the file again.

One less ball in the air, Caine thought and set the archive tablet to the side of the desk. He sat back in his chair and thought of what to do next. The threads were unraveling, he thought, but it was still early enough to control everything. He would have to act quickly.

He turned to his computer again, brought up the phone, and dialed.

"Yes, sir," a voice crackled from the speakers. A moment later the video streamed in of a pale dark-haired man sitting at a desk. Behind him were rows and rows of computer servers, their lights flashing rhythmically.

"Balkar," the Lawyer said, "any word on our two guests?"

"Nothing since Venice. The signal was there one second, then it was gone. Nothing for," he checked a screen off to the side, "twenty-five hours now. It's like they smashed the tablet or something."

"Or got it wet," Caine suggested, remembering Adriana's conversation.

"Yeah, that would do it," Balkar said.

"Keep an eye on it. If you get any signal, call me immediately. Interrupt whatever I'm doing."

"Of course," Balkar said.

Caine clicked "hang up" and the call ended. He rubbed his eyes. Slobodan Balkar was one of the few people that Caine had a healthy respect for. He was definitely one of the people you want on your side, thought Caine. People like Balkar that knew the hidden alleyways of computers, that knew how to track an individual tablet anywhere in the world, were useful. And dangerous. Caine had no problem being cordial to him. Of course, the large bonuses did not hurt, either. Money may not buy happiness, but it certainly bought people.

Caine rubbed his eyes again and stared out of the window at the steadily building Miami traffic. His computer chimed. It was his secretary. "Yes?" he called out without looking.

"Phone call, sir," Mildred called out through the speakers.

"Dammit, I said hold all calls," he barked out.

"Yes, sir. It's Rudolph Lahmbrecht, though, sir."

Caine sat up in his chair. "Why didn't you say so? Put him through." Caine scooted up to the desk.

A window popped up on Caine's screen and he clicked on it. The handsome, square-jawed face of Valenti, Lahmbrecht's assistant, popped into view.

"Good morning, Mr. Caine, hold for Mr. Lahmbrecht, please."

"Certainly," Caine said and waited for the firm's biggest client to appear.

The screen flickered and the wrinkled weathered face of Rudolph Lahmbrecht replaced Valenti's.

"Mr. Caine, you've no doubt heard of the incident in Turin," Lahmbrecht said, straight to the point as always.

"Yes, sir, most tragic," Caine said with just the right amount of regret and concern.

"As owner of the company funding the project, and the employer of many of the dead, there are certain liabilities and details that your firm must attend to."

"Of course, sir."

"I think it would be prudent for us to meet. Face-to-face," Lahmbrecht said.

"Certainly, sir. When would you like to meet?" Caine asked with trepidation.

"As soon as possible. There is a jet at Miami airport ready for you," Lahmbrecht said, staring intently at the screen and watching for Caine's reaction.

Caine tried to swallow, but his mouth had gone dry. Lahmbrecht was highly paranoid, probably with good cause, and hardly ever discussed important matters over the phone. Anything worth talking about meant talking face-to-face, he insisted. And that meant a trip.

"Sir, any words from the survivors?" Caine asked carefully. "I heard there were some on the news," he lied.

Lahmbrecht's creased face gave an almost imperceptible twitch. "Yes. They are on their way to Manchester, to Dr. Lancaster's genetics lab," he said.

"Yes sir. Good to hear that," Caine said and tried not to smile.

"I will see you soon, yes?" Lahmbrecht asked.

"Yes. I will send word when I'm in the air," Caine said.

Lahmbrecht hung up and the screen went dark. Caine slumped back in his chair, thought for a second, then buzzed his secretary.

"Mildred, cancel the next three days. Lahmbrecht wants to see me in England."

"Yes, sir. Shall I book a flight?" she asked through the speaker.

"No. I've got a ride," he said and clicked off the intercom.

Caine picked up the cell phone and turned to face the window again. He dialed Asad. No answer. He frowned. He set the phone down and took out another cell phone from his drawer.

He pressed the button, held the phone to his ear, and leaned back in his chair, closing his eyes. The phone connected.

"*Pronto?*" the silky voice said in Italian.

"Miss Nyx, how are you?" Caine asked, his voice soft and calm despite the beating of his heart.

"Skip it," she said, impatient. "I've been waiting for your call. Any word on the two?"

"Sorry Miss Nyx, the tracking is down, I apologize, please forgive me," Caine said, eyes still closed.

"Quit your useless groveling. Where are they?" she asked, her voice sharp.

Caine paused a second, savoring her words, drinking in the tone of her voice. He tried to clear his swooning head and focus. "They were outside Oviedo. They're on the way to Manchester," he told her at last. "Where are you?" he asked.

"In Barcelona, waiting for the train to Oviedo," she said, clearly annoyed.

"Never mind that. Forget Oviedo. Get to the airport, get to Manchester. I'll send you more details as I know them."

"Shouldn't I try to catch up with them?"

"No. The big Moor is after them. He'll press from behind, you lie in wait for them in the front," Caine said, having quickly thought it all out.

"Very well. I will be there by tonight," she said.

"So will I."

"What?" she exclaimed, both surprised and annoyed.

"I'm going to England. I'll be there later tonight. Tomorrow your time," Caine said and waited for her response.

"Hmmm," Adriana hummed out, thinking about this.

"Maybe," Caine said before Adriana responded, "we can get together, afterwards. Do some celebrating," Caine said with a trace of hope.

"Careful what you wish for. I am still angry with you after that *sporco* Venice hotel. There will be," she paused a breath, "consequences for that."

"Yes, Miss Nyx," Caine said, his eyes still closed.

"I will see you soon," she said in a seductive voice, and hung up.

Caine lowered the phone and allowed himself a minute to enjoy Adriana's voice still fresh in his ears. *"Consequences,"* she'd said. He let his mind wonder for another minute what she meant by this – *which one of her cruel surprises did she have in store for me?* At last, he reeled himself back in.

He opened his eyes and looked out from his perch high above Miami. He gazed at the Atlantic far beyond as the morning sun painted it with gold. Beyond that sun, on the other side of the ocean, she waited for him. Lahmbrecht waited for him. *Business first*, he thought. He readied himself mentally before setting off for the airport.

CHAPTER 2

Monsacro, the Sacred Mountain, Spain
May 23, 2025 2:57 p.m.

A sad labored up the last part of the trail. He was fit, but still a large man, and the air was thin. After an hour of climbing, his mind had begun to clear from the wreck and the conversation with the Lawyer. The hour of solitude and quiet had allowed him to think, and his mind kept going back to the priest, to Father Martin in that barn. To his pleadings to God for forgiveness for the man torturing him. For himself, Asad thought; forgiveness for *himself.* Without thinking, he clenched his fists as the old wounds, received so long ago, seemed to itch. In the peaceful solitude, he wished he could perform the *salat* and clear his mind, but he was unclean. He thought again of Father Martin in the barn, then pushed all these thoughts away and focused on his job.

This, it slowly dawned on him, was a fool's errand. He was sure the two scientists had the Sudarium, that it was getting farther and farther in that green Fiat. This business up the mountain was just a loose thread. It was something that needed taking care of, but still, just a thread.

Asad rounded a bend in the mountain and there, in the distance, was the octagonal shape of the Hermitage. He redoubled his pace, eager to get it over with. In no time, he was at the last part of the steep and scrabbly path leading up to the Hermitage. He had briefly looked up the history of this place on the drive up and thought of the irony of him, a Moor, finally making it here after so many years. And the bigger irony of him probably walking out empty-handed.

He turned to the final stretch of path leading up to the heavy wooden door, which was ajar. His senses grew sharp in anticipation, as they always did, even though he did not expect much trouble or resistance.

Asad neared the door, listening for any movement inside. There was nothing, only the wind whistling up the mountain, the buzzing of insects and the occasional distant lowing of cows. He peered inside without opening the door, careful to remain quiet. The stone walls flickered with red light from dancing candles. In the middle of the room was a kneeling figure in a black robe, the priest that had brought the Sudarium here, no doubt. Father Goya, he recalled. Asad edged towards the door, almost touching it.

"Please, enter," the kneeling figure called out in Spanish without turning around.

Asad winced, caught off-guard. It was something that seldom happened. He swung the door open, which protested noisily on its hinges. The kneeling figure slowly rose and turned towards him.

"Welcome. I am Father Goya," he said, putting a hand to his chest, "and what you seek is not here."

Asad was taken aback again, but quickly regained his composure. "If not here, where is it?" he asked, skipping the pleasantries.

"It is gone. I do not know where it is, and if I did I would not tell you," the priest said. His thin but vigorous face, lined with age, but seemingly all the stronger for it, was resolute.

"I believe you," Asad said, nodding his head.

"Tell me, why is it you seek the Sudarium?" Father Goya asked.

Asad stopped, surprised at the question. "There are men that want it," he said vaguely.

"There are men that want to destroy it, yes," Father Goya said. "But why? Why do *you* seek it?"

"It is part of the war. The *jihad*. I am only a soldier, I do not make those decisions," he said, though, in the back of his head he was thinking about the millions of euros motivating him.

"You make those decisions every time you act. Those decisions are what define your life," the priest said in a kindly and understanding tone.

"The West is immoral," Asad said, repeating the line he'd heard so much.

"I agree," Father Goya said. "And you think destroying this will help? You think killing innocents will help? Or do you think it will only add to that immorality?" he asked with sincerity. It was an honest question; there was no patronizing or condescending tone in the priest's voice.

"Do not try to change my mind, priest," Asad said. "I know what I need to do — what I must do."

Asad took a step towards him.

"Wait," Father Goya put up his hand.

Asad stopped.

"There is something I must tell you," the priest said, and paused. The silence in the small Hermitage was palpable.

"Yes?" Asad asked after a time, his deep voice filling the ancient stone building.

"While I was praying, a word came to me, a word from God."

Asad straightened up, curious but wary. Again the priest paused, waiting for Asad to ask the question.

"What did the word say?" Asad asked at last.

Father Goya smiled and paused again. "To find what you seek, you must go back to the beginning."

There was silence for a few seconds.

"What does that mean?" Asad asked.

"I do not know. It is a message for you," the priest admitted.

Asad nodded. "This was your God that told you this?" he asked skeptically.

"He is not my God. He is everyone's."

"There is no God but Allah and Muhammad is his Prophet," Asad said automatically.

The priest looked upon him with a kindly and sad face, but said nothing.

Asad shook his head. The priest was only trying to delay him, he thought. He contemplated the old priest; his face was thin and weathered, but his eyes shone like a newborn's. He stepped towards him, blocking him from the door and blotting out the light that was shining on the robed man. Father Goya did not try to get away. Instead, he knelt down.

"You know what I need to do?" Asad asked him with a trace of, what was it — regret?

Father Goya nodded solemnly. "What you must do, do quickly," he said with the trace of a wistful smile on his face. The reference was lost on Asad.

Asad marveled at the man. It was a pity to kill a man such as this. Asad respected him from the short interaction they had had. Nevertheless, he was a loose thread and had to be clipped.

Father Goya lowered his head and prayed silently. Asad stepped over him and wrapped his arms arm the priest's neck.

"Today, I will be in paradise," Father Goya whispered.

"I certainly hope so," Asad said under his breath.

With a quick and practiced move, Asad yanked up and twisted. The crunch of bone was loud in the small stone church. Father Goya went limp and Asad gently set him down on the cold floor. Asad took a deep breath, and closed his eyes, this death weighing on him in a way that none ever had.

He cleared his mind and set about the work of searching the church for the Sudarium. It was a quick search, as there was practically nowhere to hide anything in the sparse building. He looked under the altar, at the empty stone cut-out, and sighed. As he suspected, the Sudarium was gone.

Asad stood over the altar, surveying the scene. Father Goya lay slumped on the ground, his black robes gathered loosely around him like a shroud. The red candles ringed the octagonal room, filling it with the golden red light of a sunset. With the stone altar in front of him, the whole scene had a sacrificial quality to it. And a sacrifice had been made, he supposed.

Asad took a moment to think things out. The couple had the Sudarium, of that he was sure now. With a two to three hour head start, it would be difficult, but not impossible, to catch them. In any case, he did not know where they were going, though he had his suspicions. The woman, he recalled, lived and worked in Manchester, and her lab was there. That was the logical place for them to go. But there were many ways of getting there. He hoped that the Lawyer would have more information. He checked his phone again, but there was no signal here in the remote mountains.

Asad clenched and unclenched his fists, the old wounds protesting in the cool mountain air. He took another look at the priest. He thought he heard his voice still, and the message that he had for him. *"To find what you seek, you must go back to the beginning,"* he'd said. Asad contemplated this, trying to figure out whether it meant anything or whether it was the ramblings of a desperate old man stalling for time. That feeling returned to him, not quite regret, not quite guilt.

On impulse, Asad walked out from behind the altar. One by one, he went around the room, stooping down to blow out each candle. Gradually, the warmth left the stone room and it turned colder, harder. When he was back where he started, at the beginning, he glanced once more at Father Goya. No great revelation came to Asad, though.

A single candle remained on the altar. Asad blew this out as well. The Hermitage had a different character now, an ancient and patient slumbering feel. It was uncomfortable, and Asad had no problem leaving. He closed the creaking door behind him and started the long hike back, glad for the solitude to clear his roiling mind. The priest's supposed message from God had shaken him, though he did not understand why. He did not know what it meant, but the words disquieted him.

Asad scrambled down the steep path. He turned and looked once more at the octagonal Hermitage far up the hill. The clouds that had begun to roll in made it look like it was set in cotton. He took a deep breath, turned his back on it and walked on quickly.

Inside the dark Hermitage, the mountain wind whistled against the door. A cloud parted and the sun shone past, sending a shaft of light through the bars of the door's window. The shaft of light poured onto Father Goya's body, lighting it intensely, warming it. A shadow from the bars on the window painted a cross on him, barely visible against his black robes. The light remained there for a long time, until a cloud came and darkened the Hermitage once again.

CHAPTER 3

El Prat Airport, Barcelona, Spain
May 23, 2025   5:44 p.m.

Adriana Nyx unclipped her knives from her boots and put them in the brown Coach carry-on she'd bought at the airport luggage shop. She felt naked without them already, and the thought of checking her bag filled her with unease. She hated air travel; with the body-scanning, even ceramic knives were out. Still, this was the only way of getting to Manchester ahead of them with enough time to settle in and plan. She finished packing the bag with the rest of her purchases, all expensive and all courtesy of the Lawyer. She thought of him and was filled with revulsion as well as a small thrill at getting to see him again. She hoped to spend some quality time with him. *I'll flay his pasty white skin*, she thought, and smiled a crooked half-smile.

Adriana zipped up the bag and washed her hands at the sink. She looked at herself in the mirror. Her short jet-black hair was spiked up in the latest style. She wore an elegant silver and white blouse and pencil-thin black pants. A tailored black Roberto Cavalli jacket finished her ensemble. Respectable businesswoman with money, the outfit said. She kept the leather boots, though. She neared the mirror and examined the side of her head. There was no trace of the bruise the man had given her in Venice. But it was most certainly there under the makeup. She vowed again to herself to repay him. Slowly.

She smiled confidently to herself, unlocked the door of the bathroom, and stepped out into the busy airport terminal. Adriana strode to the British Airways ticketing office and in no time had a first-class to Manchester, leaving in an hour. She stepped up to the check-in agent, bypassing the coach travelers, and presented her ticket.

"Any bags to check?" the agent, a short pretty blonde woman, asked.

"One," Adriana said, reluctantly setting the leather Coach bag on the belt.

Boarding pass in hand, she walked through Barcelona Airport's impressive new terminal. Brushed nickel corkscrews spiraled up into the sky, getting smaller and smaller as they neared the roof. The roof itself was a mesh of multicolored glass, giving the impression of a kaleidoscope sky stretching to the heavens. Adriana approached the short first-class security line, once again bypassing the coach travelers. The x-ray body-scan strip-searched her and soon she was on the airside of the terminal.

She went to the Admiral's lounge and sat, sipping a *cortado* and browsing on her phone for a hotel in Manchester. She picked the most expensive one, a suite at the Hilton, and made the reservation. She then dialed the Lawyer.

The phone took a few seconds to connect.

"Hello?" the voice came through barely audible.

"Where are you?" she asked. "It is very noisy."

"On the runway," Caine yelled into the phone. "I'll be in England in," he covered the mouthpiece and yelled a question to someone, "eight and a half hours," he finished.

"I'll be at the Hilton in Manchester," Adriana said.

"Good. I'll call when I'm near. I'm sending you some information. The address to the lab and Lancaster's home address," he yelled out over the spooling jet engines.

"*Molto bene,*" Adriana whispered to herself.

"The lab is very secure from what I hear," Caine went on. "Probably not the place to try anything. They'll be arriving by car is the last information I had, but I don't have their exact location yet."

"This is all very useful," she said, actually pleased with him for once.

"Try to catch them before they get to the lab," Caine yelled out.

"If you pick up their position, let me know," Adriana said.

"Of course," Caine yelled out.

"And get ready. I want to spend some time with you after," she said in a seductive tone and smiled a wicked smile to herself.

"Yes, Miss Nyx," Caine said in a softer, calmer voice.

She hung up, still smiling, and chuckled to herself. *Men are so easy,* she thought with disdain.

She leaned back and took a sip of the strong coffee. Adriana worked her phone and checked for the messages. She opened Caine's message with the address to the lab, Tabor Applied Genetics Corporation. She clicked the link and mapped it out, studying the map and committing it to memory. She clicked on the street-view and virtually walked around the streets, familiarizing herself. The lab was a large non-descript square brick building in a rather industrial-looking area near the downtown core. Adriana next checked the message with the doctor's home address.

"301 Deansgate, Unit 4611," she whispered aloud. She furrowed her brow. The address looked familiar, but she could not quite place it.

She searched it on her phone and brought up the street-view. The Beetham Tower, Manchester's tallest building came up. The top half of the building housed Manchester's most exclusive condominiums. On the first twenty-three floors, however, was the Hilton hotel.

Adriana almost laughed. They were going to be neighbors.

Miami International Airport
May 23, 2025 12:24 p.m. EST

The door to the Gulfstream G750 sealed shut, cutting off the noise from the runway. Robert Bale Caine settled into the thick leather padded seat.

"Scotch on the rocks," he told the stewardess before she'd even approached him.

She went to the back of the opulent cabin to prepare the drink. The pilots in the cockpit busied themselves with the pre-flight check.

The co-pilot turned to Caine, who sat in the middle of the cabin. "We'll have you in the air very soon, sir," he called out.

"Good," Caine said, and brought out his phone.

The stewardess returned with the drink. "Here you are, sir," she said and handed him the drink. "Will there be anything else?"

"No," Caine said curtly.

She gave him a forced smile and went to the cockpit to check on the pilots.

Caine took a sip, then a slug of the Scotch, and dialed the Old Man.

"Yes, Mr. Caine," Valenti, the assistant, answered. "Hold please."

Caine waited nervously, taking another pull from the tumbler. It was good Scotch, this, he thought.

"Mr. Caine," Lahmbrecht's slow and meticulous voice arose from the speaker.

"Hello sir, I'm on the plane now."

"Excellent. I will have a driver for you when you arrive."

Caine thanked him.

"I look forward to our meeting. We have much to discuss," Lahmbrecht said.

"Yes, sir," Caine said nervously.

The phone went dead as Lahmbrecht hung up.

Caine slumped back in his seat and drained the rest of his drink. Lahmbrecht was the one man that made him nervous, even more so than the hired killers he dealt with. Those could be paid off with money. But a man like Lahmbrecht no one could pay off. A man with that much money, an order of magnitude more than even Caine had, could make anything happen. A man like that would not take kindly to betrayal.

"Waitress, another," Caine held up his glass and rattled the ice cubes.

The stewardess turned her attention from the cockpit with a face that said she'd rather deal with a planeload of tourists than this one man. She painted on a smile and dutifully fetched him his drink. Caine took it and nodded to her. "You're welcome," she said under her breath, and went to the back to sit.

The co-pilot turned again. "We've just received clearance, so please sit back, belt up, and enjoy the ride."

Caine took a deep breath as the small jet picked up speed down the runway. Slowly, they left the ground and downtown Miami got smaller and smaller beneath them. The plane banked and headed east over emerald waters that stretched out to the horizon. Caine raced towards the oncoming night, hoping it would not be his last.

CHAPTER 4

Monsacro, the Sacred Mountain, Spain
May 23, 2025   4:24 p.m.

Asad Hasan rounded the last bend and the village came into view. The sun had made the last stretch hot, and he wiped the sweat from his brow with a handkerchief. He neared the retaining wall lining the tiny central plaza. Samir, thankfully, was waiting for him, standing beside the rental car.

"Good," Asad said to himself and hurried down the stairs to the plaza.

Samir saw him and greeted him.

"Another Audi?" Asad asked him, looking at the blue A4 rental.

Samir shrugged. "It's a diesel hybrid. Long range, but not nearly as fast as my RS4."

"You'll get another one, brother."

"I'll get a faster one," Samir said and grinned.

"I'm sure. Let's get going."

The two got in the car, with Asad relaxing into the front seat. It felt good to sit after the long hike and the fast pace he'd kept.

"Where to?" Samir asked as he put the car into drive and they whooshed off silently.

Asad had been thinking about this for the past hour, and he'd finally made a decision. "France," he said. "Calais. If they are driving to England, they will have to cross the channel by ferry or train."

Samir nodded. "Makes sense."

They drove down the winding mountain road past where the big Audi had sailed into the ravine. The break in the dense foliage was almost imperceptible.

"Stop the car," Asad said.

"Why?" Samir asked, slowing and pulling over on the narrow shoulder.

"Cleanup."

Asad got out and scrambled down the hillside. He looked around with his keen eyes for the body of the truck driver. He found it crumpled against the tree a few meters away into the foliage. Leaves had already begun to cover him. Asad went to the body, grabbed it by the legs, and dragged it up the hill towards the road. Even with his mighty strength, it was a difficult climb.

Asad broke out of the tree line, checked to see if the road was empty, and motioned to Samir, who was standing by the car further up the road.

"Bring the car back here," he called out.

Samir backed the car up, the crunching of the gravel on the shoulder the loudest sound around.

"What are we doing?" Samir asked as he got out of the car.

"Open the trunk. Help me move him," Asad told him.

Samir looked at the body and glanced around nervously.

"Hurry," Asad said with a trace of impatience.

Samir went over and together they picked up the man, hauling the body into the trunk.

Asad snapped the trunk shut. "Let's go."

After they got into the car, Samir, turned to Asad. "What are we doing with him? Why pick him up?"

"Do you want anyone to find a dead man next to your crashed car?" Asad asked. "A fast car going off a mountain road, that can be explained. But a body—" his voice trailed off.

"Yes," Samir said, nodding. "So what do we do with him?"

Asad shrugged. "Dump him in some secluded spot far enough away from here."

Samir pushed the drive button and the car set off silently. They drove down the solitary mountain road, passing only one other car.

"Stop here," Asad said as they drove through a particularly densely forested and steep mountainside.

Samir pulled over and popped the trunk. Quickly, they lifted the body and tossed it unceremoniously down the ravine. Asad peered down and saw no trace of it. Satisfied, he wiped his hands.

"Let's go. If we hurry we can catch up to them in Calais."

On the E-80, Spain – France Border
May 23, 2025 8:47 p.m.

The little green Fiat sped down the coastal highway. The cold foreboding waters of the Bay of Biscay lay to their left and the Pyrenees, tall and impenetrable, rose in the moonlit night to their right.

"Voilà, we're in France," Jonathan told Leigh as they crossed the border on the way to England.

"Hmm?" Leigh looked up sleepily.

"I said we're in France, miss sleepy."

"Oh goodness, I dozed off again," she said. She'd been trying to stay awake to keep him company on the long drive.

"Hey, I don't blame you. It's been a hell of a day. Actually, I was thinking of risking my life and letting you drive," Jonathan said with a grin.

Leigh scowled. "If I wasn't half asleep I'd hit you," she said.

"Hey relax, grumpy bear, just kidding."

Leigh turned to him and smiled. "Pull over. I'll drive some, you rest."

"At the next rest area, I promise." Jonathan was silent a moment as he stared at the road unfurling beneath him. A slight tingling began at his temples. "Ah, crap," he said.

"What?" she asked, concerned.

"It's happening. Can you take the steering wheel, just in case?"

Leigh reached over at once, holding the car steady and pointing forward. "The Shutter?"

Jonathan nodded. He stared straight ahead, then blanked out for a second. He took a deep breath. "Okay, I'm back," he said.

"You alright?" Leigh asked, hand still on the wheel.

"Yeah. I'm okay now."

"Can I let go?" she asked, still cautious.

"Yeah, I got it."

Leigh hesitantly let go of the wheel.

"There's a beautiful memory I can relive forever. Endless highway," Jonathan said with sarcasm.

"Hey, at least I was in it, right?" Leigh asked.

"Let me check." Jonathan closed his eyes for a second. "Yep. There you are. I can just see your hand on the wheel."

Leigh laughed.

"I can see the edge of your tattoo also," Jonathan said. "Show me the rest," he added.

Leigh stared at him. "If you keep begging, maybe I'll relent? Is that your strategy?"

"So far, yes. Is it working?"

"In a few years, who knows?" she said and smiled coyly.

"If that's how long I need to wait," Jonathan said with a grin.

They passed a sign reading "*Aires d'autoroute.*"

"Hey, rest stop, *monsieur*," Leigh pointed at the sign.

"*Oui, oui,*" Jonathan said.

They pulled off the highway, slowing down into the large service plaza.

The service area was busy with cars and trucks going every which way. A row of cars lined one side of the service area, each with a cord sprouting from their snouts connecting them to the Hi-Volt charging stations.

"How we doing on gas?" Leigh asked.

"We're good."

Jonathan parked far away in an almost empty parking lot. They got out and stretched their legs and Jonathan topped off the brake reservoir.

"Okay, let's try this again," Jonathan said. They switched places.

Leigh adjusted her seat and mirrors. "Okay, teach me, professor," she said, gripping the steering wheel.

"Just push the clutch in, put it in gear, accelerate gently, and slowly let the clutch out."

Leigh fumbled with the gearshift, trying to shift into first. There was a loud grinding noise. "Darn it," she said, frustrated.

"Clutch first," Jonathan said patiently. He put his hand over hers on the gearshift.

She pushed the clutch in and with his help it snuck into first.

"Now, easy," Jonathan said calmly.

Leigh let the clutch up too fast and the car shot forward ten feet and stalled. "Oof. Stupid car. No wonder they don't make these anymore."

"It's a lost art, driving these. Just try again, you'll get it," Jonathan encouraged her.

Leigh composed herself, pushed in the clutch, and started the car again. She put it in first and slowly released the clutch.

"Give it a little gas," Jonathan said gently.

She revved and the car eased forward. Leigh turned to him with a huge grin. "It's going!" she said excitedly.

"Okay now shift into second," he said.

She pushed in the clutch and the engine revved wildly, shifted, and released the clutch. The car lurched but settled into the gear.

"Okay, a little smoother next time, but you've got it," he said.

Leigh pointed the car towards the entrance ramp and with intent concentration shifted into third, smoother this time.

"There, you're getting it," Jonathan said.

Leigh grinned broadly as she picked up speed, easily putting it into fourth. She accelerated down the entrance ramp and merged onto the highway, then shifted to fifth.

"There," she said, satisfied.

"Very well done. Next I'll teach you how to heel-and-toe downshift."

"One thing at a time, cowboy," she said.

"Certainly. And now, if you can handle it, I'm going to pass out now," Jonathan said and tilted the seat back as far as it would go, shifting the reliquary to the other side.

"I'll wake you if anything happens," Leigh said.

"Mmmhmm," Jonathan mumbled, but he was already half-asleep.

CHAPTER 5

Manchester, England
May 23, 2025   9:30 p.m.

Adriana Nyx settled in the back of the Mercedes she'd hired to drive her to the hotel. She unzipped the leather Coach bag and glanced up at the driver of the car. She caught him peeking in the rearview mirror at her.

"Keep your eyes on the road," she warned him. *Men,* she thought and sighed.

The driver turned his attention back to the road. Adriana brought her stilettos out of the bag and sheathed them back into her boots. She closed the bag and relaxed, happy to have them back.

She looked out the window at the Manchester skyline approaching, lit up like a Christmas tree. She saw, in the distance, the Beetham Tower, easily the tallest building. The big grey-green monolith was floodlit in the sparkling night. As they approached, she started to think about the preparations she would have to make. She then thought of the woman and the man, and started picturing them at her mercy. She smiled a malevolent smile that reflected off the window of the car, and watched the Beetham Tower loom larger and larger.

On the A-10, near Poitiers, France
May 24, 2025   1:11 a.m.

The long empty highway stretched infinitely on in front of Leigh. She rubbed her eyes and spotted a service area coming up. She pulled in and tried to downshift to fourth. The car protested with a mechanical grinding noise.

"Right. Clutch," she mumbled to herself.

She pressed the clutch down and tried to shift again, but missed fourth and went into second. The engine revved wildly and the car lurched forward.

"Oh, bother," Leigh said, frustrated, and fumbled with the gearshift lever again.

"What?" Jonathan sat up, half asleep.

"Nothing. Go to sleep for a minute," she said and ground the gears again.

Jonathan shook his head, clearing it. "Why are you trying to kill my car?" he asked sleepily and yawned.

"Hush, you. It doesn't like me."

Leigh put it into neutral and let the car glide in. Slowly, it rolled into a parking spot in front of a brightly lit convenience store. Leigh shut the car off.

"Where are we?" Jonathan asked, rubbing his eyes.

"We passed Bordeaux about an hour ago. I was doing fine in a straight line. It's this downshift thing I can't get."

"I don't even want to know what you did to the car while I was asleep," Jonathan said with a little smile.

Leigh narrowed her eyes. "Hey, I got us here."

"Let's see where here is," Jonathan said and opened the door.

He got out and stretched. The gas and charging station was virtually deserted. Blue neon ringed the circular store in front of them, giving everything a cool futuristic glow. A lone man stood by his car at a Hi-Volt station, waiting for it to charge.

Leigh got out and stretched in the cool night air. "Brrrr. I'm getting a hot chocolate," she said, and went towards the store.

Jonathan followed. They walked in and looked at a lonely clerk sitting behind the counter. The clerk gave them a bored smile and went back to his tablet.

Leigh stepped up to the hot-drink vending machine. She took some coins out of her computer bag, which she'd slung across her chest. Soon, the machine was pouring a respectable-looking hot chocolate.

"You want anything?" she asked Jonathan.

"Double espresso, and a cappuccino," he said.

"Someone wants to wake up," she noted and smiled.

One by one, the machine prepared the drinks. Jonathan combined his and they took them and walked around the store, picking up snacks for the trip. They walked in front of a newsstand.

"Jonathan, look," Leigh pointed at the electronic newsreader on the rack.

The headline scrolled across the screen of the ePaper. "TERROR SPREADS TO OVIEDO," the headline blared. Below it was a slideshow of pictures of the damaged Cathedral. Jonathan picked up the ePaper from the rack and scrolled through it.

"Does it say anything about the Sudarium?" Leigh asked.

"Just that it is safe, nothing new," Jonathan said. He gazed out the plate-glass window to the Fiat sitting outside, keeping an eye on it.

The clerk motioned to them. "Are you going to buy that or just stand there and read it all night?" the clerk asked in accented English.

"I'll get it," Leigh said. She turned to Jonathan. "I've been dying to check my email anyway."

She set the cheap plastic ePaper and the rest of her purchases on the counter. The clerk rang them up.

"Add one-hundred euros of gas on there," Jonathan said.

"That will be one-hundred twenty-nine euros," the humorless clerk said robotically. Jonathan paid him.

They walked out into the cool night and Jonathan brought the car around to the pump and topped it off, adding brake fluid as well. Leigh stood outside the car, busily typing her email address into the ePaper. Jonathan gazed at her.

"You know, I kind of miss newspapers. You know, actual paper," he said.

Leigh looked at him quizzically. "Why? They never made any sense. All those resources to print up something that was obsolete before it was even delivered? I never really understood why people even read them."

"Well, us old farts liked them," Jonathan said.

"I don't know why. You couldn't check your email on paper," she said, as she continued typing onto the cheap plastic buttons of the reader.

"Yeah, well, I liked the real papers better," Jonathan insisted. Then he asked, sheepishly, "Can I check my mail after you're done?"

Over the Atlantic
May 24, 2025 1:21 a.m. GMT

The phone danced on the small polished wood table, buzzing insistently. Caine opened one sleepy eye and looked at the phone, then glanced down at his Patek Philippe watch. It was still on Miami time, he remembered. He opened both eyes and glanced around, momentarily disoriented and sweating. The interior of the Gulfstream was filled with the comforting hum of the engines and the soft lighting that made it look like an expensive lounge. The phone, insistent, kept vibrating on the table. Caine, half-awake, picked it up and looked at it. It was Balkar. He swiped it on and tried to clear his head from the terrible dreams he'd been having.

"Caine here," he answered groggily.

"Sorry to bother you on your trip, but you said to call if I picked up their location," Balkar said.

"You got them?" Caine exclaimed and sat up in his seat, suddenly wide-awake.

"Yessir."

"Where at?"

"I've got a ping just outside Poitiers in France, near Bordeaux. Looks like a gas station or service plaza of some sort. I can't be sure, but I think it's them."

"What do you mean you can't be sure?"

"I picked up an ePaper activation with the girl's information."

"What?" Caine asked, not understanding.

"She bought a newspaper," Balkar said, impatient.

"How did you manage to figure that out? I gotta know," Caine asked the man, impressed.

"Simple, really. When she bought the ePaper, she activated it with her email. I had a sniffer in the DMZ grepping for her login. The next part is too much to get into. All you need to know is I'll be able to track her as the ePaper updates itself or when she accesses the web."

"You are a genius, Balkar. I don't understand a word of what you said, but you are a genius," Caine gushed.

"I know. I'm sending you the exact data. I'll keep you updated."

Caine hung up and his thin lips stretched into a smile. He dialed Asad.

On the A-10, south of Bordeaux, France
May 24, 2025 1:26 a.m.

The phone rang in the quiet car, momentarily startling Asad. He looked over at Samir, who was driving fast, eyes glazed, on the darkened highway.

"Yes?" Asad answered.

"Leon, I've got their position," Caine's voice, tinny and distant, called out to him from the phone.

Asad sat up, alert. "Where?"

"Service station about an hour north of Bordeaux, near a place called Poitiers. I'm sending you the exact coordinates. Where are you?"

Asad poked at the navigation system. "We are south of Bordeaux. They are less than two hundred kilometers ahead." Asad closed his eyes, calculating. "We may be able to catch up by the time they reach Calais, if that's where they're going."

There was a pause from the Lawyer. "Calais. Yes. That makes sense. Quickest way to England by car."

"That's what I thought," Asad said.

"I'll let you know if there's any change," Caine said and hung up.

Asad turned to Samir. "Drive as fast as you dare. We can catch them."

The hybrid Audi's engine kicked in and the car's speed crept up. They sped down the smooth black ribbon of the French superhighway, which was practically empty at this late hour. The distance to their target closed.

On the E-402, 50 KM South of Calais
May 24, 2025   6:33 a.m.

Jonathan and Leigh sped down the highway in the little green Fiat. The sky was liquid silver in front of them as the sun rose to the east.

"Are we there yet?" Leigh asked, looking up from the ePaper she'd been intently studying the last hour.

"Almost," Jonathan said. "Anything interesting in there?"

"Plenty. The plane that crashed into Turin definitely belonged to Sheik Al-Khaifa or something like that. Turns out that the Sheik lived in London and took off for Bahrain before he could be questioned. There's a big row over it," Leigh filled him in.

"Anything more about Oviedo?" Jonathan asked as he kept his eyes on the road.

"Yes. ETA, the separatists, said it wasn't them. Some group called Islamic Reclamation Front has claimed responsibility," Leigh said and paused. "What the heck are we in the middle of, Jonathan?" she said, her voice thick with concern.

"I don't know. When I told you that you were bound to make some enemies, this isn't what I had in mind," Jonathan said, recalling the conversation of three days ago.

As the sun rose, Jonathan reflected back to these last three days. By all accounts, he should be exhausted, but the rising sun energized him and the nap had done wonders. *Was there ever a time before Turin?* he asked himself. These last three days had been so intense. He thought back to his quiet life before all this. He stared vacantly out on the road, when an uninvited vision crept into his mind. There, in perfect clarity in front of him, his first love lay dead in her casket. Jonathan tried to will the vision away, to stand perfectly still and wait for the uninvited visitor to go away. Slowly, it receded, though a faint outline of her face, her mask, hovered over the road like a ghost. He cursed his memory, cursed his gift, and lusted for a drink.

"You okay?" Leigh asked, breaking the spell.

"Yeah, never better," Jonathan said automatically and painted a smile on his face.

"Alright," Leigh said skeptically. "You just looked a little, I don't know — distant."

"I was just reminiscing," Jonathan said with that forced smile on his face. "No worries," he added.

He pressed the accelerator and sped towards the horizon and the newly dawning day.

CHAPTER 6

50 KM from East Midlands Airport, England
May 24, 2025   7:35 a.m.

"Sir, we're about to land," the stewardess said to the passenger, probably a little more gently than she wanted or should have. Though she disliked him, she was still a professional.

Caine, tossing and turning on the broad leather seat, woke up startled, eyes wide open and sweating, as if he'd been in the middle of a terrible dream. The stewardess took a step back, surprised.

"Sir, we're about to land," she repeated after she composed herself.

"Yeah, alright," Caine said brusquely.

The stewardess retreated to her seat in the back of the plane.

Caine brought up his seat and sat up. He glanced at his expensive watch. Two-thirty in the morning, yet there was the rising sun right outside the window. He stared out the window at the sun, set like a clean gold pearl in a cerulean blue horizon. He adjusted his watch forward to England time, and the sun made sense now.

The intercom crackled. "We've just received clearance to land and we'll have you on the ground in a few minutes," the co-pilot called out.

The Gulfstream descended through the crystal clear skies into a white pillowy blanket of clouds and the world went dark. After a minute or so, the clouds thinned and a patchwork quilt of greens and browns, washed out by the gray skies, appeared below them. The plane continued its descent, banking sharply and showing Caine the clouds they had just traveled through. The pilot leveled it out and lined up the plane with the runway. The indistinct patches of the quilt grew detail as houses and buildings and cars emerged. The ground grew large, no longer a faraway thing, but an all-enveloping and magnetic force.

The Gulfstream gently hovered over the runway, then the pilot touched down, feathering it onto the ground. It was a masterful landing, but Caine didn't notice, preoccupied as he was with meeting the Old Man. The jet engines whined as the thrusters that had been propelling them forward worked to slow them now. The pilot deployed the spoilers and the deceleration pulled Caine forward into his seatbelt before it relented. The plane then lazily taxied to their hangar.

The stewardess appeared from the back. "Sir, immigration will meet us at the gate and then—"

"Save it, sis," Caine held up a hand. "It's not my first time at this rodeo."

The stewardess gave a forced smile, took one breath, then said, "Very well, sir," before returning to the back.

The plane slowed to a crawl, then stopped. The engines powered down and the silence suddenly flooded them.

Caine unbuckled and took his Armani coat from the empty chair in front of him. He readied his passport and grabbed hold of his silver Rimowa carry-on from behind his seat.

The co-pilot emerged from the cockpit. "I trust it was a smooth flight," he said as he readied the cabin door.

"Very," Caine said curtly.

The co-pilot opened the door and extended the stairs towards British soil. "Midlands Airport," he said, extending his hand.

Caine walked down the stairs, unsteady and holding onto the handrail. It was still the middle of the night to him, regardless of what the pale sun shining behind the clouds said.

A uniformed officer waited for him at the bottom of the stairs. "Mr. Caine?" he asked, in perfect and proper English.

"Yeah, that's me," Caine said and handed him the passport.

The uniformed officer swiped it on an electronic handheld reader. He read the screen for a second then looked up at Caine. "Very well, sir. Welcome to Great Britain," he said.

"Great to be here," Caine said, without so much as a smile on his face. The fact was he hated this dreary country. Too much fake politeness and superiority complexes here, he thought. Miami was crude, but refreshingly so, and he felt at home there.

He stepped away from the plane. At the edge of the hangar was a black Bentley Brooklands, huge and imposing. His ride to the Old Man's, no doubt. He stepped over to the car.

"Mr. Caine?" a sharply dressed man asked.

"Yes?"

"I'll be your driver, sir." The man opened the back door and took Caine's suitcase.

Caine stepped into the backseat of the Bentley. The driver shut the door with a vault-like thud. Caine relaxed into the supple leather seat. He took a deep breath, smelling the leather and wood of the car, the unmistakable smell of money. He never tired of it.

The driver stepped into the car. "We'll have you there in about an hour, sir, depending on traffic," he said, then turned to the business of driving.

Caine brought out his phone and swiped it on. He checked his messages. Balkar had left a message saying, simply, "Call me." Caine did.

"Mr. Caine," Balkar answered.

"What do you have?" Caine asked, mindful of the driver who was no doubt listening.

"They've been standing still for about half an hour."

"Where at?"

"I'm sending the coordinates. It looks like the Euroshuttle loading terminal, according to the map. Though they must have paid cash, because I haven't picked up any credit card activity."

"Great work. Keep me informed," Caine said and hung up.

He dialed Asad, who answered on the first ring. "Leon, buddy, how are things?" Caine asked casually as he eyed the driver of the Bentley.

"Good. We are near Calais," Asad answered, and picking up on the Lawyer's strange and casual tone.

"That's great. The Euroshuttle is definitely the fastest way across," Caine told him.

"They're going on the Euroshuttle?" Asad confirmed, mindful that apparently the Lawyer could not speak freely.

"Definitely. I hope you can catch up."

"We are almost there."

"That's great. I hope we can get together and celebrate," Caine said with a big fake smile on his face.

"Yes, of course. I will call with an update."

"Great, talk to you later," Caine said and hung up.

He relaxed back into the seat and gripped the phone tightly as he sped closer and closer to the Old Man. Caine hoped Asad would take care of things. He should have little trouble hunting them down in a train underground, Caine thought.

CHAPTER 7

Euroshuttle Terminal, Calais, France
May 24, 2025 7:51 a.m.

Jonathan guided the little Fiat on the platform connecting to the train. He drove slowly, through the huge door on the side of the train, and then inched down the enclosed railroad car, snuggling right up to the front of the auto in front of them. He shut off the Fiat and watched as another auto edged right up to their back bumper. Slowly, the train car filled up in this fashion, the autos parking inside and settling in for the trip across the channel.

"This is strange," Jonathan said, hunched over the steering wheel and looking up at the ceiling through the windshield. The Euroshuttle looked like an oversized subway car, albeit one filled with automobiles instead of people. There were a few folding seats at intervals along the wall.

"It's not so bad," Leigh said. "I've been on it a few times to visit France. Let's get out and walk around."

"Good. I'm sick of sitting in this tiny car, as much as I like it," he said and slipped out.

Leigh opened the door and got out, joining the other passengers that were doing the same thing. She looked up at a LED sign that said *"EST. 15 Min. Before Departure."*

"It takes forever to load these," she said, and walked around the Fiat and stood by Jonathan.

Jonathan glanced around nervously. "This feels strange," he said.

"Are you okay? You seem nervous," Leigh asked him.

"Yeah, I'm fine," he said and smiled. His smile weakened as Leigh continued to stare at him. "Actually, no," he admitted. "Truth is I hate tunnels. The thought of being in one for half an hour," he shook his head and exhaled. "All that rock and water above us—" he trailed off.

"Relax," Leigh said, putting a hand on his arm. "I've been through it a few times. You won't even know you're in a tunnel. There are lights the whole way."

"Thanks," he said. "I'll be okay."

Leigh gave him a coy smile.

"What?" Jonathan asked.

"Nothing," she said, still smiling.

"That's not nothing. What is it?"

Her smile broadened. "It's just nice to see some vulnerability there. I was beginning to think you weren't afraid of anything."

Jonathan grinned. "I'm just very good at hiding it. There's plenty I'm afraid of."

"Oh? Like what?"

"Well, tunnels," Jonathan said, counting out on his fingers, "spiders, karaoke singers, British food. Deadly afraid of that."

"Oh, stop it, you," Leigh said and playfully punched him on the arm.

Jonathan laughed. "Hey, speaking of food, is there a cafeteria or dining car on this train?"

"Yes, in the middle. At least there was last time I rode."

"Let's go get a coffee," Jonathan suggested.

"You go. One of us should stay with," she gestured at the car and whispered, "you know, the priceless relic."

"Yes, of course. What do you want?"

"Something big and strong," Leigh said.

"You've already got that, baby," Jonathan said, leaning in closer.

Leigh rolled her eyes.

"I know, I know," Jonathan said, putting up his hands, "that was bad."

"Very," Leigh said. "Go on, you."

Leigh opened the door to the Fiat and sat in the passenger's seat. She took out the ePaper and started reading the news, clicking on its buttons.

Jonathan walked down the broad train car, which was filled with autos, all of them snuggled close front to back. At the end of the car was another LED display, reading, "*EST. 11 Min. Before Departure.*" A set of stairs led to the top floor. *This is an amazing train*, thought Jonathan. Two decks of hundreds of automobiles rolling under the English Channel every hour. Jonathan shook his head, trying not to think of the tunnel part.

He came to a pneumatic door. Jonathan pushed the button, and it slid aside to reveal a sealed space between the two long train cars. Here, there was a hinged floor that allowed for movement, and thinner accordioned walls that still kept away the elements. He stepped through and pushed the button into the next car, even as the first door swooshed shut. Another long train car stretched out in front of him, mostly filled with autos and people settling in for the trip. At the tail end of the car, more autos were being loaded, driven in carefully by their owners as the train employees guided them in. Jonathan approached one of the men, hard to miss in his bright yellow reflective vest, and asked for the dining car.

"Bar Car is four cars down, in the middle of the train," the man said hurriedly and turned his attention back to loading the train.

"Bar Car," Jonathan said to himself. He glanced at the wall display and checked the time. 8:01 a.m. He wondered if he could get a gin and tonic at this hour.

Outside the Euroshuttle Terminal, Calais, France
May 24, 2025 8:01 a.m.

Asad stared out the window at the line of cars passing through the gate. He glanced at the clock on the car, and dialed the Lawyer, who answered at once.

"What's their position?" Asad asked into the phone.

"Let me get back to you on that," the Lawyer said and hung up.

Asad sighed and looked up, impatient.

"Shall we go in?" Samir asked from the driver's seat of the Audi.

"Hold on for a second. This was their last position, but we want to make sure. We do not want to board the train if they are not on it. There's no turning around once we start."

The two sat in the Audi, parked on the side of the road leading into the Euroshuttle terminal. It had been a long night of fast driving, but they had made it. Samir rubbed his red eyes. Asad was fidgeting with the phone when it suddenly vibrated in his hand. He answered at once.

"Yeah, Leon, hope you can make it up here. The Euroshuttle is still the best way across. All our friends take it," the Lawyer said in a forced tone from the back seat of the Bentley.

"They are on the train?" Asad asked.

"Yeah, that's right," the Lawyer said.

"Excellent," Asad said and hung up. He turned to Samir. "Go."

They merged onto the traffic leading into the terminal and passed the big tollbooth, paying the fifty-euro fee and showing the car's rental registration. The attendant gave it a cursory glance and waved them through. The Audi followed the road as it snaked to the loading area. An attendant waved them into one of the side lanes, which led to a ramp sitting alongside the large train.

"The Lawyer says they are on this train," Asad said to Samir, who was waiting at a red light to proceed. "We have half an hour to find them," he continued, then paused and looked through his phone. He scrolled to the files he had on all his targets. "This is Jonathan Tremaine," Asad said and showed Samir the picture, pressing a button and transferring the files to Samir's phone. The younger man studied it, then Asad scrolled to the next file. "And this is Dr. Leigh Lancaster."

Samir studied her picture as well. "She is pretty," he said.

Asad pointed up at the light, which had turned green while Samir was gazing at her picture. He turned his attention to driving and eased the Audi through the opening at the side of the train, entering inside. He pulled up to the car ahead. The attendant motioned for them to stop, and the car behind him did the same. Samir powered the car down.

"You know what the Fiat looks like," Asad told him. "Stay on the top level of the train, I will take the bottom level. If you see them, call me but do not approach them. They do not know you."

"Very well," Samir nodded.

They exited the car and split up. Asad went down the stairs at the end of the train car. Somewhere in front of him was the last loose thread, the last thing standing between himself and a very large sum of money. He sharpened his senses and moved forward in an inexorable press towards the front of the train.

Euroshuttle Train, Calais, France
May 24, 2025 8:09 a.m.

Jonathan settled into the barstool at the near end of the Bar Car. Sure enough, it was a proper bar, with bottles of booze lining the shelf behind the bar and a real espresso machine. He spotted the Bombay Sapphire immediately and looked around. He was the only one sitting down. The bartender busied himself stacking sandwiches in a refrigerator and stocking the shelves. Other people were beginning to stream in now that they had parked their cars and had settled in. Jonathan waved the bartender over.

"We don't start service until we start moving," the bartender said impatiently, pointing at an LED display at the head of the car reading, *"EST. 3 Min. Before Departure."*

"Aw, come on," Jonathan said and grinned. "I'm a thirsty man." He set down a fifty-euro bill on the bar.

The bartender looked at the bill then glanced around.

"What would you like?" he said guardedly.

"Gin," Jonathan held open his thumb and forefinger, "tonic," he closed them, holding them less than an inch apart. "And two large cappuccinos, double shot."

"Certainly, sir."

Jonathan slid over the bill. "Keep the change."

The bartender, surprised, took it quickly. "Thank you very much."

"No problem," Jonathan said, and it wasn't. It wasn't his money anyway, and, if one is going to tip big, best to do it at the beginning.

The bartender packed a tumbler with ice, then practically filled it with the Bombay, adding a splash of Schweppes from a fresh bottle and leaving this by the drink.

"Lemon?" the bartender asked.

"This is fine," Jonathan said and eagerly took the drink, which was cool in his hands.

The bartender turned to prepare the coffees and Jonathan took a sip, then a big swallow of the gin.

"Ahh," he sighed. He'd been craving that for what felt like a very long time. Jonathan relaxed, letting the gin warm him, and leaned on the bar. He studied the people around him and finished the drink quickly.

"Another, please," he said to the bartender, who poured him another two shots of gin into the same glass.

Jonathan felt a slight movement, then the train started rolling forward. He looked out the window, sipping his drink, as the train slowly gathered speed. In a short time, the walls started rising as the train descended into the tunnel. The walls rose and rose, drowning out the daylight and plunging, for a few seconds, into darkness. Soon, the train reached the yellow and white LED lights that lined the tunnel and now these flashed by at intervals as the train sped up in earnest.

Jonathan shuddered as the tunnel swallowed them. He took another pull on his drink and turned back to the bartender, who was busy frothing up the milk for the cappuccinos. More people were entering the Bar Car now from both sides. The bartender finished with the coffees and set them down on the counter.

"Anything else?" he asked.

"Yeah, I think I'll have anoth–"

Jonathan's words were taken from his lips.

His blood went cold. At the far end of the Bar Car, the door swished open, revealing the big Moor filling the frame.

Jonathan quickly turned his face away, turning his back to the assassin.

Did he see me? Jonathan's mind raced. He took the cappuccinos and, as casually as he could, walked away from the bar. He approached the door on the opposite side of the car, the one leading back towards Leigh and the Fiat. He peered into the reflection in the glass of the door, not daring to turn around. The big Moor was making his way through the Bar Car quickly, searching the crowd.

He didn't spot me, Jonathan thought.

Jonathan hurried through the door, which took seemingly forever to close behind him. He slid the next door open and walked quickly, almost running, with the coffees still in his hands. He walked briskly up the train cars, seeing the lights outside the window blurring by, then started running, oblivious of the stares of the people milling around. Some people pressed against the walls as he ran by, giving him strange looks. Each door Jonathan came to took an eternity to slide open. He kept glancing behind him, sure that the big Moor was going to spring up at any moment. But the killer was far behind, still searching the train cars Jonathan had just run through.

Jonathan sprinted through four more train cars, thinking furiously all the while as to what to do. At last he came to their train car and spotted the small green Fiat at the front of the line.

Jonathan dashed to it, right to the passenger's window, and was running so fast that he slammed into it.

Leigh, sitting inside calmly reading her ePaper, let out a yelp of surprise and dropped the plastic ePaper onto the floor. Jonathan pounded on the window like a maniac, the coffee sloshing out of the cup he still held in his hand.

"Geez, cowboy, you scared the crap out of me," Leigh said, muted, through the window.

"Get out. Get out," Jonathan called out to her. People around them stared.

"What is it?" Leigh asked, still in the car, her surprise slowly turning to concern.

"It's him. The big Moor. He's here."

Pale as she was, Jonathan swore he saw the color drain from her face. She cracked the door open, and Jonathan took hold, swinging it completely open. He dropped one of the coffees, which splashed on the ground and rolled under the car, emptying itself onto the train floor.

"Get out," he told her again.

Leigh snapped out of her momentary paralysis and sprang out of the Fiat. "My computer!" she cried out, and turned back to the car to pick up her bag which she'd left on the seat.

"I'll get it," Jonathan said, adding, "here," as he handed her the remaining coffee. "Now go!" he called out to her.

"Where?" she asked.

Jonathan folded the passenger's seat forward and leaned into the car to grab the reliquary, tossing the dirty rags from the car repairs aside. He glanced at Leigh who was still standing there.

"Go. Go upstairs. I'll follow," he said.

Reluctantly, Leigh hurried to the stairs at the end of the train car and went up. She waited nervously at the top of the stairs, glancing around for any sign of danger. She moved the hot coffee from one hand to the other.

"Where are you?" she said to herself, fidgeting from side-to-side. She ran her free hand over her shoulder, which felt strangely naked without her computer bag at her side. That computer held the last remaining direct samples of the Shroud data, and she felt irresponsible leaving it behind. She glanced around for a clock.

"Oh, bloody hell," she hissed to herself, and decided to go back down and collect her bag. As soon as she started moving, she heard someone coming up the stairs. Leigh stepped back as Jonathan darted up the stairs, spooking her a bit. He carried the reliquary in one hand, and her computer bag in the other.

"There you are," she said. "What took you so long?"

"Never mind that now. Here," he handed her the leather computer bag, which she took and slung over her shoulder. "Let's go," he said and grabbed her hand.

"Where?" Leigh asked.

"Honey, I'm making this up as I go," he said, and glanced down the long train car, which was mostly empty. For the most part, it was a near duplicate of the bottom level of the car, though not as packed. A few autos were parked here, and a number of people milled about outside them. The yellow lights from the tunnel flashed through the windows in a fast continuous blur as the train, blazing at full speed, barreled under the English Channel. Jonathan looked away from the window and tried not to think of the tons of rock and water above.

"This way," he said and led Leigh back towards the tail of the train. "We'll double back above him, get behind him. He won't look for us where he's already been."

They almost ran down the train car, pausing to open the door at the end. Leigh stopped a second.

"Hey, can I toss this?" she asked, glancing down at the coffee in her hands. She looked around for a rubbish bin.

"No. Hold on to it," Jonathan said.

"Why ever for?"

"I don't know. Gut feeling," he said. "Let's go," he said, hurrying through the door, feeling the eyes of all around on him. They made a motley and suspicious couple, with Jonathan carrying the ornate and gilded reliquary and practically running through the train like they'd stolen it. They paused in between the train cars; the rumble of the tracks below was loud.

"Okay, let's be more casual about this," he told Leigh, pausing for breath. "People are going to think we stole this thing if we keep running through here," he said and held up the reliquary.

They opened the door to the next train car and walked briskly.

"Where was he?" Leigh asked as they walked.

"What?" Jonathan asked, distracted by the walls of the tunnel zipping by outside.

"The big Moor, where was he?"

"The Bar Car. He walked in the door but didn't see me. I don't think he did, anyway."

They arrived at the next door, slid it open, and walked into another compartment between cars.

"We're probably above him now," Jonathan said over the noise of the tracks speeding by underneath.

He slid aside the next door and entered the next car, heading towards the tail of the train. Jonathan scanned the crowd to make sure the big Moor hadn't doubled back himself. Something caught his eye and he slowed. There, at the end of the car, was a young man staring at them. The man looked vaguely familiar and Jonathan saw — *what? recognition?* — in his dark eyes. Jonathan turned away quickly.

"Jonathan, that guy at the end of the car is—"

"Staring at us," he finished her sentence. "Yeah, I saw. Just keep walking, and don't look at him."

The young man, Samir, dark-haired and handsome, stood at the end of the train car by the door. They walked casually towards him, pretending not to notice him. Jonathan turned to Leigh as they neared him, trying to keep the man in his peripheral vision. The man looked down at his phone and back up at them.

"I'll have that coffee now, dear," Jonathan said casually, almost whispering it.

Leigh handed him the coffee, a quizzical expression on her face. They approached the man.

"You mind carrying this a bit?" Jonathan asked, handing over the reliquary to Leigh, with a big smile painted on his face. They were almost to the end of the car, where Samir stood by the door.

Jonathan leaned closer to Leigh and whispered. "I'm going to feel real bad about this if I'm wrong."

"Real bad about wha—?"

Before Leigh could finish her sentence, it happened, and fast.

Jonathan flicked off the lid and threw the hot coffee in the young man's face. Samir dropped his phone and brought his hands to his face, taking a step back and bumping into the wall. In one smooth move, Jonathan stepped up to him, grabbed the man's head by the hair with both hands, and brought it down hard against his knee, which he had thrust up at the same time. Samir dropped to the ground, limp.

Leigh had to stifle a yelp of surprise. It had happened so fast and so viciously, but so quietly also. She glanced around her. No one appeared to have noticed. No one except an elderly couple standing outside an old

Mercedes, staring straight at them. Their eyes met. Leigh tried to smile, and she hoped it didn't come out looking like a grimace.

"Jonathan," she said through the clenched teeth of her forced smile. "Those old folks over there are staring at us."

Jonathan gave them a glance and tried to smile. "Let's get him out of here," he said softly, his lips barely moving.

He pushed the button on the door and it slid open. Grabbing Samir, he dragged him through to the compartment between rail cars.

"Grab the phone," Jonathan told Leigh as he hunched over Samir's unconscious form, searching him.

Leigh, burdened with the computer bag and the reliquary, leaned down and grabbed for the man's phone, which was covered in frothy cappuccino. The entire time she kept looking at the elderly couple, smiling.

"He, uh, fell. I'll — I'll go help him," she stuttered at the elderly couple. "I'm a doctor," she added, without thinking, and smiled even more. She took the phone and, dragging the reliquary and almost slipping on the coffee all over the floor, she went through the opened door. It slid shut.

She turned to Jonathan, the smile falling off her face.

"Are you mad?" she called out, excitedly. "You could warn me, you know. Next time you can let me know ahead of time when you're going to assault someone. What if he's not one of them? What if he was only checking me out? Guys do that, you know, check me out," she said with rapid-fire speed.

"I'd say he wanted to check you out. With this," Jonathan said, and pulled out a gun from under the unconscious man's coat.

Leigh took a step back and pursed her lips together. "Oh," she exclaimed, suddenly at a loss for words.

Jonathan searched the man's pockets, pulling out a wallet and an E.U. passport. He opened the passport, reading it aloud. "Javier Gonzalez. Fine Spanish name," he said, sarcastically.

"I'd be surprised if that was his real name," Leigh said, regaining her composure. She set the reliquary down.

"Very surprised," Jonathan said. He pocketed the wallet and passport. He checked the gun, made sure the safety was on, and tucked it in his belt.

Leigh looked down at the man's cell phone, still in her hand. Her blood ran cold as she stared at herself.

"Jonathan, look," she showed him the phone.

"That's not a good picture of you."

"Very funny."

"Let me see that," Jonathan said. Leigh handed him the phone. He tapped on the picture.

"Your résumé," he said, showing her the phone.

"Good heavens," she exhaled. "Let me see that," she said, taking the phone back and scrolling through the file. "Look at all this," she said. "My whole life is in here."

"Mine too, I bet," he said and shook his head.

"Jonathan, who are these guys?"

"I don't know," he shrugged. "Terrorists, *jihadists*, something. Remember the thing with the Danish paper?" he asked, recalling the destruction of a newspaper building in Denmark and the subsequent killings of most of the staff from a few years ago.

"Look," Leigh said, still poking around the phone. "It's all the other scientists. Why go out of their way to kill us?"

"I'm not sure," Jonathan admitted. "But they are trying, and succeeding. And one of them is below us somewhere. And there may be more. Lets get moving. Keep your eyes peeled."

"What about him?" Leigh pointed at Samir's unconscious body.

Jonathan rubbed his stubbly chin and glanced around. There was nowhere to hide him, just a couple of small access doors to machinery. "Bathroom," Jonathan said. "There's a bathroom at the front of every car, right?"

"Right," Leigh agreed.

"Go check."

Leigh left the reliquary leaning against the wall and opened the door to the next car. "The coast is clear," she said, and pressed on the "Door Open" button again to keep it open. She grabbed the reliquary again.

Jonathan leaned down and hefted the unconscious man into the next car and into the bathroom, where Leigh was holding open the door. All three of them crowded into the bathroom and Leigh shut the door. Jonathan set the man down none too gently on the toilet and his head hit the back wall with a loud thump.

"Jonathan—" Leigh called out disapprovingly.

"What? He was going to kill us."

"Still—"

"Well, he's going to come to sooner or later," Jonathan said, thinking of what to do. He suddenly started unbuckling the man's belt.

"Umm, what are you doing?" Leigh asked.

"Slowing him down when he comes to," he said. "I don't quite have the stomach to put a bullet in him," he added.

Jonathan pulled off Samir's belt, slumped the man forward and started wrapping it around his wrists, tying them behind his back.

Leigh shook her head. "You're doing that wrong. Here, let me."

She switched positions with Jonathan in the crowded bathroom, brushing up against him as she did so. Leigh took the belt, cinched it around one wrist, then the other, then looped it all back through the buckle and locked it off. Jonathan stood and stared.

"What?" Leigh asked, seeing Jonathan's gaze.

"Where'd you learn that?" he asked, raising an eyebrow.

Leigh gave him a half-smile. "Maybe I'll tell you one day, cowboy," she said and opened the door to the bathroom, walking out with a smirk on her face.

Jonathan shook his head and smiled, then stepped out, leaving the unconscious Samir bound inside.

"Let's get going," Jonathan said and took hold of the gilded reliquary and began walking briskly down the mostly empty train car, Leigh at his side. They walked to the next train car. Jonathan paused a second when the door slid open.

"Now that is a fine automobile," he said, pointing.

At the tail end of the empty rail car, sitting by itself, sat a sleek silver Aston Martin Vanquish. The owner, a gray-haired impeccably dressed man, sat outside on a bench typing idly on his phone. Jonathan stared at the car as they walked by. The owner did not even look up at them. Jonathan paused and ogled the car once more before they stepped into the next car.

"Come on," Leigh said, pulling him. "Boys and their toys," she muttered.

Euroshuttle Train, Under the English Channel
May 24, 2025 8:29 a.m.

Asad opened the door and instantly spotted the little green Fiat at the head of the car. His senses sharpened even more. He scanned the whole compartment. It was filled with autos, parked nose to tail, and their passengers which milled about outside for the most part. No scientists, though. He carefully walked towards the Fiat but could tell from here that they were not in there.

Asad cursed under his breath. *Where were they?* He took a deep breath and walked up to the Fiat, peering inside.

Nothing. No Sudarium, no reliquary. Nobody around. He stood there a few moments, staring at the LED display on the wall in frustration. *"Arrival in 15 minutes,"* read the display.

Asad took out his phone and dialed Samir, even as he walked through the door to the next, and front-most, rail car. The phone rang and rang. Asad, holding the phone to his ear and waiting for an answer, scanned the rail car. He walked through it with a predatory intent, searching for his targets, but they were nowhere to be found.

Jonathan and Leigh reached the upper level of the Bar Car. They walked through the door to the upper bar, which was deserted and closed. As they walked through the empty bar, Samir's phone buzzed in Leigh's hand. Startled, she juggled with it, almost dropped it, then caught it. She stopped and held it out to Jonathan.

"What do I do?"

"Well, don't answer it," he said. "I don't think it's his mother calling."

She held the phone in her hand, each vibration sending a shiver of dread through her. At last, it stopped and went silent, with only a "missed call" message flashing on the screen.

"What now?" Leigh asked.

Jonathan looked around the deserted bar. "Go downstairs and have a drink?"

"Very funny, mister."

"Let's keep going, then."

"What are we going to do if he finds us?" Leigh asked with great worry.

Jonathan shrugged. "Run."

"That's your plan?"

"So far, yes."

They continued through the deserted bar as the tunnel lights outside flashed in a continuous blur as the train sped forward.

Asad reached the front of the train and frowned. *Their car was here, they were not, not on the first level anyway.* And Samir was not answering. That was the most troubling thing of all. Asad checked his phone. There was plenty of signal here; the train was equipped for cell communication. He stood a moment, thinking.

Asad started backtracking quickly on the lower level. He thought about setting up an ambush at the Fiat; they'd have to return to it eventually. But he needed Samir. Asad made his way back to the Audi. With any luck, Samir would either pick up the phone, call, or return to the Audi himself. He hustled back through the cars of the train, ever mindful of the LED displays ticking down the time to arrival. He slid door after door open, keeping a sharp eye out for the two, and checking the bathrooms on the way back as well just in case they were hiding in one.

Asad waited for the door to the Bar Car to slide open, and stepped through. The bar was filled with people now, and he quickly walked through the crowd. He walked briskly down the next few cars and reached the tail end of the train. Asad climbed the stairs two at a time and went up to the second level to where they had parked the Audi. The LED display reminded him again of the time running out, and he started nervously clenching his fists. *Nine minutes.* He stood by the Audi, took out the phone, and tried Samir again.

Jonathan opened the door leading out of car number eight.

"So far, so good," he said.

"We'll be there soon," Leigh said, looking at the LED display. "Shouldn't we get back to the Fiat?"

Jonathan exhaled, scratching his stubbly chin with his free hand. "I don't know. If he was making his way through the train, he spotted our car no doubt. I don't think it is safe. And besides, there may be more of them."

They walked through the compartment between the cars. When Jonathan pressed the button to open the door, the cell phone vibrated again in Leigh's hand. She startled and put a hand up to her chest.

"This thing's going to scare me to death," she said, and looked at it. "It's him again."

Jonathan, waiting for the door to open, looked down at the phone, then looked up through the door as it opened. Past the rows of parked cars and people, he saw the big Moor standing by a blue Audi, holding a phone up to his ear.

Their eyes met.

Asad, waiting for Samir to pick up, saw the door at the front of the train car slide open. His eyes went wide with surprise. Standing at the door was the man, holding the gilded reliquary at his side, and the woman standing beside him peering at a phone, the screen bright and flashing. Asad lowered the phone, mouth open. They stood staring at each other in disbelief for a second or more. Asad couldn't believe it. Right in front of him, not one-hundred feet away, was everything he needed to finish the job. The scientists, the Sudarium, the end of his labors.

Asad launched himself towards them, sprinting down the rail car.

Jonathan took a step back through the doorway, searching futilely for some way to shut it. Leigh looked up from the phone at that moment and gasped, dropping the phone. The big Moor was sprinting towards them, closing the distance fast.

Jonathan yanked on the door again and, whether due to his efforts or due to a timer, the door swooshed shut.

"Run!" Jonathan yelled.

Leigh turned and furiously pressed the button for the door behind them. It slid open and she ran through it, Jonathan was on her heels as he ran, awkwardly carrying the reliquary. They sprinted down the rail car, past the few people standing there. Leigh reached the door first and pounded on the button.

"Come on, come on!" she yelled at the door.

Jonathan glanced behind him. The door at the far end of the car slid open and the big Moor sprinted through.

"Hurry! He's catching up," Jonathan cried out.

The door slid open with agonizing slowness. Leigh ran through and on to the next door even as Jonathan worked on closing the door they'd just run through.

Leigh sprinted down the next car, which was virtually empty, and Jonathan followed closely. She snuck a glance at the LED display at the front of the car as she neared the next door.

Five minutes to arrival. *May as well be five years with this killer chasing us*, she thought.

She ran to the door and punched the button, sweating now from exertion or fear or both. Behind them, at the other end of the car, Asad slid the door open and ran towards them. They repeated the drill at the next door, and stepped into the empty upper level of the Bar Car running as fast as they could towards the front of the train. Before they were even at the next door, Asad was entering the Bar Car.

"He's getting closer!" Jonathan yelled out.

Leigh worked on the door right when Jonathan got to her and they both spilled into the connector between the cars. Jonathan looked around for something, anything, to jam the door, but there was nothing.

Leigh opened the next door and they ran through. They were back at the solitary Aston Martin and almost ran into it. The silver-haired man, sitting on a fold-down seat at the side, looked up from his phone. Jonathan peered through the window behind him at the big Moor bearing down, then looked up at the Aston Martin sitting there. He decided his plan in an instant.

"Get in," he told Leigh.

"What?"

"Get in the car!"

"Are you serious?"

"Do it!" he cried out and ran towards the driver's side of the car, which, he remembered, was on the right side. The car, as Jonathan suspected, was unlocked with the keys in it.

Jonathan opened the door, threw the reliquary in, and jumped in the car. Leigh opened the door and tumbled into the passenger's seat.

The silver-haired man stood up, open mouthed, looking on with incredulity at the two strangers jumping into his car.

"What now, mister?" Leigh asked, practically yelling.

Jonathan pressed the red glowing "Start" button and the big V12 roared to life. He pulled the small silver lever into drive and floored it. The exhaust thundered in the enclosed train car as the Aston Martin leapt forward. Leigh held on to the grab bar above her. The front of the train car loomed in front of them as the lights from the tunnel outside flashed. In a matter of seconds, they covered the length of the train car.

Asad raced in the door at the back only to find the two gone and, incredibly, the Aston Martin speeding down the compartment. He paused a second, staring in disbelief. He pulled out his gun.

Jonathan slammed on the brakes, stopping just short of the wall. Leigh braced again against the leather dash.

"Get out!" Jonathan cried out as he opened the door.

Leigh scrambled out of the car and ran towards the train's door. A bullet whizzed overhead. Jonathan slipped out of the Aston Martin and glanced back at Asad, who, after standing still for a second and firing, had begun to race towards them again, gun in hand.

Jonathan looked around. There was nothing to stop the big Moor with. He pulled out Samir's gun and aimed, but the silver-haired man was right behind Asad. Jonathan didn't trust himself to shoot, and feared hitting the innocent man.

What he decided next he did without much thought. Jonathan took the reliquary and shoved it into the footwell of the car, jamming down the accelerator and the brake pedal. He wedged the reliquary against the seat. The Aston Martin's big V12 roared and thundered, the tachometer bouncing off the rev limiter. As he shoved the reliquary in, the gun slipped out of his grip and jammed between the seat and the sill. "Crap," he hissed, and looked over at Asad bearing down. Still leaning half inside the car, he grasped for the gun, but there was no time. Jonathan pulled the silver transmission lever into reverse, and dove out of the way.

The next few seconds happened in slow motion, it seemed.

The tires of the Aston Martin smoked and squealed as the whole car shot backwards through the train car. The big engine overpowered the brakes and the auto gained speed, flying driverless in reverse with the driver's side door still open. It veered to the side and the door caught against a folded seat cropping out from the wall of the train. The door snapped back and off, flying and scraping down the floor as the Aston Martin relentlessly gathered speed towards the astonished owner of the car and towards Asad, who had stopped dead in his tracks.

Asad snapped out of it and ran away from the oncoming car, back towards the door he'd just come through. The silver-haired man was at his heels as the Aston Martin came towards them both.

The Aston Martin started to veer more to the right. The back corner hit the side wall of the train car and, suddenly and violently, the Aston Martin jackknifed sideways. There was a horrible scraping noise as the back end of the Aston Martin punched through the aluminum skin of the train, like a child punching a toy car through tin foil. The outside roar of the train, blazing through the tunnel at a hundred and fifty miles an hour, practically drowned out the insistent roar of the big V12 and the squealing tires of the car. The tires smoked as the Aston, with a seeming suicidal will of its own, tried to drive itself out of the very hole it had punched in the side of the train.

Asad and the silver-haired man raced through the door to the compartment between cars. Asad glanced back and, seeing the car jackknifed and imbedded in the side of the train, stopped. The silver-haired man continued running, not turning to look, and disappeared through the next door.

The Aston Martin kept inching out of the train sideways, its tires smoking and clawing at the floor. Suddenly, a metal support on the train gave way and the car punched halfway through. The rear tires, now hanging out the side of the train, spun impotently in the air. The car rested precariously, half-in and half-out of the train. The engine revved and howled, but was drowned out by the thunder of the train speeding down the tunnel.

Jonathan was on the floor where he'd landed, coming up to one knee as he looked on at the sports car dangling out of the side of the train. Leigh stood behind him, open-mouthed, staring in disbelief at what Jonathan had done.

The reliquary, she thought. *The Sudarium.*

There was another frighteningly loud noise. What happened next happened with savage speed.

The train, speeding down the tunnel towards a pinpoint of light, passed a signal pole, flashing green. The Aston Martin, hanging halfway out of the speeding train, slammed against the signal pole with metal-crushing violence. The impact jolted the train. The collision sent the Aston Martin tearing a gash down the train's side and towards where Asad stood watching.

Operating on pure survival instinct, Asad dove backwards towards the closed door of the next train car. The Aston Martin yawed and twisted, caught by the pole, and ripping sideways through the train's aluminum skin. It careened towards the thin wall separating Asad from the train compartment. Scraping metal and sparks showered the interior through the long gash that had opened in the side of the train. The car, the twisted metal of the train, and the whole wall at the rear of the train car were thrown rearward by the force of the impact. It all came down upon Asad, who dove to the ground. The last thing he saw was the back wall of the train collapsing on top of him, and then there was darkness.

Jonathan stood up by Leigh. They had been watching as the Aston Martin rocketed back and punched through the train when the impact with the signal pole sent a tremendous shudder through the entire train. They struggled for footing as the train started oscillating in a worrisome way. The lights of the train flickered and, somewhere, alarms started to sound.

Jonathan grabbed Leigh's hand as she stood mesmerized by the destruction. "Let's go," he tugged at her.

She pulled her hand away, slipping away from him. "The Sudarium," she said and started running towards the wrecked Aston Martin and the shredded metal that was the other side of the train car.

Jonathan grabbed hold of her hand again, tighter this time, and pulled her back. "Don't worry, let's go," he insisted. He held on to her hand, not letting her go.

"But Jonathan," she protested.

"Trust me," he said, calmly.

The tone in his voice, a deep and sincere calm in the middle of this storm of chaos, convinced her, at least for the moment.

They ran towards the front of the train. Red emergency lights flashed and they could feel the train slowing as the brakes dug in. A great shudder came from behind them and the train gave another sickening oscillation, like it was going to tip to the side. They ran to a set of stairs leading to the first level and carefully but quickly made their way down.

The first level was full of people. There was apprehension at the emergency lights and the bumps the train absorbed. Tension was beginning to fill the air, but panic had not set in. Yet.

"We've got to get as far forward as possible, get off this train as soon as we can," Jonathan said.

"But the Sudarium," Leigh protested again.

"Don't worry," he assured her.

Leigh took a deep breath and clutched at the bag at her side. At least she had this, she thought.

They ran, jostling past people. Jonathan looked out the train window. The train was slowing now, but the walls were lighter with — what? — sunlight? Yes, it was sunlight, he noted. They were nearing the surface.

He redoubled his pace, pressing through the train cars and the increasingly panicked passengers, Leigh following close. They soon reached their car, the little green Fiat still there at the front. Jonathan ran past it, Leigh in tow.

"What about the car?" she asked, tugging at Jonathan.

"Leave it. Look," he pointed out the window at the tunnel wall. "These cars aren't going anywhere. Not for a good long while."

The train finally came grinding to a halt. A distant circle of light shone far off, the exit of the tunnel.

A pleasant and calming recorded voice came on the loudspeakers, imploring everyone to proceed calmly to the emergency exits. Jonathan and Leigh were near the front of the train, already there.

The door opened and steps unfolded down. They hurried down the steps onto the utility access pathway that lined the side of the tunnel. The gathering crowd of passengers pressed behind them and many were pouring out of the exits in front of them. They hurried through the mob, towards the mouth of the tunnel, towards the daylight. Jonathan was grateful for the light shining in; it quelled his fear, which, now that they were in flight mode, had started to rise in him again.

"You up for running?" he asked Leigh.

"Try and catch me," she said.

They ran towards the daylight, with not a clue as to what they would do when they reached it.

CHAPTER 8

Euroshuttle Train, Folkestone, England
May 24, 2025   8:49 a.m.

Asad blinked once, then opened his eyes, trying to make sense of where he was and what had happened. A distant alarm blared, yellow lights flashed from somewhere, blocked by something huge on top of him. He tried to move but was pinned down. *What was it?* He struggled to think, to replay the last moment before he'd lost consciousness. The wall of the train, the separator between compartments, had been ripped apart by the force of the impact with the auto. That's what was on top of him now. He took stock of his body. The left leg. A jolt of pain shot through when he tried to move it.

Asad placed his hands on the collapsed wall resting on top of him. He gave a tremendous push with his considerable strength. The wall inched up and caught on something, allowing him precious inches to move. He scooted back, his leg screaming at him. He ignored the pain as best he could. Behind him was the door to the adjacent train car; he scooted back towards it, towards light and freedom. Pushing back with his good leg, he spilled into it.

He leaned on his back for a second, collecting himself and looking at the roof of the train car, which was bathed in yellow emergency lights. Asad leaned up onto his elbows and stared at his leg. An ugly shard of aluminum jutted from his left thigh. He examined it. Blood was oozing out, darkening his pants. With a deep breath, he took his belt off and cinched it tight around his thigh. Asad took another deep breath and in one quick move yanked the shard out of his leg. His vision clouded for a moment but he willed himself back to consciousness.

Asad allowed himself a moment to collect his senses, then rose up slowly, grabbing hold of the wall to help himself up. In front of him was the door to the ruined train car, bisected halfway up by the wall that had collapsed and had pinned him down. He looked down at the space he had been in, the space that had saved his life. Above that, he could see the entire ruined train car. A huge gash ran alongside the wall and the tunnel's emergency lights were visible through it. Below him, underneath the sirens, he could hear the murmur of people as they evacuated. The Aston Martin, almost cut in half by the impact with the signal pole, was jammed diagonally, imbedded in the side of the train.

Asad shook his head at the surreal scene. He gingerly tried out his leg, putting weight on it. He could walk, but barely. He closed his eyes again, playing back what had happened. *The man, Tremaine.* He'd stuffed the gilded reliquary into the car. Asad had seen it, he was sure, before all hell had broken loose.

He limped over to the door, his wound oozing blood. With some effort, he crawled over the ruined wall that bisected the door. He hitched his bad leg over, then his good one, then slid down the partition, tumbling awkwardly. Asad regained his balance and stood. He limped over to the Aston Martin, to the driver's side. The door had been ripped open and rested fifty feet down the train compartment. Asad peered inside, and, sure enough, he saw the reliquary jammed in the footwell against the seat. He reached in and, with a shove, unjammed it. He brought the reliquary out of the smoking ruin of a car and took hold of it with both hands. Limping, he made his way up the train car, past the Aston Martin's door resting on the ground, and over to the stairs.

At least he had the Sudarium, he thought. The scientists he could catch up with again. But the main thing was the Sudarium, the holy relic that he should have destroyed back in Oviedo. Asad paused a moment amid the flashing lights and insistent sirens. *Why did the man leave it?* In a rising panic, Asad set the reliquary down and worked the ancient latches. He expected to find it empty, but was pleasantly surprised when the reliquary opened and sitting inside was the stained cloth so precious to these people. Asad breathed a sigh of relief, closed the ancient box and carefully clasped it shut again.

He resumed his long walk down the train car and labored down the stairs to the lower level. Already, the train car was empty, the passengers having mostly evacuated from here. He looked out the window at the line of people walking hurriedly up the tunnel, no doubt coming from the tail end of the train. They were evacuating, and he had to leave too. The Audi was a lost cause now; it would be hours before the train was taken back up to the loading ramps.

Asad thought suddenly of Samir. He brought out his phone and dialed it again. No answer. He thought for a moment. With his leg like this, it would take all his strength to evacuate the train and the tunnel. He could not afford to go looking for the young man. Samir could take care of himself, wherever he was.

Holding onto the railing, Asad stepped one leg at a time down the steps to the tunnel floor. Mercifully, the train had stopped within sight of the mouth of the tunnel. He limped, reliquary in hand, towards the distant pinpoint of daylight at the end. He dialed the Lawyer to let him know the good news.

Euroshuttle Terminal, Folkestone, England
May 24, 2025   8:50 a.m.

Leigh and Jonathan walked right past all the emergency workers attending to the wounded.

"No time for any of that," Jonathan said as they went past.

The two walked quickly to the end of the tracks to the unloading ramps where, had the train arrived, the autos would be offloaded.

"Where are we going?" Leigh asked, with frustration in her voice.

"Manchester, silly," he said, smiling.

"I can't believe you left the Sudarium on the train," Leigh said.

Jonathan smiled slyly. "What makes you think it's on the train?"

"I saw you shove it into the car, right before—" Leigh waved her hands in the air, "right before all the craziness." She stopped and stared at him. "I still can't believe you did that. What were you thinking?" she asked in an excited and loud tone.

"I wasn't thinking," Jonathan said.

"I'll say."

"No one's ever accused me of being much of a thinker. I'm more the doer type."

Leigh rolled her eyes, then fixed her gaze on him. "So how about it, mister?"

"How about what?"

"You told me not to worry about the Sudarium. So, here I am, not worrying." Leigh said this and stood in the middle of the road, arms crossed, where normally the train would be unloading the autos.

Jonathan grabbed her hand and walked on towards the end of the road with her in tow. "Don't worry," he said. "It is safe," he added.

"Where? Where is it safe?"

"Look in your bag," he said, with an amused smile on his face.

Leigh stopped again. She unclasped the bag at her side and stared down into it. She glanced up at Jonathan, then back down into the bag. "You dog, you," she exclaimed.

Jonathan laughed.

"You took it out," Leigh said, "out of the reliquary." She reached into the bag and brought out her tablet, wrapped with the Sudarium. It was surprisingly supple and soft, like a well-worn and loved pillowcase. Leigh stroked it, staring at it in the pale silvery English sun. "You dog, you," she repeated. "You switched it."

Jonathan nodded. "I had a feeling it would be safer at your side than in that big golden case. That thing was a walking target."

"That's why you took so long coming upstairs in the train," Leigh said, still trying to figure it out.

"Yes."

"You could have told me, you know," she said with a disapproving look on her face.

"What? And have you be all nervous about carrying it?" Jonathan shook his head.

Leigh stood a moment and carefully put it back in her bag. "So what's in the reliquary, then?"

Jonathan laughed. "A rotten surprise," he said with a smirk. Jonathan glanced around them. "Come, let's keep moving."

They veered away from the loading ramps and walked down the road the cars normally would take. Arriving from the opposite direction was a string of ambulances and fire trucks.

"Everywhere we go—" Jonathan said and shook his head.

They walked further past the road and saw a long line of cars waiting to load the train for the return trip. A terminal building sat to the side. Spotting a taxi sitting alongside, they made their way to it.

Leigh went up to the taxi, a tall black cab in the typical English style, and knocked on the window. The cabbie, half asleep, rose up and lowered the window.

"Hello there, lass," he said in a Scottish accent.

Leigh smiled. "We need to get to the passenger railroad station, and quickly," she said.

"Well, hop on in then," the cabbie said, and they did. He punched the button to start the fare and set off in a silent electric hum. "I hope you were not in that mess I heard about on the radio," he said as Jonathan and Leigh settled into the ample back seats.

"Actually, we were," Leigh said, and cast a glance at Jonathan, then whispered under her breath so only he could hear, "actually, we caused it."

"Oh my," the cabbie said.

"Not to worry," she said. "We got through it in one piece."

They drove down the road, out of the Eurotunnel deboarding area.

"Where you off to?" the cabbie asked.

"Manchester," Leigh said. "Home," she added with a smile.

"Nearest place to catch that train is at Folkstone," the cabbie explained, pulling onto the Motorway.

"Sounds good," Leigh said.

They rode for a short while, exiting the Motorway, and pulled into the Folkstone station.

Leigh and Jonathan got out of the cab.

"Thank you," Leigh said, leaning into the cab and handing him a twenty-euro bill. "Sorry, we haven't had time to change to pounds. Keep it."

"No worries," said the cabbie. "And thank you."

The taxi pulled away, leaving Jonathan and Leigh at the entrance of Folkstone train station.

Jonathan took Leigh's hand and walked in. "First train heading north we're on, okay?" he said.

"Agreed."

The station was practically empty. Most passengers that passed through here were on through-trips from the continent, and not many people started or ended their voyage here. Jonathan scanned the board, and in a matter of minutes they had pounds in hand and tickets for the high-speed to Manchester, connecting in London, and departing in fifteen minutes. They went towards the track and waited.

After minutes of comfortable silence, Leigh regarded Jonathan.

"What?" he asked her.

"Nothing. Good move back there. A bit daft — but good. Thanks for taking care of me," she said with sincerity.

"Anytime," Jonathan said and smiled.

A chime rang and an LED sign lit up over the track.

"Our ride," Jonathan said.

The sleek modern train pulled into the station and Jonathan and Leigh climbed onboard and settled into their seats, facing each other.

Jonathan peered around, examining his surroundings. "I think we're reasonably safe here," he said.

After a short stop, the train started to move silently out of the station. For the first time in seemingly forever, they both relaxed. They stared silently out the window at the English coast as the train relentlessly gathered speed.

"Can I see your phone?" Leigh asked. "I want to touch base with the Old Man."

"Here you go, jellybean," Jonathan said and handed her the phone and the battery, which he had taken out.

Leigh gazed at him silently.

"What?" he asked.

She leaned across and kissed him quickly on the lips.

"What was that for?" Jonathan asked.

"It's all chemicals," Leigh said and smiled.

PART 5

Peter and John walked back to the tomb that afternoon, leaving the others arguing with the women. He was alive, some of the women had claimed. John walked towards the tomb, grateful to be outside. As they approached, he brought out the bag. "I will gather up the burial cloths. I am already unclean," John said, thinking back suddenly to his wrapping the cloth around the Master's head, to the blood on his hands two days ago. "I do not care," Peter said sullenly. They both walked into the empty tomb. "They are still here," John said. The burial Shroud still lay flat against the stone. Carefully, John rolled it up. He wept as he saw the bloodstained stone beneath, the white limestone discolored red and pink with the Master's blood. Peter took the Sudarium from the nook. They placed both the Shroud and the Sudarium in the bag and carried it back to the others.

CHAPTER 1

The Peak District, England
May 24, 2025 8:50 a.m.

The Bentley Brooklands glided down the hedge-lined narrow road. Caine, in the backseat, nervously fidgeted with the phone. The train should have arrived, and Asad should have called by now. He started fearing the worst.

As he thought this, the phone buzzed in his hands. He hurriedly answered it. "Leon? Are you here yet?" Caine asked Asad.

"There's been — an accident," Asad said through a crackly bad connection. "But, I have the Sudarium."

Caine breathed a sign of relief. "That's great news, buddy. We'll have to go celebrate."

"The two got away, though," Asad quickly told him.

Caine cursed. "Well, that's not so good news. Where are they?"

"They left on foot. I do not know. I'll keep working my way to Manchester, and if you have any information, let me know," Asad said. Caine could hear the man laboring for breath a little, as if he were under some duress.

"Are you okay? You sound — different."

"I was hurt. I'll be fine," Asad said as he continued up the tunnel on his bad leg. "Shall I destroy the Sudarium?" he asked. That was, after all, the job.

Caine thought about it. This new change in circumstance could be played to his advantage. After all, why destroy a priceless relic? Why not sell it? *Because you'll be killed if you don't finish the job*, a part of him thought.

"No," he heard himself saying, despite his misgivings. "Hold on to it. Make your way to the Hilton in Manchester with the — thing I ordered," Caine said, pausing and mindful of the driver. "I'll meet you there."

He hung up and slumped back into his seat, analyzing the situation. He could keep the Sudarium and, if he were caught, only then would he destroy it. Until then, he would keep silent. He would wait and see how things played out. In the near term, he was not risking much. He could always talk his way out. He stared out the window contemplating the countryside.

"Is it much further?" Caine asked the driver.

"Actually, sir, we're here. We've been in Mr. Lahmbrecht's estate for five minutes. It'll be a few more until we reach Voland Manor."

"Voland Manor?"

"Yes, sir," the driver said without taking his eyes off the narrow road. "Mr. Lahmbrecht bought these lands ten or so years ago. Not so popular with the locals to have, well, a foreigner, if you pardon my expression, come in and buy up the place."

Caine nodded. He'd met Lahmbrecht before, but had never been summoned to his estate.

Caine stared out the window. The hedgerows lining the road thinned out and they entered a forest. To his right, a stag eyed the car warily before retreating into the dense woods. The Bentley rolled silently through the bucolic surroundings. The forest grew sparser and then a large expanse of green lawn came into view, which gave way to manicured gardens. They passed a low stone wall. Caine noticed a few security cameras set up at intervals, though there were no guards to be seen. *Minimal personnel*, Caine remembered a conversation with Lahmbrecht years ago. The man was distrustful to the extreme. Even at the firm, only Caine and his assistant were allowed to handle all but the smallest transactions for Lahmbrecht and his many companies.

The road curved and, past a copse of trees, Voland Manor came into view. Huge and sober, the big stone manor house dominated a rise in the land.

"Here we are, sir," the driver said. He pulled the Bentley right into a carriage house at the side, itself as huge and elegant as a mansion. The car came to a stop.

A uniformed man materialized at the car door and opened it. Caine exited, stiff-legged after the long ride from the airport.

"Mr. Caine? This way, sir," said the uniformed man, the butler, Caine presumed.

Caine gathered his bag and the butler offered to carry it.

"No, thanks," Caine said, and held onto the bag protectively. He followed the butler down a stone court to a side entrance in the manor house. He walked in, trading the silvery morning radiance of the outside for the dim reddish glow inside. There was a long oriental runner lining the lengthy narrow non-descript hallway. *The servant's entrance*, thought Caine with disdain.

He followed the butler down the long hall, past closed doors. All the walls were paneled in rich oiled wood. The whole place smelled ancient, of old library books and sandalwood and must. The butler opened a door and they came out into a large room, a receiving hall, filled with antiques. The room looked like it had been decorated in the 1700's and, Caine supposed, it probably had been.

"With your pardon, sir, Mr. Valenti will take you from here," the butler said and quickly disappeared back down the hall.

Caine was left alone in the room. He gazed at the heraldic portraits of long-dead people, and their eyes, which seemed to follow him around the room. He walked to one wall, filled with framed pictures of the Old Man with various heads of state and dignitaries. *Jesus, is that Putin?* Caine asked himself, staring at the picture of Lahmbrecht standing dourly alongside Russia's newly re-elected President. There was Lahmbrecht next to former president Obama, former president Johnson, and the current president, shaking her hand. There was another picture of him standing shaking hands with Bono at some sort of ribbon cutting in what looked like Africa. Caine shook his head. He knew the man was well-connected, but it still impressed him.

Caine continued looking around the room, waiting. On the mantle of a fireplace, he spied a grand ornate clock. Curious, Caine went to it. A great dragon slumbered at its base, its head and tail meeting in the middle. A nearly naked woman sat, back arched, holding up the clock face in her hands. Gold, precious stones and pearls adorned her and seemed to drip over her sides and fall on the dragon as well.

He certainly liked surrounding himself with the trappings of old money, Caine thought. Even though he knew Lahmbrecht was anything but old money. Caine should know; he'd been representing Lahmbrecht since the man was a mere multi-millionaire.

A door at the end of the long room opened. Out walked Valenti, Lahmbrecht's assistant. Caine recognized his face from the many videoconferences over the years, but was not prepared for the man in person. He was square-chested, and, even in his impeccably tailored suit, one could tell that an athletic body lay underneath. His face was model-handsome, but with a cruel disinterested sneer on his lips.

"Mr. Caine, it was a good trip, I trust?" Valenti asked.

"It was long," Caine said curtly.

"Right this way," Valenti said through a forced smile.

They walked through the door, down a broad hall lined with even more paintings on one side, and windows looking out to perfectly manicured gardens on the other. Caine tried to ignore the opulent surroundings and mentally prepare himself for the meeting with Lahmbrecht. There were still loose threads. Caine closed his eyes a second and steeled his mind.

They neared the end of the hall and stood in front of a heavy wooden door. An electronic touchpad with a fingerprint scanner was embedded inconspicuously in the wood paneling by the door. Valenti typed in a code and set his thumb on the pad. A green light flashed and the door clicked open. Valenti held the door open.

"After you, sir," he said.

Caine walked in.

Lahmbrecht's study was lined with antique books from floor to ceiling. What was not covered by shelves of books was lined with oak paneling. A painting of water lilies that looked suspiciously like a Monet, Caine noted, hung on one wall. A window to the side looked out at the formal gardens of the estate. The Old Man himself sat at a huge desk on the far side of the room. His hands were on the desk and he sat perfectly still.

"Thank you, Valenti," Lahmbrecht's voice, low and deep and slow, rang out in the library-silence of the room.

Valenti retreated through the door.

"Please sit," Lahmbrecht said, extending a palm at the antique chair across the desk.

"Thank you, sir," Caine said. He hurried to the chair, placed his bag on the ground, and sat.

"I have summoned you here, at great expense, because it is the one place I know we can speak freely," Lahmbrecht said in his slow, meticulous voice.

It sounded to Caine like the man was dictating into a machine. *Hell, like he was a machine*, Caine thought.

"Yes, thank you. It's a lovely house," Caine said nervously, not knowing what else to say.

Lahmbrecht ignored him.

"I have heard the news reports of the plane of Sheik Al-Khaifa flying into Turin Cathedral, and of his fleeing to Bahrain. I have heard reports of confusion in Spain, of Basque terrorists denying the blame for the bombing of the Oviedo Cathedral, and have heard reports of a group called Islamic Reclamation Front claiming responsibility."

Caine smiled ever so slightly. That last one had been his idea. It had a nice ring, he thought.

Lahmbrecht went on, with a scowl on his face now. "But it is what I have not heard in the news that interests me." Lahmbrecht stopped speaking and his stare bored into Caine.

The lawyer shifted uncomfortably in his seat, as if a great laser was burning through him.

"I have heard no news of the two that escaped Turin — unharmed," Lahmbrecht sneered. "No news of those very same two making their way to the lab with the Sudarium of Oviedo in their possession. The Sudarium you were tasked to destroy." Lahmbrecht paused. "I do not abide failure," Lahmbrecht continued, hammering each word against Caine. He let the effect of the words linger in the air.

Caine, unaccustomed to being on the receiving end of anger, squirmed again. It would be wise to tell him now that the Sudarium was in Asad's possession. Caine thought of the promise of riches though, of perhaps being able to sell it. "I've got my man working on it," Caine said, vaguely.

Lahmbrecht held up a wrinkled hand. "Spare me the details," he said. "I want no details. Only results."

Caine began to say something, then stopped. He sat in uncomfortable silence. The distant tick of a clock was the only sound in the richly appointed room.

There was a soft knock on the door.

"Yes?" Lahmbrecht called out, the tone of his voice still harsh.

Valenti cracked the door open and poked his head in. "Sorry to disturb you, sir, but it is Dr. Lancaster on the phone. Voice only."

Lahmbrecht gave a twinge of a smile, really just an upturn of the corner of his mouth. "Put her through," he said. Lahmbrecht composed himself, turning to stone again, and picked up the phone. "Dr. Lancaster, good to hear from you," he spoke into the phone. His voice had the same slow deliberate tone, but with none of the harshness he had shown against Caine, at whom he stared intently now. "Yes. Good. Thank you," he continued on in the conversation.

Caine leaned forward in his chair, eager to hear the other side of the conversation. There was a long pause from Lahmbrecht.

"Well I am glad to hear that you are both safe," Lahmbrecht said. His eyes bored into Caine. "And the Sudarium?" he continued. "Oh, you still have it, safe and sound? Good. When will you be at the lab?" He nodded. "Very well. I look forward to the results."

He hung up and stared at Caine, who was visibly discomfited. "Your man is working on it?" Lahmbrecht asked with disdain.

"I — I can explain—" Caine stuttered, but no words came out. His mind raced furiously as he assimilated this new information. *Why would Asad tell me he had the Sudarium?* Caine asked himself.

"Be silent and listen," Lahmbrecht told him. "They are on the train headed to Manchester Victoria Station with the Sudarium. They are headed to the lab. I do not need to tell you that they must not get to the lab, do I?"

"No sir. They'll be neutralized. I've already got someone in place."

"It is good to know you have at least thought ahead," Lahmbrecht said, but his tone was anything but complementary.

"And they said they had the Sudarium?" Caine asked guardedly.

Lahmbrecht eyed him. "Yes, they did." Though he didn't betray any emotion, Caine's question caused Lahmbrecht to grow suspicious.

"Do you have access to explosive?" Caine asked. "I had not planned for the destruction of the lab, though it's something we should do now, I think."

Lahmbrecht stared ahead, thinking. "I will need to make some calls," he said at last.

"I didn't think it'd get this far," Caine shook his head. "These damned scientists," he cursed under his breath.

"Indeed," Lahmbrecht said.

"I'll need to get to Manchester, sir. To supervise and make sure they are neutralized," Caine said.

"The driver will have you there within the hour. He is at your disposal," Lahmbrecht said, still eyeing him intently.

Caine picked up his bag and rose to leave, anxious to escape the Old Man's gaze.

"Caine?" Lahmbrecht called out as the Lawyer was leaving the room.

"Yes?" He turned around.

"Do not fuck it up," Lahmbrecht said, each word a hammer.

Lahmbrecht's face was an impassive mask, though seething anger roiled underneath. Caine quickly turned and went out the door, glad to shut it behind him.

Valenti stood in the drawing room, hands clasped in front of him. "This way, sir." He walked back to the door where they had entered and Caine followed. "William will take you from here," Valenti said, extending an arm. The butler, William, stood in the hall waiting.

"Thanks," Caine said, not meaning it. He hurried, eager to leave Voland Manor.

Valenti's phone buzzed twice. He turned and walked back to Lahmbrecht's office to see why he was being summoned. "Yes sir?" he asked as he walked in.

Lahmbrecht stood by a wall of the ancient books, idly perusing an old tome from Sir Walter Scott, an original. "Caine will need a truck. A full truck. A repeat of Oviedo."

"Here, sir?" Valenti asked, frowning.

Lahmbrecht nodded grimly. "Yes. For the lab. The sooner the better."

"I'll reach out, see what I can find," Valenti said, still frowning.

"One more thing. Remember that contingency plan we talked about?" Lahmbrecht asked without looking up.

"The clean-up plan? Of course."

"Get it ready."

"Right away, sir," Valenti said, and rushed off.

Lahmbrecht, left alone in his study, held up the two-hundred-year-old book. He read out loud from *Marmion*: "Oh what a tangled web we weave, when first we practise to deceive." The words rang loud in the silence of the study.

CHAPTER 2

Near Ashford, England
May 24, 2025 9:35 a.m.

Jonathan glanced over at Leigh, who sat across from him on the train. She hung up the phone.

"Anything new with the Old Man?" Jonathan asked.

"Nothing. He said to give him a call when we get to the lab."

Jonathan shook his head.

"What is it?" Leigh asked.

"I don't know," he admitted. "There's just something about that man I don't like."

"Jonathan, he's a philanthropist. His foundation gave I don't know how many millions for food and water projects in Africa last year. I should know, I'm on one of the boards. He even funded my water project in Haiti," Leigh said, tucking a stray lock behind her ear.

"Tell me about Haiti," Jonathan asked.

Leigh sighed, her lips tightening. "I don't know."

"Aw, come on. I told you my great hurt," Jonathan said. "You can tell me," he added gently.

"I suppose you're right." Leigh took a deep breath, gazing out the moving window of the train. "It was back in 2010 when I went. I –" she trailed off.

"It's okay," Jonathan reassured her.

Leigh took a breath and continued. "I'd been working for Tabor for three years, virtually non-stop. I'd been working there half the time I was in school too, mind you. I was burned out, losing my edge, losing my desire. My boss, Barnette, God bless him, was understanding." Leigh smiled, reflecting. "That man was almost a second father to me. He suggested I take time off, go do something I'd always wanted."

"And that was when you went to Haiti?" Jonathan asked.

Leigh nodded. "I'd always wanted to go work with the disadvantaged. Get my hands dirty and all that." Leigh smiled wistfully, staring out the window at the blurred scenery. "I got them dirty alright—" she said and trailed off.

"What happened?"

"I was working near St. Marc, helping out with water filters like I'd told you."

Jonathan nodded.

Leigh took a long breath. "One day we went into Port au Prince to pick up a new shipment of supplies. One day—" Leigh paused and took long breath, as if steeling herself, "one day — January 12, I'll always remember."

Jonathan gazed at her eyes as they went far away; he knew he wore that same look when he remembered.

"That day," she continued, "was when it happened. The earthquake. We were in the truck, driving back. At first, I thought someone had hit us or that something was wrong with the truck. We stopped and I got out. I remember—" Leigh paused and wiped away an errant tear that had welled up at the corner of her eye, "I remember the ground shaking, me trying to find my footing. There were screams, confusion, people darting out of the buildings all around us. One of the buildings crumbled. It happened in seconds. It was there one second, the next it was a cloud of dust." Leigh stopped and took a deep breath.

Jonathan put his hand on hers.

"It was a school," Leigh continued. "We dug. Oh God, how we dug. With our bare hands, trying to move the twisted steel and broken concrete. Everyone around us worked furiously. We managed to get a few students out. But there was one," Leigh took a quick breath, stifling a sob, "Angeline. We couldn't get to her. We could hear her; we tried our damnedest to reach her, chipping away at the concrete as day turned to night and night turned into day. For three days I was there, praying, talking with her, keeping her company when I wasn't digging. One night — the third night — she started singing." Leigh's voice broke and she took a deep breath. "I remember thinking all that day that there couldn't be a God, not a good one, anyway. Not one that allowed things like this to happen. One that didn't answer my prayers for this little girl. And then — Angeline started singing. Her voice was angelic. She sang in Creole, and at first I didn't recognize the hymn."

Leigh sang the words in broken Creole in a soft and tremulous voice. The hymn was familiar to Jonathan, though he couldn't quite place it. Leigh switched to English.

"This is all my hope and peace, Nothing but the blood of Jesus," Leigh sang quietly, almost whispering the broken words. "Angeline sang that night, in the pitch dark. I was so exhausted by then, I thought I was imagining it. She kept on singing throughout that dark night, singing me to sleep. I woke up and it was morning. I called out to her, but there was nothing. For hours I tried calling out to her, but I never heard that sweet voice again." The corner of Leigh's lips quivered and two tears rolled down her cheeks.

Jonathan was silent for a time. "That must have been awful to live through," he said at last.

Leigh shook her head. "No, I'm glad I was there. It was awful, but I'm glad I was there — there for Angeline."

Jonathan nodded solemnly.

"The thing that amazes me to this day was that girl's faith. She wasn't angry, or questioning, or anything else. She just sang to God. I wish," Leigh paused and dabbed at her eyes with her hand, "I wish I had that faith."

"Me too," Jonathan said softly. He reached over and, with his thumb, gingerly wiped away another tear that had rolled down Leigh's cheek.

Leigh smiled a tight smile, trying not to cry. "Thanks," she said. She took a deep breath. "I suppose I'm trying to prove it to myself with all of this," she said, tapping the bag with the Sudarium. "To find something to prove that faith. Something concrete. Something that makes sense."

Jonathan nodded. "You'll find it, that faith I mean. One way or another."

"I hope you're right," she said, and put her hand on his.

CHAPTER 3

Ten miles South of Manchester, England
May 24, 2025   9:58 a.m.

Robert Bale Caine looked on at the Manchester skyline in the distance, approaching rapidly.

"To the Hilton, okay?" Caine, nervously fidgeting with his cell phone in one hand, told the driver.

"Yes, sir," the driver said as he piloted the big Bentley up the A-6, easily passing the slower traffic.

Caine took a breath and dialed the phone. He closed his eyes, waiting for her to answer.

Adriana answered at once, her Italian accent unmistakable. "*Pronto.*"

"Darling, where are you?" Caine asked jovially.

"Darling?" Adriana asked with equal parts amusement and annoyance.

Caine gave a forced laugh, not wanting to mention any names in front of the driver.

"Well, I am at the hotel, if you must know," Adriana said.

"Great. I'll be there in—" he cupped his hand over the phone and asked the driver, "fifteen minutes."

"You do not give a girl much time to get ready," she said with annoyance.

"Ah, yes. I almost forgot," Caine continued, "our friends are coming by train."

"Oh?" she asked, paying close attention to this change in information.

"Yes. They left Folkestone about an hour ago."

"I see," she said.

"It'll be great if you can meet them at Victoria Station."

"You can count on that. I'm looking forward to getting very intimate with them," Adriana said.

Even over the phone, Caine could hear the ice in her voice. It sent a shiver through him, one part excitement and one part fear. "I'll see you soon," he said and hung up.

Caine looked absently out the glazed window of the Bentley at the building morning traffic of the highway. He wanted desperately to call Asad, to clear up the confusion regarding the Sudarium. Either Asad had it, as he had said he did, or Lancaster had it, as she had told Lahmbrecht. Caine would have to wait for more privacy to make that call, though.

Euroshuttle Terminal, Folkestone, England
May 24, 2025 10:11 a.m.

Asad set down the reliquary and rested a moment alongside the terminal. Behind him were a few stragglers from the train evacuation. He'd seen no sign of Samir, and he tried him again now, but there was still no answer. Something nagged him, some thought that his brain refused to process.

Another emergency responder, dressed in a bright yellow jumpsuit, approached him. "Are you alright, sir?" he asked.

Asad, his train of thought interrupted, was about to wave him off as he had the last two that had approached him. His leg, though, throbbed insistently. It would be wise to take care of this now. No use in chasing his prey like this, he thought. "Actually, no. I hurt my leg," Asad told the EMT.

The man came closer and examined the leg. "We're going to have to take care of this," the man said, and called for an ambulance from the walkie-talkie at his lapel.

"Make it quick. I've got — a meeting to attend," Asad with hesitation.

"We'll have you on your way as soon as we can." As he said this, a small electric ambulance pulled up to them. Another EMT got out.

"Where are you hurt?" the man exiting the ambulance asked.

"Leg," Asad said and pointed at his left leg. "A piece of aluminum penetrated," he explained. "It did not hit a vein, but it was bleeding. I applied a tourniquet."

The EMT guided him to the back door. Asad's size dwarfed the already small ambulance. He gingerly got in, placing the reliquary inside first. They set off, passing the evacuating passengers, and quickly arrived at the clinic. The building, off to the side, had a big red cross painted on the outside. They went inside to the white, gleaming, and mostly empty interior, and Asad sat on an examination table.

"Thank God it was a minor accident," the first EMT said. "Just bumps and bruises. As a matter of fact, you're the first one we've had to sew up today," he said casually as he cut the bloodied pant leg away.

"Any idea what happened?" Asad asked, knowing full well what had happened.

"Not sure. They're saying a car rolled away and unbalanced the train. It's a bloody wonder it wasn't any worse. This is going to hurt," he added, almost as an afterthought. The EMT liberally poured alcohol over the wound, then dabbed at it with gauze.

Asad sat impassively still, controlling the pain. He'd had worse. Far worse.

The EMT examined the bottle to make sure it was indeed alcohol. "That should've hurt," he said with surprise.

Asad gave the barest trace of a smile. "It did. You can sew it up and I'll be on my way."

The EMT chuckled. "I wish all my patients were like you."

He cleaned and probed the wound, making sure there were no shards of metal left in it. "You really should get this x-rayed to make sure there's nothing broken or nothing broken off in there."

"I understand. I'll take care of it in London," Asad lied.

"Ready?"

Asad nodded.

The EMT sprayed anesthetic on it and started to sew the wound shut. Asad closed his eyes and accepted the pain, placing it far from him. The EMT was skillful and finished quickly. Asad glanced down. It was good work, he thought.

"Try to stay off of it," the EMT counseled as he bandaged the leg.

"I will," Asad said, adding, "Say, any chance I can get a ride to the railroad station? I must catch up to some friends."

The Hilton, Beetham Tower
Manchester, England
May 24, 2025 10:29 a.m.

Adriana Nyx sat in the glass-walled lobby of the Hilton Hotel. From her vantage point at the edge of the bar, she had a clear view of the whole lobby, as well as the porte-cochère outside. She sipped her Bordeaux, watching the people come in and out of the hotel.

A black Bentley pulled up. From it, she saw the Lawyer emerge. She steeled herself for his advances. It had been a few months since she'd seen him in person, when he'd flown her to Miami. He looked pudgier. Not obese, but somehow bloated, as if his pasty skin had stretched and filled.

"*Mama mia,*" she whispered to herself, and tried to think of the money.

The driver of the car retrieved a small silver suitcase from the trunk and handed it to him. The Lawyer clumsily took it, dragging it along and fumbling with his coat, which was draped over his other arm. He spun through the revolving door and the Bentley pulled away to park.

Adriana rose up gracefully, her long legs encased in tight black pants. Her boots clicked on the marble floor and she strode purposefully towards Caine.

He saw her at once. She was hard to miss, prowling catlike through the lobby. Despite his need to stick to business and be professional, his desire for her rose up in him. He smiled at her, gazing at the inky black pools of her eyes.

"Darling," she called out to him in a loud voice from halfway across the lobby, mocking his tone from their earlier conversation.

His smile faded and he cast his eyes downward. He could hear the menace in her voice, the underlying danger that thrilled him. "It's good to see you," he said diplomatically.

"It has been too long," she said, getting close. "You look pale. We need to get that blood of yours pumping." She ran a finger along his temple to behind his ear, tucking his hair back.

Caine closed his eyes at her touch, feeling the familiar electricity go through him. She took hold of his ear and, smiling like she was greeting a long lost lover, cruelly dug her fingernails into the sensitive flesh of his ear.

Caine stood in the middle of the busy lobby and tried not to show his distress. "Later—" he managed to say through clenched teeth, even as tears started to well in his eyes.

Adriana contemplated him with a half-smile playing across her face. She squeezed harder, then suddenly let go.

"All work and no play is going to make you a dull boy," she cooed, and turned and walked back towards the bar.

Caine took a good look at her lean legs wrapped in tight and stylish leather pants. He fumbled with his suitcase and coat and hurried after her.

Adriana sat at her chair and crossed her legs, taking hold of her globe of Bordeaux, swirling it, and sipping it nonchalantly. Caine set the suitcase down, dropped the coat, and pulled up a chair. He picked the coat back up and sat down, breathing loudly. He fumbled with the coat and finally laid it across his lap.

"Are you nervous?" Adriana asked, amused.

"You always make me nervous," he stammered.

"Is that a bad thing?" she asked.

"No. Not at all," he said, composing himself, and even managing a smile. Caine took a deep breath. His trysts with Adriana were always one part fear, one part excitement, and they always left him battered and bruised, literally and figuratively. He craved them and craved her cruel attentions. But this was business; there was much to be done and time was crucial. Business before pleasure, he told himself. *And pain*, he thought.

Adriana stared at him dispassionately, as if she were contemplating a lobster in a tank. Caine glanced up at her, then back down, unable to meet her gaze. He looked at his watch.

"Their train should be here in two hours or so. Do you have a plan?" he asked.

"I do," Adriana said, straightening up and turning her mind to business. "I found something very interesting from the information you sent me."

"What's that?"

"Where our good friend Doctor Lancaster lives."

"And where's that?"

Adriana took a sip of her wine, pausing for effect. "Here."

"In the hotel?" Caine asked.

"No, you imbecile. Not the hotel. Above it," she lashed out at him.

Caine looked confused. Adriana rolled her eyes.

"The hotel," Adriana explained, "only goes up to the twenty-third floor, which is a posh bar. The floors above that are residences. Very exclusive residences. Doctor Lancaster lives in 4611." Adriana smiled when she'd finished revealing this. Her lips were stained red by wine. "The only thing is," she continued, "security is tight. Many celebrities live there. It will be difficult to enter. The elevators, the entrances and all apartments are controlled by fingerprint locks."

Caine looked pensive, then shook his head. "That won't work. They'll probably go to the lab first. We have to keep them from going to the lab."

Adriana frowned. "I've been by the lab. It is near here. There is a gate, security. If they take a cab from the station, they'll be in the gate before I have a chance at them."

"That leaves the station, then," Caine reasoned.

"That will be difficult — they know me."

"It's your only chance."

Adriana took another sip of her wine, thinking about the station. "I really need another man. Where is the big man?" she asked.

"I'm not quite sure," Caine admitted, shaking his head. "He missed them on the train," he added. *Like you did in Venice,* he thought, but didn't say.

Adriana's eyes suddenly brightened. "I have an idea — and I'll need you," she announced.

"Me?"

"*Porco!* Yes, you," she spat out at him. "It will be easy, do not worry," she said, then turned calmer, with a half-smile on her face.

"What?" Caine asked, seeing the change of expression.

"What do you think I'll look like as a blonde?" Adriana asked. Her lips parted in a cruel grin.

CHAPTER 4

Manchester, England
May 24, 2025 12:31 p.m.

Leigh shook Jonathan's leg. "Wake up, sleepyhead."

Jonathan blinked, looked out the window, disoriented for a second. The red brick nineteenth-century warehouses and gleaming steel and glass modern buildings of Manchester filed past the train's windows. "Are we there yet?" he asked sleepily. He'd been dozing for the past two hours.

"Almost. We're pulling into Victoria Station."

Jonathan sat up. "So this is home?"

"Yes," Leigh said, with a look of relief on her face at being back among familiar surroundings.

"A bit dreary, isn't it?"

"Hush, you. It has its charms."

Jonathan watched as the train went past more old brick factories and warehouses, most of which had been converted to condominiums and shops. There were huge skyscrapers as well, a mixture of modern and old that did have its charm, Jonathan admitted. Through a gap in the buildings, he caught sight of a huge white Ferris wheel, the Manchester Wheel, which then disappeared as it was blocked by more buildings. The train slowed and they pulled into the industrial-age black iron and glass canopy that enclosed Victoria Station. Leigh sat on the edge of her seat, looking out the window.

"You excited? You look excited," Jonathan noted.

"It feels good to come home," she said. "It's been a long time, you know? A long few days."

"It certainly has. But it hasn't been without its charms," he said and gave her a small wink.

Leigh smiled at him and put her hand on his. She then took out the cell phone and swiped it on. "Calling Tony," she said to Jonathan, cupping a hand over the receiver. "Tony?" she called out into the phone, holding a hand over her opposite ear to block the train's insistent announcement that they were arriving. "Hey Tony," she said. "Yes. Fine. We're here. Is everything ready?" she asked, pausing. "Wonderful. See you soon."

Leigh hung up and handed the phone back to Jonathan.

"Everything alright, I take it?" he asked, pocketing the phone.

"Yes. He's great, Tony is. My right hand," she said.

"Is the lab far from here?"

"Not too far. Twenty minute walk or so."

"Walk?" Jonathan asked, raising an eyebrow. "I pictured some huge modern compound out in the middle of nowhere."

Leigh laughed. "Hardly. You'll see. It's rather modest. We call it 'The Brickhouse.' It suits us well, though."

The train finally stopped and people around them rose, taking up jackets and bringing down suitcases from the compartments above the seats. Leigh stood up, holding her bag at her side containing the precious Sudarium and her tablet computer. Jonathan got up and stretched.

They made their way out of the sleek bullet train, which seemed out of place in the decidedly more Victorian surroundings of the train station. They followed the crowd down the platform towards the exits, strolling briskly past the passengers encumbered with luggage. The noonday sun shone brightly through the glass roof.

Leigh looked up. "It's beautiful out. We don't get many days like this," she noted.

"I'll have to take you to the park later, have a picnic when we're all done. You do have parks here, don't you?" Jonathan asked.

Leigh laughed. "Yes, mister, we have parks. And trees. It's not all buildings and bricks."

They neared the edge of the platform, where the huge station lobby began. The high arched ceiling rose over them, an industrial cathedral of steel and stone, blocking out the sun.

Jonathan glanced up at the ornate ceiling, then back down. Ahead of him, a man holding a sign caught his eye. With surprise, he saw their names printed on the sign. He paused, grabbing hold of Leigh. "Look," he nudged Leigh.

A pasty-skinned man in a suit stood at the edge of the platform, holding up the printed sign with both of their names. The man glanced at them, then looked away and stared straight ahead.

"Did you order a limo?" Jonathan asked.

"No," she answered.

"Maybe Lahmbrecht sent it?" Jonathan suggested.

"Maybe," Leigh said. The hair on the back of her neck stood up as they walked cautiously towards the man.

The man turned to them as they approached and stretched a smile across his pale face. "Dr. Tremaine?" he asked.

Jonathan glanced around. "Yes, that's me. That's us," he said, pointing at the sign the man was holding.

"Ah, good. I was afraid I'd miss you," the man said, and extended a hand. "I'm Robert Bale Caine, Mr. Lahmbrecht's attorney."

Still cautious, Jonathan took Caine's hand, which was cold and clammy. He shook it once and let go. Caine offered his hand to Leigh, who shook it and forced a smile onto her face.

"Attorney? Are we in trouble?" Jonathan asked.

"Goodness no," Caine said and gave a forced chuckle. "Mr. Lahmbrecht thought it would be nice to have a ride to the lab. There are also some legal matters we need to discuss, regarding Turin, and the Sudarium. Mr. Lahmbrecht said you were in possession of it?"

Leigh glanced at Jonathan. *No*, he said with his eyes. "We — have some samples," Leigh said vaguely.

Caine stared at Leigh, trying to read her. "Well, we can discuss it on the ride down," he smiled again, showing his small teeth.

Jonathan nodded. "Very well. Let's get on with it."

"Right this way," Caine extended a hand, pointing the way.

"Oh, Jonathan, can't we walk? It's such a nice day," Leigh said, tugging at his arm.

"Leigh, he needs to talk to us," Jonathan said.

"I do," Caine said, turning around and smiling. "Besides, this will get you to the lab quicker."

Leigh took a deep breath. "Alright," she said, and walked reluctantly on after them.

They made their way through the station, past the crowd of people, to a less-used side exit. The three walked out to a narrow side street. A large grey stone building loomed in front of them.

Leigh glanced around, but the street was mostly empty except for a few people walking. "Where's the car?" she asked.

"Oh, I had to park down the street there," Caine said, and pointed. He tried to smile, but it came out all wrong. The man looked nervous, and it was making Leigh nervous.

They walked to the end of the street and onto an even smaller street, almost an alley, off to the side of the station.

"Right through here," Caine said and walked into the alley. "It's hard to find parking around here, they tow you everywhere," he added.

Jonathan followed him, but Leigh hung back a little. At the end of the alley sat a big black Bentley. They walked towards it, down the long alley, surrounded on both sides by the big grey stone buildings.

As they neared the Bentley, Leigh thought she heard footsteps behind her. She stopped and turned. At the entrance to the alley, she saw a blonde woman walking briskly towards them.

Caine turned and stood by the Bentley. He also looked at the blonde walking towards them. "Ah, Ms. Jones," he said, noticing that Leigh had turned and spotted her. "My legal assistant," he added quickly.

Adriana, dressed in a sharp and professional jacket and pants suit, wearing rectangular reading glasses and a blonde wig, hardly looked like herself. Her boots clicked on the red brick of the street. She knew she did not have to make the deception last for long, just long enough for her to get close to the two. She walked towards Jonathan and Leigh casually, but her muscles were tensed, ready to spring.

Leigh gazed at the legal assistant walking towards them. The click of her boots made Leigh look down. She stared at the woman's boots as she walked down the alley. *Those are nice boots*, she thought. Then, something clicked in her brain. Some recognition. What was it? She thought, closing her eyes a moment. *Venice.* The word flashed into her mind and, suddenly, the memory of her frozen in fear in the corner of the hotel room staring at Adriana in her boots was vivid.

Leigh took a step back, then another, walking backwards away from the blonde, and tried to keep a smile on her face. She bumped into Jonathan.

"Excuse you," he said jokingly and grinned.

Leigh turned to face him. The smile from her face dropped and the expression of terror that replaced it made Jonathan's grin vanish. She made a sideways gesture with her eyes. *Look at her*, she seemed to say.

Jonathan looked over Leigh's head at the approaching blonde, but he didn't recognize her. He glanced down at Leigh, who was pressed close to him now. "What?" he asked, and shrugged.

"It's her," Leigh whispered. "The woman from Venice."

Jonathan looked up again and stared at her, into her eyes. Past the glasses, past the blonde hair, it was those same obsidian eyes, shark eyes, from Venice.

Jonathan forced a smile on his face and tilted his head, greeting the woman. He glanced around, taking in the situation instantly. *Be aware of your surroundings*, he heard his father tell him, as if he were whispering the words in his ear. There were only two openings into the alley. In one end of the alley was the woman, in the other end was the car with Caine standing beside its opened door. He saw now that it was a good trap, and they were the ones trapped. He thought quickly, and nudged Leigh towards the Bentley.

"Say, that sure is a neat car; what kind is it?" Jonathan asked Caine loudly as he turned and walked the three steps to the Lawyer, who was standing at the door of the car.

Jonathan acted quickly. He glanced at Leigh and nodded and, as if by some unspoken understanding, they both started running. Jonathan drove his shoulder hard into Caine, knocking him back and against the open door of the car. Leigh sprinted ahead of him and Jonathan, regaining his footing after the tackle, followed.

Adriana saw all this and reacted instantly, sprinting after them.

Caine, who laid half-sprawled on the ground and half-leaning against the door of the car, made a feeble attempt to grab at Jonathan, but missed.

By the time Adriana reached the Bentley, Jonathan and Leigh had reached the end of the alley and had turned right, out of sight.

"You fool!" Adriana called out. She ran past Caine. "Get to the lab!" she yelled.

Leigh ran as fast as she could, thankful she knew these streets well. Jonathan caught up to her, running alongside her. "Follow me — stay close," she said.

"Gladly," Jonathan huffed out.

They turned back towards Victoria Station and ran down the street, past a parking lot and towards a red brick building. Here, at one of the main exits of the station, the people coming out filled the street. They sprinted across the street, mercifully empty of crossing cars at the moment. The Printworks, a big restaurant and nightclub entertainment complex, loomed to their right. The streets were filled with residents and tourists alike enjoying the beautiful late spring day.

Leigh deftly dodged the people crowding the sidewalk, and Jonathan followed close behind. They ran past a green-tinted glass building. From the corner of her eye, Leigh saw their reflections running beside them, following them. She snuck a glance behind her. Adriana, less than a block away, was catching up. Leigh jumped the curb and sprinted into the street to avoid the sidewalk crowded with shoppers. This road, she knew, was just for buses and taxis. The road narrowed and a taxi headed towards them. Leigh hopped back on the sidewalk, which opened up here into a broad square.

The huge Manchester Wheel, which Jonathan had seen from the train, dominated the square. The Ferris wheel rose high in the air, turning slowly with pods full of tourists. They ran past it, past the gleaming steel and glass façade of the Arndale Shopping Centre, and down the road. The buildings here turned from modern glass and steel to the traditional golden Spinkwell stone façades typical of the city.

"This is a hell of a tour," Jonathan breathed out at Leigh who was running furiously, running on adrenaline.

Leigh paid no attention, intent as she was on running as fast as she could. She started breathing hard, and cursed herself for not having kept up on the jogging she normally did every morning. Some people stared at them as they ran, but most were hypnotized by the stores and paid them no mind.

Jonathan craned his head back. Adriana was close — no more than half a block and closing. The road narrowed again and they ran into the shadows of the encroaching buildings. *She's going to catch up*, Jonathan realized.

They ran to a fork in the road and the street widened before suddenly opening up to Albert Square, the center of Manchester. Hundreds of people filled the large square, lazing about in front of the majestic Town Hall with its big bell tower rising to the sky like a slightly smaller version of Big Ben. The clock struck one, and a loud bell sounded out in the square.

Jonathan made a decision.

"Keep going to the lab. Don't stop for anything," he yelled out to Leigh.

"What? Wait!" she called out.

At that moment, Jonathan peeled off to the left, running into the crowded square.

"Wait, you!" Leigh called out again, slowing down. Then, realizing that Adriana was bearing down on her still, and that she was now alone, Leigh redoubled her pace. *I hope to God you know what you are doing*, she thought to herself as fear and adrenaline propelled her forward.

Adriana ran furiously, fists pumping. She'd ripped the reading glasses off her face earlier and now sweat was beginning to bead on her forehead. The two were in front of them, dodging the crowds through the streets. She was close now, so close. As they entered a large square, the man suddenly ran off to the left, into the crowd in the square, leaving the woman running down the road by herself. Adriana slowed for a second, not expecting them to split up. Deciding quickly, she stayed on the woman. She had the bag, and she would be the easier of the two anyway. Adriana smiled and sprinted as fast as she could, closing the distance.

Jonathan dove through the crowd, losing himself in it. He looked over the heads of the people. As he suspected, the woman stayed on Leigh's trail. Jonathan paused for a second, right by a fountain of a gargoyle spitting water, and caught two breaths. He then ran through the crowd, parallel to Adriana. He almost kept pace with her, but was slowed by the crowd. As the crowd thinned out, he ran free.

It had been a long time since he'd played football in college. *You do something enough, you never forget it*, he thought now, the words of his father echoing in his mind. Jonathan sprinted as fast as he could. He picked his route, his approach on her blind side. Jonathan angled back towards her, closing the distance between himself and Adriana. *Just like college ball*, he thought.

Leigh took a chance and looked back again. Her heart sank. The assassin was at her heels. Leigh pumped her arms, running, literally, for her life. She ran out of Albert Square and back into a narrow street. Leigh could hear the woman behind her, the sound of her boots clicking on the pavement.

Adriana was almost there. She extended her arm, reaching for Leigh's hair, the bag strap, anything. Her hand brushed Leigh's hair, and the woman gave a little scream. Adriana savored this, the chase, her prey's fear. She lunged forward and grabbed hold of Leigh's hair. Her hand tightened around it and she began to pull.

Suddenly, Adriana felt a crushing blow from behind, and she tumbled to the ground, tangling with whoever had hit her. As she fell, she realized it was the man that had tackled her. She sprawled on the ground and scrambled to get back up, dazed. Suddenly, everything went white. She tried to get up, but her ears rang and a great pain bloomed in her head. The pain started to get far away and the white started to turn into darkness. She willed herself to remain conscious. She welcomed the pain, tried to take hold of it, to keep her awake and aware, but it was no use. A warm sensation on the side of her head tried to lull her to sleep, beckoning her into velvety darkness. She followed, and all was dark.

It was a perfect tackle, Jonathan thought. *She never saw me coming.*

Right between the shoulder blades, he'd lined her up and leapt at her. He connected and they tumbled together to the ground, hitting his elbow hard as he landed. He ignored the pain and sprang up quickly. Adriana was dazed, sprawled on the ground, and trying to get up. Jonathan, already standing, grabbed the woman by the head and rammed it down against the hard cobblestone street.

It felt and sounded awful, Jonathan thought. Like dropping a Pyrex glass bowl on the ground and having it not quite break. A hollow yet full sensation.

Jonathan knelt down on one knee, examining her. Adriana tried to get up, then her black eyes rolled and she slumped down on the street.

Leigh, having shaken Adriana's grasp, had resumed running. She turned to look and paused, staring at the woman on the ground a few paces back. Jonathan knelt beside the woman, looking like he was praying over a fallen comrade. He was breathing hard and his hair was disheveled. He glanced up at Leigh and gave her a small and tired grin. He rose up and walked to her.

"You okay?" he asked, putting his hand gently to her face.

"Are *you* okay?" she countered, adding, "That was a nasty spill."

"Yeah, I'll be fine," he said, rubbing his elbow.

"What about her?" Leigh asked, pointing at Adriana's unconscious body. A trickle of blood was pooling on the ground where her head lay.

"I don't think she'll be much trouble now," Jonathan said, looking around. A few people from the square further back down the street were staring at them and pointing. "Let's get out of here," he said, noting the unwelcome attention. Jonathan took Leigh's hand and led her away. "How much further is the lab?" he asked.

"We're close — can you jog?"

"Try and catch me," he said, and started off down the street.

CHAPTER 5

Manchester, England
May 24, 2025 1:07 p.m.

Adriana contemplated the sideways world. Her head throbbed. She blinked, looking straight at a curb and the rough cobblestone street. Disembodied voices came from somewhere above her. She tried to move and managed to sit up, helped by strangers that she was just now noticing.

"Are you okay?" a voice asked.

She wasn't, but willed herself up and mumbled something. She stood on unsteady legs, helped up by the good Samaritan at her side. Adriana's head throbbed insistently. She put a hand up to her temple and drew it back wet with blood. She must have looked a sight. *Respectable businesswoman assaulted near Albert Square*, she imagined the headline.

"Which way did they go?" she heard herself ask the small crowd that had gathered around her.

A broad-chested man pointed down the street and hitched his thumb to the right. "They turned there on Peter Street, they did," he said in his thick Manchester accent.

Adriana tested her legs, taking a step, then another. She was dizzy, but recovering fast.

"Hold on there, miss," a young woman said, gently taking her elbow. "You've just had quite a wallop. The police will be here soon."

At the mention of police, Adriana came back fully to her senses. She shook off the concerned woman and broke free of the crowd, jogging down the street. She broke into a run as she recovered and whipped around the corner to Peter Street.

She ran down the eclectic street, a mix of old buildings and modern green glass and steel construction. Though there were a fair number of people walking and going about their business, Adriana thought she could see, far down the street, blocks away, two tiny figures running. Adriana smiled, letting her anger fuel her and ran hard after them. She vowed to herself once again to repay the man. She would watch him bleed to death while she practiced her carving.

Manchester, England
May 24, 2025 1:23 p.m.

"You going to make it?" Leigh asked as they jogged down the pretty leafy residential street on the way to the lab. She slowed to a fast walk to let Jonathan catch up.

Jonathan tried to play it cool, but he was breathing hard. "I don't do the long distance thing. More of a short burst type of guy," he managed to say as he caught up to her.

"I'll try and remember that," Leigh said with a smirk on her face.

Jonathan rolled his eyes and broke into a faster jog again. "How much further?"

"The lab's in Potato Wharf, just a few blocks," Leigh said as they ran side-by-side.

They jogged past the Museum of Science and Industry, past the stares of people in the crowd gathered at the front.

"Here's a shortcut," Leigh said and turned down an alley which ran the length of a block.

They neared the end of the alley, where a pile of trash sat on the side under a sign reading "No Rubbish" painted on the wall.

Jonathan chuckled as he jogged past.

"What's so funny?" Leigh asked.

"Well, that," he turned and pointed at the mound of illicit garbage behind them. He glanced past the garbage to the entrance to the alley and froze. "Crap," he said.

Leigh turned around. "Oh, you're kidding me," she exclaimed.

At the end of the alley, Adriana appeared, running fast towards them.

Leigh and Jonathan glanced at each other and broke into a run. They burst out of the alley onto a road lined with red brick warehouses and converted condominiums. Leigh turned and ran ahead towards a large steel and brick Victorian railroad bridge in the distance. Then, as they crossed an intersection, it all went wrong.

A car, driving fast down street, slammed on its brakes and screeched to a halt. Leigh, ahead of Jonathan, managed to avoid the car, but it caught Jonathan, who was two steps behind her. He was thrown on the hood even as a cloud of dust and smoke from the brakes wafted over them.

"Jonathan!" Leigh cried out.

He landed, sprawled out on the hood face down. Jonathan lifted his head groggily. Through cloudy and disbelieving eyes, he stared right at Robert Bale Caine, sitting at the wheel of the big Bentley.

Caine stared back with a mixture of shock and surprise, then, a slowly dawning realization that he'd not accidentally hit a pedestrian, but instead had hit the very person he was looking for. Caine floored the accelerator. The big Bentley shot forward.

Jonathan rolled towards the driver's side and fell off before the car had gathered too much speed. He landed hard on the curb.

Leigh rushed to help him up. "Hurry," she called out as she tugged on him and kept on eye on Adriana running towards them down the alley, less than a block away.

Jonathan stumbled up, regained his footing and started running, helped on by Leigh. Dazed, but operating on pure instinct, he followed Leigh down the road.

Behind them, there was more screeching of tires as Caine struggled to turn around the big car on the narrow road.

Leigh, urging Jonathan on, said, "Not much further, just a couple of blocks." She cast a glance behind her.

At that very moment Adriana Nyx came running out of the alley. She skirted the Bentley, which Caine was still struggling to turn around, and ran straight towards them.

"Okay, come on, mister," Leigh said, pulling Jonathan along, who was starting to limp.

They ran past a row of brick warehouses, down the weed-strewn and dilapidated industrial street, running alongside a canal filled with brown murky water.

"Almost there," Leigh encouraged him.

Towards the end of the road sat a huge perfectly square red brick warehouse surrounded by imposing metal fencing. A small stainless-steel sign, haloed with blue neon from behind, read "Tabor Applied Genetics

Company." They ran towards the entrance, towards a small guardhouse with a red and white striped gate.

They were close, no more than a football field in length from it. Then, Jonathan tripped and stumbled on the ruined pavement. He caught himself. Rather, Leigh caught hold of him and steadied him. He regained his footing.

As she helped him, she glanced back. The woman was close, but more troubling was the big Bentley barreling down behind her.

Caine blew the horn and Adriana angled to the left as she sprinted, allowing him to pass.

"Move it, cowboy!" Leigh ordered. Jonathan gritted his teeth and redoubled his efforts. As they neared the guardhouse, Leigh yelled, "Tommy!"

The muscular and stocky guard came out of his little shack. He stared in disbelief at a woman — *Dr. Lancaster was it?* — running towards him. At her side was a large man limping along, trying to run. And, even more incredible was the big black Bentley speeding down the road, looking for all the world like it was intent on running them over. Behind all that, another woman ran after the lot of them. He ran his hand over the close-cropped hair on his head.

"Tommy!" Leigh yelled out again.

It *was* his name he'd heard, and it *was* Dr. Lancaster. Tommy went on high alert and sprinted towards them. On instinct, he drew his sidearm.

"Dr. L?" he yelled out.

"Tommy," she called out as they neared. "Help us," was all she could think to say.

Tommy ran to them and they met in the middle of the road. Leigh kept running, helping Jonathan along, towards the gate. Tommy brought up his Beretta 9MM and trained it on the Bentley heading at them.

The car slowed, then came to a screeching stop and started backing up. Tommy kept the gun pointed at the car. The Bentley, far down the street now, skidded to a halt and the woman who had been running opened the door and got in. The car continued backwards before turning and disappearing past the warehouses at the far end of the street.

The danger having passed, Tommy turned and ran back to the guardhouse, where Leigh and Jonathan had stopped and were watching the showdown from the small window.

"Dr. L, what the shit is going on?" Tommy asked, agitated.

"It's a long story. Let's get inside and I'll tell you."

Tommy picked up a phone on the wall and pressed a button.

"Casey, wake up," he said gruffly into the phone. "It's a Code 2. Yes, Code 2," he repeated and paused. "No, I'm not bloody joking — right. Just get over here."

"Everything okay?" Leigh asked.

"Yes, Dr. L. Just give him a minute to get here, we'll whisk you off in no time."

Leigh turned to Jonathan. "Are you alright?" she asked.

Jonathan managed a weak smile. "Never better," he said, and winced. "Actually, that's not exactly true. I'm pretty banged up."

Leigh looked him over, focusing on his head, which sported a nasty bruise on the temple. She touched it.

"Ouch."

"Well, that answers that question. I'll have a good look at you when we get in."

A small windowless van pulled up to the guardhouse. Casey, a lanky young man, got out and came over to them.

"You could be quicker, you know," Tommy said, still holding the gun at his side.

Casey saw it and stepped back. "Jesus, Tommy, guns and all?"

"Don't be a jessie. I said Code 2," Tommy said impatiently.

"I know you said it. I didn't think you'd meant it, you know?" Casey said.

"Well I did and I do. Stay here, and watch for anything untoward. Like a big bloody Bentley," Tommy told him.

"And Italian women assassins," Jonathan added.

"You hear that, Casey? No Italians," Tommy said, then turned to Leigh and shrugged. *What is he talking about?* his expression said.

"I'll explain inside," Leigh said.

"You okay to walk, mate?" Tommy asked Jonathan.

"Yeah, I'll be fine."

Jonathan walked to the van with Leigh's help, and Tommy went to the driver's side. They all got in.

Casey, inside the shack, looked on anxiously. "Be back soon, okay, mate?" Casey called out to Tommy, who nodded as he began driving away.

Inside the van, Jonathan and Leigh finally started to relax. They did not fully let go of their adrenaline edge until they entered the side of the big brick square and the garage door closed them off from the outside world. Only then, when the door closed, did they deflate into each other's arms. They held each other for what seemed like a very long time.

"We made it," Jonathan whispered to Leigh.

CHAPTER 6

Manchester, England
May 24, 2025 1:34 p.m.

Adriana turned her bruised head to Caine.

"Why didn't you get them?" she spat out.

"Why didn't you?" Caine shot back, then, remembering who he was talking to, added, "Sorry."

Adriana ripped the blonde wig off her head and threw it against the Bentley's dash. She let out a terrifying primal scream of frustration and anger. Her face turned hard, almost demonic, before returning to her normal self.

They both stewed in silence in the interior of the car. Caine dared not speak; she was liable to turn on him. He drove back towards the hotel, where he'd left the driver when he'd borrowed the car.

Caine's mind raced through the situation and the few options open to him now. He let out a long sigh.

"I'm screwed," he said, softly, to himself. "We won't get them now. Not in there."

"There's still a chance," Adriana said, staring straight ahead, regaining control.

"What chance?"

"She still needs to come home sometime. And I think I know how to get in," she said with the trace of a sneer on her face.

"That's something. But Lahm—" he stopped, catching himself, and continued, "my employer is going to be furious that they got to the lab," Caine said as he piloted the Bentley down the city streets. He glanced over at Adriana. "Jesus, you're bleeding."

Adriana touched the side of her head and looked at the blood as it dried on her fingertip. "I will be fine. I need to get cleaned up."

"If you say so," Caine said, and stared absently at the road, dreading the phone call to Lahmbrecht, and wondering where the hell Asad was.

He pulled out the cell phone and dialed Asad, keeping one eye on the road.

London, England
May 24, 2025 1:45 p.m.

Asad settled into his First Class seat on the train. He set the black duffle bag he'd bought at the luggage shop in the station on the empty seat opposite him. It contained, after all, a precious relic, and he wanted to keep his eye on it. He relaxed into his seat, and the phone buzzed in his pocket. He brought it out and looked at it.

Caine. He closed his eyes and answered it.

"There you are, where the hell are you?" Caine said before Asad spoke.

"I'm leaving London now."

"You screwed up, Leon, you screwed the pooch." Caine said.

"What are you talking about? I have the Sudarium," Asad said as he stared at the bag.

"I'm not so sure," Caine said. "My sources tell me that the doctor has it, in her lab no less."

Asad frowned, confused. "Hold on," he said.

Asad picked up the duffel bag and headed to the train's bathroom. There, in the privacy afforded him, he unzipped the duffel bag and took out the gilded reliquary. Carefully, he unclasped the latches. His right hand trembled as he did, and he realized he was breathing hard, afraid of what he would find. He'd glanced in there before and the Sudarium had been in there — hadn't it?

Asad opened the reliquary and drew back the purple cloth covering the relic. With sick dread, he examined the stained cloth. He flipped it over and his stomach dropped. A tag was attached to the side of the dirty cloth. The man had switched it.

Everything made sense now, though it was faint comfort. Asad cursed, and hit his big fist into the plastic wall of the bathroom. From far away, he could hear Caine's tinny voice coming from the phone where he'd rested it on the counter. He picked it up.

"—and now they're in the lab," Caine said in mid-conversation.

"They have the cloth. They have the Sudarium," Asad said in a disheartened voice.

"That's what I've been trying to tell you."

"They must have — never mind. It's not important now," Asad said, thinking about what to do. What he *could* do.

"How can we stop them now?" Caine asked.

Asad thought. "I don't know," he admitted. "If we had a repeat of Oviedo, maybe. Can you get — supplies?" he asked guardedly.

"I'm working on that, but I don't know yet. Get to the lab as soon as you can. If I do get the supplies, you'll have to set them off. You may have to drive it in," Caine said, waiting for an answer.

Asad took a deep breath. *So this was it*, he thought. The sacrifice he'd told himself over and over that he was willing to make. *At the hour of judgment, there is no escape*, he though of the old saying now. "What must be, must be," he said into the phone automatically.

"Good. I'll keep you updated. Call me when you get to Manchester," Caine said and quickly hung up.

Asad pocketed the phone and leaned on the counter. He gazed at the mirror in front of him, staring into his own eyes. He saw doubt in them for the first time. And this scared him more than anything else.

CHAPTER 7

Manchester, England
May 24, 2025 1:54 p.m.

Jonathan stepped out of the van into a large loading bay, the remnants of a turn-of-the-century warehouse that had been restored. He glanced around the large open space. Used scientific equipment lay piled up on one side, and a duplicate of the small van was parked on the other side of the room.

"This is your high-tech lab?" Jonathan asked Leigh as he took her hand coming out of the van.

"No silly. This is the garage. Truthfully, I can't remember the last time I was in here," Leigh said.

Tommy shut the driver's door and came over to them. "You alright, mate?" he asked Jonathan, who had a bruise on his head and was holding one arm with the other.

"I'll live," Jonathan said, smiling. "Hey, thanks, man. For back there."

"No problem, mate. Just doing my job," he said, pronouncing it "me job."

Jonathan looked at Tommy closely now. The man looked tough, and had the scars on his closely shaved scalp to prove he was more than words. Jonathan liked him if only for the respect and care he showed to Leigh.

"Tommy," Leigh said and held out her arms. They hugged. "Thanks," she whispered.

"Glad you're okay, Dr. L. We heard about that business in Turin and were worried sick," he said.

"That's not all the business," Leigh said.

"Apparently," Tommy said, running a hand over the stubble on his head.

"I'll have to fill you in later, though. I need to talk to Tony, and quickly," she said.

"Let's go then," he said, and began walking. "We'll go have a pint or two when you settle down, yes? All of us," he added, glancing back at Jonathan.

"Brother, that sounds just about perfect," Jonathan said.

Tommy gave a short good-natured laugh.

They walked across the garage to an old black steel door set into the red brick wall. Tommy opened the door, keying it with his badge, and they all walked into a long brick hallway to another door.

"I'll take it from here, Tommy," Leigh said. "Thank you for everything," she added.

"No problem, doc." He turned to Jonathan. "If you need anything, let Tommy know."

"Hey, thanks again, man. You saved our bacon," Jonathan said.

Tommy laughed at the American expression. "Hey, any friend of Dr. L's is a friend of mine, right?"

"Right."

They shook hands, two hard grips testing each other for strength, it seemed. Satisfied, Tommy let go. He walked back down the hall towards the garage. Leigh and Jonathan watched him go.

"He seems like a good guy," Jonathan whispered to Leigh.

"Yes, he is. He's protective of me. Of all of us, really."

"He's got a hell of a grip, too," Jonathan said, flexing his hand.

Leigh gave a little giggle. "He's probably checking you out, making sure you're up to snuff for taking care of me."

"Am I?" he asked, grinning at Leigh.

"You're holding your own," Leigh said with a sly smile.

She fished through her bag, still scarcely believing that she had the priceless relic in there. She brought out her key card, put it in the slot, and pressed her thumb to a pad. The door buzzed.

"That's some high-tech security," Jonathan said.

"This whole building was designed to protect us from industrial espionage. I never thought we'd need it to protect us from assassins."

Leigh opened the door and they walked into a small room, gleaming white with bright LED lights lining the ceiling. The contrast between the Victorian-era warehouse and the sleek white room was jarring, Jonathan thought.

"Wow," he said.

"You haven't seen anything yet," Leigh said with a smile.

They walked down a gleaming white hall to a door that read "Sampling and Imaging." Leigh put her thumb to a pad by the door and it too buzzed open.

"My office," Leigh said, and, with a sweep of her arm, invited Jonathan in. They entered.

Jonathan stood open-mouthed. The room looked like a small version of the NORAD control center. The whole front of the room was lined floor to ceiling with a huge OLED television, as big as a movie theater. Along one wall was a bank of sequencers, the big black boxes with the flashing lights that Jonathan had seen in Turin. Half of this wall was glass, with what looked like a surgical operating room on the other side. Sleek workstations, about ten in all, lined the opposite wall. About half the stations were occupied with workers busily sifting through their computer screens. Two bigger workstations stood in the center of the room, presiding over everything.

"Don't just stand there, come in," Leigh said, obviously at ease here and happy to be back in her familiar, and safe, surroundings.

Jonathan moved forward into the lab. The door clicked shut behind him. At the sound of the door, a couple of faces turned from the workstations to look at them.

"Hi, Doc," one said to Leigh.

"Good to have you back," said another.

A dark-haired, dark-skinned Indian man turned from one of the two workstations in the center of the room. "Leigh!" he cried out, his face beaming. A big white smile radiated from him. He rose and walked to Leigh and hugged her.

"Tony," she said, still hugging him. "It's good to see you."

Tony let go and turned to Jonathan. "Is this the cowboy?" he asked, eyeing Jonathan up and down.

"I'm not a cowboy. Jonathan's the name." He smiled and extended his hand.

Tony took it, placing his hand in Jonathan's. "Well it's good to meet you, Mr. Not-Cowboy. Leigh's told me a lot about you," he said.

"I'll bet she has," Jonathan said, casting a glance at Leigh, who was blushing pink on her pale face.

Tony laughed.

"So, Tony? Is that a nickname or something?" Jonathan asked.

"You mean because I'm Indian, right? That Hindu people can't have a name like Tony, right?"

"Well — no," Jonathan said, feeling awkward. "No. Yes. Well — yes, actually," he stumbled over his words, embarrassed.

"Oh relax, cowboy," Tony gave a big smile. "I'm just taking the mickey on you."

Jonathan screwed up his face, not understanding. "Mickey?"

"Yes. How do you Americans say it — pulling your leg. I was born in Prestwich, honey," Tony said, still smiling.

"I take it that's not near New Delhi?" Jonathan asked with a wry smile.

"Ah, a kidder! We're going to get along famously, you and I," he said.

"Stop exasperating the man, Tony," Leigh chimed in. "We've got work to do."

"All work and no play," Tony chided her.

"That's what I've been telling her," Jonathan added.

"Don't start, you two. Let's get things going. I want to get the sampling started and then check out Jonathan here," she said.

"Oh?" Tony intoned in a suggestive voice.

Leigh rolled her eyes. "Not what you think. He got banged up on the way here."

Tony looked at Jonathan with concern.

"It was nothing," Jonathan shrugged. "I just got run over by a Bentley," he said, deadpan.

Tony's eyes opened wide.

"I'm fine," Jonathan added.

"Come on, you two. Let's get the sampling going," Leigh said, and walked towards the glass wall of the room and the operating room on the other side. Jonathan and Tony followed.

Leigh poked at a button and a glass door swooshed open. A blast of air came out. Jonathan looked dubiously inside. It was a tiny room with a grated floor and a glass door on the other side. The whole thing looked like an old-fashioned glass phone booth, and was not much bigger.

Leigh stepped inside, as did Tony. It was crowded with them in there.

"Well, you coming?" Leigh asked Jonathan.

"What, in there?"

"Yes, in here. Come on. There's plenty of room."

Jonathan hesitated.

"Oh, is this like the tunnel thing?" Leigh asked. She turned to Tony. "He's afraid of tunnels."

"I'm not afraid of tunnels," Jonathan protested. "I just don't like them. More so now."

He crowded into the glass chamber. Leigh pressed a button and the door swooshed shut.

"We're not going to teleport or anything, are we?" Jonathan asked, glancing around the tiny enclosure.

"Should we tell him?" Leigh smiled deviously at Tony.

"It's the rule. First time in the Dyson, he does not get told," Tony said.

"Get told what? What's a Dyson?" Jonathan asked, his gaze darting around nervously inside the tiny glass fish tank. He barely noticed the red button that Leigh's hand was hovering over.

"Weee!" Leigh called out with glee and pressed the button.

A circuit clicked somewhere outside and an electric motor spooled up. Suddenly, a great whoosh of air came from above them, like a hurricane blowing in from the sky. Jonathan was startled for a second, though he tried hard to hide it. Slowly, he understood, and relaxed. They were entering a clean room. The deafening gale was washing the debris and dust from them. The circuit clicked again and the wind died down.

"Please close eyes," a recorded voice intoned from a speaker overhead in perfectly proper English.

"What?" Jonathan asked.

"Close them," Leigh replied.

Jonathan did. An ultraviolet light flashed in a quick electrical snap, like a bug zapper.

"Thank you," the recorded voice called out.

The door to the inner room whooshed open.

"You can open your eyes now," Leigh said, looking at Jonathan with an amused smile.

"Am I going to still be able to have children?" Jonathan asked her, returning her amused smile.

She chuckled and they all exited the small room into the Operating Room, as they called it.

"This," Leigh swept her arm over the room, "is where it all happens. Well, the beginning of it, anyway."

She walked over to a stainless steel table. The back wall behind her was neatly stacked with test tubes and centrifuges and other instruments that Jonathan did not recognize.

"We've got to make sure the samples aren't contaminated," Tony explained. "Plus, we deal with some nasty bugs sometimes, and we wouldn't want them to get out."

"We're only a Level 3 here," Leigh added, "so we don't work on the really nasty stuff, Ebola and the like. Most of what we do is pretty routine, though. Here, I'll show you."

Leigh went to a cabinet in the back wall and grabbed a few items. "Here, give me your hand," she said.

Hesitantly, Jonathan put out his right hand, palm up. Tony looked on, amused.

Leigh quickly rubbed Jonathan's thumb with alcohol, took hold of it and squeezed it, then pricked it with a small lancet. A large bead of blood bloomed from it.

"Ouch," Jonathan said, not really meaning it. "You don't have much of a bedside manner, did I ever tell you that?"

"Yes. Once already. Be quiet."

She took what looked like a thin glass tube and put it against the drop of blood. The blood started to go up into the tube by capillary action.

"I knew you were a vampire," Jonathan said.

Tony laughed.

"Shush," Leigh said. "Almost done."

With a practiced hand, she slipped the glass tube into a plastic container, which looked like a small computer thumb drive, though longer. She handed Jonathan a piece of gauze.

"Press it until it stops bleeding," she said.

"No lollipop?"

"I'll buy you a drink later," she said, and Jonathan's face lit up. "*If* you behave," she added, and his smile dropped a little.

Leigh handed the plastic sample case to Tony.

"What are we doing? The whole G?" he asked.

"No, just twenty-two," she said.

Tony went to the far side of the room and inserted the sample case into what looked like a very expensive toaster, only with a dozen or so small openings instead of toast slots. He picked up a tablet from the counter, typed in a few commands, and the machine elicited a small whirr.

"Now what?" Jonathan asked, holding the gauze to his thumb. "What's a twenty-two?"

"The twenty-second chromosome. It's one of the shortest. We'll be checking to see if you have Emanuel Syndrome, among other things."

"What syndrome?"

"Emanuel. An error in the twenty-second chromosome. It causes mental slowness, retardation, etcetera," Leigh said, clinically.

"Very funny," Jonathan said.

Leigh smiled. "Just kidding. Well, not really. We really are reading your twenty-second.   Just to show you how it works, and to calibrate the machines."

"Oh? How long does that take?"

"Four minutes and fifty-three seconds," Tony said, reading the information from the tablet.

"Great. We find out if I'm a moron in less than five minutes."

Tony laughed, and Leigh cracked a smile. "Let's get working for real," she said. "You feel okay?"

"Yeah. Don't worry about me. I just banged up my elbow. It's nothing," Jonathan said dismissively.

"What about your head?" Leigh asked.

"I've got a thick skull, if you haven't figured it out by now."

"Quite." Leigh nodded. "Right, then." She unhooked the bag from around her shoulders and placed it on the stainless steel table.

"It's in *there*?" Tony said incredulously.

"Yes. It's a long story," Leigh said as she donned surgical gloves.

She opened the bag and carefully brought out the Sudarium. She held it in her hands reverently, gazing at it in the bright lights of the lab. Again, she was amazed at how soft it felt, like her old favorite pillowcase. The cloth seemed to glow a deep honey color, that is, where it was not stained the dark faded ochre color of the ancient blood.

Was this really the blood of Jesus? Leigh wondered. *Am I really holding the cloth that wrapped Jesus' head after the crucifixion?* She asked herself, scarcely believing it.

Leigh took a deep breath, suddenly overcome.

Something like a cold electric feeling coursed through her. It was not unpleasant; on the contrary, it was *too* good. It made her feel like she was going to overflow. The events of the last three days were flooding back to her now in a torrent. The fears and feelings she'd kept packed away leapt over the walls of her defenses. She realized she was crying, the tears plopping down on the stainless steel table.

"You okay?" Jonathan asked softly.

She felt Jonathan's strong but gentle hand on her shoulder. She looked up at him through her flooded eyes, taking her gaze away from the Sudarium.

She nodded her head, the tears still falling. "Yes," she sniffled out, and tried to compose herself. "Yes," she repeated, with more conviction.

She carefully and reverently set the Sudarium down on the table, far from her tears. Hands free, she hugged Jonathan, nestling into his body. He gently stroked her hair as she regained her composure. Tony looked upon them both and smiled.

"Right, then," Leigh said at last, returning to herself. "Let's start this. Tony, can you start the sampling? You're better at it anyway."

Tony nodded, the playful smile he usually wore replaced by a determined and businesslike set in his face. "Use the Shroud protocol?"

"Yes," Leigh said, her eyes still puffy with tears.

"Don't worry, I'll take care of it," Tony said reassuringly.

Leigh smiled and wiped away the last errant tear. "Thanks," she said sincerely.

"You go get some rest. You've got to be exhausted. Both of you. Why don't you go home?"

Leigh shook her head. "I can't rest now."

"This will take a while, you know that," Tony said.

"I've got to keep going. I'll go home later, when the first samples come back. Promise," she said.

Tony nodded.

"Oh, I almost forgot," Leigh said as she grabbed her bag and took out the ruined tablet. "We need to get the data out of here."

"Talk to Karen," Tony said. "She'll get everything sorted. I've already spoken with her; it's all arranged."

"You're the best," Leigh said, and hugged Tony.

"Go. Relax. You've got some time to wait," Tony said, and busied himself gathering the materials for the sampling.

Leigh nodded and turned to Jonathan.

"Let's go," she told him. "Let's get this thing fixed, and read your DNA."

"Do I get to ride that vacuum cleaner again?" Jonathan asked with a grin.

CHAPTER 8

Manchester, England
May 24, 2025 2:01 p.m.

Caine pulled the big Bentley into the car park by the hotel. He pulled in through the exit, forgetting he had to drive on the left. A tiny Smart car stood in front of him, beeping the horn.

"Crap," he hissed, backing up in the tight garage.

Adriana glared at him. She had calmed, somewhat, but was still livid and looking for any excuse to vent.

"Imbecile. Drive in the correct lane," she hissed.

Caine backed it up and went into the entrance. He pulled in, taking two parking spots, and shut the car off. Putting his hands on the steering wheel, he leaned forward and lowered his head. He felt as if it would explode if he lifted it. Caine's thoughts spun. He had not planned for this situation. He rubbed his eyes, aware of Adriana studying him.

"You say you can get into the woman's apartment?" Caine asked without looking up.

Adriana frowned. "It may be possible. I studied it before you came. There are two entrances — the front lobby, and the one on the 23rd floor, at the bar. Both are guarded, but the residents come and go. The elevators and the door locks are all fingerprint coded. No keys. The bar entrance on the 23rd floor will be the easier one. After work, many residents come down for drinks. It may be possible to slip through."

Caine listened and analyzed her plan. He looked up at Adriana. "But you'll still need a fingerprint to get on the elevator and in the room," Caine pointed out.

"Or a finger," Adriana said with a cruel smile spreading across her face.

Caine gave an involuntary shudder and held up his hand. "Stop. I'd — rather not know any more. Let's go."

They got out of the car and walked through the old parking garage, which looked to be an old arched bridge that had been walled in at some point in its history. They walked down the alley at the side of the Beetham Tower and through the revolving doors into the Hilton.

They paused at the elevator, waiting. The elevator doors opened and Adriana pressed the button for the 22nd floor. Caine and Adriana stood alone in the silent elevator, the air tense.

"How's your head?" Caine asked with genuine concern, breaking the silence.

"It's fine," Adriana shot back, a momentary flash of anger peeking through.

She was like lava that had skinned over, Caine thought. She might look solid, but underneath it was roiling death and danger.

The elevator dinged and the doors slid open. The two walked silently to the executive suite that Adriana had booked. She opened the door and they went in.

The room was filled with sleek modern furnishings and lined with floor-to-ceiling windows. Adriana threw the keycard on the table and headed to the green-glassed bathroom. She stared in the mirror, at the wound on her head, and resisted the impulse to smash the glass. Splashing water on her face helped calm her, and she took a deep breath. Adriana thought of her plan, of lying in wait for the two. And, most of all, of being able to take her time with them. The thought relaxed her and caused a sideways smile to creep onto her face.

Caine slumped into an Ekornes recliner by the window. He sighed and listened to the running water in the bathroom. He took his phone from his pocket and fiddled with it, staring blankly out the window at Manchester spread out below him. The call to Lahmbrecht was the thing he dreaded the most now, but it was something he had to do. Caine closed his eyes and decided to put it off a couple more minutes. He savored the temporary peace, knowing it would not last.

Tabor Applied Genetics Lab
Manchester, England
May 24, 2025 2:02 p.m.

The wind died down and door to the clean room slid open.

"That was fun, now that I know what to expect," Jonathan said.

"Never gets old," Leigh agreed.

Leigh strode across the large room, Jonathan following. "Karen," she called out.

A thin and lanky woman with square glasses sitting at a computer terminal turned around and a big smile spread over her face. "Hi Leigh," she said. "It's great to see you. I thought you were coming back two days ago. We were worried sick."

"It's been quite a ride — and that's only half the story," Leigh said, glancing at Jonathan.

"I'm looking forward to the other half," Karen said.

Leigh brought out her poor abused iTablet from her bag. "Tony said you could fix it. It's got the direct feed from the Shroud sampling in it, from right before—" she trailed off.

Karen took the cracked, dirty and water-stained tablet and poked at it. "Wow, what did you do to it?" she asked.

"I sort of went swimming with it. In a canal. In Venice."

Karen looked up, eyes open in surprise. "You're kidding."

"I wish I were," Leigh said.

"Well, the computer is probably rubbish, but the memory is most likely good. Give me a few minutes. I bought you a shiny new one. I'll do a brain transplant and you should be good as new."

"Brilliant. You're the best, Karen," Leigh beamed.

"That's what everyone keeps telling me," she said and smiled.

Leigh thanked her and walked over to the center of the room, to the larger workstation. "Here, pull up a chair," she said to Jonathan as she sat down.

He grabbed a chair and sat at the sparse desk, populated only with an aluminum keyboard, a trackpad, and an Apple widescreen display. "This is your desk?" he asked with a look of amusement.

"Yes. Why?"

"Looks like you just moved in. No pictures, knickknacks."

"I like it sparse. It helps me think. Besides, everything is on the computer," she said.

"You should see my office. It's the complete opposite of this," he said, and chuckled.

Leigh turned to him, putting a finger to her lips. "Let me guess — lots of dark wood, huge desk, books — real books — everywhere."

Jonathan looked surprised. "Wow, you been in there?"

Leigh smiled. "Call it intuition." She turned to her keyboard and the computer came to life. "Well, we've got some time to kill here. Let's see if your sample is done," she said, and tapped out a couple of commands.

Jonathan scooted closer. "Is this when we find out if I'm a moron?"

Leigh chuckled. "No comment. Well, actually — one comment." She turned to him. "You stole a car, you drove it, on a train mind you, for a hundred feet, then you wrecked it." She tilted her head, staring at him.

"It was a nice car," Jonathan wistfully recalled.

Leigh shook her head. "Cowboy," she whispered and tapped on the trackpad. "Ah. Here we are." She swiped at the trackpad and brought up a file on the screen. "Here's your file. The sequencer is still reading your blood, but we can see what's been processed already."

She clicked open the file. The window on the screen filled with a seemingly random collection of A's, T's, G's, and C's.

Jonathan scooted even closer to the screen. "Is that it? Is that — me?"

"A tiny part of you, yes."

"It's all gobbledygook to me," he said.

"Watch this," Leigh worked the trackpad, and each letter turned into a colored square. "And, watch this," she said and pressed the trackpad. She sat back in her chair triumphantly.

The huge movie screen that lined the wall in front of them flickered for a second, and then was filled with a kaleidoscope of colors.

"That's cool," Jonathan said, staring up.

"That's your genome. Your 22nd chromosome. Some of it, anyway."

The large screen, running the length of the room, was filled with red, white, purple and gold squares, each color representing a different letter of Jonathan's genome.

"So what does this mean?" Jonathan asked.

"Watch, we're going to find out if you're hopelessly moronic or not," Leigh said with a playful smile on her face.

She typed on the keyboard, then, with the trackpad, zoomed out and selected a swath of DNA on the computer screen.

"This," Leigh pointed at the wall at the region that was highlighted, now so zoomed out that it was just a mosaic of color, "is twenty-two 'q' eleven two. A section of your 22nd chromosome. We're going to compare it to a normal strand."

Leigh pressed a button. A green square flashed on the screen.

"Well, that's strange," she said, pausing.

"What?" Jonathan leaned forward. "What is it?"

Leigh was silent for a moment, keeping Jonathan in suspense. "It says here you're perfectly normal," she said at last, a smile creeping onto her face.

"Very funny, Miss Doctor," he said.

Leigh leaned back in her chair and sighed. "Amuse me, cowboy," she said.

"Oh?"

"Yes. I need to keep going. If I stop I'm going to crash," she said.

"I hear you. Why don't you show me your tattoo while we're waiting? You know, to kill the time?"

"You wish," she said and smiled.

"I do," Jonathan whispered, and leaned in close to kiss her.

Karen walked over and coughed. "Excuse me you two," she said. "I don't mean to interrupt any of your — work — but I'm done."

Leigh sprang up out of her chair. Jonathan, the target for his kiss now gone, smiled and shook his head. "All work," he whispered under his breath.

"You're kidding. Already?" Leigh asked Karen breathlessly.

"Yep. All I had to do was swap the old memory into the new unit. She fired right up," Karen said, satisfied.

"You're a genius. Thanks," Leigh said excitedly, taking the new iTablet. She swiped it on. "It's all here," she said.

"Of course. Enjoy it," Karen said and walked back to her station.

Leigh poked and scrolled through the computer. "All the data from Turin, it's all here," she said to Jonathan excitedly. With renewed energy, she pressed a few buttons and started downloading the data into the main system.

CHAPTER 9

Voland Manor
The Peak District, England
May 24, 2025   2:13 p.m.

Rudolf Lahmbrecht waited impatiently at his desk for the phone call. By his calculations, the scientists should have been neutralized by now. The silence could only mean failure. People, especially Caine, were quick to communicate success, he'd found over the years. Failure was an orphan, as the saying goes.

"Mr. Valenti?" Lahmbrecht called out on the intercom for his assistant.

Valenti, sharply dressed in a tailored suit that clung to his chiseled physique, came into the study. "Sir?"

"Get me Caine on the phone. Video if you can get it. I want to see his face. And get my car ready. I suspect we'll be going to Manchester very soon."

"Yes, sir," Valenti excused himself and stepped out.

A minute later he chimed in.

"Sir, Caine is on the line. I'm putting him through."

Lahmbrecht turned to his computer and pressed the button. Caine's pasty white face filled the screen. The video was jittery, as if he were holding the phone with unsteady hands. Nervous hands, Lahmbrecht noted.

"Mr. Caine, I am waiting to get word on our latest — acquisition," Lahmbrecht chose his words carefully, ever paranoid of anyone intercepting his calls.

Caine looked nervous, even scared. His face gave him away, but Lahmbrecht waited patiently for the words.

"Yes, sir, there's been a — a," Caine stammered and trailed off.

"Setback?" Lahmbrecht offered.

"Yes. They made it in. With the Sudarium," Caine blurted out. "They escaped and—"

"Stop," Lahmbrecht cut him off with a hard bark. The Lawyer was becoming unhinged. "I think it best if we continued this conversation in person. I will notify you of my arrival."

Lahmbrecht hung up.

The fool, Lahmbrecht thought. Not only had Caine botched things up, but now he was talking loosely over a cell phone. A complete breach of protocol.

Lahmbrecht turned in his opulent chair and stared out the window to his manicured gardens, stretching practically as far as the eye could see. The late spring sun was making its way towards the horizon, painting everything an intense shade of gold. Time was running out. He needed to talk to Dr. Lancaster. He could no longer afford to wait.

He buzzed the intercom for Valenti.

"Yes, sir?" the assistant answered.

"Get me Lancaster."

"Right away, sir."

Lahmbrecht turned to the computer again and waited patiently.

"She's coming through now," Valenti's voice called out.

Leigh's pretty face appeared on his computer screen. From the background, she was indeed in the lab.

"Doctor Lancaster, good to see you safe and sound."

"Thanks," Leigh said.

"I see you have arrived at the lab."

Leigh turned to look behind her. "Oh, yes. We got here okay," she said and gave a hesitant smile.

"How is the research going? Have you been able to sample the Sudarium?"

"We're working on it. It could take a couple of hours or a couple of days, but we'll get it done," Leigh said with a tired smile.

"Excellent work. Keep me updated on your progress," Lahmbrecht said and hung up.

They have not found it yet, Lahmbrecht thought. *There is still time.*

The fortunes seemed to be turning his way again. He buzzed the intercom again.

"Valenti, come in."

"Right away, sir," he answered.

A moment later, Valenti was at the door, hands clasped in front of him.

"Is everything ready?" Lahmbrecht asked.

Valenti shook his head and frowned. "No sir. It — is being worked on. We should have it in position by late tonight."

"Why the delay?" Lahmbrecht asked gruffly.

"We had trouble with one of the suppliers. Seems he is under surveillance by Scotland Yard. I'm working on another source."

Lahmbrecht harrumphed.

"The device will be ready by tonight, I hope," Valenti continued nervously. "But we should still have a driver if we're to go through with it. Detonating it at the gates of the lab may not be sufficient."

"Caine has the driver. If he does not, he will be driving the damn thing in himself." Lahmbrecht allowed himself a flash of anger. For a moment, and only a moment, his normally implacable face turned into a visage of a great pent-up rage.

Valenti took half a step back, then caught himself. He was not used to seeing anger, or frustration or, well, any emotion at all from the Old Man. It had only lasted a second, or less, but it scared the hell out of him.

"See it gets done," Lahmbrecht said.

"Of course, sir."

"And what of the contingency?" Lahmbrecht asked.

"The cleaning crew is ready. Where will this take place?" Valenti asked.

"Manchester. Call Nigel Clevin, the Beetham's property manager. Tell him I need the 23rd Floor. Call it — a charity event. High-end dignitaries, very private, that type of thing. Tell him the other venue fell through and we need it last minute. Apologize, offer money, you know," Lahmbrecht waved his hand dismissively. As a minority shareholder in the real estate fund that owned the building, he had a certain pull.

"I understand," Valenti said.

"Let me know when you are ready."

"Yes, sir," Valenti said. He turned and left.

Lahmbrecht stood at the huge window, arms clasped behind his back, contemplating the gardens and remembering back. History was repeating itself, again. He thought back to the last time. To the time when the first team had found it. He'd stopped it then, he'd sure as hell stop it now. His future depended on it.

Tabor Applied Genetics Lab
Manchester, England
May 24, 2025 3:27 p.m.

Jonathan stood in front of the glass room where Tony was busy sampling and knocked on the window.

Come out, he motioned with his hands, mouthing the words. Tony set down the tablet he was working on and stepped into the Dyson, as he called it. Jonathan stood by, amused, as he watched the wind blowing Tony's longish jet-black hair around and his clothes flapping with the force. The machine turned off and air lock hissed open, expelling a little puff of air. Tony stepped out, combing his hair with his fingers and smoothing out his clothes.

"That thing messes up my hair every time," he complained.

"You know, you're right. That is an amusing sight," Jonathan said with a smile.

"Funny, Mr. Cowboy. What did you want?"

"The boss is calling for you," Jonathan said, hitching a thumb at the center desk.

They walked over together towards Leigh.

"Tony, look," Leigh said. "All the Turin data is here," she pointed at the screen.

"Wonderful," he said. "I knew Karen would get it sorted."

"How's the Sudarium sampling going?" Leigh asked.

"Very well. I'm getting tons of data. There's the typical degradation you would expect, but there are a lot of data points. Whatever that cloth was, it was soaked with human blood at some point."

"Excellent," Leigh said.

"Now then," Tony pointed at the screen. "I've been wanting to get my hands on this, to compare."

"Against the Shroud samples I emailed you?" Leigh asked.

"Yes. I think they were corrupt. That's the only thing I can think of to explain those anomalies."

"You mentioned that," Leigh said, brushing a stray lock behind her ear. "Show me."

Tony sat at his workstation, as Leigh wheeled over in her chair. Jonathan stood behind the two, looking on in fascination.

Tony swiped at the trackpad and tapped out a couple of keystrokes on the keyboard. "Let's see — here we go. Here are the Shroud samples from Turin that you sent," he said as he brought up a display on the screen. "I ran the twenty-second chromosome first, of course, to see if we had enough to piece it together." Tony scrolled through until he reached the area he was looking for. "See?" he asked, pointing at the screen.

Leigh stared at the screen full of "T" bases, punctuated here and there by "A" bases. "Put it up on the big screen, as graphics," she told him.

Tony tapped a couple of buttons and the room flooded with red light from the screen. Red, the color-code for the "T" base, filled the wall-sized television, punctuated at intervals with white squares from the "A" base. "See?" Tony repeated.

"Yes, that's not right," Leigh said, frowning.

"At first I thought it was a telomere, maybe a mutated one, so I ran the analysis of this section against a known. Nothing," Tony said.

"Maybe it's a LINE?" Leigh offered.

"I ran it against that too. Nothing, too."

"It looks like a Pribnow box," Leigh said, thinking out loud. "But it's too long."

"That's why I'm leaning towards transmission error. We'll know soon enough when we compare your samples from the horse's mouth, as it were."

Jonathan coughed. "Excuse me," he said. "I know I'm just a simple cowboy and all, but can one of you explain what in the hell you're all talking about?"

Leigh turned in her chair. "You got a couple of hours?" she asked.

"Can you give me the five-year-old version?"

Leigh smirked. "Okay. See this?" she asked, pointing at the screen. "It's supposed to look like this." She pressed a few buttons and brought up a multicolored array, like what she'd shown him before. "This is you, your twenty-second chromosome at the same spot."

Jonathan gazed at the kaleidoscope of colors he'd seen before.

"That's you, that's normal," Leigh reiterated. She clicked on the computer again and the screen returned to the transmitted Shroud sample, the red filling the screen and bathing the room in its light. "That's not," she said, shaking her head.

"It's got to be a transmission error," Tony said. "Like it got hung up and repeated the same letter over and over."

"It can't be right," Leigh agreed. "Go finish up on the Sudarium samples. I'll work on comparing the Shroud samples. These are straight from the horse's mouth, as you said," Leigh held up the iTablet, "they should be okay."

"Will do," Tony said. He put his computer to sleep and headed off towards the clean room.

Jonathan scooted closer to Leigh. "Anything I can do? I feel more useless than a one-legged man at an ass-kicking contest."

Leigh laughed. "That's a charming expression. And no, there isn't. This is my job now."

"Mind if I look around?" he asked.

"Please do. But don't get in trouble. And for goodness' sake don't touch anything."

Jonathan laughed. "I promise," he said, holding up a hand.

Leigh turned and started clicking away on her computer.

Jonathan got up and wandered around the lab, up to the big black boxes humming with energy and blinking with lights. *Why all these lights?* he wondered to himself. He put his hand on top of one of the machines. It was warm and gave off a slight vibration.

"No touching," Leigh called out from across the room, with a serious stern expression.

"Yes, Doctor," Jonathan said.

Her face softened and a smile spread across it. She turned back to her work.

Jonathan walked over in front of the glass wall, gazing at Tony busy inside. The Sudarium lay unfolded on the table with some kind of device, the sampler, he imagined, perched over it on a gooseneck, like a huge fancy kitchen faucet. Jonathan put his face up to the glass, getting as close as he could.

Jonathan stared at the Sudarium. He marveled at the cloth, so ancient, sitting here in this modern lab in Manchester. The contrast was striking. He looked closely at it, studying it. The long-ago bloodstains covered the cloth, painting it like some ancient Rorschach test.

What does it mean to me? he asked himself.

For the first time, he had time to think, and the enormity of everything struck him. He thought of the trail of destruction that had followed them, followed the Shroud, and followed the Sudarium. It was willful ignorance to think it had stopped at their doorstep. The destroyers, whoever they were, would try again.

The Sudarium, lit from above, seemed to almost glow with a golden-honey light. He knew the history of the relic as well as anyone alive. Historically, he could only trace it back with certainty to the year 600. But to the time of Jesus? At the end of the day, Jonathan was convinced all the testing in the world wouldn't be able to prove that this was the blood of Jesus. At the end of the day, it was a question of faith. As he stared at the cloth, he asked himself if he had that faith.

His head went dizzy, and he leaned on the glass. Jonathan closed his eyes and reopened them. He saw, lying on the table where the Sudarium had been, his long-dead Julie and her not-quite-right face. He rubbed his eyes, hoping to banish the vision, the memory that haunted him. It disturbed him every time it appeared.

Forgetting would be nice, he thought, though without much hope of it happening. He'd settle for a drink, though there was not much hope of that, either.

Tony, inside the clean room, saw him staring in and gave a quick smile and small wave. Jonathan gave him a weak smile in return, and Tony went back to his work. He shook the vision of his dead love away, and it faded reluctantly back into the depths.

Jonathan turned and gazed at Leigh. She was busy on her computer, intently staring at the screen. She was cute and smart and personable, and she scared the hell out of him. During their time in Venice, he'd felt a fantastic connection with her, like she could be the one.

The next one to die on you, some reptile in Jonathan's brain whispered. Jonathan closed his eyes. He chased the reptile away, and walked over to her.

"Excuse me, Doctor," he said.

"Hmmm?" Leigh said absently, tapping away on the trackpad.

"I'm suffering from a case of terminal boredom. You either need to give me something to do, or directions to a pub."

Leigh looked up at him. Her face, hard with concentration, softened. "You poor thing," she said. "Here, sit."

He did, taking a chair beside her. "So what are you doing here? Playing solitaire?"

Leigh smiled. "Just setting up the processing. See this?" She pointed at the screen.

Jonathan nodded.

"This is a broken strand of DNA, and it has errors. That's what all the dark spots are. The computer will search for this same pattern from another pass of the DNA. The two samples will have different errors."

She clicked a button. On the screen, the two graphics were overlaid, and a few squares flashed.

"These that are flashing are the missing pieces. The computer overlays the samples, and stitches them together for a more complete picture," she explained.

"And it does this until you have the full picture?" Jonathan asked. The graphical representation helped him understand.

"Yes, you got it," she said, smiling.

"So how long does this take?"

"Not long now. I'm almost done setting it up. Then the big computer will take it and sort it out."

Jonathan watched as Leigh's delicate hands danced over the trackpad, swiping and pinching and dragging.

"There," she said at last. "All done."

"Now what?" Jonathan asked.

"Now, we wait."

CHAPTER 10

Hilton Hotel
Manchester, England
May 24, 2025   6:36 p.m.

Adriana Nyx twisted the lipstick, watching it rise. She pressed it to her lips and glided it across, one side first, then the other. She kissed her lips together and looked in the mirror, tufting up her hair on the side of her head where the man, Tremaine, had battered it into the sidewalk. She bared her teeth at the mirror.

"*Presto, il mio ragazzo,*" she whispered and placed the lipstick down on the vanity.

She smoothed out her short Roberto Cavalli waistcoat, black with leather accents, and stared at herself in the mirror of the vanity where she sat. She shifted her gaze deep into the mirror to the reflection of Caine behind her. He lay curled up in a ball on the bed among crumpled sheets. She'd had her way with him this last half-hour, venting her sadism upon him. He loved it and hated it, begged her to stop and for more. Now, she suspected, he just wanted her to leave so he could pick up what was left of his dignity scattered around the room.

She looked away from him and back at herself in the mirror. She gave a sly seductive smile. She looked good, both bait and hook.

Adriana leaned over and slipped her boots on, feeling the stilettos sheathed in each. She zipped them up and rose up taking one last look in the mirror. She took her key from the table and walked towards the door.

"Do clean up, you filthy *porco,*" she told Caine with derision, and walked out of the hotel room.

Adriana slinked down the long hallway to the elevator, and took it one floor up to the 23rd floor. The Cloud 23 bar and club shared the floor with executive offices and, most importantly, the secondary entrance of the condominium side of the building.

Adriana exited the elevator and took a look down at the lobby, to the security guard station and, beyond it, the private elevators leading up to the posh condos. She caught the security guard's eye and smiled. The guard, a young well-built man with the closed-cropped hair that seemed to be the *de rigueur* haircut of Manchester men, smiled back at her. She stepped towards him.

"Where is the bar?" she asked, with a dose of extra Italian accent in her voice.

"Right back that way, Ma'am," the guard told her, pointing back behind her.

"*Grazie*. Thank you," she said, taking special care to slur her words and stumble towards the bar.

The guard watched the shapely, and apparently already a little tipsy, woman walk towards and into the Cloud 23 bar.

Adriana paused, standing at the opened door to Cloud 23. Floor-to-ceiling windows showed off all of Manchester in its late afternoon glory, the stone and glass buildings lit by the brilliant golden light of the setting sun. The thing that startled Adriana, though, was the glass floor.

Cloud 23 sat on an outcropping of the Beetham Tower, which was one large rectangle of a building stacked upon another rectangle, offset by about twenty feet. The place where they offset, where the top rectangle lay precariously over the bottom rectangle, was the 23rd floor, right at Cloud 23. It was a marvel of engineering and allowed Cloud 23 to have a glass floor.

Adriana stepped hesitantly onto the glass. The hostess at the front of the bar welcomed her in.

"Good afternoon, Ma'am. Feel free to have a seat anywhere. And don't mind the floor. It's all tempered glass with another layer of tempered glass beneath it as a safety net. We've had thousands of people walk on it for over five years now. You could drive a lorry on it, it's so strong," she said, giving her canned and practiced spiel.

Adriana walked across the glass floor, seeming to float twenty-three stories up. The bootheels clicked on the glass, and she went and sat at a low chair by the window facing the city. A waiter came over.

"Your best Bordeaux," she told the waiter before he asked.

"Yes Ma'am," the waiter smiled and left. He returned a short time later with a big globe of the wine.

"2019 Leoville Barton," the waiter said, placing the large wine glass on the small table by her low chair. Adriana handed him the room key and the waiter swiped it and handed it back.

Adriana took the globe of red wine, swirled it, and sipped, looking out at the Manchester skyline. The big Manchester Wheel turned in the distance as the sun dropped towards the horizon. The buildings were beginning to light up, as if anticipating the darkness about to engulf the land.

Victoria Station
Manchester, England
May 24, 2025 6:37 p.m.

The Six-Thirty from London pulled into Victoria Station, seven minutes late. Asad stepped off the sleek train and walked down the platform with a slight limp. The rest during the train ride had done him good, and the paramedic had been skillful in his treatment. He tested the leg now, walking slightly faster. There was slight pain, but nothing bad. He walked towards the baggage check with the empty reliquary inside the black duffel bag. He checked it, storing it for later retrieval; the reliquary was ancient and must have some value, even empty. It was a small consolation, but he intended to salvage what he could.

Asad walked out of the station into the Manchester late afternoon. He walked towards a stand of taxis when the phone buzzed in his pocket. He looked at it. *Unknown number*, it read. He answered it cautiously.

"Asad?" the voice on the other end sounded tiny and far away.

"Yes. Samir?"

"Yes. It's me brother. I just got out," he said. There was much noise in the background and it was hard to hear.

"Out of what?" Asad asked, turning back towards the building and covering his other ear to try and hear better.

"They got me. The man. He knocked me out, locked me in a bathroom. One of the rescuers found me. There had been an accident, they said. Was that you?"

"No. The man caused it. I was there. Where are you calling from? It is noisy."

"The train station. They are still waiting to unload the cars. There are many angry people here."

Damn him, Asad thought, *using a public phone.*

"It's no use coming here now," Asad told him. "I think the party will be over by the time you get here. Buy a cell phone and call me. I will let you know if anything changes."

"Very well — and Allah be with you," Samir said and hung up.

Indeed, Asad thought, and resumed his walk towards the taxis, and towards the lab.

Tabor Applied Genetics Lab
Manchester, England
May 24, 2025 6:47 p.m.

Leigh pressed a button on the cappuccino machine. It whirred, grinding beans and filling the small kitchen with the delicious aroma. Jonathan glanced around the kitchen, which was as sleek and modern as the rest of the lab.

"You know what you need here? A beer tap," he said.

"Very funny. Here, have a coffee," Leigh said, handing him a cappuccino from the machine.

"It'll have to do. Thanks," he said and took the cup.

"Don't mention it," she said, and took her own from the machine.

"How are you holding up?" he asked her, absently tucking a stray lock behind her ear. He lovingly stroked her head.

Leigh smiled. "Good. Tired, but excited. I can't wait for the sequencers to be done. This is what we've been waiting for, after all," she said. She paused and stroked his hair gently where he'd hit his head. "How are you doing?"

"I'll live. My elbow's banged up. I'll never play the guitar again."

"Because you never played the guitar — right?"

"Darn it. You're onto me." Jonathan grinned. "I'm going to have to change up my shtick."

Leigh rolled her eyes. "Off with your shirt," she said.

"What? Here?"

"I want to check you out, silly boy," she said, tilting her head.

"Sure you do."

"Your bandage, cowboy," Leigh said as she stepped to the sink and washed her hands.

Jonathan pulled up his shirt, revealing his midsection. Leigh kneeled down, peeling away the bandage and examining the wound.

"What's the diagnosis?" Jonathan asked as he stared down at the top of Leigh's head.

"Looks good. She really only grazed you. Just an inch closer and—" Leigh trailed off.

"Best not to think of that," Jonathan said.

"Yes, best not to," she said.

The door to the kitchen swung open and Tony walked in. He looked at Jonathan standing, holding his shirt up, and Leigh kneeling, her face close to his body.

"Sorry — I can, um, come back later, if you like," he said, turning away.

Leigh stood up, embarrassed.

"It's not what it looks like," she said, her pale face flushing light pink.

Tony put his hands up. "Hey, it's fine. It's about time you had a boyfriend."

"Tony!" she scolded him.

"We've been trying to get her a boyfriend for a little while now," Tony said, turning to Jonathan, who was looking on with an amused smile.

"Okay Tony, I'm sure Jonathan doesn't want to hear about your little projects," Leigh said with embarrassment.

"Actually, I do," Jonathan chimed in. "Tell me about the last one," he said as he taped the bandage back on and smoothed his shirt over it.

Tony shook his head. "Oh, you don't want to know."

"Alright, that's enough you two. Did you actually want something, Tony?"

"Why, yes. Your Turin samples are done processing."

"What? Why didn't you say so?" Leigh asked excitedly. She practically darted out of the kitchen and towards the lab.

Tony and Jonathan looked at each other and shrugged.

"After you," Jonathan said, extending his hand.

"You're such a gentleman," Tony said with a smile.

They walked down the hall, chasing after Leigh, who was almost running. She stopped at the door to the command center, pressing her thumb impatiently on the pad. The door swooshed open and she made her way through the large empty room, the other workers having gone home for the day. She made a beeline to her workstation in the center. By the time Tony and Jonathan caught up, she was already swiping away at the computer's trackpad.

"Bring up the 22nd," Tony said.

"Way ahead of you," Leigh said. She tapped away at the computer. In front of them, the big screen covering the wall came to life. It filled with letters. "One second," Leigh said. She tapped a button and the screen changed to colored blocks as before.

"Okay, now zoom in here," Tony said, hovering over her and pointing at Leigh's computer screen.

"I've got it," Leigh said impatiently, brushing his hand away.

The image on the screen, full of miniscule squares, zoomed in. The room darkened as the screen filled with the red squares of the repeating "T" bases. The predominant red was sprinkled with the white squares of the "A" base, like snowflakes on a field of blood.

"Is this the old sample, the one you emailed?" Tony asked.

Leigh furrowed her brow, typing on the computer. "No—" she hesitated, "this is the new one from my iTablet. From the horse's mouth." She checked again. "Yes. This is the Shroud sample, direct from my tablet," she said, pointing at a line of code on the screen.

Tony scratched his head. "It's the same. Same anomaly."

They all stared up at the big screen, filled with thousands of red squares. They were silent for a minute, both Leigh and Tony thinking through possibilities and trying to troubleshoot the problem.

"So what does this mean?" Jonathan asked, breaking the silence.

"I'm stumped," Leigh said at last. "It must have been a problem with the sampling itself."

"Maybe it was a problem with the transmission. It was feeding wirelessly, right?" Tony suggested.

"If it's a problem with transmission, then why only this one—" Jonathan began to ask, but trailed off, suddenly dizzy.

He leaned forward, catching himself on the back of Leigh's chair. His vision blurred, then brightened and snapped into perfect clarity for a moment. He took in everything around him. The tilt of Leigh's head, the light glistening off her jet-black hair, her hand resting on the silver trackpad. Tony leaning over, staring intently at Leigh's computer screen. The curved wall in front of them, filled almost floor to high ceiling with the big OLED screen, lit in red squares, interspersed with white squares. A small line of text at the corner read: "*Turin Shroud Sample, Composite reading, 5/19/25 — 5/21/25.*"

"You okay?" Jonathan heard from somewhere distant. A hand shook him.

"Yeah," Jonathan heard himself say automatically.

Leigh turned in her chair. "Jonathan?" she asked.

"Yeah. I'm okay. I'm back."

"The Shutter?" Leigh asked.

"Yeah," Jonathan said. He shook his head, as if something had come loose that he was trying to shake back into place.

"The what? What just happened?" Tony asked, confused.

"I've got a condition — a gift some say. It's like photographic memory, but I can't control when it happens. I probably fell off my horse too many times as a little cowboy," he joked.

"Weird," Tony said.

"Thank you for the honest appraisal. It *is* weird."

"Well, if you're okay," Leigh said, "then be quiet, both of you. I'm trying to think."

"What I was saying before," Jonathan whispered, "is that if it's a problem with the transmission, why is only this section that is screwed up? Wouldn't the whole thing be screwed up?"

"Most likely yes," Tony said.

The three stared at the screen.

"Let me try something," Leigh said. She tapped out on her keyboard. "Just running a comparative analysis on you both," she said, talking at the screen. She leaned back. "There."

"What did you do?" Jonathan asked.

"I'm comparing the two samples, the one I sent to Tony and the one direct from my tablet. This will tell me if there is any divergence."

"Five-year-old version?"

"Any divergence. If the samples are different anywhere."

They waited, watching Leigh's screen as the computer processed and compared the data.

"It's like watch a tea kettle boil," Tony offered.

"Or paint dry," Jonathan added.

"Quiet you two," Leigh hushed them.

"What? The machine is thinking now?" Jonathan asked.

Leigh's serious determined face softened with a little smile.

The computer sounded a small chine.

"There," Leigh said and hurriedly turned to face it.

"What is it? What's the diagnosis?" Jonathan asked, leaning forward.

"I'm reading," Leigh said, looking at the screen. "Three."

"Three? Three what?"

"Three points of divergence out of almost three billion." Leigh scratched her head. "According to this, the two are virtually identical."

"Which means what exactly?" Jonathan asked.

"That there is no transmission error. Whatever we're looking at was in the samples we took from the Shroud," she explained. "Of course, without the Shroud actually here, or anywhere else for that matter, we can't confirm it."

"Bring it back up," Jonathan said.

"What?"

"The anomaly. The 22nd chromosome thing."

Leigh typed out on the computer. "There."

The room filled with the red glow again. Jonathan stared at it. They all did.

"T," Tony mumbled. "T, T, T, T."

"T for Tony?" Jonathan suggested.

"Funny. Be serious," Leigh said. "Why all the T's? Why so many?" Leigh wondered aloud.

"It's not all T's. There are little white specks in there. The A, was it?" Jonathan asked.

"Yes, A. It's negligible, though," Leigh said. She sighed and sat back in her chair. "Maybe the sample was too old."

They stared up at the big screen for a little while, silent. At last, Leigh got up and stretched.

"How are the Sudarium samples coming?" she asked Tony.

He stepped to his workstation and picked up a tablet, swiping at it.

"Processing still. It's at eighty percent. You can help me run some tests if you want to give your mind a rest from this," Tony said, pointing up at the big screen.

"I'd be glad to," Leigh said. She took her tablet and went over to his workstation.

Jonathan, looking on, asked, "What kind of tests?"

"Science-type tests," Leigh said dismissively.

"Funny. No, really. I'm interested in this stuff, you know."

Leigh smiled. "We compare the DNA sample we have against other known DNA sequences to check for accuracy. We all have many genes in common. For example, everyone has the same tumor-suppressor genes at chromosome 17. Gene p53 it's called. We'll check the samples against that. When they start matching up, we can tell we're getting close to an accurate full sample."

"Got it," Jonathan said. "Thanks – now, what can I do?" Jonathan asked.

"Coffee?" she asked.

Jonathan laughed. "Errand boy." He nodded. "Got it. Got to start somewhere, I suppose."

"I'm serious. I forgot it in the kitchen. Be a dear, please?"

"Right away, doc."

Jonathan walked out of the command center and down the hall. The red from the bright screen was still burned in his memory. He blinked, trying to pack it away into memory, but it was insistent, overlaying the reality before him in a transparent red film. A drink would help tamp it down.

He walked on down the hall. Something tickled at his subconscious, some nagging detail that he could not quite place. He entered the kitchen, took Leigh's coffee and warmed it in the microwave. Jonathan stood watching the numbers count down. *27, 26, 25, 24, 23, 22.*

"Twenty-two," he said out loud to himself in the solitude of the kitchen. He closed his eyes and saw the command center again, saw the big OLED screen lit up red. Leigh's jet-black hair, the tilt of her head. The squares of red and white on the screen. There was some nagging thought there at the edge of his consciousness, some synapse that would not close.

The microwave dinged, snapping Jonathan out of his trance.

He took the hot coffee, walked back down the hall and into the nearly empty command center. The big screen was still showing the 22nd chromosome, filling the room with red light. For a second, the ghostly memory-image that persisted in Jonathan's vision and the scene before him lined up perfectly.

Leigh was sitting over at Tony's station, tapping away on her tablet.

"Here you go, miss. Would you like cookies or a biscotti?" he asked, setting the coffee down.

"That would be great," Leigh said absently.

"That was a joke," Jonathan said.

Leigh looked up from her work. "I'm sorry, dear. Thanks for the coffee," she said, and returned to her work.

Jonathan shook his head, gazing at her as she tapped away on the computer. He wandered over to Leigh's empty workstation and sat at her seat, twirling around once. He stared up at the big screen and the thousands of red square "T's" covering it. Again that nagging feeling came back, like he was staring at something he couldn't see.

"Enough of this," he muttered under his breath.

He pulled up his chair up to the desk, eager to do something. Anything.

"Let's see," he said, running his hand over the trackpad. He pinched his fingers together and zoomed wildly out on the DNA image, making the squares infinitesimally small. He spread his fingers and zoomed back in, the squares growing larger, then started moving around the image, scrolling it up and down.

"Cool," Jonathan he said.

He played with the computer, scrolling through the genome, looking at the different colored squares and, occasionally coming upon those large red areas of T bases. The big screen flickered with the moving squares as they flashed around wildly.

"What are you doing over there, mister?" Leigh asked, noticing the flickering.

"Playing. I mean, working," Jonathan told her.

"I thought I said no touching."

Jonathan smiled sheepishly. "I just had to see something."

"Oh? What?" she asked, turning her chair to face him.

"I don't know. Something."

"That's not much of an answer," Leigh said.

"I don't know. Ever since that screen flashed onto my brain back there, I keep seeing it, but not seeing it. Like I'm trying to find my keys and they're right in front of me but I can't see them."

"Well, let's see what you were trying to do," Leigh said, rising from her seat. She walked over and stood behind Jonathan, looking at the screen.

"Oh, I don't know I was actually trying anything. I don't have any idea," he said.

"Hmm, you were zooming in and out," Leigh said, looking at the movement log on a small window on the side of the screen.

"Yeah, like I said — playing," he said.

"Let me teach you."

Leigh reached over to the trackpad, getting close to Jonathan, almost pressing up against his back. She spread her fingers slowly and smoothly, zooming in on the image.

"See, it requires a gentle touch," Leigh spoke softly. She turned her head and smiled. They were close enough to kiss.

Jonathan looked at her elegant hand working the trackpad. The edge of her tattoo peeked out from under her sleeve.

"Show me your tattoo," he whispered.

"No. Pay attention," she said softly.

"I am. Kiss me, then." He could feel her warmth.

"Not here," she whispered.

"Then let's go somewhere else," he whispered.

"And this is how you zoom in," she said, louder. She'd glanced over at Tony and caught him looking at them. He gave her a knowing smile.

"Thank you, Doctor," Jonathan said in a loud and official tone, picking up on her ruse.

Leigh pursed her lips, trying not to laugh, then she did, letting out a chuckle, then a laugh. It was infectious, and soon Jonathan was laughing too.

Leigh straightened and wiped a tear from her eye. "Oh, I'm getting right giddy, I am," she said.

"We both are. We need rest. It's getting late and it's been a hell of a day. Hell of a week," Jonathan said.

"Soon. We'll be done soon," she said. "Now, back to this. Be gentle with the controls, and have a look around. Whatever you do, don't delete anything."

Jonathan tried his hand at it, and seemed to get the knack quickly. "There. See, I'm a natural," he said.

Leigh smiled at him and walked back to Tony's workstation. Tony cocked an eyebrow at her.

"What?" she asked, blushing.

"You like him," Tony said.

Leigh nodded. "Let's get back to work here."

Jonathan sat watching the exchange, amused. He peeled his attention back to the computer.

He scrolled through the chromosome, quickly getting the feel for the sensitive controls. Zoomed out as he was, he could plainly see the anomaly, a large red section in the otherwise multicolored section of chromosome. He zoomed in on the area slowly, as Leigh had showed him. The big screen filled with red squares. As he zoomed in, more and more of the little snowflakes, the white "A" squares, became apparent. Jonathan zoomed in slowly, watching the pattern change as the squares got bigger and filled more of the screen.

Pattern.

That feeling tickled Jonathan's brain again. *There's a pattern there,* he thought, though he could not see it. He scrolled in and out slowly, searching. The pattern of the white squares against the red squares shifted as their size grew or shrank, taking up more or less of the screen.

Unexpectedly, Jonathan felt a great shiver go through him, like someone had walked over his grave. This was not the Shutter, though, but something different, as if a great energy had swept through the room. He stared at the screen, hypnotized as he zoomed in and out.

Suddenly, and only for a moment, all the white squares lined up in a perfect row. As he zoomed past, they went right back to being those seemingly random snowflakes.

He paused. He zoomed back ever so slowly, looking for that pattern. *There.* Again, all the white squares lined up in a perfect column, from top to bottom of the screen, the rest of the screen filled with red.

He froze.

That chill went through Jonathan again. *A pattern.* At that level of magnification, the white "A" squares stood out on the screen, one to each row, with the rest of the row filled with the red "T" squares, all the way through the screen. Jonathan carefully took his hand off the trackpad.

"Leigh, look at this," he said.

Leigh looked up at him from her tablet. "What is it?" she asked.

"Look," Jonathan pointed up at the screen.

Leigh looked up and tilted her head, staring up at the white column running down the otherwise red screen. "What is that? What did you do?"

"Nothing," Jonathan said. "I was just zooming in and out like you showed me."

"That's strange," Leigh scratched her head. "It must be an artifact from whatever sampling error made that anomaly."

"Five-year-old version, please," Jonathan said.

"Like a CD skipping at the same scratch. You remember those, right? CD's?" she asked with a sideways smile.

"Ouch. I'm not that much older than you. And besides, I don't think that's what it is."

"Oh? Why do you say that?" Leigh asked.

Jonathan shrugged. "Gut feeling."

Leigh looked up at the screen again, at the wall of red with a single white stripe running top to bottom. "Hmm," she hummed to herself, searching her mind for some scientific reason for why that would be there.

Tony stood up and interrupted her train of thought. "All done," he called out.

"What?" Leigh asked, turning her attention to him.

"All done. The Sudarium sample is done processing," Tony said.

"Run a comparative analysis with the Turin sample," Leigh said. The first thing she wanted to find out was whether the blood on the Shroud and the blood on the Sudarium came from the same man.

"Already on it," Tony said, almost talking over Leigh. "It'll be done in," he paused, looking at his computer screen, "four minutes to ninety percent."

"Ninety percent?" Jonathan asked.

"Ninety percent certainty. It'll take a few hours to get to one-hundred percent," Leigh explained. "But once you're at ninety percent, you can be relatively sure."

"The rest you take on faith?" Jonathan asked, smirking.

"Something like that," Leigh said, returning his smirk. "Now, back to this," she pointed up at the big screen. "What do you make of this, Tony?"

He stared at the screen. "Interesting," he muttered. "There's definitely a pattern there."

"I still say it's a transmission artifact," Leigh said.

"Could be," Tony said, "but why only in this section? Why only at the 22nd chromosome?" he asked.

Leigh stared up at the screen, a finger on her lips, her face wrought with concentration. Suddenly her face brightened.

"I've got an idea. Bring up the time stamp," she told Jonathan who was still sitting at the computer.

"Bring up the what?" he asked, confused.

"Here, switch with me," she said.

Jonathan got up and Leigh settled into her seat. She started deftly working the trackpad and keyboard.

"Each sample has a time stamp," Leigh explained to Jonathan, sensing his curious gaze. "It records the time when each base, each T or A or G or C, was sampled. If this section of chromosome is some kind of transmission error, each base will have similar time stamps."

"In other words," Tony added, "if it was an error, it would have happened at about the same time. Bah, I should have thought of that," he said, slapping his forehead.

Leigh highlighted a section of the screen.

"Wait," Jonathan said. "Before you go away from this screen, can you take a screenshot or save it or something?"

"I've got the data saved right here," Leigh said, pointing at a small window. "See, Magnification 401, Position 2,316,431."

"What's that mean?" Jonathan asked.

"Position is the place in the chromosome where the data shown begins. The 401 means 401 columns across," Leigh swept her arm from the left side of the screen to the right.

"Hmm, 401," Jonathan whispered to himself. That nagging feeling was tickling him again.

"So," Leigh went on, talking softly at the screen, "you were sampled at 05232510473717, and," she clicked a button, scrolling through the sample, "your mates here were sampled at—" she worked the computer and read the data, "totally different times. So you're perfectly normal."

Tony, looking over her shoulder, said, "Interesting. So it's not a transmission error."

"Doesn't look that way," Leigh said and leaned back in her chair. "Well, I'm fresh out of ideas."

"Bring the other screen back up," Jonathan said.

Leigh selected the coordinates from a menu and typed.

"Magnification 401," she said to herself, and pressed the button.

The screen came back, filling the room with red with that single white stripe running down the side.

"Hmmm, 401," Jonathan whispered to himself. "So," he went on, trying to work loose the nagging mental block in his head. "There's one white square, an A, followed by 400 red squares, the T. One A, 400 T's, over and over." He stared intently at the screen, then closed his eyes, though he could still see it scrambled in his memory. The big empty lab was silent as all three were occupied by the mystery before them.

Tony's computer beeped.

All three turned to look at it.

"It is finished," Tony said as he walked to it.

"What is it? What's the result?" Leigh asked excitedly.

"Hold on a second," Tony said, examining the screen and tapping at his trackpad. "Right."

"Well? Tell me already," Leigh said impatiently.

"It's a match," Tony announced triumphantly.

The words took a moment to sink in.

"A match?" Leigh asked, not believing.

"Within ninety percent probability. We'll be at a hundred percent in a few hours."

Jonathan walked over to Tony's station, temporarily forgetting the screen in front of him.

"Wait a minute," he said, incredulous. "Just so I understand — you're saying the blood from the Shroud of Turin and the blood from the Sudarium of Oviedo are the same? They came from the same man?"

"To a ninety percent certainty, yes. Ninety-one, actually," Tony corrected himself as the screen updated.

Jonathan grabbed a chair and sat down, face ashen. He, more than anyone, instantly knew the implications.

"This — this is—" he trailed off, speechless.

"This is incredible," Leigh said in a hushed voice.

"What's the big deal?" Tony asked.

"You don't understand," Jonathan said from his seat. "Historically, there's no evidence of these two relics ever being together. Well, except once—" he trailed off again.

"Where? Where were they together?" Tony asked, still not fully comprehending.

"In the tomb of Jesus Christ," Jonathan said in an awed voice.

PART 6

John and Peter entered into the crowded room, setting down the bag with the Shroud and the Sudarium. Simon and Cleopas had arrived, and they sat and listened to their story. Now they too were sharing the womens' visions, claiming they too had seen Him on the road to Emmaus. Peter rose, about to protest, when there was a sudden wind that blew through the room. As Peter began to speak, suddenly He was there. The Master. "Peace be with you," Jesus said. The men shrieked, terrified and frightened. John cowered, staring at the spirit. Then Jesus spoke. "Why are you troubled? And why do doubts arise in your hearts?" He said in a kindly voice. Slowly, the crowd calmed down. Jesus showed his hands and feet, the wounds there. The men neared but did not dare to touch. Jesus spoke again. "Have you any food here?" The men glanced at each other, bewildered. At last, John brought out a piece of a broiled fish and some honeycomb. All watched silently as Jesus ate. When He finished, He spoke many more things, opening up the scriptures to them. In the corner, forgotten for the time being, sat the burial cloths, their trip through history just beginning.

CHAPTER 1

Cloud 23
Manchester, England
May 24, 2025 7:58 p.m.

The waiter, a handsome dark-haired man, Adriana noted, walked up to her.

"I'm sorry Ma'am. We will be closing in half an hour. The club has been rented for a private function," the waiter said apologetically.

Adriana shrugged nonchalantly. "It is fine," she said. It was time for her to get on with it anyway.

"Would you like another before then?"

"No, I will just finish this," she said, swirling the Bordeaux in her globe. She watched the waiter walk away and savored the rest of her wine, mentally preparing herself. She gazed out the window at the last traces of light on the horizon and the panorama of the twinkling city.

It is time, she thought.

She leaned over and felt at her boot for the stiletto sheathed there and smiled. Adriana rose from her chair and strode towards the bar door across the glass floor. She looked down at the darkened Manchester streets twenty-three stories beneath. The tiny streetlights shone yellow on the sidewalk far below. She paused at the door and readied herself for the act.

Adriana swung the door open and stumbled out towards the condo's elevators and the guard sitting at the podium. The security guard, a thin but muscular man with a boyish, almost delicate, face, looked up at Adriana walking tipsily towards him. He rose up and stepped from behind the podium. Adriana gave him a drunken smile and staggered to him, almost falling into his arms.

"Whoa there, lass," the guard said, catching her. "Where are you off to?"

"I'm staying with a friend," Adriana slurred out. "Up in 46. Yes 46. I think I may have had too much to drink." She smiled at the guard, letting her touch on him linger.

The guard glanced around him. "Well, let's just get you up there then, yes?" he said.

"Mmm, I would love that," she said, running a hand down his chest.

The guard guided her to the elevators. "Alright love, thumb on the scanner," he said.

Adriana stole a glance around her. The elevator lobby was empty, but two people were walking out of the bar and could see them. They were watching them, actually, watching the spectacle of the drunk woman being helped home. Adriana swiped at the sensor pad in front of the elevator, missing.

"Sorry," she giggled.

The guard stifled a laugh. He'd dealt with drunken residents before, but this lady took the prize, he thought.

The guard held up Adriana with his left arm. He placed his right thumb on the sensor pad, calling the elevator. Adriana clung to him, giggling and running her hands over the guard's chest. The elevator dinged and the door slid open. He stepped in, helping Adriana who stumbled along at his side.

"Alright, darling, I need your thumb for real now," the guard said, taking her hand.

"*So do I*," Adriana whispered under her breath.

She brought up her hand behind his head and stroked his closely cropped hair. Adriana tensed and straightened herself, rising up to kiss the guard. Her lips brushed his. The guard froze, not expecting this, but not pushing her away either. The door to the elevator slid shut.

Adriana pushed the guard back against the wall and pressed herself to him. A smile played on the young guard's face as he put his arm around her waist. She brought up her right leg, running it up his thigh like a python coiling around its prey. Adriana went to kiss him again and brushed her lips against his for a second. She turned her head to the side and flicked her tongue lightly down his cheek, even as she silently brought the stiletto out of her boot sheath. Adriana curled her lips and kissed the guard's cheek. He started breathing hard with excitement. At that moment, Adriana bared her teeth and bit down fiercely on his cheek.

The guard froze, scarcely believing the sudden pain or the source of it. On instinct, he tried to push her away but Adriana was latched on tight, her hand clasped to the back of his head and leg curled around. Blood ran down the guard's cheek and Adriana savored the salty taste. He began to thrash around, feeling at his belt for his Taser.

"No time for fun, *bambino*," she whispered in his ear and sunk the stiletto underneath his armpit.

The guard tensed in her grip, then relaxed. His eyes went wide then stared right past her, through her, and on through to forever. She set him down gently.

She twisted the blade and the body gave a small jerk, then went completely limp. Adriana drew the stiletto out, wiping it clean on the guard's uniform. She took a moment and licked her lips still stained with his blood.

She crouched over his body and took the guard's limp right hand. She brought the stiletto to it, laying the blade against the thumb. Adriana curled her lip and, with a crunch of bone, the thumb was off. She let the hand drop. It fell limp and oozed a tiny bit of blood onto the red carpets of the elevator.

Adriana rose and set the thumb against the elevator's fingerprint scanner. As she suspected, the security guard was keyed to all floors, and probably all apartments as well. The elevator chimed softly and ascended, gliding up silently to the 46th floor. Adriana knelt and cleaned her blade again on the guard, then sheathed it in her boot.

The door slid open as the electronic voice announced their arrival. Adriana peeked her head out and looked down the empty hall. She dragged the guard's body halfway out the elevator, leaving him blocking the door. She ran down the hall to Apartment 4611, Leigh Lancaster's apartment. Adriana took a breath and held the security guard's thumb up to the fingerprint scanner on the door. For one tense second, nothing happened. Adriana adjusted the thumb, and the apartment door clicked open. She smiled.

Hurrying, she went back to the elevator. With her considerable strength, she took hold of the guard, and half-dragged, half-carried him down the hall and into Leigh's apartment.

Adriana shut the door, breathing hard and smiling her cruel smile. All she had to do now is hide the body, hide herself, and wait.

CHAPTER 2

Tabor Applied Genetics Lab
Manchester, England
May 24, 2025   7:58 p.m.

"**J**esus Christ?" Tony asked skeptically. "*The* Jesus Christ?"

"The one and only," Jonathan said. "Water to wine, raise the dead, walk on water, resurrected in three days — you know — Jesus Christ."

"Wait a minute," Leigh chimed in. "You can't be sure of that. You only know that it belonged to the same person and that it's at least 1,400 years old."

"Ah, you're a skeptic now?" Jonathan raised an eyebrow.

"No. Yes. Wait," Leigh stammered. "I'm just being scientific. Analytical and all that."

"See? Belief doesn't need science," Jonathan said with a smirk.

"It does," Leigh protested. "It does," she repeated softly, almost to herself.

As if by some unspoken word shared only between them, Leigh and Jonathan got up and walked to the glass wall of the sampling room as Tony looked on from his desk. The two stared at the cloth inside as it sat on the stainless-steel table. The dimmed lights accented the edge of the cloth, gilding it in soft golden light.

"I believe," Leigh spoke softly. "At least I did. I just want to prove it — to prove it real. I want to prove it to everyone. And to myself, too."

Jonathan nodded. His eyes lingered on the ancient cloth.

"I want you to prove it too. To me," he said softly, speaking directly at the cloth beyond the glass.

His hand at his side reached out to Leigh's, just as hers reached to his. They held hands comfortably, lightly. Jonathan pushed away old hurts and visions of the past that bubbled at the surface of his mind. He squeezed Leigh's hand, feeling the soft delicate skin, and smiled to himself. She squeezed back.

"Let's prove it," she said. "Back to work, mister. Let's look at God's DNA."

Leigh went back to her workstation with new energy. "Right," Leigh limbered up her fingers. "Tony, start running an ethno-scan. Let's find out where this blood comes from."

Jonathan sat at her side. "Ah, the brave new world of genetic archeology," he said, knowing something about this field. There were certain genetic markers, he knew, that could be used to trace a person's bloodline and ethnicity.

"Well," Tony said, "we already know it's type AB, so that narrows it down."

"How so?" Jonathan asked.

"Type AB is rare, appearing only in about three percent of western populations. But among Jews it's closer to ten percent."

"You learn something new every day," Jonathan said.

Tony busied himself at the computer.

"Now," Leigh wiggled her fingers, "let's get back to that anomaly. With any luck, this fresh Sudarium sample will clear everything up."

Leigh cut and pasted the location of the anomaly on the Shroud sample from her computer and brought up the same location on the new Sudarium sample. She tapped a button, fully expecting the normal kaleidoscope of colors. Instead, the big screen filled with the same red squares of T's, interspersed with the white squares of the A's.

"And, it's the same," Leigh said to herself, perplexed. "Of course, it would be if the two samples were a perfect match," she chided herself. She stared up at the screen, shaking her head. "I must be tired," she said, shaking her head.

"Can you do the magnification thing?" Jonathan asked. "To see if they all line up the same?"

"Sure," Leigh tapped out a few commands and the squares magnified to 401 columns across. The one white column was there, running all the way down the screen.

"I don't understand this," Leigh admitted.

That nagging feeling returned to Jonathan. He shook his head. "It's the strangest thing. I feel like I've seen this but, I hate to say this, I can't remember it. Like I've seen it in pieces somehow but I can't put it together."

"Well, I've never seen anything like it," Leigh admitted.

"How long does this go on for?" Jonathan whispered to himself, holding a finger up and counting the rows.

"There's a better way to do that, cowboy," Leigh said. With her trackpad, she selected the beginning to the anomaly, and copied that line. "Now we're going to search how many times this line, this pattern, appears."

Leigh pressed a button. Seconds later, "Search Complete" appeared on the screen. Leigh looked at the long list of results.

"Hmmm," Leigh muttered to herself.

"What?" Jonathan asked.

"This line here repeats 31,685 times in the whole genome. But in this section, and this section only, it repeats 400 times," Leigh said, pointing at the white followed by the red squares. "Clustered right here, repeating 400 times in a row," she said, her face pinched with concentration.

"Red squares, 400 of them. Repeating 400 times in a row. Don't you think that's a bit strange?" Jonathan asked.

"It's bloody strange," Leigh said. "But I haven't the faintest idea why it's like that." Leigh rubbed her eyes, the exhaustion beginning to set in.

Jonathan rubbed his chin. "Hmm — 400 red T's, 400 times. One white A, 400 times," he mumbled to himself.

"Leigh?" It was Tony.

"Yes?"

"Got something."

Leigh got up and stood behind Tony. "Already? What did you find?" she asked.

"Well, I ran it to check the most likely probability first. It's male, Jewish lineage. Most definitely Jewish."

Jonathan glanced over at Tony, listening. He felt strange, like he was going to have another episode of whatever had hit him before. Pieces floated in front of his vision, each a disparate fact that somehow went together. "Jewish," he whispered to himself. He stared up at the big screen at the 400 T's all in a row.

Then, it clicked.

"Of course!" Jonathan practically yelled out.

Startled, Tony and Leigh turned to him.

"What's wrong?" Leigh asked, surprised.

"Aleph and Tav. One and 400. Don't you see?" Jonathan exclaimed, almost leaping out of his chair.

"No, I don't. What are you on about?" Leigh asked, tilting her head.

"Okay, in Hebrew, you've got 22 letters. Aleph, Bet, Gimel, all the way to Tav, the last letter. Traditionally, each letter was associated with a number.

The Hebrews had this whole numerological system, gematria it's called. Aleph, the A, is one. The first letter. Tav, the T, is 400. The last letter. A is one, T is 400." Jonathan pointed up at the screen. "See?"

Leigh shook her head. "No. That's impossible," she said.

"It's right there," Jonathan pointed up at the screen.

"That's just coincidence. There's got to be a rational explanation for this anomaly," she said with a shake of her head.

"I'd welcome one if you have it," Jonathan said. "You said yourself that this junk DNA is normally random."

"Yes, I did — but this, this is just—"

Jonathan cut her off. "Just what? Impossible? It's right there," he pointed again at the screen.

"But it's not scientific," she protested. "A pattern like this just doesn't crop up."

"The science is right there. Maybe, just maybe, this sample is different. Because the man it's from was different," Jonathan argued.

Leigh shook her head, still trying to find a rational scientific explanation. "Why A and T, then?" she asked, stalling for time while she tried to think of a less fanciful reason for the anomaly.

"I am the Alpha and the Omega, the beginning and the end," Jonathan intoned in priestly voice as he quoted from Revelation.

Leigh gave a small laugh. "I never thought you would be the one quoting scripture at me. And I also never thought that was — you know — literal."

"Me neither."

"Still, it's an interesting thought, but it's not proof," Leigh said.

"You can't prove belief, babe. You either believe it or not."

"That's Doctor 'babe' to you, mister," Leigh said and smiled tiredly at him.

Jonathan smiled back, then frowned and turned serious, as if another thought was trying to force its way into his consciousness.

What was it? Jonathan asked himself. It was something Leigh had said. *Why A and T, then?* she'd asked. Jonathan thought about it. *Why not other letters? Had they checked for other letters?*

Jonathan closed his eyes, trying to recall the Hebrew alphabet. *There.* It was an old memory. *College. Dorm room. His walls plastered not with posters but with pages and printouts of information. History books ripped apart and stuck on the walls, all there to read anytime he wanted to remember. There was more. That feeling of being 21, of being young and invincible. And Julie, his dear dead love, alive and well and coming to meet him in fifteen minutes. Her picture in the center of the wall, framed by the ripped apart histories. She smiled at him from that picture, her dark and beautiful eyes filled with love. That feeling of new love, so overwhelming.* Jonathan pushed that away and focused on the wall. *There, from his Hebrew Studies class, was the alphabet. The alefbet, he corrected himself. Aleph, Bet, Gimel, Dalet, the whole alefbet. And next to it was each letter's numerological value. One, two, three, four, every letter paired up.*

Jonathan slowly opened his eyes.

Leigh came into focus, her face beautiful but with a concerned expression weighing on it. "Are you okay?" she asked.

Jonathan nodded and smiled. "Remembering is hard."

Leigh's face softened and she breathed out a sigh of relief. "You were gone a long time there, mister."

"I needed something," Jonathan said. "I've got an idea."

"Another gut feeling?" Leigh asked.

"This one's a little higher," Jonathan said with a grin. "You said before that the pattern appeared a bunch of times?" he asked her.

"Yes. Four-hundred times in a row here in the 22nd Chromosome and 31,685 elsewhere in the whole genome," Leigh said, checking the computer.

"Where elsewhere?" he asked.

Leigh worked the trackpad, searching. Her brow furrowed. "That's strange. All the rest are scattered in the 23rd chromosome. The Y chromosome," she explained. Leigh pointed at a line of code that looked like gibberish to Jonathan.

"Okay. Now, can you zoom in on that section where those appear? I mean aside from this one here in the 22nd."

"Of course," Leigh said. She spread her fingers apart on the trackpad and pressed a button. She typed on the keyboard and her computer screen changed to the new section. "This section here, in the 23rd," Leigh said, almost talking to herself, "is more junk DNA."

As she zoomed in, the squares grew more distinct. Right away she could tell it was an odd section. It was all red and white squares, A and T bases exclusively, all jumbled up in no discernable pattern.

"Is that it?" Jonathan asked.

"Yes. And it's damned odd," Leigh mused. "Tony, look at this." She brought the image up on the big screen.

Tony, who had been busy at his computer, proofing the DNA samples, looked up.

"Wow. Where is that?" he asked.

"It's a section of junk DNA in the 23rd chromosome," she responded.

"So this is different than normal too?" Jonathan asked.

"Very much so. For one, there's no C's or G's. In a sample this large, there should be some, at least."

"Is it — you know — human?" Jonathan asked with hesitation.

"Oh, it's one-hundred percent human," Leigh said with certitude. "All the working bits are there. The code that knits the body together is all there. It's just these chunks of junk DNA that are strange."

Leigh zoomed out on the Sudarium sample, filling the screen with it. "So, what was your idea?" she asked.

"Can you search for different patterns?" Jonathan asked quietly.

"Of course. That's what this system is designed for, to search for patterns," Leigh responded.

"Good. Let's start at the beginning, then. Search for one A and one T here in this anomaly in the 23rd chromosome."

Leigh furrowed her brow. "I'm not sure what you're on about, but okay."

She tapped out the commands.

"Millions of occurrences. It's everywhere," she said.

"Hmm—" Jonathan ran a hand across his face. "Okay. Try one A, one T, and one A," Jonathan said.

Again, Leigh tapped out commands on the computer.

"OK, that one comes up 275,376 times. What are you trying to do?"

Jonathan ignored her. "Now do one A, two T's, and one A."

"If you'd just tell me what—"

"Trust me. Try it," he cut her off.

Leigh took a deep breath. "Alright." She tapped out the commands. "Okay, that sequence comes up 48,614 times."

"Can you bring it up on the screen?" Jonathan asked.

Leigh tapped out a command. The section of red and white DNA came up on the screen, zoomed out so much that the squares were not even visible. The whole thing dissolved into a pinkish blur.

"Okay, cowboy, tell me what you're on about," Leigh said, turning to face him with a determined set in her eyes.

Jonathan told her, explaining his hunch.

When he was done, Leigh stared at him, disbelieving.

"That's just—" Leigh trailed off. She was about to say "silly," but that chill went up her spine again, stopping her words. Instead, she shook her head, said nothing and looked intently into Jonathan's eyes.

"So is there any way to do it?" Jonathan asked.

Leigh scratched her head. "I don't know. I think so. I'll need Tony for that. We'll need to do some reprogramming, and that's his area." She turned to him. "Tony," she called out.

He looked up from his computer. "Yes?"

"Need you again, love," she said.

Tony rolled his chair to her workstation.

Leigh explained to him what they were trying to do.

"You're not serious, are you?" he asked after she had detailed the job.

"Yes," she said, glancing at Jonathan.

"I've got a gut feeling," Jonathan chimed in. "More than gut, actually. Can you do it or not?"

Tony thought, staring up at the high ceiling of the lab. He nodded. "Yes. I can insert a subroutine in the reader code and have it output to a separate file. It shouldn't take too long."

Jonathan nodded. "Great, buddy. Get to it."

Tony wheeled back to his computer and started typing.

Leigh stared at Jonathan.

"What?" he asked.

She shook her head. "That's a hell of a hunch," she said with a far away look in her eyes.

"What's wrong?" he asked, reading the strange expression on her face. "You look, I don't know — afraid."

"I suppose I am," she admitted. "What if you're right?"

"Well then, I would think that's the proof you were looking for," he said.

Leigh took a deep breath, scarcely believing the events of the last three days and what they had found so far.

"If you're right, Jonathan, it's going to change the world."

CHAPTER 3

Cloud 23
Manchester, England
May 24, 2025 9:38 p.m.

Rudolph Lahmbrecht, hands clasped behind his back, walked on air over the Manchester skyline. The heels of his Bontoni handmade shoes clicked loudly on the glass floor of the empty Cloud 23 club. He stood at the plate glass window and surveyed the city, pausing to look at the buildings he owned or had an interest in. The Beetham Tower here was his favorite, though.

"Sir?" Valenti's quiet voice interrupted the silence.

"Yes?" Lahmbrecht said without turning.

"The area has been secured," Valenti said. He stood ramrod straight in his tailored suit, holding his hands in front of him.

"And the cleaners?" Lahmbrecht asked, still facing the glass.

"Also ready."

"What is the status on the van?" Lahmbrecht asked, his slow and deliberate words edged with steel.

Valenti hesitated. "It is close." He saw Lahmbrecht's face harden in the reflection of the window.

"How long?"

"The package will be in position in an hour or less," Valenti said with an edge of nervousness to his voice.

Lahmbrecht's face flashed with anger for a second. He caught a glimpse of himself in the reflection of the window and became impassive again, accepting the circumstances. He had a contingency for the contingency, after all.

"Very well. Have it in place as soon as possible."

"Of course, sir," Valenti said, then paused. Hesitantly, he asked, "When can we expect our guests?"

"Call the lawyer, get him in here. I'll call the good doctor myself."

"Are we doing the lawyer?" Valenti asked with trepidation.

Lahmbrecht stared impassively at the night. "I have not decided on him yet."

"But Lancaster and Tremaine, yes, right?"

"Eventually. I need to speak to her before, though," Lahmbrecht said coldly.

Valenti withdrew to the far side of the club. Lahmbrecht dialed Leigh's number but there was no answer. He tried again but got her voice mail again. He left a message.

"Doctor Lancaster. Rudolph Lahmbrecht. Call this number at your earliest convenience. It is of utmost importance."

Lahmbrecht hung up and took a breath. Hopefully, they hadn't found it, but he needed to know. He needed to talk to her. Lahmbrecht quieted his mind and considered every contingency he could think of. Everything was in position to neatly clip off all the loose ends. He glanced over at Valenti who was standing by the bar and was dialing the Lawyer.

Hilton Hotel
Manchester, England
May 24, 2025   9:48 p.m.

The phone vibrated on the nightstand of the hotel room, buzzing insistently. Caine opened a bleary eye and saw it dance. He reached for it, opened both eyes, and looked at the screen.

The Old Man.

"Crap," he hissed.

He forced himself awake and sat up, groaning as he did so. Adriana had been exceptionally cruel with him, more so than usual. He took a breath and answered the phone.

"Yes?"

"This is Valenti. Mr. Lahmbrecht would like to see you."

Caine sighed. "Sure thing," he forced himself to say. "When?" he drawled out, the sleep still clinging to him.

"Now."

"Now?" Caine's heart raced, forcing him fully awake.

"Yes, now," Valenti said impatiently.

"I'll call the driver," Caine said.

"No need. Mr. Lahmbrecht is upstairs."

"What?" Caine asked, sitting up on the side of the bed, incredulous.

"We're in Cloud 23, upstairs."

"Holy crap," Caine said, forgetting himself.

"I suggest you get here presently," Valenti said.

"I'll be there in fifteen minutes. I need time to get ready," Caine said.

"Very well. I will let him know."

Caine hung up, throwing the phone on the rumpled sheets of the bed. He rubbed his eyes, got up, and walked on unsteady legs towards the shower.

He turned on the water and waited for it to warm. Caine looked at himself in the mirror, turning to look at his back. It was a roadmap of pain, long welts and scratches where Adriana had dug with her sharp nails. Testing the water, he stepped in the shower with trepidation.

"Mother—" he blurted out, his curse cut short by the involuntary gasp he took when the hot water hit his back. He turned it colder, letting the water refresh him, and waited for the pain to die down.

Caine thought about the situation. *What could the Old Man want?* Did Lahmbrecht find out about his aborted plan to keep the Sudarium? Surely not. Could the Old Man be tidying up? The thought crossed his mind, though it was hard to believe after the long and fruitful relationship they'd had.

Caine had to gather himself up, call Adriana and Asad, find out their status. Get one or both of them in here to accompany him. He was safer with backup, he thought.

Caine shut the water off and gingerly toweled himself dry, wincing as he did so. He dressed hurriedly and took a moment to collect himself before calling Adriana. There was no answer, not even going to voice mail.

Reluctantly, he called Asad. The man answered on the first ring.

"Leon," Caine said in a somewhat less grating tone than normal.

"Yes?" Asad replied curtly.

"What is your status?"

"Sitting here in the cold. No movement. They haven't left the lab," Asad said as he stood in the shadow of a nearby building, his eyes trained on the lab.

"Well, they'll leave eventually. And when they do, they'll come home to a surprise," Caine told him.

"Surprise?" Asad asked, then added, "Never mind. I do not want to know."

Caine paused for a long while, so long that Asad thought they had been disconnected. Caine weighed things out. At last, he spoke. "I need you here, at the hotel," Caine told him hesitantly.

"Oh?" Asad was surprised, not only by the request but also by the tone in the Lawyer's voice.

"Yes. At the hotel. Meet me in the lobby as soon as possible. I've got a meeting with — the principals, and I'd rather you be there," Caine said. *I trust you more than Lahmbrecht right now, even if I don't trust you all that much*, Caine thought.

Asad sighed into the phone. His mind chewed on this. It was not good to meet the principals, he thought. The less you knew, the better chance you had of remaining alive. Still, it would be good to meet the Sheik, an honor actually. Maybe the Sheik wanted to congratulate him, to reward him, even.

"Very well. What is the situation there?" Asad asked at last, having made his mind up.

"I don't know," Caine said honestly. "He wants to see me and I want to make sure there is no trouble. Just being cautious."

"What of your lady friend?" Asad asked.

"She is busy."

"With the scientists?"

"Yes. She is waiting for them," Caine explained.

Asad understood. Adriana was lying in wait at the doctor's apartment, most likely.

"Very well. I'm on my way," Asad looked at the Beetham Tower in the distance and was already walking towards it through the darkened city streets. "I will be there in ten minutes."

"Great, I'll meet you in the lobby," Caine said, sounding almost polite.

"One more thing," Asad said, even as his mind worked out the new information. The Lawyer was taking a great risk meeting in person, which meant he was desperate. And desperate people made poor choices. "The money. I would like to be paid for the rest of the job."

"The job isn't done yet," the Lawyer said.

"My job is done. Spain was taken care of. Your faulty information was the reason the cloth escaped," Asad said firmly.

Caine was in no mood to argue. "Fine. You'll be paid. Paid extra for your troubles." Money was cheap, after all, thought Caine.

"Very well," Asad said cautiously.

"See you downstairs," Caine said and hung up.

Caine took a deep breath, smoothing out his hair in the mirror. He walked out of the room and down the hall. He dialed Adriana but there was still no answer. Caine pressed the button to the elevator, waiting for the car. A good stiff drink in the lobby bar while he waited for Asad seemed like the best idea in the world at that moment. He dreaded the meeting with Lahmbrecht, and hoped he'd done the right thing by bringing Asad in.

CHAPTER 4

Tabor Applied Genetics Lab
Manchester, England
May 24, 2025 9:49 p.m.

Leigh's tablet rang twice as it sat abandoned on Leigh's workstation. Jonathan and Leigh, across the room and unable to hear the buzzing, stood in front of the clean room. They both stared at the Sudarium, the bloodstained cloth laid out flat on the table and lit from above.

"I can't believe all this," Leigh said softly.

"What?" Jonathan asked.

"This," she gestured at the Sudarium. "What we've found. And your theory."

"I'd hardly call it a theory."

"Well, your hunch, then." Leigh shook her head. "I feel like we've left science behind and are in some other realm."

"*If* I'm right," Jonathan reminded her.

"If you're right, it will change everything," Leigh said in a hushed tone.

"I've been thinking about that. I don't think it will," he said, shaking his head.

"How can it not? How can you think that?"

"Because history repeats itself. People don't change. They'll either believe or not believe," he said.

Leigh shook her head. "No, that's pessimistic. If what you think is right—" she trailed off. That chill went through her again.

"That's a big if," Jonathan said.

They stared silently at the ancient cloth for a moment.

"Let's see how Tony is making out," Leigh said.

They turned and walked to Tony's workstation and stood behind him.

"How's it going?" Leigh asked softly.

"Almost done. I'm troubleshooting a couple of lines of code, but it's mostly ready."

"So this program will convert the DNA code to the alefbet like we discussed?" Jonathan asked.

"Yes. Look," Tony said. He selected one of the lines from the anomaly, the white A followed by the 400 red T's. "now, according to you, this line of 400 should be a Tau?"

"Tav," Jonathan corrected him.

"Right. Tav." Tony tapped a button. "*Voila.*"

He pointed at the screen where the Tav, the last letter of the Hebrew alefbet, appeared. The window of the screen read: "*Transcription complete. Result: ת.*"

"Is that right?" Tony asked, unsure of the Hebrew.

"That's it. That's the Tav," Jonathan confirmed.

"Cool. Let's fire her up," Leigh said, eager to get it done.

Tony selected the huge swath of anomalous junk DNA from the 23rd chromosome, the section full of seemingly random A's and T's. He tapped the "convert" button.

"How long will it take?" Jonathan asked.

"It's done," Tony said. "These are fast computers," he added with a smile.

"I'll say," Jonathan said, impressed.

"Put the results up on the big screen," Leigh said as she practically leaned on Tony trying to read the smaller screen.

The big screen filled with a jumble of Hebrew letters. The three stared up at it.

"Okay, you're the only one here that reads this, professor, so what does it say?" Leigh asked.

Jonathan stared at the screen, brow furrowed, faced etched with concentration. A look of confusion crept over him. He shook his head sadly.

"Nothing," he said, crestfallen. "It's all gibberish."

Leigh's shoulders slumped. She thought Jonathan was crazy or grasping at straws, but deep down she wanted him to be right. She wanted his crazy hunch to actually be true.

"I'm sorry," she said, with a heartfelt sad smile on her face. "I wanted you to be right."

Right, Jonathan thought. Something was off. His hunch had felt so sure, so certain. *So right*. There was something he was missing.

"Right," he whispered, then, snapping his fingers, loudly exclaimed, "of course!"

"What? What is it?" Leigh asked.

"Right," Jonathan said with excitement. "Tony, can you flip all this around? Invert it?"

"Flip it around?" Tony asked, confused.

"Yeah. Make it decode right to left. Hebrew reads right to left."

Tony put a finger to his lips, thinking.

"Yes. Just a couple of modifications."

He typed furiously on the keyboard, modifying the program. After a few tense moments, he was done.

"There," he said.

"Now do the conversion again," Jonathan told him excitedly.

Tony tapped on the "convert" button. "Here it is, from the beginning of the anomaly," he said.

The screen filled up with a new set of Hebrew letters.

Jonathan read intently, then went dizzy. His face turned ashen and he groped around for a chair. He found one and slumped into it.

"Jonathan, are you alright? What is it?" Leigh asked, concern and excitement and expectation all fighting for supremacy in her.

"It's—" Jonathan trailed off, unable to speak. A great chill went through him, like he'd just seen the most beautiful sunset ever, amplified a hundred-fold. A thousand-fold.

"What? What is it, Jonathan?" Leigh asked, taking hold of his shoulders and gently shaking them.

"It says — I can't believe it — it," Jonathan stammered, almost literally speechless.

"What? What does it say?" Leigh insisted.

Jonathan told her, speaking the words out in a tremulous voice.

Leigh grabbed hold of the side of the workstation, her knees going weak.

"This can't be," she almost whispered.

Her tears fell on the table. Leigh realized she was crying, not out of sadness or happiness, but out of sheer awe.

Hilton Hotel
Manchester, England
May 24, 2025 9:59 p.m.

Caine sat downstairs at the lobby bar of the Hilton, waiting for Asad. He sipped on his scotch, scanning the door. He saw the big man walk in through the revolving doors, unmistakable. A custom tailored wool blazer framed his huge shoulders. Caine drained the rest of his scotch and walked to him.

Asad spotted him at once, recognizing him from the many video calls over the past year. The Lawyer looked heavier in person, puffier than he expected. Their eyes met and Caine signaled to him. They met in the side of the lobby.

"Leon," Caine said, "good to meet you in person. I'm the Lawyer." He extended his hand.

Asad took it, enveloping it in his huge strong hand. The big man nodded. "What's the situation?" he asked, straight to business.

Caine sighed. "I received a call from the principal, the man funding all this," Caine said, shaking his head. "It was — unexpected, and he wanted to meet right away. Now. Here." Caine shook his head. "I don't know. I've got a bad feeling — call it instinct," he said.

Asad nodded. For the first time since he'd known him, he thought he heard something resembling civility or humanity coming from the Lawyer.

"You are probably right to trust your instinct," Asad said.

"Are you ready? I'm already late."

Asad tapped his side and the gun holstered under his coat. "I'm ready. Where is the meet?"

"Upstairs, at a bar. Cloud 23."

Asad curled his lip in distaste. He disliked bars. Even now, he could smell the liquor on Caine's breath.

"Very well," he said with resignation.

They walked to the front elevator that serviced the 23rd floor exclusively. They got on and the elevator shot up in the air. The door dinged and they exited.

The elevator lobby was empty. A little guard's podium sat unmanned. Beyond this there was another bank of elevators. A sign read "Residents Only." The cool sheen of the brushed stainless-steel walls contrasted with dark wood accents, giving the lobby a classically modern and expensive feel.

Caine walked to the door of the Cloud 23 club. A serious-looking and beefy gentleman in a sharp suit stood at the door, arms folded in front of him.

"Mr. Caine?" the guard asked.

Caine winced, even as Asad took note of his handler's name.

"Yes," the Lawyer said. "Is he ready for us?"

The guard nodded, then looked past Caine to Asad.

"He's with me," Caine said, and gave the guard a humorless smile.

The guard stepped aside and opened the door. Caine and Asad walked on to the glass floor of Cloud 23, and towards the Old Man himself.

Tabor Applied Genetics Lab
Manchester, England
May 24, 2025 10:11 p.m.

Leigh, Jonathan and Tony sat in the kitchen, each cradling a hot tea in their hands. They all stared downward at the dark brew.

"I can't believe it," Leigh said, breaking the silence.

"Me neither," Tony said quietly.

"I can't believe it either," Jonathan said. "I mean — if someone told me this, I wouldn't believe them."

"But it's all right there," Leigh said. "Right there in the blood."

"The blood," Jonathan repeated.

They sat silently, occasionally stirring the tea.

"I had no idea," Tony spoke softly. Of the three, he looked the most distant, the most shell-shocked. It was as if his whole belief system had been upturned. And it had been. He had tears dripping from his eyes that he was scarcely aware of, as if some great truth was working deep within him and had hit a vein of water. "I had no idea that all this was — true," he said.

"I hear you, buddy," Jonathan said tenderly. He shook his head. "I always wanted a reason to believe, something to hang my hat on, but this—" he shook his head again, and tried to continue, "this—" he trailed off, the words not coming to him. He turned to Leigh. "I guess you've got the proof you wanted."

"No one is going to believe us," Leigh said. She had been distant, locked in deep thought and working over in her mind the incredible revelation of the past hour. She was also so exhausted that she even suspected she might be dreaming.

"You need to send this out to other labs," Tony said. "We need independent confirmation."

"You're right," Leigh nodded. She took out her iTablet and swiped it on, so distracted and tired that she did not notice the blinking message icon in the corner. "Who should we send it to?"

"Pacific Bioscience, Illumina, Applied Biosystems, Oxford Tech, Emory, Dr. Sawyer at Johns Hopkins," Tony counted off on his hand, "and that's just for starters."

"Good, get me a contact list while I prep this. Let's see what kind of cover letter I can possibly send with this data," Leigh said.

She tapped out a letter on her tablet, while Jonathan looked on, sipping his tea occasionally.

Dear sir or madam: Our lab would like independent analysis and confirmation of the following samples. In particular, note the anomalous sections in Chromosomes 22 and 23, at the following locations . . . .

When Leigh was done typing, she started selecting the files to send. She frowned. "Well, this raw data is going to take hours to send," she said.

"Hours?" Jonathan asked.

"Yes. It's not like you can add this whole genome in raw data as an attachment to an email. You have to stream it in over hours to an open connection." She turned to Tony. "You've got those addresses yet?"

Tony tapped away at his own tablet. "I'm putting them on your desktop now."

With a flick of the wrist, Tony sent the addresses of the various labs to Leigh's iTablet. Leigh set up her tablet, and pressed a button.

"There," she said, stifling a yawn. "It's started. It'll finish downloading the Sudarium samples on the other lab's computers in a few hours. I should wait here and make sure it all gets there," Leigh said with a sleepy voice.

"Nonsense," Jonathan said. "It's late. Let's get home. We have all our lives to work on this. Hell, it'll take all our lives to work it all out."

"I don't know if I can sleep," Leigh said. "This is like Christmas."

"If you don't sleep, Santa Claus won't come," Jonathan joked. "Besides, you'll get sloppy, and no one wants a sloppy scientist."

"You're right," Leigh said, looking at the clock on the microwave. "I can barely think straight." The adrenaline was long spent and the incredible last three days were a whirlwind in her head. Her bed sounded like just about the greatest thing in the world right then.

"Let's go," Jonathan said, getting up. "Tony, you mind driving us there?"

"No problem," Tony said with a smile, but it was a distant and forced smile.

"Just one more thing. I just want to make sure," Leigh said, checking her iTablet again to confirm the computers of the various labs were connected and talking to each other. The data was all streaming. Satisfied, Leigh shut down the tablet. "Okay," she said with a tired smile.

They all walked out of the kitchen and passed by the lab, pausing to take one last look at the Sudarium bathed in light inside the clean room. Leigh stepped to her workstation. The big screen, still full of Hebrew letters, went dark. Already, it seemed like a dream.

CHAPTER 5

Cloud 23
Manchester, England
May 24, 2025 10:12 p.m.

Lahmbrecht sat in a large chair against the backdrop of the twinkling Manchester skyline. The door to the bar opened and in walked Caine and, unexpectedly, a very large darker-skinned man. No doubt this was the Moor that Caine had in his employ. Lahmbrecht frowned at the man's presence. He saw Valenti meet the two men at the door and frisk them. The big Moor handed over a semi-automatic to Valenti, a Heckler & Koch it looked like from this distance. Valenti took it and finished frisking the man. He pointed over at where Lahmbrecht was sitting.

Caine started to walk, then noticed the glass floor and hesitated a step. Gingerly, he stepped on the glass and walked 23 stories above the street below. Asad followed, hesitant, eyes open and on high alert.

The men approached Lahmbrecht, who sat impassively and regally on his chair facing them. With the glass floor and plate glass windows behind him, he appeared to be floating over the bottomless darkness. The king of the air on his throne, surveying his dominion.

"You are late," Lahmbrecht admonished Caine. His voice was edged with steel. He took a cursory glance at Asad and turned his attention to the Lawyer. "Sit." Lahmbrecht said, pointing at a chair facing him.

Caine looked at the chair with its back to the rest of the bar. With its back to Valenti, Caine noted. Lahmbrecht's word was not a request, and Caine took the seat reluctantly.

Asad stood behind him, turned a little off to the side, with Valenti in his peripheral vision. Asad eyed Lahmbrecht, then scanned the room. *That is not the Sheik. An intermediary, perhaps?* Asad's mind raced, trying to recall snippets of information. Though the Lawyer had never directly told him who was funding the job, it had to be the Sheik. Who else but the Sheik would finance the destruction of two Cathedrals and the two holiest relics in Christendom? The feeling began to creep over Asad that he did not have all the information and that maybe, just maybe, he was a pawn in a game he was scarcely aware of.

Lahmbrecht was silent for a long time as Asad contemplated these thoughts. At last, the Old Man spoke.

"Things have not gone exactly according to plan," Lahmbrecht said methodically to Caine. "Have they?" he added, with venom.

Caine took the accusation in stride, saying, "Things are under control."

"I fear it may be too late. They have been at the lab for hours working on the cloth. I fear the worst," Lahmbrecht said then fell silent. He turned to Valenti. "What is the status on the van?"

"No more than fifteen minutes and the van will be in position near the lab," Valenti said.

"You got the van? Filled?" Caine asked.

Lahmbrecht nodded. "Yes. But detonating it at the gates will not be sufficient. We were not able to obtain enough explosive for that. It will need to be driven in," Lahmbrecht said and looked over at Asad.

Asad took a deep breath. From the beginning, he had been willing to die for the *jihad*. Was he to back out now? *At the hour of judgment, there is no escape*, he thought again of the saying from his youth. Was he willing to die even though he did not have all the answers? Asad nodded, but said nothing.

Caine tried to imagine what Lahmbrecht was so intent on destroying. Surely it could not be a mere scrap of cloth. Throughout the last few months, as the plan had come together, Lahmbrecht had revealed only what Caine needed to know. Never had Lahmbrecht revealed his true intentions, or the reasons for the destruction of these relics. Caine, though curious, had been satisfied to put his questions aside and count the massive amounts of money he was making. Now, though, he could not resist asking.

"What is it?" Caine asked Lahmbrecht. "What is it they are looking for? What's in that cloth?"

Lahmbrecht, deep in thought, ignored him.

"Before we destroy it, I need to speak to Dr. Lancaster. To find out if she has discovered it, if she has told anyone," Lahmbrecht said, almost to himself.

"That will be difficult," Caine said. "The doctor and the man are being taken care of as we speak."

"What? Call it off!" Lahmbrecht practically yelled, a rare show of emotion from him. "I must speak with her."

"Okay, okay," Caine said, raising his hands in front of him. He took out his cell phone and dialed Adriana. The phone rang and rang, not even going to voicemail. "No answer," he said, looking up at Lahmbrecht.

"Try again," Lahmbrecht said with a trace of desperation in his voice. Caine dialed.

Beetham Tower
Manchester, England
May 24, 2025 10:22 p.m.

Tony's Ford Focus E glided silently down Deansgate and turned. He pulled up to the Beetham Tower's residential entrance. The car stopped.

"I appreciate this, Tony," Jonathan thanked him.

"Anytime. No bother at all, really," he said.

"We'll see you tomorrow, bright and early, yes?" Leigh asked.

"Yes, Doctor," Tony said and tried to smile, though his heart was heavy. The incredible revelations of the night were still weighing on him, working on his mind.

Leigh, sensing his disquietude, reached up from the back seat and put a comforting hand on his shoulder. "If you need anything or just want to talk, call, yes? Don't be afraid to wake me," she said.

"Thanks, Leigh. I will."

Jonathan and Leigh stepped out of the car and waved goodbye. Tony's car set off silently and disappeared down the street.

Jonathan craned his head up and gazed at the skyscraper in front of him. "So this is home?" he said.

"Yep. Well, actually, the lab is home. This is where I sleep."

"Nice."

Jonathan contemplated the building, which was floodlit and lined with gray-green plates of glass in various shades. He noticed the lip sticking out 23 stories up. "What's that?" he pointed up.

"That's Cloud 23. Posh bar. It's quite amazing, actually. We'll go there tomorrow and I'll buy you that drink," Leigh said.

"Promise?"

"Promise."

Jonathan held the door open for her as they entered the building.

"Thanks."

"Anytime," he said with a smile.

Leigh walked up to the front desk. A guard looked up from a tablet he was reading. "Dr. Lancaster. It's been ages. Where have you been?" he asked.

"Hi, Mark. You wouldn't believe me if I told you."

Mark, the guard, glanced at Jonathan who was standing behind Leigh.

"Oh. My friend, Jonathan," Leigh introduced him.

Jonathan lifted a hand in greeting and smiled.

"Did you want to register him?" Mark asked.

"Register?" Jonathan asked, arching an eyebrow.

"To get in and out," Leigh explained. "The whole building is on a thumbprint ID system."

"Are you giving me the keys to your place already?" Jonathan asked with a grin.

"Watch it, cowboy," Leigh said with a smile. "It's in case I send you out for take-away."

Jonathan laughed. "Alright, alright. What do I do?" he asked and stepped to the desk.

"Just put your thumb here, sir," the guard said and pointed at a small pad.

Jonathan did.

"And your name?"

"Jonathan Tremaine."

"Got it. You are all set," the guard said.

"Shall we?" Leigh said, pointing towards the elevators.

"We shall," Jonathan said and extended his hand.

They walked through the stylish lobby towards the bank of elevators. Leigh placed her thumb on the elevator keypad and the door chimed and slid open. They went in.

"You want to try it?" Leigh asked as they stood in the elevator.

"Sure. What floor?"

"Forty-six."

He pressed the 46th floor and put his thumb on the keypad. The keypad lit up green and the elevator doors closed. The elevator rose quickly and quietly, pressing them to the floor with its speed. The numbers flashed by and soon it slowed as it reached the 46th floor. A chime sounded and the door slid open.

"After you," Jonathan said with a sweep of the arm.

Leigh walked out into the hall. Jonathan followed.

"It's down here on the right," Leigh said.

They walked on down the hall.

Adriana tried to stay alert and fought off the boredom by imagining what she would do once they arrived. She had everything prepared. The dead guard, safely stowed in the tub, had unwittingly made her job much easier. On his belt she'd found a pair of handcuffs and a Taser.

She fondled the Taser now, feeling its sharp barbed tips. She had initially planned on killing them both quickly, not risking complications. Now, though, in the privacy of this apartment, and with this Taser, she would be able to take her time with both of them.

Adriana froze. There was a noise outside the door. She brought out her stiletto in one hand and gripped the Taser with the other. She crouched to the side of the door and tensed her muscles, readying herself to pounce.

"My humble abode," Leigh said and put her thumb on her keypad. The door clicked open. Leigh swung it open and they walked in. She tapped a pad at the side of the wall and the lights turned on.

"Nice place," Jonathan said and walked in.

The apartment was small but smartly furnished with a low-slung Scandinavian couch in the center of the living room. Floor-to-ceiling windows twinkled with the lights of the Manchester skyline.

Leigh closed the door and froze in terror.

Standing behind the door was Adriana Nyx with a cruel grin on her face.

She pounced instantly, before Leigh had time to react or even call out. Adriana swung her right arm around Leigh's neck, wrapping the arm around her throat and putting her in a headlock. In Adriana's hand was the stiletto, which she pressed to the back of Leigh's neck.

Leigh gave a yelp at the feel of the pointed steel.

Jonathan, who had been admiring the view, turned immediately at the sounds of the scuffle. He took the situation in at once. The woman from Venice, from earlier that day, held Leigh in a twisted embrace. One arm was wrapped around Leigh's throat. In her other hand, she held what looked like a Taser, pointed straight at him.

"*Calma*," Adriana said, as if soothing a baby.

Jonathan tensed and suppressed his first instinct, which was to leap at her.

"Be still," she repeated in heavily accented English. She tightened her arm, pressing the stiletto ever so slightly into Leigh's skin. Leigh cried out in pain.

Jonathan froze. His mind raced, trying to think of what to do, of some kind of plan, but he came up empty.

Adriana's lips curled. From the corner of her eye, she spied a bead of blood welling up at the tip of the stiletto. She inhaled, taking in the mix of Leigh's sweet scent and the metallic tang of the blood. She turned slightly and stared straight at Jonathan.

"I'm going to shoot you now," Adriana said to him matter-of-factly. "It is going to hurt." She savored the look of fear and resignation on Jonathan's face and lined up the Taser.

She pulled the trigger. Jonathan braced himself, watching it all in slow-motion.

There was a pop and the two steel barbs shot out of the Taser, followed by thin filament wires. They dug through Jonathan's shirt and pierced him. He tried to be strong and remain standing but his muscles stopped working. He dropped to the ground, clenching his teeth. With no control of his body whatsoever, he curled into a fetal position and gasped at the pain shooting through every nerve. The last things he saw before he passed out were Leigh's frightened expression and the cruel sneer of Adriana as she held down the button and unleashed the electricity throughout his body.

Cloud 23
Manchester, England
May 24, 2025 10:33 p.m.

"Try her again," Lahmbrecht told Caine.

"I've been calling," Caine replied. "She must have her phone off."

"You have got to go up there then. I need to speak to Doctor Lancaster. I need to know if she has told anyone," Lahmbrecht insisted.

"Told anyone what?" Caine asked.

Lahmbrecht ignored the question. "Take Valenti. He's got elevator access," he told the Lawyer.

Caine sighed. He cast a glance back at Asad, who stood staring at him with an intense frown on his face, then looked over at Valenti behind the big man.

"Bring them here," Lahmbrecht said to Valenti. "And bring her computer if she has it."

The man nodded and motioned to Caine. "Let's go," Valenti said.

Caine huffed. "You're coming too," he said to Asad, who merely nodded.

The three walked through the club. The entered the lobby and stood by the elevators, waiting impatiently to get to Leigh's apartment.

There was a sharp stab of pain as someone kicked him in the ribs. Jonathan opened a bleary eye. His mind snapped to attention. *Leigh.* He started to spring up, but his hands refused to move. Confused and dizzy, he blinked and looked around. He sat sprawled on the floor of Leigh's kitchen. His hands were pinioned above his head to something. He glanced up. Handcuffs, attached to the handle of the stainless steel stove. He shook his wrists but the cuffs held fast. He tried to sit up straight as best he could and winced in pain. Every part of him hurt, but, above all, there was a sharp pain at his chest. He looked down and saw the barbs of the Taser still clinging to him, digging into his skin.

"Are you awake, *bambino*?" Adriana asked him with a malevolent grin on her face. She stood in front of Jonathan and held Leigh by a fistful of hair in her left hand. Her right hand held the stiletto. Slowly, Adriana played the edge of the knife over Leigh's neck. "I wanted you to see before I start."

"Jonathan!" Leigh cried out, both a plea for help and a cry of concern for him. She reached out her hands, bound with zip ties, in a pleading gesture.

"Let her go," Jonathan said automatically.

Adriana laughed, mocking him. "You are cute. But you forget your position." She brought the hand holding the stiletto down to the kitchen counter. On the counter sat the Taser, the thin filament wires still running to the barbs imbedded in Jonathan's skin.

"Aw, crap," he said, and steeled himself.

Adriana pressed the trigger, holding it down a few seconds. Jonathan gritted his teeth and his body tensed as 50,000 volts ran riot through him.

"You bitch!" Leigh yelled out and swung her bound fists at her.

Adriana tightened her hold on Leigh's hair and quickly brought the stiletto back up to Leigh's throat. Leigh stopped struggling at once, going perfectly still.

"*Buono*," Adriana smiled. "Now that we know everyone's position, we can start."

Adriana dragged the tip of the sharp blade over Leigh's throat and around her neck to the base of her skull. Leigh froze, holding perfectly still. She tried to stifle a sob.

"See, if I cut here, she dies," Adriana explained with cold calculation. "That is no fun. *Veramente palloso.*"

She tightened her grip even more on Leigh's hair, pulling her up and her neck taut.

"And down here," Adriana continued and dragged the blade down the back of Leigh's neck, the sharp tip leaving behind a welt, "down here — she is paralyzed. She would feel nothing, and that is *veramente palloso* also. Very boring."

Jonathan looked on, helpless. Leigh started breathing shallow and fast, sick with fear.

"But if I go down here—" Adriana said, trailing off and letting the words linger in the air. With a quick flick of her wrist she caught Leigh's thin black cardigan and brought the blade up, ripping the cloth in a clean line right along Leigh's spine.

Leigh cried out. Jonathan gave a tremendous jerk trying to break free of the cuffs, but they held tight. He tugged again, not even feeling the pain as the cuffs dug into his wrists.

"If I cut here," Adriana continued, running the blade down Leigh's spine, pressing a little harder now, "here is where the fun begins." She lined up the blade between Leigh's shoulder blades and pressed a little more. "One push here and her legs die," Adriana said with a twisted smile, "and you get to see me have fun all night, *bambino*," she finished, imagining Leigh helpless on the ground as she carved into her flesh.

"No—" Leigh pleaded in a soft and tremulous voice.

Jonathan jerked on the cuffs again, nearly breaking his wrists. He reached out impotently with his hands, like a wild animal with its leg caught in a trap.

Adriana's eyes went wide and her pupils dilated as she savored the helplessness of the two. She pressed a little more with the stiletto, breaking the skin, and tightened her grip on Leigh's hair.

Adriana froze. There was a knock on the door. A loud insistent knock.

"*Vaffanculo!*" she cursed and glanced at the door. Another knock, louder, rang out.

"Adriana!" she heard her name muffled through the door. It sounded like the Lawyer. It had to be the Lawyer.

"*Testa di cazzo,*" Adriana hissed. *What could he want? Why now?*

Adriana let out a growl of frustration and went to the door, dragging Leigh along by the hair. Leigh stumbled and crawled and struggled to follow, bound as she was. Adriana cracked the door open.

"What the hell do you want?" she spat out at the Lawyer.

Caine forced the door open and walked in. A well-dressed man Adriana did not know followed him in, and behind the two was the big man, the Moor. They all entered and Asad shut the door.

Caine saw Adriana standing in the foyer, holding Leigh by the hair in one hand and the stiletto in the other.

"Stop, Adriana," Caine pleaded. "We need them alive."

The fury built inside of her and for a moment she considered stabbing Caine in the side of the neck. He was in range. She took a deep breath, held it for a second, then let out a deep animal growl of rage that frightened even Asad.

CHAPTER 6

Cloud 23
Manchester, England
May 24, 2025 10:45 p.m.

Lahmbrecht sat in the darkened empty lounge, waiting. The club had a strange and ominous feel without people or music. Lahmbrecht contemplated the situation and waited impatiently. At last the door into Cloud 23 opened. Caine walked in, holding Leigh's computer bag. Jonathan, who looked dazed and was walking tentatively on unsteady legs, followed him in and paused. Leigh, hair disheveled, face still ashen with fear, and hands zip-tied, was at his side, as much holding on to him as holding him up. Behind them, Valenti, gun drawn, gave Jonathan a slight push to get him moving forward into the bar. They continued inside. Adriana followed them in. Her face was sullen, but it was a mask hiding pent-up rage. The last to enter was Asad, his face keen and studying everything around him, as if sensing and preparing for trouble.

"What's going on?" Leigh whispered to Jonathan. "Who are these people?"

"Shut up," Caine barked out, turning around.

They walked through the bar. Jonathan looked down at the glass floor in surprise, and at the street far below them where Tony had dropped them off earlier. They rounded the edge of the bar and Leigh and Jonathan stopped in their tracks. Their blood ran cold. Standing there by the window was the Old Man. Rudolph Lahmbrecht.

Leigh and Jonathan glanced at each other, bewildered.

"Doctor Lancaster, Doctor Tremaine, please, have a seat," Lahmbrecht said in a cordial voice and pointed at two chairs in front of him. Valenti gave Jonathan another shove and they moved forward and sat in the low chairs. Valenti stood behind them, arms folded in front of him, gun in one hand.

"I trust you are not hurt," Lahmbrecht said.

"No. Yes, actually. What — what the hell is going on?" Jonathan stammered.

"It was an error. A mistake. The woman acted without permission," Lahmbrecht lied.

"Permission?" Jonathan's eyes bored into him. "From who? From you? Are all these bastards working for you?"

"Everyone works for me," Lahmbrecht almost interrupted him, spitting the words out. "Even you." He composed himself again. "And you too, Dr. Lancaster," he said, turning his steely gaze towards her.

"I don't understand," Leigh said, trying in vain to assimilate all this new information.

"You don't have to understand. All I want from you now is facts. A report, if you will."

"A report?"

"Tell me what you found. Tell me what you found in the blood," Lahmbrecht said, leaning forward in his chair in anticipation.

"Wait a minute," Jonathan interrupted. "We're not saying a damn word until you tell us what's going on," he said, stalling for time. Jonathan's senses were returning to normal after the repeated shocks with the Taser. He silently sized up the situation, checking his peripheral vision and the reflections in the windows, and noting the position of Valenti and the others.

Lahmbrecht gave a short humorless laugh. "What is going on is that I asked Doctor Lancaster a question. And I fully expect an answer. Now, Doctor, what did you find in the blood?"

Leigh glanced at Jonathan seated beside her. Their eyes met and she took strength from his. She turned back to Lahmbrecht with a defiant glare and remained silent.

Lahmbrecht nodded. "I see." He paused a moment. "Mr. Caine," he called out.

"Yes?" asked Caine, who had been standing off to the side along with Asad and Adriana, observing.

"Perhaps your lady friend can persuade Doctor Lancaster," Lahmbrecht said.

Caine looked at Adriana, who smiled, curling up one side of her mouth. She stepped forward, the click of her heels loud on the glass floor of the empty club.

"I get her afterwards, yes?" she asked Lahmbrecht, who simply nodded once.

Leigh shot a frightened glance at Jonathan.

With each click of her heels, Adriana neared Leigh.

"No—" Leigh cried out and tried to get up from her chair with her still-bound hands. Valenti, who was standing behind her, pressed her back into it.

Jonathan began to leap up to defend her. Valenti showed him the gun, pointed at Leigh's thigh. The well-built man shook his head. "Don't," was all he had to say, and Jonathan sat back down.

Jonathan gritted his teeth and tried to remain calm. Angry people make mistakes, his father had taught him, and right now he was fuming. He took a deep breath and tried to clear his mind and wait for any opening.

Adriana prowled around the chair and stood in front of Leigh. *I get to have my fun with her after all*, she thought. She leaned over, gently stroking Leigh's hair.

Leigh froze at her touch, still feeling the blade at her throat from earlier in her apartment.

Adriana swung her leg over, straddled Leigh, and sat on her lap facing her. The assassin's lips stretched into a cold smile as she gently stroked Leigh's face. Adriana got close, leaning forward as if she was going to kiss Leigh, then she did, barely brushing her lips against Leigh's. Leigh tried to turn away but Adriana, with cat-like speed and strength, locked her hand at the back of Leigh's head, grabbing a big fistful of hair. Leigh let out a little yelp.

Adriana pressed her closer and kissed her, even as the assassin's free hand slid down to her boot. Adriana silently drew the stiletto out of its sheath and brought it up to Leigh's face. She let the tip of the knife play ever so lightly over Leigh's cheek.

Jonathan, watching all this, leaned forward in his chair, ready to spring. Valenti was watching him with an eagle eye and pointed the gun at him now. The man shook his head. "Don't," he said softly.

Jonathan again tried to control himself. He was willing to die for Leigh right then, he realized. He also knew that he would not do much good to her dead.

Leigh let out a little cry as Adriana teased her with the blade. Leigh closed her eyes, as if everything would go away if she did so. "Okay," Leigh breathed out. "Okay — okay," she repeated over and over, her voice getting softer and softer.

Adriana studied Leigh's face, her fear, and savored it.

"Caine, call your lady friend off," Lahmbrecht's strong authoritative voice rang out in the tense silence.

Adriana frowned and glared back at Lahmbrecht, shooting him a spiteful look.

"Later," Lahmbrecht told her.

She turned back to Leigh, still letting the blade play over her cheek.

"Adriana," Caine said gently, with trepidation.

Just as suddenly as she'd grabbed Leigh's hair, Adriana let go and backed off. She gave Leigh a smile that was more animal than human, baring her teeth with a curl of her lip. Adriana sprang up, dismounting Leigh and turning casually, as if nothing had happened. She prowled to a low chair off to the side and relaxed into it, draping one leg over the arm of the seat. She leaned back and lounged, keeping an eye on everything and idly playing with her stiletto.

Leigh, still whispering, "okay," over and over, opened her eyes.

"Dr. Lancaster," Lahmbrecht called out.

"Y — yes?" she stammered.

"Are you ready to discuss your findings now?"

"Yes," she croaked out, trying to compose herself.

"Tell me. Tell me what you found in the blood," Lahmbrecht leaned forward in his chair, his creased face coming into the beam of an overhead LED spotlight.

"There — there was an anomaly," Leigh said, regaining her composure. "In the 22nd chromosome."

"Go on," Lahmbrecht leaned back into his chair, as if he were listening to a story he'd heard many times. "An anomaly you say."

"Yes. Hundreds of T bases, all in a row," she said.

"Four hundred," Lahmbrecht said. He paused, watching the reaction of Leigh and Jonathan.

"Y — yes. How did you—" Leigh trailed off, suddenly confused. She furrowed her brow. "How did you know?"

"Do not mind that. Go on with your findings," Lahmbrecht insisted.

"Yes. Four hundred T's and one A base. Repeated over and over, four hundred times. Jonathan noticed the pattern, and thought it might mean something," Leigh said.

"Indeed," Lahmbrecht said, though he did not sound surprised. "What is that?"

"The Aleph and the Tav," Jonathan spoke up. "The one and the four hundred. The Hebrew numerological designations for Aleph and Tav."

"Amazing," Lahmbrecht said with a condescending sneer on his face. "That should have been amazing enough, but did you find the rest?" Lahmbrecht asked, his voice patronizing.

Jonathan tilted his head. "You know. You bastard, you know. I can see it in your eyes." Jonathan exchanged a quizzical glance with Leigh.

"You are right, of course, Dr. Tremaine. I do know. I am impressed, though, that you and Dr. Lancaster found it in so short a time. You did in one night what took many intelligent and dearly departed people over two years to do, including your predecessor, dear Doctor Barnette," Lahmbrecht said, turning to Leigh. His thin lips struggled to curl into a smile, though it was one of amusement.

"Wait," Leigh said, confused. "You knew? You know? You know about what we found in the 23rd chromosome? How?"

"The male chromosome," Lahmbrecht said with a short chuckle. "The male chromosome from a man born to a virgin." Lahmbrecht let the implication of the statement hang in the air.

A silence filled the room. Both Jonathan and Leigh gave a little shudder. That same chill went down their backs, as it had earlier in the lab.

"How did you know?" Leigh stared at Lahmbrecht in wonder.

Lahmbrecht remained silent.

"Know what?" It was Caine, breaking the silence. "What is it?" he asked, desperate to find out what his employer had been keeping from him.

Lahmbrecht ignored him. "So you found it," Lahmbrecht said, nodding his head. "Impressive."

"What did they find?" Caine asked again. He turned to Leigh. "What did you find?" he asked her.

"Silence," Lahmbrecht called out, anger welling up in him.

"A pattern," Jonathan said, ignoring Lahmbrecht. "A code," he told the Lawyer.

"In the very DNA," Leigh picked up. "In a huge section of junk DNA in the 23rd chromosome. Only it's not junk DNA. There is a code there. There is a message."

"What message?" Caine asked Leigh, desperate to know. He turned to Jonathan. "What message?" he asked again.

"Be silent!" Lahmbrecht called out.

"It's Hebrew," Jonathan said, ignoring him. Then, in a reverent voice, he spoke. *"B'rê'shiyth bârâ elôhiym 'êth shâmayim 'êth 'erets."*

"What the hell does that mean?" Caine asked.

Jonathan was silent, barely able to speak the words.

Asad leaned in closer, listening intently.

"What?" Caine practically yelled out.

"*In the beginning, God created the heavens and the Earth,*" Jonathan announced to the stunned room.

The room was silent. Everyone stared at Jonathan in disbelief.

Asad, standing to the side in a daze as the realization that he was not working for the Sheik sank in, went lightheaded at the words. He recognized them immediately. The words of Father Goya from the mountain came to him, then, in a flood. They resounded loud in his head as if God Himself were speaking them. *To find what you seek, you must go back to the beginning.*

"Wait." It was Caine who finally broke the silence. "What is that? What does that mean? What do you mean it's a code in the blood?" He rattled off the questions, bewildered.

"It's the Bible, Mr. Caine," Lahmbrecht called out with something between derision and amusement in his voice. "Genesis, to be exact," he added.

"Yes, Genesis. And the rest of it, too," Leigh said. "The whole Bible. All there, encoded in the blood. Each letter encoded in a section of the chromosome."

"What do you mean encoded?" Caine asked, still not understanding.

Lahmbrecht shifted uncomfortably in his chair.

Jonathan spoke up. "One T for Aleph, two T's for Beth, three for Gimel, thirty for Lamed, the whole thing, all the way to four-hundred for the Tav. Each letter separated by an A. The Aleph and the Tav, the alpha and the omega. The Hebrew gematria, all encoded in the DNA."

"How's that possible?" Caine asked, dumbfounded.

"I don't know," Leigh admitted. "A miracle? But it's there. It is in the blood and anyone can study it and confirm it."

"Enough!" Lahmbrecht voice was harsh and filled the club.

"And you," Leigh said, turning her attention to Lahmbrecht and ignoring his command. "Why?" she asked. "Why didn't you tell us you knew? Why fund the study into the Shroud at all?"

Lahmbrecht gazed at Leigh, steely eyed. "It was the only way of getting the Shroud out of its protective case. Inside that case, it would have survived even the fire."

"But why? Why destroy it?" Leigh insisted.

The room fell silent again.

Lahmbrecht's eyes bored into Leigh's. He gave a short chuckle. "You really do not see, do you, Doctor?" Lahmbrecht asked, as if speaking to a child. He went on, not waiting for a response. "They say confession is good for the soul, do they not? I suppose since you will not be on this Earth much longer—" he trailed off, leaving the room in silence once again.

Leigh and Jonathan exchanged a worried glance.

"You're right, of course," Lahmbrecht continued, all ears listening. "I did know. Twelve years ago."

"How?" Leigh asked, incredulous.

"There were samples taken from the Sudarium in the year 2000. Of course, back then all they could determine was that it was human blood and type AB. I obtained the samples twenty years ago, at great expense, I might add, and funded research into them, quietly. I funded Tabor Labs and your predecessor, Dr. Barnette, before you were there. That it has been a very profitable side business is merely a bonus. What I wanted was a way to decode this ancient DNA."

"But how did you know?" Leigh asked again.

"My team was able to sequence most of the genome over a year and a half. As you know, Doctor Lancaster, we started on the 22nd chromosome because—"

"Because it is the shortest," Leigh completed his sentence.

"Exactly. We found the anomaly easily enough. But it baffled everyone. Of course, we did not have the illustrious professor Tremaine on staff. Too many geneticists, not enough linguists or historians. But we eventually figured it out." Lahmbrecht gave a short laugh.

"What's so funny?" Jonathan asked, even as he studied Valenti's reflection in the floor-to-ceiling windows, waiting for him to let his guard down.

"What we found. You're right, of course, Dr. Lancaster, it is a miracle. But I was not looking for a miracle."

"What were you looking for?" Jonathan asked, wanting to keep him talking.

"The secret of life," Lahmbrecht said with a resigned look on his face, as if the one thing he had wanted was the one thing that had eluded him. "I was sure. Sure that if Jesus really had risen from the grave, there must have been a medical explanation. Perhaps something in the genome that turned off death." Lahmbrecht drew in a breath. "But I didn't expect what we found. What you found," he said, turning to Leigh.

"But why destroy it? Why not tell the world?" Leigh asked earnestly.

Lahmbrecht sneered. "You really are naïve, are you not, doctor? Do you have any idea what my companies do?"

"Well," Leigh said, taken aback, "bio-engineering, for one."

Lahmbrecht gave a dismissive wave of the hand. "A side business. The real money is in defense, in weapons. I own a controlling share in Universal Dynamics, MEP, Spartan — well, you get the picture. Many defense contractors. Companies that would not fare well if peace and morality suddenly broke out."

Jonathan laughed.

"Is something funny, Doctor Tremaine?" Lahmbrecht asked, annoyed.

"Yeah — you," he chuckled. "You are a bigger optimist than I thought."

Lahmbrecht curled his lip, not used to anyone laughing at him. "Do tell," he sneered.

"You think this will change the world?" Jonathan asked him with disdain. "This won't change a damn thing. People will either believe or not believe, same as always."

Lahmbrecht, and Leigh, looked at him disapprovingly.

"I hope you are right," Lahmbrecht said. "But I can not take that chance."

"So you're going to destroy it, then?" Jonathan asked, stalling.

"Yes," Lahmbrecht said with typical directness. "And everyone who knows about it."

Asad, who had been standing to the side listening intently, grew alarmed.

"But enough of this," Lahmbrecht said. "What I really want to know, Doctor Lancaster, is who? Who did you tell? Who have you discussed your findings with?"

Leigh clammed up, thinking of Tony.

"Doctor Lancaster," Lahmbrecht said impatiently. "Would you like to discuss the matter with Caine's lady friend?" he asked, gesturing at Adriana, who was still lounging in the chair.

When he pointed to her, Adriana sat up straight and was in rapt attention.

Leigh glanced at Adriana, then at Jonathan. He nodded his head slightly. *Tell him*, his face said.

"Everyone," Leigh said. "By tomorrow morning, all the major genomics labs in the world will know. They'll confirm our findings. No matter what you do, word will get out."

Lahmbrecht's face hardened as he absorbed this information. "Tomorrow morning," he repeated. "So you have not finished sending it yet?"

Leigh froze, cursing herself.

"Mr. Caine, hand the good doctor her computer," Lahmbrecht waved his hand at the Lawyer.

Caine, who himself was standing in a sort of daze trying to make sense of all these revelations, snapped out of it at the mention of his name.

"Ah, yes," he said absently and handed the bag to Leigh. She took it hesitantly and awkwardly with her bound hands.

"Doctor Lancaster, if you please," Lahmbrecht said with a supremely confident look on his face, the look of a man who was not to be disobeyed.

Leigh looked at the computer bag in her lap, then gazed up at Lahmbrecht.

"No," she said with confidence and strength.

"Doctor Lancaster, stop those transmissions," Lahmbrecht commanded with increasing impatience.

Leigh shook her head.

"Do it!" Lahmbrecht's face flashed with a terrible red anger. Just as quickly as the anger had come, it disappeared and his face became impassive again.

"You're going to have to kill me," Leigh said, defiant, drawing from some hidden well of strength she didn't know she had.

"As you wish," Lahmbrecht said. "Mister Caine," he called out, "have your lady friend persuade the good doctor."

Adriana was up before Caine could say anything. She was on Leigh in an instant, batting the computer bag aside and pouncing on her, straddling her as she had before. Adriana's hand whipped around to the back of Leigh's head, holding her hair in a twisted lover's embrace. Her left hand held the stiletto to Leigh's neck. Leigh did not yell, but tried to put on a strong and defiant face. Despite her best efforts, a tear welled out of the corner of her eye, rolling down her cheek. The corner of Leigh's mouth quivered.

"Remember, I need her alive," Lahmbrecht reminded Adriana.

"Oh, she will live, for a long time. Though she will pray for death," Adriana said with a sneer.

Leigh's eyes darted in panic from side to side. She saw Jonathan in the very edge of her vision, ready to pounce but held back by Valenti's gun.

Adriana pressed the tip of the stiletto to the side of Leigh's neck and turned it ever so slowly.

Leigh let out a cry of pain, loud in the silence, then settled into a soft sob.

Adriana smiled malevolently as she turned the blade, intently watching a small rivulet of blood running down Leigh's neck.

"Don't," a deep baritone voice called out in the quiet of the room.

It was Asad. He looked on with pity at Leigh's face, which was twisted with fear and pain. The revelations of the night still played out in his mind; the words of Jonathan repeated over and over in his mind. *In the beginning . . .*

"Don't," he called out again louder, insistent.

Adriana glanced up at him, her attention diverted for a moment.

Jonathan saw her in the corner of his eye. In the reflection of the window, he also saw Valenti turn his attention to Asad. It was the opening he needed.

"Ah, hell," Jonathan whispered under his breath.

He did not hesitate. With every muscle and every fiber of strength he had, Jonathan leapt out of the chair at Adriana. He rammed his shoulder into her chest as he split her and Leigh apart. Leigh went sprawling backwards, chair and all, and fell onto the glass floor and hit her head hard on the floor as she landed, dazing her.

Adriana, caught unaware and in an awkward position, fell backwards on the glass floor of the club. She landed on her back with a hard thump and grunted as Jonathan landed on top of her.

Adriana was quick and strong, though. She arched her back, lifting at the hips and throwing Jonathan to one side. Jonathan rolled, caught himself, and scrambled to his feet. Adriana sprung to her feet, knife in hand, only to be met by Jonathan's charge. She twisted and absorbed the blow and now they were intertwined. Jonathan grabbed hold of her left wrist, bending it painfully and trying to make her drop the knife.

Adriana countered with the grace of a dancer, ducking under his arm, stepping through and untwisting the hold. Like a partner in some deadly tango, she was now behind him. Caught by surprise by the move, Jonathan tried to swing her around or flip her over, but she held fast, swinging her free arm around his neck. She squeezed, choking the air out of Jonathan. His vision began to grow blurry and his grip faltered.

Desperate, he swung his head back blindly and caught her with a glancing blow. It stunned her and the arm coiled around his neck slackened. In an instant she tightened it again.

The others were watching the struggle intently.

"Shoot them both," Lahmbrecht told Valenti. His voice was loud, rising over the scuffling, grunting and heavy breathing of the two fighting.

Both Jonathan and Adriana froze and looked up at Valenti, who swung his Sig Sauer P300 up towards them. The dark eye of the silencer stared up at its victims.

Adriana saw and acted immediately. She uncoiled her arm from Jonathan's neck and swung down with all her might at Jonathan's groin.

Jonathan's vision turned white in an explosion of pain and he crumpled to his knees, letting go of his grip on Adriana's knife-wielding hand.

What happened next happened very fast. Adriana, freed of the grip, brought her arm back and threw the stiletto at Valenti with amazing force. The stiletto flew through the air like a spear before imbedding itself deep in Valenti's neck. Valenti's arm dropped and he fired off rounds wildly, punching holes in the glass floor around Adriana and Jonathan.

The bullets sprayed everywhere. One shot landed between Jonathan's legs as he knelt winded on the floor, and sent little shards of glass spraying up. Cracks began to spider out from the holes.

Lahmbrecht, sitting in his high-backed chair, cried out in distress as a stray bullet ricocheted and pierced him in the leg. The Old Man cursed and clutched at the wound. He groaned out in pain.

Asad dropped to the ground, taking cover behind a couch. Caine scrambled away, making for the bar to hide behind.

Valenti, in shock already, dropped the gun and brought both hands up to his neck to try in vain to staunch the flow of blood. His eyes went wide with surprise and slowly settled into fear, then they rolled, hiding his pupils and showing nothing but ghastly white. Within ten seconds, he was losing consciousness. He fought, but his body failed him and he crumpled to the ground right beside Leigh, who was still dazed and sprawled on the ground where she had fallen and hit her head.

Leigh blinked, coming back to awareness. She opened her eyes and beheld the visage of Valenti, eyes white and rolled back in his head and throat gurgling and spouting blood. She screamed.

Jonathan, recovering from the blow, barely registered what had happened. Suddenly, Adriana was on him again from behind. Her arm coiled around his neck. She brought up her free hand and placed him in a bar-arm choke. Jonathan swung wildly with his fists, trying to connect but missing. Adriana stood behind him, her face frozen in a feral bloodlust as she squeezed the life from him. Jonathan wheezed, desperate for air.

A tiny part of Jonathan's brain registered the fractures on the glass floor that were spreading from the bullet holes beneath them. In between his ragged breaths, the sickening crunch of breaking glass filled the silence. He gasped for breath.

Suddenly, the glass gave way and they both plunged down.

Leigh, who had just recovered her composure from seeing the dead Valenti, watched in horror as Jonathan and Adriana both disappeared, falling through the floor.

"Jonathan!" Leigh screamed.

Jonathan and Adriana plunged through the shattering glass floor and landed on the second safety layer below, almost six feet down. They hit the safety glass with a hard thump, both of them momentarily stunned. Crystal raindrops of the shattered pane of glass above rained down and lay all around them.

Jonathan struggled to one knee, and the glass underneath him crunched. Dazed, he took a moment to catch his breath. With dismay, he saw tiny cracks in the glass spreading from small holes on the floor. *The bullets went through the lower glass too*, he thought. He glanced at the dark night 23 stories beneath and regained his senses.

Jonathan scrambled to his feet and looked desperately for a way out. The floor of the club was now above him and, when he stood up, he was almost eye level with it. He stepped gingerly over to the edge of the broken pane of glass, to the metal flashing that had held it in place. Sharp jagged shards of glass jutted out from the edges at eye-level. He glanced around for a handhold. A steel support beam ran vertically from the floor of the top layer to the floor of the bottom layer where he was standing, but it afforded no handhold. He thought of trying to jump up to the top, but reconsidered as the safety glass crunched under his feet. If he missed and landed back here, it might just give way.

Jonathan stuck his head out and called out to Leigh.

Leigh, horrified and thinking that he had plunged to the street below, gave a tremendous sigh of relief when she saw him. She scrambled over towards him.

"Leigh," Jonathan called out. "I need something to hold on to or something to break away these shards of glass."

"Okay," Leigh said, breathless and in shock. She quickly scanned the club for something, anything. It was chaos.

Caine had braved his way out from behind the bar and was now running to the exit. As he reached it, the stout beefy guard that had been stationed outside ran in, alarmed by the gunfire and almost ran into Caine. The guard tangled with Caine, holding him until he could make sense of the situation.

Lahmbrecht, meanwhile, was out of his chair and limping towards the exit. He walked very slowly, dragging his wounded left leg and dripping blood.

Asad, who had sought cover at the first sign of trouble, was now up and running. Leigh gasped as she realized with dismay that the big man ran straight for her. She gave a frightened cry, but Asad ignored her and ran right past. He dove to the floor and reached for Valenti's gun, which was where the dying man had dropped it.

Leigh processed all this in seconds. There was nothing to hand Jonathan. She leaned over the big empty square where the floor panel had shattered. Jonathan was standing six feet below, working at the jagged glass with his bare hands, desperate for a handhold.

"I can't find anything," she said in a panic. "I don't know what—" Leigh cut her words short and screamed, "Look out!"

Adriana rose up behind Jonathan, brandishing the small curved blade she'd unsheathed from her belt. She held it up and, with a sneer, rushed at him. The heels of her boots crunched the broken glass beneath them and she let out a growl. She flew towards him, arm outstretched, meaning to eviscerate him.

Jonathan spun to avoid her, then it all happened.

There was a low and sickening cracking noise and, suddenly, there was nothing beneath them as the bottom pane of glass shattered and rained down on the street below.

Jonathan, finding himself suddenly falling, threw his arms around the vertical steel support beam in front of him. He embraced it for dear life as the floor disappeared from under him.

Adriana plunged downwards. She dropped the blade and grabbed wildly and instinctively for anything around her. As she fell, she snagged hold of

Jonathan's leg and gripped tight as she dangled in the cool night air. The chilly wind outside rushed in the opening, whistling and howling.

Jonathan locked his arms around the support beam, holding on desperately. He glanced down at Adriana, who glared up at him malevolently. She grabbed both of his legs and began to pull herself up.

"Leigh!" he called out, looking up at her as she peeked over the side of the hole.

Leigh had watched in horror as the safety glass had given way and Jonathan had grabbed on to the post at the last second. She could see Adriana below him, hanging on his legs and working her way up. Leigh leaned over the hole and reached out as best she could with her still-bound hands. Jonathan, five feet below and dangling half out of the building, hung far out of her reach. The wind rushed through the opening and blew Leigh's black hair around.

Adriana labored, pulling herself up with that adrenaline-fueled strength that pushed a body away from death. She grabbed hold of Jonathan's belt and pulled herself further up.

"Leigh!" Jonathan pleaded for help again.

Leigh rose up and scanned the area. She saw her computer bag peeking from underneath an upturned chair. She grabbed it and leaned over the hole, dangling the strap off the side. *Too short.*

She glanced desperately around. Then, her eyes fell on the stiletto jutting out of Valenti's neck. She closed her eyes a moment. *It's the only way,* she thought.

She crawled to Valenti. He looked dead. Probably was dead. As she crawled, Leigh's bound hands landed in a warm, wet pool. *Blood.* Leigh tried to focus, to put on her medical game face. She took hold of the handle of the stiletto with her slippery hands and pulled. It slid out easily. The wound oozed a little blood then stopped. *He* is *dead*, some clinical part of her mind thought. She crawled back to the hole, leaving a streak of Valenti's blood on the glass floor.

"Jonathan, the knife!" she shouted down, leaning over the edge on her belly as far as she dared. She tried to hand the stiletto to Jonathan so he could use it against Adriana.

Jonathan saw and reached up, straining to reach it. He grimaced, his arms growing tired. "Get — off — me," he yelled out. Adriana, now almost at his waist, grabbed hold of his shirt and, he could swear, laughed malevolently.

Leigh leaned down a little further and, carefully holding the blade, extended the handle to him. Jonathan, holding on with one arm wrapped tight around the support beam, gave one more great effort and reached up for the knife. His fingers stretched, inches away from the handle. Leigh leaned down a little more.

The stiletto slipped.

Leigh saw it happen in slow motion. Her hands, slick with blood, lost their grip on the blade, and it fell. Jonathan grabbed for it and just grazed the handle with his fingertips, but the stiletto kept falling, turning end over end now. It fell past Jonathan and landed, point first, into Adriana's right shoulder.

It was not a deep wound, but it was enough. Adriana howled in surprise and pain. Her right arm involuntarily contracted and she lost her hold on Jonathan. She tried in vain to hold on with her left hand, clawing at Jonathan's shirt and back.

The shirt ripped, and she lost her grip. Shrieking, Adriana Nyx plummeted into the darkness outside. Her feral scream followed her down, fading more and more until there was nothing but the silence of the rushing wind.

Jonathan took a big breath. Relieved of the extra weight, he hoisted himself up. He crawled onto the adjacent bottom pane, which was, he hoped, intact. He sprawled out on his back and caught his breath, his feet still dangling over the edge into the night sky.

Jonathan stared up at the glass floor above him and at Leigh, lying face down and gazing back down at him through the glass. Her hair was a mess and she had a trickle of blood running from her neck and she was the most beautiful thing he'd ever seen. He smiled up at her and she smiled down at him. They lay there a moment, like astronauts drifting in space, weightless on a wave of relief and love.

CHAPTER 7

Cloud 23
Manchester, England
May 24, 2025 11:11 p.m.

A loud yell startled them both out of that quiet moment. Chaos erupted in the room once again. Leigh bolted up.

Jonathan saw her alarmed expression and her rising to her feet. He viewed everything, surreally, from six feet below as he lay on the safety glass.

"Hold on!" Leigh yelled down at him. She ran to a large cocktail table and, with her still-bound hands, dragged it over to the edge of the hole.

Jonathan tentatively stood up, careful not to hit his head on the floor above him. The legs of the table were poised at the edge of the missing pane. Jonathan carefully stood at the edge and grabbed hold of the table leg with both hands.

"Grab hold and get up here, mister," Leigh cried out to him as she braced herself and grabbed hold of the table.

"Don't let go," he told Leigh.

"I'll never let go," she said.

Jonathan tested his grip, and the table leg seemed steady. He took one look down at the gaping darkness below him, said a quick prayer, and pulled himself up. For one sickening moment, his legs dangled in the air. He pulled himself up level with the floor of the club. With a grunt, he threw his leg on the floor and scrambled on top. He pushed himself back, away from the missing pane leading into the dark night outside.

Leigh rushed to him, falling on him and embracing him with her bound hands. Jonathan threw an arm around her and hugged her tight. She helped him up.

Jonathan stood, scanning the room and quickly taking stock of the chaotic situation.

Lahmbrecht braced himself against a chair, holding his injured leg. The stray bullet had not gone deep, but the wound pained him. He tried to keep his face impassive, but the pain was evident in the downturned corner of his mouth and the slight grimace he wore.

Caine still tangled with Lahmbrecht's security guard. The beefy man held Caine, preventing him from darting out the exit. Caine yelled curses at him.

Meanwhile, Asad, having picked up Valenti's gun off the ground, walked steadily towards Caine and the guard.

The guard glanced at the big man. "Stop!" he yelled.

Asad kept coming towards them and the guard raised his weapon. Still walking, Asad leveled the Sig Sauer at the guard. He squeezed the trigger. The soft distinctive pop of the silenced weapon sang out in the empty club.

Caine, standing by the guard, cried out in shock when a hole opened up in the guard's forehead. The guard slumped to the ground, instantly dead, and his weapon fell to the floor with a loud clang. Caine stood still for a second, stunned. He then glanced at the exit and darted towards it. A big hand grabbed him by the collar of his jacket, stopping him. Caine tried to twist away but Asad's huge hand held him fast.

"You lying pig!" Asad bellowed out, shaking Caine like a doll. "You said all this was for *jihad*! For the Sheik!" Asad continued shaking him.

"Leon," Caine cried out, "your money."

Asad stopped. He let go of Caine, who tried to regain his composure, smoothing out his suit. Asad thought of the millions yet owed him, and he controlled his anger and calmed himself.

Caine shook his head and laughed. "You hypocrite," he said with disdain. "I never said anything about *jihad* or any of your other religious bullshit," Caine spat out at him. "It was about the money. It was always about the money. You know it, I know it." Caine straightened his coat, regaining his lawyerly demeanor.

"That's not true," Asad said, but weakly and without confidence.

"The hell it's not," Caine sneered at him. "Think about it. I hired you. *I* did. For the money that you would've gotten if you hadn't screwed it all up."

"But the Sheik—" Asad protested.

"What about the Sheik? Yes, I told you it was his plane. And yes, I told you he was my client. That's it. And both true. You chose this job for the money. And lots of it. Everything else you invented in your head. You told yourself what you wanted to hear."

Asad took a step back, the words hitting him hard. Deep down, he knew that Caine was right. Asad had assumed that the Sheik was the one planning the mission. That it was his will, and Allah's will, being done. That's how it had been sold to him, Asad thought back. With innuendo and the promise of millions.

Asad backed off. Caine still owed him millions for the job. Killing him would do no good.

Caine studied the expression on Asad's face. The Lawyer gave a short mocking laugh. "That's what I thought," Caine said, nodding his head. "You need me and you know it," he sneered. He glanced around the big man, past him, some movement catching his eye. "Well, holy shit," Caine said in surprise as he saw Jonathan standing there with Leigh at his side. "I thought you both died," he said to them. If Caine was upset at the death of Adriana, he did not show it.

Jonathan ignored him, though, and stared right past him. Caine turned to see what he stared at.

"Lahmbrecht!" Jonathan yelled out.

The Old Man, taking advantage of the argument between Asad and Caine, had left the chair and was once again hobbling towards the exit.

Jonathan walked intently and single-mindedly towards Lahmbrecht. Leigh trailed behind, keeping a wary eye on Caine and Asad.

Jonathan closed the distance. He passed Asad and Caine, casting a glance at them, but they seemed to be regarding him, curious to see what he was going to do. He spied the gun on the ground from the slain security guard. Jonathan bent down, not breaking his stride, and scooped up the gun. The words of his father sounded in his head. *Never point a gun at anything you don't want dead.* Jonathan felt for the safety with his thumb. It was off.

"Lahmbrecht!" Jonathan yelled out again, still walking across the club. "Stop! Or I'll—"

Lahmbrecht stopped. He turned around, standing ramrod straight and looking remarkably fit for a man of 70 or more that had been shot in the leg. "Or you will what?" Lahmbrecht asked, spitting out the words at Jonathan with disdain.

Jonathan raised the gun. The silencer changed the balance, he noted, and adjusted. He pulled the slide back on the gun, the sound loud and distinctive in the emptiness of the club, and pointed it at the Old Man.

Lahmbrecht stared at Jonathan with steel-grey eyes that seemed to penetrate him, to see right through him.

"Stay right there," Jonathan said, hoping he sounded more confident than he felt.

"You fool. For what?" Lahmbrecht asked in a condescending and mocking tone.

"You've got to answer. For all this," Jonathan said, waving his free hand. "For Turin. For Oviedo. For all the dead."

"What are you going to do, Doctor Tremaine? Arrest me?"

"Yes," Jonathan said with conviction.

Lahmbrecht laughed. "Doctor Tremaine, I did not picture you as the naïve type."

Jonathan stared at him, keeping the gun trained on him, but said nothing.

"Do you really think they will arrest me?" Lahmbrecht asked, not waiting for an answer. "I have contributed more money to the government here than you will see in your lifetime. To say nothing of the United States." Lahmbrecht gave a short humorless chuckle. "Yes, one call and I will be on a plane to D.C. I will be in Nantucket while you are still answering questions in Scotland Yard."

"And what about what we found? What we found in the blood?" Jonathan asked.

Lahmbrecht shrugged. "There is always the media. Your findings will be discredited. A fabrication by an overzealous scientist," Lahmbrecht said with a cold set in his eyes.

Leigh spoke up from behind Jonathan. "But the samples, the Sudarium. Other labs will confirm our findings," she said confidently.

Lahmbrecht glanced down at his watch. "Very soon, there will be no Sudarium, nothing left of your lab. It will be your word alone."

Leigh turned paler than she already was. "You wouldn't," she said.

Lahmbrecht smiled, showing his small teeth, and ignored her. "Now, if you do not mind, I grow rather tired of standing here. I have some unfinished business, and I never leave things unfinished."

Lahmbrecht started shuffling towards the exit again.

Jonathan stepped closer.

"Stop, or I'll shoot," Jonathan said with all the force he could muster. He held the gun in both hands and aimed it at the back of Lahmbrecht's head.

Lahmbrecht gave a dry laugh.

"What's so funny?" Jonathan asked.

"You," Lahmbrecht said mockingly and turned around. He shook his head. "You still do not understand people, least of all yourself."

"And you do?" Jonathan asked.

"Yes. It is my gift to understand human nature. Take my attorney Caine over there and his big friend," Lahmbrecht said, pointing over at the two. "Motivated by money, pure and simple, the both of them. The big Moor does not shoot the hand that feeds him, and Caine does the same for me. I feed them all, you see, even you. And that is why I will walk out of here."

"I don't want your money," Jonathan replied.

"Quite right. You are motivated by something else, Doctor Tremaine. By a sense of right and wrong. By that morality that is deep in you that you try to shrug off. It is ingrained in you — part of your DNA, you could say," Lahmbrecht said with a short chuckle. "And it is your weakness. You are weak. It is why I know you will not shoot," Lahmbrecht said with a terrible sneer, his eyes full of contempt.

Jonathan stared at Lahmbrecht. His finger itched on the trigger.

The muffled pop of the silenced gun rang out in the quiet of the club. A small red hole appeared in the middle of Lahmbrecht's forehead. For the first time in years, and certainly for the last time, a look of utter surprise spread across the Old Man's face. He slumped to the floor, the strings of the marionette cut. A dark pool of blood spread rapidly from the back of his head.

Jonathan, in shock, stared at his gun.

"He was right," the deep baritone voice of Asad said from behind Jonathan. "You would not have shot."

Asad thumbed the safety and put the gun in his belt. He stood, towering over even Jonathan.

Leigh ran past Asad to Jonathan and fell into his arms, then turned to Asad.

"Don't you hurt him. I'll kill you myself," she said defiantly, trying to take the gun from Jonathan, who stopped her.

Asad almost smiled, but stopped himself. He admired the woman's courage and resolve.

"Is it true, what you found in the blood?" Asad asked.

Leigh, taken aback by the question, glanced up at Jonathan. She relaxed a little and turned to the big man.

"Yes, of course," Leigh said at last.

Asad nodded. "In the beginning," he whispered, almost to himself. He closed his eyes and a look of what could only be described as peace, mixed with equal parts regret, spread over his face. At last, he opened his eyes. He gazed at Leigh, looking deep in her emerald eyes. Asad's mouth, normally set and impassive, gave the barest hint of a smile. He looked at Jonathan, staring deep into his eyes with a soulful gaze, and nodded with respect.

Asad turned around and started walking back towards the Lawyer. Caine saw him and turned and ran towards the exit. Asad calmly took out the gun and fired a couple of rounds past him. Caine fell to the ground and cowered.

"I only want to talk," Asad said. "We have some — online banking to take care of."

Asad reached Caine and almost picked him up off the floor with his immense strength. He held him by the scruff of the neck and they disappeared through the exit and went towards the bank of elevators.

Leigh clutched Jonathan with her bound hands. He still held the gun in his hands, pointing it forward. The club was completely quiet now, save for the soft whistling of the wind flowing through the broken floor pane. They glanced around the room. They were the only ones left, the only ones alive, anyway.

Jonathan lowered the gun, not allowing himself to fully relax. He held on to Leigh with his other arm. He could feel her heart beating against his chest.

"Are they gone?" Leigh finally broke the silence.

"Yes. I think so," Jonathan said in a soft voice.

"Is it over?" Leigh asked in a whisper.

"Yes, I think so," he repeated, softer.

They were quiet for a long time and stood embracing each other.

"Look, Jonathan," Leigh said, pointing down.

Through the glass floor they could see the street beneath them. Blue flashing lights were gathering far below.

"They'll be here soon," Jonathan said. "Best get rid of this," he said, tossing the gun onto a nearby lounge chair.

They held each other close, not saying anything, and enjoyed the silence.

"I love you," Jonathan whispered to Leigh.

"I love you too," Leigh whispered back.

Jonathan hugged her tighter and they were silent for a time.

"How can you be sure this isn't all chemicals," Jonathan asked, with the trace of a smile.

"It *is* all chemicals. *We're* all chemicals. We're DNA," Leigh said, with a coy smile on her face.

They faced each other and kissed, standing on air above the cool Manchester night.

EPILOGUE

Tangiers, Morocco
June 21, 2025 11:11 a.m.

The old Land Rover Defender, caked with dirt and sand from its long desert trek, wove through the chaotic streets of the city. Cars honked and pedestrians blocked the road occasionally, but Asad Hasan was not in a hurry. His large body filled the seat despite the modifications he'd done to the Landy. Asad hunched over the steering wheel, peering up through the windshield at a street sign overhead. He reviewed the map in his head, having long ago given up anything with a GPS chip. Paper maps and a sense of direction were fine by him.

Asad turned right through the chaotic traffic, edging out another car trying to cut the corner. There, at last, was his destination. The large brown UPS sign was clean and stood out in stark contrast to the dusty signs of the other shops on the street. It was probably washed daily, Asad thought idly.

Asad parked the Landy on the side of the road and stepped out. He walked to the back door and opened it. Carefully, he took the package out. The large brown cardboard box had been methodically wrapped earlier. He put it under one arm and shut the Land Rover's door.

Asad walked down the street to the UPS office and entered, thankful for the cool air-conditioning inside. The office was practically empty at this time of day. He waited behind an older gentleman sending an express envelope. Soon it was his turn.

Asad went to the counter and placed the large package on top.

"Hello," the clerk said in Arabic as he eyed the large package with suspicion. "Where are you sending this?"

"Spain. Oviedo," Asad replied. "Here is the address," he added, sliding over a sheet of fine linen stationary with the address to the rectory of the Cathedral printed out in neat handwriting.

The clerk took a cursory glance and pulled out a form.

"You will need to fill this out and sign it," he said, as he'd said thousands of times.

"Of course," Asad said and complied.

He filled out the customs form with his real name, though the address was false, of course. Finished, he handed the paperwork back to the clerk.

The clerk read it, and frowned when he came to the space labeled "Contents."

"What is this word here?" he asked, pointing at the space.

"Reliquary," Asad replied with a smile.

The clerk tilted his head. "What is that?"

"It is a case Catholics keep relics in. Holy items," Asad explained.

The clerk gazed at the package as if he could see through it, curious.

"What is it? The holy item, I mean. What is the holy item inside?" the clerk asked, more out of curiosity than anything else.

Asad shook his head. "Nothing. It is empty."

"Empty?" the clerk asked.

"Yes," Asad said, and paused. "I already took what I needed from inside," he said with a wistful smile.

The clerk shrugged. "It will be 825 Dirham," he said as he weighed the box.

"Here," Asad said and handed him 5,000. "Keep it, and see that it takes off safely."

The clerk opened his eyes wide. "Thank you!" he said with excitement.

"Think nothing of it," Asad waved his hand dismissively. "I recently came into some money," he added with a smile.

The clerk took the box and carefully prepared it for shipping.

Asad took one last look at the box and walked out onto the hot street. He walked back towards the Land Rover, but passed it by and walked instead to a teahouse down the street. It would be nice to have a tea here in the city before the long drive back home, he thought.

He sat at an outdoor table in a patio under the shade of an awning and ordered a mint tea. While the waiter prepared the tea, Asad took from his pocket the small book he carried everywhere. He opened it up to the front, as he always did, and read the first page softly, to himself.

"In the beginning God created the heavens and the Earth," he read and smiled.

The tea arrived. He set the book aside and wrapped a napkin around the hot handle. With skill, he raised the small silver kettle and poured full a tiny glass. He inhaled the delicious aroma of the minty brew. He gave sincere thanks to God for being alive, and sipped the tea.

Asad picked the book back up and turned to where he'd left off last time, the place marked with a red ribbon. He read softly to himself.

"*In the beginning was the Word, and the Word was with God, and the Word was God . . . .*"

Venice, Italy
June 21, 2025 11:11 a.m.

Jonathan stood on the dock of the San Cassiano Hotel, dressed in a cream-colored linen suit, his shirt open and collar up. He leaned on the post and peered out through his Ray-Ban Aviators at the sparkling green waters of the Grand Canal. He took a sip from his espresso and set the cup down on the table among the flowers. The hotel's small dock had been decorated, at his request, with hundreds of flowers and plants.

In the distance, he saw a polished wood taxi boat, sleek and elegant, come into view. At the prow, like a maidenhead of old, stood a beautiful woman, her short black hair blowing in the Venetian breeze. He smiled and smoothed out his suit.

The boat plied the waters and closed in on the hotel. Leigh saw him now on the dock. She smiled and waved excitedly, her face alight with joy. The boat turned and slowly drifted towards the dock.

Jonathan could see Leigh closely now. She looked resplendent, dressed in a long flowered sundress with a thin long-sleeved cardigan thrown over as a guard against the cool morning breeze. She practically was jumping up and down, eager to get off the boat and into Jonathan's arms.

The boat bumped against the dock and the captain quickly tied it off.

Leigh stepped up onto the dock, taking Jonathan's hand.

"*Bon giorno, bella.* You look beautiful," Jonathan said, admiring the bright colors on her.

"Jonathan," she said, and hugged him. "It's good to see you," she whispered in his ear, not letting go.

Jonathan squeezed her. At last, they let go, but held each other's hands.

"Look at you, cowboy," she said, standing back and eyeing him.

"Like it?" he asked, turning around and modeling the outfit.

"I do. Very elegant, but leisurely elegant."

"I was bored waiting for you and went shopping. I got carried away," he said.

"I know. I'm sorry," Leigh apologized.

"No need to apologize. I've got to share my superstar scientist with the rest of the world," Jonathan said and smiled.

Leigh shook her head in exasperation. "I am so sick of the media. You had the right idea getting out of town when you did," she said.

"Here, have a seat," Jonathan said, offering her a chair.

They sat at the table on the dock overlooking the Grand Canal, the waves practically lapping at them. Leigh glanced around the dock.

"They certainly decorate things nicely here," she said, admiring the flowers.

"They must have heard you were coming," Jonathan said with a sly smile.

"Hush, you," she said and brushed a stray lock away from her eyes.

"How are things in Manchester?" Jonathan asked.

"Good. Busy. Every day some other lab confirms our findings and I have to do another interview. I left Tony in charge. I think he likes the attention."

Jonathan laughed. "I bet he does." He stared at Leigh, smiling. They were quiet for a moment, their eyes locked together. "I saw you on the news here a few days ago," Jonathan said at last.

"Oh yeah?"

"Yes. The whole thing with the Vatican studying your findings."

"*Our* findings," she corrected him. "Goodness, the Vatican is taking its sweet time," Leigh huffed.

"They will. They'll take years. Decades." Jonathan looked out on the water, contemplating the light dancing on it. "You know, it's funny," he said with a pensive expression.

"What is?"

"I was sitting in a plaza drinking a cappuccino when I saw you in the paper at a newsstand. You were in all the ePapers here. I remember the headline of the Herald Tribune. 'Evidence of God?' it read." Jonathan stared out at the water. "I remember seeing all these tourists walking obliviously by. Life going on as normal." Jonathan sighed. "I hate to say it, but I think I was right. People don't change."

Leigh put her hand on his. "Give them time," she said tenderly. "Some people change," she added.

"Ever the optimist," Jonathan said, looking at her and smiling.

"Ever the optimist," Leigh repeated and returned his smile.

"You think this will change the world?" she asked very seriously.

Jonathan shrugged. "We'll just have to wait and see." He stared out at the water a moment.

They sat in silence for a while.

"How about you, cowboy?" she asked, changing the subject.

"Doing good, now," Jonathan said. "Nothing like being caught with a gun in front of one of the wealthiest dead industrialists in the world to make Scotland Yard interested," Jonathan chuckled.

Leigh frowned. "It'll be funny in a month or two, maybe. I'm just glad everything got sorted out."

"That bastard Caine getting caught helped," Jonathan said.

"Yeah, they caught him in Montreal," Leigh said. "The Brits, the Italians, the Spanish, even the Americans, they're all fighting over him."

"I think the Spanish are just glad to have the Sudarium back safe and sound," Jonathan said.

"I think you're right."

"Any word on that big Moor?" Jonathan asked.

"None. He disappeared. You don't think we have to worry about him, do you?" Leigh asked.

Jonathan shook his head. "I don't think so," he said, recalling the look in the man's eyes.

Jonathan stared a Leigh for a minute.

"Damn it's good to see you," he said.

Leigh blushed. "Flatterer."

"You know it's true."

"I know," Leigh said.

"I got us a suite, of course," Jonathan said.

"Ground floor?"

"Ground floor," he said, amused.

They gazed in each other's eyes.

A waiter opened the door that led into the lobby and came to the table, breaking the spell. "Your *prosecco, signore*," he said.

"*Ah, mille grazie*," Jonathan said.

The waiter opened the bottle with a soft pop and set it down on the table. He retreated to the hotel lobby.

Jonathan poured the sparkling wine into the two flutes.

"We never did have that wine on the terrace, miss," he said to Leigh, offering her a flute.

She took it and they stared at each other.

"To—" Jonathan paused, thinking, "to the wonder of life."

"To the wonder of life," Leigh repeated.

They raised the glasses and clinked them softly.

Leigh took a sip. "Yummy," she said, smiling.

"Glad you like it," he said. "Damn, you look good," he added.

"I'm on to your lines, mister," Leigh said.

"Show me your tattoo," Jonathan said.

"Okay," Leigh said.

Jonathan sat up. "Okay?" he asked, taken by surprise.

"Okay," Leigh repeated, and gave him a coy smile. "You earned it," she said with a smirk. She set the flute down and took her cardigan off, revealing her sleeveless flowered sundress and her elaborately tattooed arm.

Jonathan stared at her, and stared in wonder at the tattoo.

His vision went cloudy and his head went light, then everything snapped into perfect clarity for a moment. Jonathan saw every detail, burned onto his memory forever.

The sun glinting off the blue-green waters of the Grand Canal, gilding the crests of the waves. The *palazzos* lining the canal, standing resplendent as the waves lapped at their sides. The gondolas plying the waters with their loads of happy people. The flowers filling the small dock like a giant window box in the spring.

And Leigh. Leigh, her black hair glistening in the Venetian sun. Her emerald eyes reflecting the water and the beauty around her. Her soft lips always turned up in a smile. And her tattoo, elaborate and wrapping itself around her arm like a painting in a museum.

"Jonathan, you okay?" she asked, taking his hand.

"Yes. Very," he said.

"So, what do you think?" she asked, showing her arm. "Is it what you thought?"

Jonathan took her hand and turned her arm slowly. He looked up and down at the familiar scene tattooed there.

He shook his head and laughed.

"I should have known," he said with a smile and kissed her hand.

AUTHOR'S NOTE

This book is a work of fiction. However, I have tried at every turn to remain close to the truth and actual history of the subject, as the subject rightfully deserves.

The Shroud of Turin has long been an object of speculation and study. I, for one, having researched it extensively for this book, was 95% convinced as to its authenticity. But I had yet to see it in person. That changed in May of 2010, when I was blessed enough to visit Turin and see it in front of me. The feeling I felt when I saw it for the first time, going by the Cathedral the night before my scheduled visit, and seeing it illuminated past the Cathedral doors, was nothing short of spectacular. It was then that I knew, I believed, that this relic was indeed real. I saw it up close the next day, and it was incredible. I remember thinking how small the image was. Jesus was no giant; He was an average-sized man. The Shroud showed me His humanity, even while the image itself and its mysteries showed me His divinity. Nowhere is the miracle of the Incarnation and the Resurrection more closely tied than on this one cloth.

Special thanks goes to Ian Wilson's most excellent study of the Shroud, *The Blood and the Shroud*, published by Simon & Schuster, as well as *The Turin Shroud, the Illustrated Evidence*, published by Barnes & Noble Books, by Ian Wilson again and Barrie Schwortz. Also informative is *The DNA of God*, by Dr. Leoncio A. Garza-Valdes, published by Doubleday.

The Sudarium of Oviedo was likewise a subject of much interest to me. Though much less celebrated than the Shroud, it is, in its own way, just as stunning a relic. Here, a thousand thanks must go to Janice Bennett and her first-rate book, *Sacred Blood, Sacred Image: The Sudarium of Oviedo*, published by Ignatius Press. Her book details the incredible evidence behind the Sudarium, and is a must-read for anyone with an interest in the subject.

There have been blood samples taken from both cloths, and they do, in fact, reveal that the blood is human and type AB. DNA studies are pending, although given current technology, it is difficult to find enough viable DNA, much less a whole genome. But, by the year 2025, who knows? Science may yet prove that the Sudarium and the Shroud have the same man's blood. And that would, in my mind, cement the authenticity of both.

The gene sequencing technology described in the book is somewhat fictional, though it has its basis in reality. Nanopore extraction techniques are being worked on by, among others, Oxford Nanopore Technologies of Oxford, England and Agilent Laboratories of California. Also informative was the article *Nanopore DNA sequencing with MspA,* the abstract of which is available at: www.pnas.org/content/107/37/16060.full.

Thanks to the website www.hebrew4christians.com, which was extremely helpful in helping with the Hebrew Scriptures.

Special credit goes also to Wikipedia, that vast repository of knowledge containing everything from articles about telomeres to the explosives favored by ETA.

A very special thank you goes to Chris Rollins of Clean Water for Haiti, whose ministry and great efforts helped inspire Leigh Lancaster's Haiti story. More information is available, and donations may be made, at: http://rollingsinhaiti.wordpress.com.

Finally, a million thanks to my crack team of readers and editors, including Mike, Papi, Jodie, Linda, Dori, Heather, and others, who helped hone the book with their comments and sharp eyes.

The Bible verses quoted come from the New King James translation. I would like to close by repeating my favorite verses, the verses that inspired this entire book:

> In the beginning was the Word, and the Word was with God, and the Word was God.
> He was in the beginning with God.
> All things were made through Him, and without Him nothing was made that was made.
> In Him was life, and the life was the light of men.
> And the light shines in the darkness, and the darkness did not comprehend it.
> Gospel of John, 1:1 – 5

L.G. Rivera

2011

Coming in 2013: The exciting sequel to The Blood!

THE BONES

The Land Cruiser sped down the desert road, bounding over the ruts and leaving a rooster-tail that wafted up towards a steel-blue sky. The truck hit a depression in the hard-packed dirt road and the suspension bottomed. Inside, Stefano Willems gripped the steering wheel and cursed. Nonetheless, he accelerated, pushing the big Land Cruiser as fast as he dared towards the white tents that dotted the horizon.

Stefano closed in on the billowing white tents that had been set up around the dig site. As he neared the crest of the hill and sawed at the wheel in the softer sand, Stefano saw a child sitting on a large rock by the side of the road. The boy stood up and waved. Stefano stopped the truck, sending a cloud of dust towards the boy, who ignored it and hurried towards him. Stefano rushed out of the Land Cruiser.

"Where is he?" he asked the boy.

"This way," the boy replied, and sprinted off down a small trail etched out of the hard mountain that comprised this region of Israel.

Stefano followed as quickly as he could, tracking the boy's footsteps down the path as it trailed steeply down the mountain. After a short while, the dig site came into view, marked off with a small sign reading "C-16." It was a hive of activity, workers going this way and that. Below him, the thin figure of Fadhi Al-Naoog glanced up, shielding his eyes from the harsh sun. Stefano paused.

"We found something," Fadhi called out as he beckoned Stefano down.

Stefano hurried down the path, passing the laborers who had carefully moved a mountain, one shovelful at a time. The workers eyed Stefano, who was impeccably dressed in a cream linen jacket, dress pants, and the cream Panama hat the man favored. Stefano hurried past them, and stepped on the wooden boards set in the down-slope, going down into the pit. Carefully, he made his way down, and to Fadhi.

"What did you find?" Stefano asked, sweating and breathless. He adjusted his thick, black-rimmed glasses, which were slipping off his nose.

"Let me show you," Fadhi said, and turned, walking towards the far end of the pit, towards the most recent excavations. Stefano followed. "The GPR showed what looked like a necropolis, a small one," Fadhi told him.

"I know that, I saw the radar images myself last night," Stefano curtly stated.

Fadhi smiled. "Ah, yes. But when one gets one's hands dirty – well, the radar could not show this," he said teasingly.

"What is it?" Stefano asked.

"Definitely first century. We've been making our way through, slowly. It's a truly astonishing find in its own right. But this..." he trailed off.

"What is it?" Stefano asked, impatient after the long drive.

Fadhi shook his head. "Best to see for yourself," he said, pausing at the edge of a square hole in the ground. The thin man slapped his khakis, sending up a little puff of dust. "Follow me," he said, and disappeared into the dark hole, clambering down a ladder.

Stefano took a look, shuddered, then gulped. It was dark and confining down there, he knew, and feared. The man took a deep breath and tried to draw from some source of strength. "Any light down there?" Stefano asked the black maw of the hole.

In response, a white glow emanated from the opening. It quelled Stefano's fear, somewhat. With trepidation, he turned and set one foot on the rung of the aluminum ladder, then the other foot, and descended into time.

After ten or so increasingly claustrophobic feet, Stefano finally reached the hard earth.

Fadhi was waiting patiently beside the ladder, and noticed Stefano's trembling legs. "Nervous?" he asked him.

"No," Stefano lied. "I just don't like this."

Fadhi looked around the small square chamber that had been dug out of the earth, supported with steel girders, and ringed with LED lights. "This," he said, inhaling the damp earthy air and smiling, "this is home to me."

Stefano shook his head. "You should get out more," the man joked, trying to hide his nervousness.

"Come," Fadhi said, and walked towards the back wall. He picked up two LED torches and handed one to Stefano. Fadhi shone it at a knee-high square hole cut into the wall.

"What, in there?" Stefano asked, fearing the answer.

"In there," Fadhi said. He sank to his knees and crawled in, holding the LED torch with his teeth.

Stefano shuddered again. He closed his eyes, took a breath, and got to his knees. He lit the torch, peered inside, and crawled into the small opening. After a few terrifying feet, he came to a smaller chamber where he was able to stand up, just. Fadhi, the taller of the men, was standing with his head bowed. He tucked his long hair behind his ears. Stefano, sweating in his now-dirty suit despite the damp coolness of the earth, adjusted his glasses and stood up straight.

"Any further?" Stefano asked, not knowing if he could handle any more.

"This is it," Fadhi said, pointing his torch at the end of the chamber. "The tomb is sealed, like the other ones that we found. But it is this," he said, pointing the torch, "that caused me to call you."

Fadhi stepped closer to the limestone wall, shining the LED on it and showing an inscription, set at about waist-level. He took a soft brush from a side pocket of his khakis and dusted the ancient stone. The dust of millennia rained down on the floor. "See?" Fadhi asked, adjusting the angle of the torch to better show the relief on the inscription.

Stefano leaned over and examined the jagged script. "What does it say?"

"I'm no expert on the ancient Greek, but I know enough. It is – extraordinary," Fadhi said with awe.

"Yes, yes," Stefano said, his patience running out. "What does it say?" He repeated the question.

Fadhi traced the letters, his fingers hovering over the inscription as he read it in Greek.

Stefano, not as proficient, took an exasperated breath. "Translate," he ordered.

Fadhi did.

Stefano's blood went cold. "That – that is," he stuttered.

"Extraordinary," Fadhi finished.

"Impossible," Stefano completed his thought. His mind raced. For a minute, he completely forgot his fear and trepidation at being underground. He knelt down before the inscription, repeating Fadhi's words, brushing the ancient marks with his fingers.

"Caspar will want to see this," Stefano said, absently. He cleared his head. He had to focus, to get this right. Stefano brought out his phone from his pocket and, steadying his trembling hand, took several pictures of the inscription and the door to the tomb.

"Who else has seen this?" Stefano asked.

Fadhi shrugged. "Some of the workers. I doubt any of them can read ancient Greek, though."

"Good," Stefano said.

"What about the tomb? Shall we open it?" Fadhi asked.

"No. Leave it alone. As a matter of fact, bury it. Bury it all," Stefano said, decisively.

"What?" Fadhi asked, incredulous.

"Bury it. The whole thing. The whole site," Stefano told him.

"Are you crazy? Do you know how much work this was?" Fadhi asked. "It has taken almost a month to get here."

"We'll have to do it again. Caspar will want the excavation on film. Tell the men to bury it. I'll inform Caspar myself of what you found."

Fadhi shook his head. "You tell the men to bury it. They will never dig for me again if I tell them."

Stefano shrugged. "Tell them to bury it. Then, get new men. A whole new crew. Replace them all."

Fadhi huffed. "They're a good crew. They have families, childr–"

"Replace them," Stefano interrupted, his voice suddenly hard. "It's what Caspar will want," he added, staring at Fadhi, who was glaring defiantly at him. Their gaze locked until Fadhi, resigned, finally looked away. The man nodded, but said nothing.

Stefano gave a slight smile, satisfied at being obeyed. "Let's go," he said, and began to make his way out of the underground chamber.

Fadhi took one more look at the inscription, and the tomb, then went back through the tunnel and up the ladder to the hard daylight outside.

L.G. RIVERA

THE
BLOOD

L.G. Rivera was born in Spain and loves to travel. From the top of the Eiffel Tower to the impoverished slums of Haiti, he finds beauty and darkness anywhere he goes. He lives in Florida and is the author of three novels and multiple short stories. His next novel, Z+, a zombie tale like you've never read, is scheduled for release in late 2012. You can find more information at www.lgrivera.com.

Made in the USA
San Bernardino, CA
27 November 2017